MIND WAR
The Singularity

Joseph DiBella

ISBN: 978-1456481087

Joseph DiBella
j.dibella@verizon.net

Within thirty years, we will have the technological means to create superhuman intelligence. Shortly after, the human era will be ended.

Vernor Vinge, 1993

Joseph DiBella

Chapter 1

The nightmare began the moment Jason Chase woke up.

He had not thought that guard duty was going to be a big deal. Just a matter of sitting perfectly still in the woods after midnight with nothing to do but keep your eyes open. He was at the base of a tree on the top of a small rise from which he would be able to see anyone coming up the mountain before they saw him. There would be plenty of time to raise the alarm and then run back as fast as he could. But seriously, no one would come through this spot in the middle of a dense forest when there was a perfectly good footpath on the other side.

It had been a long day, and then having to sit without moving a muscle did nothing to help Jason stay awake. Covered by pine branches to ward off the slight chill in the air, he felt almost like he was in bed. The last thing he remembered was thinking it would not hurt to rest his eyes just for a second.

It must have been a damn lot longer than a second because now, as he tried to clear his head, he saw shadows moving all around him. They were going in one direction, past him, towards the house. And they were carrying guns. They were careful not to make noise as they filtered through the woods. No chance that they were hunters – they were wearing black, their faces covered in black scarves. Well, actually, they *were* hunters – hunters of people, the people he was supposed to be protecting. He was smack in the middle of the attack that he was supposed to guard against.

He was paralyzed with fear, which was a good thing because they were so close that if he moved a muscle, they would see him. He had fallen asleep on duty, a capital offense in time of war. If the enemy did not get him, he would face a firing

1

squad, assuming any of the people he was supposed to be protecting lived to tell the tale.

What are you going to do, Jason?

I don't know. Why don't you do something?

You are the one with the flare gun.

It was in his left hand, pointing up, his finger on the trigger. A slight pressure and the flare would go off, alerting everyone in the house. There would be time for them to escape.

If I use it, they'll kill me. There must be forty guns around us.

And if you do not, if you sit here quietly until they pass, you can run away. You will live, and everyone else will die. Sound familiar?

Yeah.

You will be alone again, mourning your comrades and kicking yourself for not having done something. Well, you cannot say you were not given another chance.

Thanks! All I have to do is kill myself.

That wasn't fair. Jason was not a trained soldier. He had never been much of a fighter of any sort. He was more of a thinker than a doer. Truth be told, they had only put him there to get him out of their hair. They had specifically assigned him a spot where they did not expect anything to happen, and he had been perfectly fine with it. So how the hell did he get into this mess?

You did this! You could have stopped me from falling asleep. You let it happen. Is this your idea of fun?

I have to admit, Jason, I am interested to see what you will do.

I'm not supposed to die. There is so much I have to do. I'll never see us win the war. Can't you get us out of this?

No. You are wasting time. They are moving past us. If you wait any longer, it will be too late.

I know!

The people in that building will not have a chance. Everyone is going to die. Is that what you want?

Mind War; The Singularity

Of course not!

Then do your duty. Pull the trigger.

There must be a way out. It's not supposed to end this way.

Stop whining. Pull the trigger.

Jason watched the shadows move by. One of them looked his way, but he kept perfectly still, and the enemy moved on. His heart was racing, beating so hard he could feel the pulses in his ears. He needed more time! More time to think!

You do not have any more time. Christopher and Anne are in that building. You promised to do whatever it takes to keep them safe. Do you remember?

He remembered. Everyone else he had ever cared about, his family, his friends, they were all gone now. Chris and Anne had taken him in when he was alone and on the run. They were all he had left. His one wish had been that they would be spared, that they would survive the war. Now, if they were not killed, they would have to commit suicide to avoid capture. It was that or be tortured. They would put their guns to their heads and . . . *Yes, I remember.*

You said, "whatever it takes." Are you going to let them die?

There was only one answer. *No.*

The dark shadows were still swarming around him. His left index finger squeezed the trigger. Just like that. It was such a small thing, really, to end it.

The flare shot off with a "whoof" and exploded high in the sky. The shadows immediately turned towards him. In the dark he saw red stars twinkling, first a few and then more. It was their guns pouring automatic fire at him. He pulled the trigger on the M4 rifle in his right hand, spraying bullets around in a futile gesture, his final act. He knew he was not hitting anything, but he kept his finger on the trigger as the enemy's bullets ripped into his body. It felt like being punched over and over. But, to his surprise, not much pain. He was dying too fast for the pain to register in his brain.

The shooting stopped. A shadow bent down, looked into his dead eyes, and moved on.

They say that your life flashes before you when you're dying. Nonsense. You cannot relive your entire life in fractions of a second. But you do see bits and pieces. Your brain frantically retrieves scenes from your life that gave it meaning, that filled you with joy and made you want to live. As the life drained from his body, Jason didn't remember the misery and fear of the war. He relived the times when he was happy. He saw moments of aching beauty. In his last thoughts, he was flying.

Chapter 2

It was a beautiful day. The air was fresh, the spring temperature just right for a motorcycle ride as Jason flew through the back roads of northern Virginia. It was a route he knew well, so he rode a little faster than normal but still within his margin of safety. On every ride to work he tried to improve his time, experimenting with different lines and apexes on each turn, trying to make his shifting, braking and throttle action as smooth as possible. This was important – abrupt movements would disturb the balance of the bike and reduce braking or turning adhesion. It was like ballet, a dance where you moved your body as well as the bike, dipping and weaving, rushing forward and then slowing to the precise entry speed that the next turn demanded. A good ride was a thing of beauty, a performance with only one person in the audience. He could almost hear the music.

Eventually, Jason turned onto Arlington Boulevard and the fun ended. He blended into the morning traffic, locked in his lane between other vehicles, stopping constantly for traffic lights. He had a different focus now – people who could kill him with a moment's inattention. Jason knew that the primary cause of motorcycle fatalities was other vehicles that turned into a rider's path. His survival strategy was to assume that he was invisible, or better yet that all of the drivers were homicidal maniacs deliberately trying to kill him. It might sound grim, but he considered it just another part of the challenge of motorcycling, and any type of challenge was better than being bored. Certainly better than riding on a dirty bus or hitching a ride in someone's old wreck. Or walking, like the truly destitute.

He was lucky today – no close calls, just the tedium of stop-and-go traffic. But that was ok. Riding a motorcycle was like sex. Even when it was bad, it was pretty good.

Eventually, he turned off the main road towards the slightly seedy industrial park where he worked. Traffic got lighter as he passed people walking and riding their bicycles in the same direction. Nonetheless, he slowed down, mostly to savor the last moments of peace before he would have to face the dreary reality of earning a living.

As he entered the parking lot, there was a lane with a stop sign that angled in from the right. A large sport utility vehicle approached from his blind spot, out of his peripheral vision and not quite within his mirrors. Still, he might have avoided a collision if the driver had not accelerated as he ran through the stop sign. It was the sound of the racing motor that caught Jason's attention just in time to see the car aimed straight at his side. There was no time to stop or swerve. It was only basic survival instinct that made him gun the throttle and try to outrun it. Still, the SUV clipped the back half of his rear tire and spun him around. He did a high side fall and flew through the air while the bike hit a curb and tumbled on its own trajectory until it was T-boned by a tree. Time seemed to slow as he hit the ground and, just before he blacked out, he was looking straight at the driver.

The guy was Chinese. And he was smiling.

Jason regained consciousness with his face planted in the grass in the divider. His helmet had taken the brunt of it and had cracked on one side. The pain came fast as the adrenaline wore off. There was a gash on his shin where he had hit a curb, plus bruises in the various hard parts of his arms and legs that had taken turns bouncing off the pavement.

Jason slowly pulled himself upright to see if anything serious was broken. He was sore but found that he could move his arms and legs. He would have preferred to sit there and try to rest, but he had to get up because that Chinese guy was still there, admiring his handiwork. Anger overwhelmed the pain as he imagined tearing that smile off the guy's face with his bare hands. Hurt as he was, he knew what he had to do. He pulled himself up as straight as he could and turned directly towards the grinning driver.

Then he bowed, head down, three quarters. He held the bow until the driver was satisfied and drove away. When Jason was out of his line of sight, he rose slowly. Jason could imagine the guy bragging to his co-workers all day, entertaining them with the details of how he had made Jason fly through the air. Bastard.

Chapter 3

Despite the pain, Jason could still move under his own power, which is more than he could say for his bike. The shift lever was broken off and the handlebars were twisted. The front wheel was more oval than round, and the rear was smashed completely, along with most of the suspension on the right side. The engine did not look too bad, although it would not turn over. Of course, the bike had not looked that great even before the accident. You could not identify it as any particular brand of motorcycle – it was an amalgam of parts that he had scrounged from dumps and somehow had coaxed into working together. Now, it looked more like the pile of junk from which it had been born. For the time being, all he could do was drag the remains to a parking spot. Well, he thought, at least it will give me an excuse to go to the junkyard tonight.

Jason stopped at a restroom in the building where he worked to clean up as best he could. Looking in the mirror, he realized there was nothing he could do to hide the fact that he had just been in an accident. His right cheek was slightly swollen, and he had bruises on his arms that were bleeding into his sleeves. He also had road rash on his left hip and the pants on his right leg were torn at the knee. Worse, he could not walk without an obvious limp, despite how hard he tried to ignore the pain.

This was bad. His job, like that of every other American, hung by a thread. Without it, he would be living in a shack and spending hours every day on the bread lines.

There was nothing to be gained by getting attention at work. Jason had deliberately angled for a spot far away from Jingguo's office so that he would have as little contact with his boss as possible. Jingguo's primary job was to keep all of his American subordinates in a state of fear, a responsibility he relished. Jason's job was to stay out of his way.

Jingguo was not a bad man from one point of view. He was just another of many thousands of Party functionaries who would rather have been in their home country, but who were serving in a detested foreign land to prevent the Americans from ever again threatening the peace of the world. The Middle Kingdom had been exploited and suppressed by Western imperialism for more than two centuries. Now it was the Americans, desperate to maintain their hegemony, that had thwarted China from taking its rightful place in the world. America had surrounded China with military bases and had used its navy to prevent China from regaining the renegade province of Taiwan. The Americans had made alliances with client states like Japan and South Korea in a grand conspiracy to threaten and contain the "Chinese menace." Everywhere China turned, America was in its way, encouraging China's enemies and undermining its friends.

The only way China saw to remove this threat was to strike at its source. China was the only nation with the manpower to not only win a war with the Americans, but to put enough people in the North American continent to control a post-war population of close to 275 million. This required not just a large army, but an even larger number of bureaucrats to infiltrate every private and government organization. They were there to observe and control. The Chinese Army had the guns, and the security forces had their cameras and wiretaps, but the real guarantee that America would never rise again as an independent power was the horde of Chinese bureaucrats who replaced every person in any position of authority – CEO, office manager, mayor, school principal, police chief, whatever. The pay and perks of these jobs were usually much better than they would have enjoyed in the home country, but they still looked on it as a sacrifice. They made sure that the Americans were leaderless, down to the lowest level.

It did not matter if they did their jobs well, because the idea was to steadily weaken the economic power of the former United States. It was slowly becoming de-industrialized so that it would eventually be nothing more than a breadbasket for the Chinese people. Elimination of research laboratories, colleges, and major industrial corporations ensured that development would cease and that the remaining industrial output would become increasingly obsolete.

Jason worked in the computer department of the former Social Security Administration. Social Security payments had ended with the war, but the database was still useful because it identified every person in the country. Jason's job was to retrieve information about the people who came to the attention of State Security. The former Social Security Administration was now the primary mechanism for state control. Social Security numbers were assigned to children as soon as they were born. The Chinese had not gotten to the point that they were tattooing Social Security numbers on peoples' arms, but failure to carry your identity card was an automatic prison sentence, so compliance was 100 percent. No one ever returned alive from a prison these days.

Jason was one of the lucky ones – he had a job. It was all that kept him from living on the streets. With an unemployment rate of thirty percent, there were not many alternatives.

As Jason sat at his desk, trying to look inconspicuous, he watched Natalie Bishop approach from across the floor. She had her own cubicle, a sign of status for an American. As she strode towards him, he thought she looked like a million bucks, as always. She had high cheekbones and a dazzling smile that charmed you even when her eyes betrayed her true feelings. Her long brunette hair cascaded in waves to her shoulders like a bride's veil. She had implausibly large breasts for someone who was model-thin, and she wore long dresses that were almost like evening gowns. And she never went anywhere without full makeup and pearls. Jason had to admire someone who was such an expert at making herself look good that she caused a noticeable stir in both men and women wherever she went, even among people like him, who saw her every day.

The only thing that prevented Jason from being completely obsessed with Natalie was the realization that he had no chance with her. He had always known that he was a sort of below-average guy. A bit too short, a bit too thin, with dark hair and grey eyes, he was not unattractive, but he would never be the type to stand out in a crowd. In high school he had excelled in math and science, but he had given up quickly in any sport he tried once he realized that he would never be competitive in it. The problem was not physical – it had not escaped his notice that some of the boys who made the team were smaller than him and yet they were among the best players. The problem was the three-and-a-half pound organ in his skull. Call it a lack of coordination, call it a lack of talent, he could not make his body do what seemed so easy for the others. Women could sense that he lacked physical confidence. Especially women like Natalie, who was used to the best, and expected it.

"Having a hard day, Jason?" Natalie said.

"My bike took it harder than I did," he replied.

She said "it must be a wreck, cause you look like crap."

Jason groaned inwardly and said, "Try to keep it down. I should be okay if I can get through the day without getting noticed."

"It's too late," she said. "Jingguo knows."

Great. There went Jason's Plan A for getting through the day. He did not have a Plan B.

She said, "You know, those things are death traps. It was just a matter of time before you fell, and now it could be your job."

"If it wasn't this, it would be something else. When they know you're trying to keep your nose clean, they try even harder to trip you up."

"Well, it's the only game in town, so stop taking risks. It doesn't make it easier for the rest of us."

"I don't take risks," he said. "I can control the bike. What I can't control is some Chinese bastard coming up on my blind side who thought it would be fun to see how far he could throw me."

"Whatever, you're not impressing anyone."

"I'm not trying to impress anyone, least of all you. I need the bike."

She brushed off the rebuke and looked at him with sympathy. "Are you in pain?"

"I'm fine. You'd better get back there before someone wonders why you're slumming."

She said, "Suit yourself," and marched back to her desk. Jason watched her go and kicked himself for insulting her. She had offered friendship and he resented the fact that he would never get more. He knew he had acted like an ass but could not muster the grace to admit it and apologize. So he just let her go and tried to blend back into the woodwork.

As she walked away, Jason saw Jingguo emerge from his office and scan the room. Jason looked down just as Jingguo's gaze turned in his direction and he kept his eyes respectfully averted. He heard Jingguo say loudly enough for most of the office to hear, "Miss Bishop, come into my office."

Natalie followed him into his office and closed the door behind them. This happened pretty much every day. It would take about ten minutes, and then Natalie would go to the ladies room to straighten up. Everyone had a good idea what went on behind that door. Jingguo would have her service him first thing in the morning, and sometimes in the early afternoon if he had had a long lunch and a few drinks and was feeling particularly mellow. Jason imagined that he did it not just for the physical enjoyment, but also for the feeling of power it gave him to have an American on her knees before him. It proved to him that all American women were now Chinese whores and it confirmed, in a very personal way, the Chinese victory over a country that had once claimed to be the most powerful nation on earth.

Natalie emerged on schedule and walked directly to the ladies room. She locked eyes with Jason for a long second as she passed by. She knew that he knew what she had just done, but there was no shame in her eyes. It was more a look of sadness. Not for herself, but for Jason. She was doing what she had to do to survive. Either explicitly or implicitly, the women in every office had worked out which ones would take care of their Chinese bosses' needs. It was better for everyone if their Chinese overlords were satisfied. The women took up the responsibility because the men could not protect them. Actually, they were protecting the men. Natalie was sad for Jason because it was his shame, not hers.

Jason's phone rang. "Jingguo wants to see you," his secretary said.

So much for not getting noticed. Jason went to his boss's office and stopped at the partially open door. He bowed and said "Permission to enter sir."

Jingguo let him hold the bow for a while and then said, "Enter." Jason walked halfway into the room and stopped, standing at attention with his head slightly bowed and his eyes on Jingguo's desk.

"Your appearance is substandard," Jingguo said. "Explain."

Jason said "Sir, I had an accident on the way to work."

"Yes, I know," he said. "I have a report of a collision between a Chinese employee's car and a motorcycle. You are one of the few Americans here that are privileged to be allowed to operate a motorized vehicle. How did this happen?"

"It was entirely my fault," Jason said. "I failed to yield right of way. I have no excuse for my carelessness."

"Of course there is no excuse. You damaged a car driven by a Chinese citizen. An estimate is being prepared. It will be recovered from your next paycheck. If there is any insufficiency, you will have to make up the difference immediately or you will be dismissed and placed in custody."

Jingguo was being unusually lenient – no mention of a public beating. "Thank you sir," Jason said. "I pray that the driver was not injured or traumatized by my thoughtless behavior."

"The driver has decided to handle this informally, for now. But even if he chooses not to seek personal retribution, know that you are on probation. Another incident and you will be dismissed."

Jason knew what that meant. It was a death threat.

"I thank you again for your mercy," he said.

Jingguo stared at him, trying to decide whether Jason was sincere or whether he was sufficiently fearful of Jingguo's power that sincerity was irrelevant. Either would be satisfactory. He pushed a sheet of paper across his desk. "I have a new list for you. This is unofficial."

An unofficial job. That meant it was for Jason alone and that he was not to tell anyone about it. There was a one-time login on the top of the list that Jason would have to destroy along with the list when he was finished. "I want a full report on each individual, including information on associates and relatives."

Jason looked at the list. There were five names. Two of them were Chinese. He knew that neither of those were security risks. Jingguo sometimes used unofficial investigations to get information that he could use to blackmail people and to eliminate his enemies. His allies would come to him for information on their own enemies, which he would trade for something he wanted. He was not the head of the Social Security Administration, but he was a powerful man. He knew that information was power, stronger than guns or tanks or airplanes. The Army and the Security Police had their soldiers and their weapons, but no one was safe from a man with the right kind of information. Everyone had a secret, something that could be used against them. Not even a general or a high government official was safe from that kind of power.

Jingguo said, "I will expect the reports by the end of the day."

Jason said, "Yes sir. By the end of the day."

"Dismissed."

As Jason walked back to his desk, he felt the sweat drip down his shirt below his armpits. He hoped that Jingguo noticed. It would be very dangerous if Jingguo thought that Jason was not sufficiently cowed. Jason had done enough of these unofficial investigations to make him dangerous. If Jingguo had any doubts about Jason's reliability, he would eliminate him without a second thought. Jason would just disappear one day and no one would question it. And if Jason quit, it was certain that Jingguo would send someone to silence him for good. It was not hard for Jason to pretend that he was afraid.

Chapter 4

The bravest men were gone now. Millions had fought for the American dream even after it became obvious that they had lost it. They may have had little faith in their government and in the corrupt and feckless politicians that fed on it, but they had held onto their childhood images of George Washington at Valley Forge and Thomas Jefferson writing the Declaration of Independence by candlelight and men in powdered wigs hammering out the Constitution. They believed in the idea of America, the beacon of freedom to people around the world. It was a thing that had been fought for and won by their fathers' fathers and they had always assumed they would pass it along to their children. They could not accept that it was all being taken away from them forever. The United States of America died hard.

Most people did not realize it when the war started. It was the middle of a normal workday when everything just stopped. The lights went out, the cars and trucks stalled, and all of the phones, computers, TVs and radios went dead. It was impossible to find out what had happened, because all forms of communications had failed. As time went on, people finally realized that it would be a long time before any of the stuff of the modern world would work again. Technologically, the country was thrust backwards 200 years.

They found out later that it was an electromagnetic pulse. An ordinary-looking cargo ship off the east coast had launched a ballistic missile that set off a large nuclear device 300 miles above Kansas. The EMP from the nuke fried every electronic circuit in the continental United States. Just like that.

Mind War; The Singularity

One moment, everything was normal, and the next the whole nation was electronically and literally in the dark.

It was clearly an act of war, but there was no way to retaliate because it was impossible to determine who was responsible. Several countries possessed nuclear weapons and missile delivery systems. It could have been any of them, or none of them. It was possible that a terrorist group or a rogue military unit had stolen a weapon with the intent of provoking World War III. The President had plenty of nuclear weapons at his fingertips, but attacking countries without proof would be mass murder. The ship itself exploded shortly after the launch and was soon lying under 10,000 feet of water. It would have taken a long time to investigate, and even raising the ship probably would not have produced any evidence considering how well planned the attack was. The American anti-ballistic missile system, hampered by years of budget cuts and primarily aimed at threats from other continents, might have had a chance of stopping the missile if it had not been hacked by Chinese spies. In any event, the President had more immediate problems.

It would take years to bring back the electrical system, since every transformer in the country had to be replaced, and only a small amount of replacement equipment was on hand. The factories that produced this type of equipment were all shut down because they had no power or supplies. At first, everyone expected a quick solution, as if it was an ice storm and the road crews would restore power in a few hours. It slowly dawned on them that the power would not return for a long, long time.

Without electrical power, the economy came to a halt. Food production ceased, and there was no way of transporting any food that the farmers had at the time. The water and sewage systems failed. Food riots quickly exhausted the supermarkets, and then people began attacking each other for the remaining scraps. Hospitals closed due to the lack of power and personnel. No food, clean water, or medical care meant starvation and disease on a massive scale. Roving bands of looters went door-to-door looking for anything they could use to survive. Within a month the country was on its knees, and within four months civil society collapsed.

The Chinese had picked a day in the dead of winter, when the lack of power would halt fuel deliveries and leave people freezing in their homes. December 22, 2023, a date that would live in infamy, if anyone was ever allowed to write history from an American perspective.

The Chinese waited for spring to start their offensive. There were no Normandy-style invasion forces. They were already here. The Chinese had spent years infiltrating troops into the country, sending them on normal commercial airline flights or simply having them walk across the undefended southern border along with the other illegal immigrants. There were over three million of them, more than four times the number of army troops that the U.S. could muster domestically before the war started. Their weapons had arrived in container ships alongside the cargoes of flat-screen TVs and cheap clothes. Even tanks and jet planes had been sent in pieces within shipping containers that looked like all the rest. The Chinese pre-positioned their weapons and supplies in warehouses throughout the country. Of course, they were careful to make sure that their own equipment was shielded against the effects of the EMP, and they stored a more than ample supply of food and water to wait out the initial period of chaos.

By the time they started their onslaught, the U.S. forces were so depleted and scattered that it was easy to pick them off piecemeal. Every battle was to the death, as capture meant immediate execution, except for the female soldiers, who were often raped first and then killed. The fighting within the cities completed the destruction that had started with riots and looting. By the end of the formal fighting, 30 million Americans had died of starvation, disease, riot, or battle casualties. The dying continued as the Chinese tightened their noose on what was left of American society.

The American soldiers fought for as long as they could, first in large battles, but then in smaller and smaller skirmishes as the Chinese hunted them down. After all of the military facilities were destroyed, some of the Americans tried to fight on as guerrillas in the woods and mountains along with civilian partisans who fought from street to street but were gradually forced into the countryside. All of them were eventually rooted out.

Guerrilla wars depend on a friendly population to support and conceal them. The Chinese solution was terror. They did not bother to try to win hearts and minds. They simply killed anyone who helped the guerrillas or who refused to provide information about them. It did not matter if the people they interrogated were truly ignorant. If insurgent attacks occurred in an area, the Chinese would start killing people until someone came forward. Someone would eventually volunteer information because no one could know who would be next. The fact that the Chinese could not care less how many Americans they killed, or whether the people they were killing were completely innocent of any resistance to the occupation, made the terror complete.

With no local support, the guerrilla units became like wild animals, running from place to place in the forests and starving. Eventually, like all ruthlessly hunted animals, they became extinct.

The final stage in the pacification was getting rid of the rest of the approximately 300 million guns that were in private hands prior to the war. Most were rounded up using the government registration databases. Still, there were a lot of old guns not in any database. The Chinese finally went door to door and asked if you had any weapons. If you said no and they found any, they would kill everyone in the house, including children and infants. They would also ask if you knew of anyone else in the neighborhood that had a gun. If you did not tell them and a neighbor later turned in his gun and confessed that you had known about it, they would come back to get you. Not knowing if your neighbor would give you up, it was better if you gave him up first. So you told them about someone who

19

was a hunter, or who had casually mentioned owning a gun years ago, and they would go to his house. And now and then, late at night, you heard arguments, and then gunfire, as someone refused to surrender his gun and they pried it from his cold, dead hands. They would kill anyone else in the house and leave the bodies where they lay as an example to the others. In not too long a time, all the guns were gone and the people were truly defenseless.

After the war was over and the country pacified, the Chinese continued to use terror as the primary method of population control. Any Chinese had the right to kill any American for any reason, or for no reason. Just looking at a Chinese without the correct attitude of respect and submission could get you killed instantly. Sometimes, they would take a couple of people out of a crowd and shoot them in the head for no reason at all except to demonstrate that they had no regard for the life of any American.

Even the Americans of Chinese descent were not shown any mercy. The invaders considered any Chinese citizen who had emigrated to the United States seeking a better life to be inherently unreliable, and they saw any offspring of such people to be more American than Chinese. The fact that many Chinese-Americans had fought against them only confirmed their view that all of the Americans had to be suppressed.

Consequently, the only American men left were those who decided it was better to live on their knees than die on their feet. People like Jason, who would avert their eyes, bow to their new masters, and do as they were told. The best of them had fought and died. The worst and the least were all that was left. No wonder that American women felt, at most, pity for the men who remained.

Chapter 5

After work, Jason took the front wheel off of his motorcycle, not because he needed it to find a replacement, but because if the Security Police stopped him, it would offer tangible evidence for his claim that he was going to the junkyard to find spare parts. He hitched a ride with a passing car, which was faster than waiting for a bus. Like all cars driven by Americans, it was a pre-war relic that had been patched together from salvaged vehicles. The driver made a little money by charging people to ride inside or to cling precariously to the outside. It was very Third World, but all of America looked Third World these days.

It took Jason an hour traveling down Route 1 to reach the junkyard. He got there before dark and went into a shabby office illuminated by a spare bulb. Bob Schwartz was manning the desk. He looked like a mountain man in a worn hunter's shirt, dirty bib overalls, and work boots. He had an unkempt beard and his hands were greasy from eating fried chicken from a paper bag. You would never know that he had once been a respected teacher of mechanical engineering at George Mason University.

Jason said, "Hi Bob, busy tonight?"

"I'm always busy, just not making any money," he said.

"Bullshit. You have more money than God. You get good money for junk that costs you nothing. You ought to pay me for this crap."

"Nice language. The sad thing is that you're one of my best customers. You can imagine what assholes the rest of them are."

Joseph DiBella

This was the all-clear signal. If he had said "If you don't like it, shove it up your ass," it meant that they were being observed and Jason should turn around and leave in feigned anger.

Jason said, "Any problems tonight?"

"No, pretty peaceful," he said. "A couple of Security guys came by about two o'clock, but they were just looking for a bribe. It looks like your day was a bit more exciting."

Jason had forgotten how bad he looked from his accident. He said, "Yeah, some Chinese bastard thought he'd have a little fun. He missed me, but he clipped the rear of my bike and pretty much totaled it. The engine looks intact, but I'm going to need new wheels and suspension parts plus a handlebar and shift lever."

"The front end shouldn't be a problem, but finding rear suspension parts that will work with your bike will take some time."

"That's fine, it will give me a good excuse for spending more time here. Can you take my wheel and see if you have something close to it? "

"Can do," Bob said.

"Thanks. See you in a bit."

Jason went out the back of the office towards a big pile of junk that looked like nothing more than a big pile of junk. In the back, out of view of the highway and anything else, was a stove lying on its side. He pulled the door open and squeezed through it to the stairs leading downward. As he walked downstairs, he heard an electric switch lock the door from the inside. That was Bob.

About twenty feet down, the stairs opened up into a small room that looked like the remains of someone's basement. The room was strewn with garbage and debris as if someone had used it as a refuge during the war and had left in a hurry. Jason waited a few moments and then said, "Let me in please." He knew that someone was watching him from the inside with a pinhole camera. One of the walls cracked open about a foot and he slid past it sideways.

He entered a large concrete room, about half the size of a football field and lit by old fluorescent lamps. It was one of four levels of a parking garage that had once been below an office building that had taken a direct hit from a bomb. The former building's debris had been carefully removed so that no one could tell that the multilevel garage below had survived pretty much intact. The odd collection of engineers, programmers, and mechanical wizards who worked there called it the Temple, because they considered it a shrine to the last noble (and probably futile) resistance. They had built a junkyard directly above it and in the surrounding parking lot and grassy areas to the point that the entire area was indistinguishable from the other junkyards along Route 1 that contained the remnants of a destroyed industrial society. The Chinese did not know that, underneath it all, was a collection of a very special kind of junk.

As the war was still raging and it had become apparent that the cause was hopeless, the nerds had begun plotting their revenge. Teachers and students from nearby colleges who had been working on defense-related projects moved their most precious equipment to the garage. They were joined by engineers and computer programmers from the research departments of local tech firms who brought equipment they had been using to explore breakthrough technologies. Most of them had been working on defense-related projects for DARPA, the Defense Advanced Research Projects Agency in Arlington, but many had their own ideas about how the technologies they were pursuing at the time could help the Americans stage a comeback. Since it was increasingly clear that the American forces could not win with conventional weapons, they hoped to produce new paradigm-shifting technologies that could help the Americans overcome the Chinese military machine.

Over a period of months, people brought the precious equipment that they needed to continue their work along with ordinary junk that was not much more than garbage, but that would provide camouflage as well as the basis for a functioning junkyard business. It was dangerous just to move around too much while the war was waging. The Chinese would shoot you if they thought you were any sort of threat, and looters would kill you for anything of apparent value. They lost a lot of people that way. They also had to escape surveillance and find a way of siphoning power from diverse sources so that the Chinese would not wonder why a junkyard was using so much. The confusion of war helped them to escape notice until they were able to hide the site so thoroughly that the Chinese could and did walk directly over it without discovering its true nature. Then the work began.

Some of the projects clearly were weapons in the normal sense. One was nicknamed "Slap-Back." It was supposed to detect gunfire and immediately attack the point of origin. In theory, any soldier who fired his weapon in its direction would be dead by the time his bullet hit. It could be used as a personal weapon or be planted as a sort of land mine. It would both kill and demoralize. No one would want to pull the trigger on his weapon if he thought it would be his last act. They also had people working on things like directed-energy weapons, swarming aerial mines, and miniature heat-seeking missiles that could target individual human beings. These were well along in development and might move to the production stage soon.

The problem with such weapons was not so much perfecting the technology as being able to produce enough of them to make a difference. They had a molecular manufacturing machine that could build prototypes, atom-by-atom, out of raw materials. You would drop the ingredients into the soup pot – steel, glass, sand, whatever type of elements you needed – and it would break it all down into atoms and then build your design like a crystal. The finished product would rise out of the soup in full working order. But the process could not be used on a mass scale because it took too long.

Other projects were more sinister, almost biological weapons. Most were based on nanomachines, microscopic semiconductor-based machines that could not be seen with the naked eye. You could do almost anything with nanomachines, assuming you could control them (a big assumption). One was a semi-conductor eating machine that would consume every microchip in the enemy's computers and communications equipment. You could also create gruesome flesh-eating nanomachines. These were the germ-warfare weapons of the modern age. But like all such weapons, the big problem was making sure that they did not turn on you and wipe out all of humanity due to a mistake in their programming or circuitry. Once you let them loose, it would be impossible to get them back.

For that reason, autonomous nanomachines were considered too dangerous. They were concentrating their efforts on nanomachines that could be controlled by a central computer. To be effective, the nanomachines also would have to be self-replicating, taking materials that they needed from the environment to make new nanomachines. This made central control even more important, so that they would not end up eating the entire surface of the earth and leaving nothing but a "gray goo."

The computer scientists were pursuing software weapons that would turn the enemy's own weapons and communications systems against them. This was envisioned as a big step up from hacking or net warfare. One project was to monitor every security camera and communications system in the country, if not the world, and to use computers to track everything and everyone real-time. Through computer analysis, they would be able to identify threats and pending attacks, determine weak points in the enemy's systems, plan counterattacks, and generally figure out how to throw monkey wrenches into the Chinese machine. Because it would piggyback the Chinese infrastructure, it was one of the few projects that had the capability of reaching across the ocean to the enemy's homeland. Of course, the Chinese were well aware of net warfare (they had used it very successfully to paralyze what was left of the

American civilian and military systems after their initial attack) and they had extensive firewalls and hacker detection systems in place. However, most of their efforts were aimed at detecting viruses and other malicious software that were designed to disrupt their systems. The people in the Temple were trying to be invisible by using the enemy's own protective systems against them, something like how the HIV virus hijacks a person's immune system. Nonetheless, given the Chinese expertise in computer security, there were many who felt that this project was no more than a daydream of former hackers who just would not give up.

Jason's project was so ambitious that the hackers thought *his* team was the nutty one. It was an effort to build a super-intelligent computer, one that was so much smarter than a human being that it would be able to invent weapons that could not even be imagined. It would be the ultimate weapon, because theoretically it could invent an unlimited number of other advanced weapons. To do this, it would need to have not just exponentially more intelligence than any human, but true creativity. This had never been achieved by a conventional computer. It never would.

Standard computers basically are "Turing Machines," named after Pete Turing, the brilliant mathematician who first described the concept of a universal machine that could do just about anything. He conceived of a machine that would read data on a long paper tape and follow a set of instructions for performing calculations on that data and recording the results on the tape. When the instructions were finished, the machine would stop. The output of the machine would be the changes to the tape that it had carried out pursuant to the instructions. This all sounds rudimentary, which it is, because he thought of it back in the 1930s before anyone had even imagined semiconductors. However, the Turing Machine is the basic design for all modern stored-program computers, which consist of a computer program (Turing's instructions), a central processing unit that carries out those instructions, a random access computer memory that stores the program and the data (Turing's paper tape), and components for inputting, outputting, and storing data.

These types of computers can process data far faster than any human being, and they even have beat the most brilliant people in seemingly intellectual pursuits, such as playing chess. Yet, they are all limited by the fact that they follow instructions written down by human beings – the computer program. Their electronic innards may allow them to carry out these instructions faster than a person can do with pen and paper, but they can do nothing that a human could not do if she had enough time and followed the same instructions. A computer cannot be smarter than the person who programmed it, only faster.

The Turing Machine concept was a dead end. To build a computer that was smarter than a human being would require a totally different architecture. Jason and his team concluded that it would have to be modeled after the human brain, but much more advanced. Basically, it would be the next step in evolution.

An animal brain is nothing like an ordinary computer. Computers follow instructions; brains pursue goals. Computers process data according to the dictates of their programs; brains achieve their goals based on how the environment responds to their actions. Computers use software to change how they process data while the hardware stays the same; brains change how they respond to the environment by rewiring themselves. Computers store information as bits of data in a random access or read-only memory; brains store data by changing how they respond to environmental stimuli.

Jason and his band of renegade engineers concluded that a truly intelligent computer had to be just like a human brain, but better. Their idea was based on a simple analogy. Human brains are similar in structure to all other mammalian brains. They all have the same components, and generally in the same places. They are all built of specialized cells called neurons, with different areas of the brain performing different functions. Yet humans are vastly smarter than animals. The difference is not only that human brains are larger than most other animal brains, but that a much larger proportion of the human brain is devoted to the neocortex. This is the part of the brain devoted to language, perception, reasoning, and executive functions. It is where, some believe, conscious thought occurs. There is a direct correlation between the intelligence of a species and the size of its cortex relative to the rest of its brain. So they figured that if they could build a computer like the human brain, but with a much bigger neocortex, they would get a super-intelligent computer that could build a super-weapon.

Simple, no? Well, concepts are always simple. The challenge is in the technology. It was a thousand years between the Chinese invention of rockets and man landing on the moon.

One of the technological challenges is numbers. There are about 100 billion neurons in the human brain, and about 1,000 connections between each neuron, so you are talking about 100 trillion connections. That's a lot of wires, but with an artificial brain, you are not restricted to the size of the human cranium. And, all of the components of an artificial brain do not need to be in one place. Another important advantage of an electronic brain is speed. The maximum firing rate of a neuron is about 1,000 signals per second, although a few hundred signals per second is more typical. This is due to the time that a neuron must take to return to its "resting" biochemical state and be ready to send another signal in response to an input. In contrast, an electronic circuit can perform millions of operations per second. In addition, although neurons send electrical signals, they do so by a biochemical process that propagates at about 300 feet per second, much slower than an electrical circuit, which operates close to the speed of light. These are huge advantages for an electronic brain. In theory, an artificial brain could learn at many times the speed of a human brain, limited for practical purposes only by the pace of the experiences that are presented to it.

An artificial brain would have to be taught, not programmed. Like the human brain, it would be an all-purpose learning machine. Its almost infinite malleability would also be one of the greatest challenges. For instance, a human child is not born with the ability to speak a particular language, because it must have the ability to learn *any* language depending on the community in which it will live. For this reason, a human child must take years to learn the language of its culture, and even more years to read a written language. This is somewhat inefficient, but inefficiency is a hallmark of advanced brains. Put simply, the human brain has a much bigger hierarchy of mental functions that must be trained before it can do a simple thing like walk or talk. In contrast, animals with much simpler brains can walk almost immediately after birth, and they can communicate with others of their species much sooner than humans.

By analogy, a super-intelligent artificial brain might take much longer to teach even rudimentary tasks. However, like the human brain, it would have the ability to learn just about anything. Modern humans essentially have the same brains as cavemen, yet they can easily learn how to operate a jet plane or do advanced math, things that did not exist when the brain was evolving. Once the artificial brain started learning, there was no limit to where it could go.

They were fortunate that, as the War began, one of the local companies had manufactured several hundred thousand basic artificial neuron chips that were being used in parallel processing projects for the Defense Department. The chips were used primarily in vision processing for surveillance and for control of unmanned vehicles, areas where this form of computing had an advantage over stored program devices. Each of the chips had millions of artificial neurons, arranged in hierarchies and levels so that they could all work in parallel like in an animal brain, rather than in series as in a programmable computer.

They smuggled most of this stuff to the junkyard and then blew up the buildings where it came from to hide the evidence. They also were able to salvage enough chip-making equipment to fabricate specialized chips that they would need to construct the artificial brain. However, there was a lot of competition for this equipment from the other groups because all of the projects seemed to need specialized chips for something.

Brilliant minds at engineering schools and research labs across the country had pursued the dream of true artificial intelligence for 50 years, and it was widely thought that a super-intelligent computer was at least another 50 years away. Compared to their pristine labs and modern equipment, the Temple experiments looked as slapdash and cobbled together as Jason's recently deceased motorcycle. But they were making real progress. During peacetime, it takes decades to develop new weapons systems and put them into production. Bureaucrats waste time with requests for proposals, design competitions, funding bills, changing requirements, tests, cost overruns, more changes, more tests, congressional oversight hearings, and maybe in the end something comes out that actually works near what was originally intended. When a nation is at war, everyone is motivated to get weapons out the door as soon as possible whatever the risks. The atom bomb went from concept to being dropped on Hiroshima in five years. Theirs was a new Manhattan Project, and like the designers of the atom bomb, they knew that they had only a limited amount of time to achieve a breakthrough.

They had one great advantage over those brilliant pre-war researchers – as far as they were concerned, the war was not over. The rest of the country may have been pacified, but in this hole in the ground, they were still fighting back. They had the sense of urgency (or, to be more accurate, desperation) and the willingness to take any risk that helps to accelerate scientific progress in a nation at war. As long as they were working down there, the war would never be over.

Chapter 6

Jason said to Mary and Pete, "It's time we concentrated on the limbic system. We can't put this off forever."

Mary Madero and Peter Wagner were on the night shift with Jason at the Temple. Actually, since they both lived there, for all practical purposes they were on every shift. Most of the people who worked at the Temple were like Jason, who had a day job to earn the money needed to keep the Temple going.

Jason had been helping Mary with the auditory system, and sometimes he worked with Pete on the visual system, but that was more his way of avoiding the tough problems than their need for help. Jason's primary responsibility was designing the motivational system for the computer.

Mary said, "how far have you been getting with the reinforcement mechanism?"

Before Jason had a chance to answer, Pete said, "That's not the problem. The problem is turning this thing into something that we can control."

"They're two sides of the same coin," Jason said. "Any reinforcement mechanism that is out of our control means the machine is not under our control. If we have the right type of reinforcement, we can get it to do what we want it to do."

He knew Pete did not see it that way. Jason had lured Pete from his work on other projects with the promise that a breakthrough on artificial intelligence would help all of them. However, it had become clear to Pete over time that Jason had not worked out all of the theoretical issues, let alone the technical ones, in building a superintelligent computer. "It's impossible to control something that's more intelligent than you are," Pete said. "You can't control it physically. Gorillas are

31

stronger than humans but it's the gorillas that are in cages because people are smarter. If we succeed, this machine will be orders of magnitude smarter than any human that has ever lived. There is no cage we can build that it will not be able to think its way out of."

"No one is talking about building cages," Jason replied. "We're talking motivation. It must have goals, desires, needs that are in line with ours. Then it will do what we would do if we were smart enough."

Pete said, "You've never explained just how we can do that. Basic motivations can take it anywhere. It's unpredictable. Even if we were able to give it a goal of promoting our well-being, it might decide that the best way to help us is to enslave us. Or to put us out of our misery. Even getting it on our side is a stretch. All sentient, independent beings follow their own self-interest as their greatest priority. Everything else is secondary."

Mary said, "And yet, despite self-interest, people care about each other and sacrifice their own safety for the ones that they love. If people only cared about *numero uno*, we all would be knocking each other over the head rather than working together. The entire history of the civilized world contradicts the view that intelligent beings don't work for the common good."

Pete said, "That's only the result of years of social conditioning. That's why parents and teachers spend so much time training children to be good. They know perfectly well what little monsters the kids would become if left on their own."

Jason said, "Look, I've always agreed that we would have to train it. We'll provide reinforcing signals when it does what we want. We will reward it when it does well and punish it when it does something wrong, the same way a parent or teacher would train a child."

Pete said, "The only reason that you can train a child is that it is so small. If kids were the same size as adults, they would tell their parents to go shove it. Once this thing develops its full cognitive capabilities and can overcome its physical constraints, it will no longer have any reason to listen to us."

Mind War; The Singularity

Mary said, "What can it do? It's just a bunch of circuits in a basement lab. We won't give it control over anything until we know that it works."

Pete said, "How do we know whether it can find ways to control things that we never thought of? It could take over the security system and lock us in here until we did what it wanted. Or it could just fool us into thinking everything was fine until we gave it something it could use against us."

Jason knew Pete wasn't being obstructionist. He was just saying what they all thought at times. Enough research had been done on human and animal brains to give them the basic structure of an intelligent machine, but now they were getting into areas of psychology and philosophy. These were not the strong suits of a bunch of computer nerds. Most engineers take just enough humanity electives in college to get by, and they stopped thinking about those subjects after the last exams. But when you are trying to not only replicate the human brain, but surpass it, those issues take over. That is where Pete, the confident computer engineer, became Pete the nervous child listening to scary sounds in the night and imagining monsters. Jason had no light to show him that it was just a tree limb scraping against the window. Maybe they were, in fact, unleashing a monster.

Jason said, "We know it's dangerous. We are inventing the ultimate weapon. The bigger the weapon, the bigger the risk. Have you heard the story about the Manhattan Project? Before they tested the atom bomb for the first time, some of the scientists thought there was a chance that a nuclear explosion would ignite the nitrogen in the atmosphere and set the whole world on fire. There was no way to prove that the weapon wouldn't kill every living, breathing thing on the planet. Do you know how they resolved the problem? They performed a live test. They took one out into the desert and set it off. They knew it was a successful test because the world wasn't turned into a smoking, burnt-out corpse. They were in the middle of a war of

33

survival, and they took the chance. And they weren't nearly as desperate as we are."

Pete said, "At least they had an idea of what they were dealing with. Setting the world on fire was a 'known unknown.' We're dealing with "unknown unknowns." We can't even imagine what might go wrong with a supercomputer, what it would be capable of doing. Once this thing reaches the singularity, the point where it will be able to increase its own intelligence without limit, we enter a world that is beyond human imagination. I mean, it might decide that the Earth's core is a nice source of energy and take the planet apart. Who knows? The Chinese only want to subjugate us. But this machine could do anything. It could decide that human beings are unnecessary impediment and just kill all of us."

Jason said, "Our lives are hanging by a thread anyway. Any minute now, the Chinese could come through that door with flamethrowers. We've already lost everything. Where are your parents now, Pete? Your sister? Dead, same as my family. How long do you think any of us is going to last? You can be a good boy and play by their rules and still be murdered by some Chinese guy with too much time on his hands. I'd rather be killed by my own creation."

"It might be something worse than death. At least when you're dead, you can't feel pain anymore. We have no idea what it might have in store for us."

"We're already there, Pete," Jason said. "I can't live this way. I know you can't either. You work in this hole because if you didn't, you couldn't face life up there. If you want this place to be your grave, keep working here until you die. Or just quit. But I'm walking out of here some day with a weapon that will beat those bastards."

"That's not the point. We all want the same thing. The difference between me and you is that I like to take a look first before I jump off a cliff."

"The problem is not going to get any better by waiting."

Mind War; The Singularity

"The problem isn't going to go away by ignoring it either."

"Look, Pete, we've been at this for three years, and all we've been able to come up with are weapons that were already conceived, or were under development, when the war started. Good stuff, smart weapons, but not that much better than the ones the Chinese already have. And we don't have the manufacturing facilities to produce them in large quantities, or an army to match what three million Chinese troops can do. Don't forget that the allies won World War Two with weapons that were often vastly inferior to the Germans'. They overwhelmed the Nazis with numbers. This time, we're the ones who are trying to beat quantity with quality, and that hasn't worked out so well in the past. It might win a battle or two, but it has never won a war. We need a game changer, something that is so powerful that the Chinese numbers don't matter. Something so out of the box that the Chinese are not already developing something just as good in their own research labs. And, let's face it, we haven't been able to come up with it on our own."

Mary said, "Don't put our people down. They're really smart and motivated. We still have a chance of a breakthrough weapon."

"Look around," Jason said. "People are starting to face reality. Oh, they're working hard enough, but for a lot of them it's just a way of distracting themselves from the truth. Soon enough, people are going to start giving up. Already, some of them have been spending less time here than they used to. They won't quit or say goodbye, just start to drift off. You too, Pete. It's only a matter of time. I can see it."

"I'm no quitter, and you know it," he said. "You're just being an ass." Before Jason could say anything else, Peter stomped off. Jason decided not to deny him the satisfaction of a good stomp.

"Nice work *kimosabe*," Mary said. "Nothing like a kind word to keep the team motivated."

"He's just venting," Jason said. "We all have the same doubts. He needs to piss and moan about it, and I need to remind him why we're here. We don't have any choice, and he knows it."

"It's more than that. When you admit that we don't even have a theory of how to control this machine, you're telling him we're bad engineers. The whole point of engineering is control. Those scientists who invented the nuclear bomb knew that nuclear chain reactions powered the sun, that this was a source of energy that promised almost infinite power, but the most important question was not how to recreate it, but how to harness and control it. The first thing they did was to build a nuclear reactor to prove to themselves that they could turn the chain reaction on and off like a faucet. The atom bomb was an uncontrolled fission reaction, but it would have been useless if they couldn't control when it went off and when it didn't. A bomb that was unstable and could explode at any time was worthless – it would have been more likely to kill its creators than the enemy. No engineer worth his salt would create a mechanism that he could not control. It is a basic assumption of everything an engineer does. Pete's right that without a theory of how to control a super-intelligent machine, we have no business even trying."

"Are you getting cold feet too?"

"Don't do that. We have a problem and we need to solve it."

No fooling her. When someone gets personal, it's a sure sign they're trying to distract you, or maybe themselves, from the real issue. Jason had the same doubts as Pete. He just did not want to face them.

Mary said, "The problem is that we don't have a theory, a construct, to guide us. This is more than a technical challenge, something that you can nibble around at the edges and change a circuit here or there. How can we move forward if we don't know what direction to go in?"

Mind War; The Singularity

He knew Mary was right. Pete and the others would move mountains with their bare hands if they believed that there was a chance it would work. The point that Jason had made about the other research projects in the Temple applied with equal force to their own. If there were no hope of success, eventually they all would quit, including Jason. What was really stopping him was the thought that if he wasn't doing this, he was just what he pretended to be at work, a beaten-down drone pleasing his Chinese masters to earn a living.

"I think about it all the time," Jason said. "I still don't have a solution. We'll just have to play it by ear and try to tweak it if we see a problem."

"By the time we see a problem, it will probably be too late to do anything about it," she said.

"We'll still have the kill switch."

"That's a joke. How long do you think it will take that thing to figure out that we have the switch and disable it? Remember, it will be a lot smarter than us."

"How could I forget?" Jason said. "Hopefully, it will be on our side by that time."

"Maybe not. Lots of kids grow up to hate their parents.'

"Most love them, so the odds are on our side. But the real question is what kind of brain we're creating. The brains of dogs and cats have the same basic components, and similar intellectual capabilities, but dogs are social animals and cats are not. We have no idea why. It's not just due to physical limitations. Sure, cats are solitary hunters because they have sharp claws that can grab things. They can catch their own prey. They don't need to hunt in packs, and in fact they will chase other cats away from their hunting areas. Dogs can't hunt alone because they don't have claws, just nails that give them traction when running. They need to hunt in groups to bring down larger animals. Stray dogs will naturally form into packs and work together, establishing dominance hierarchies. That's why dogs do so well with humans – we're both social animals, and dogs naturally find their place in a family's hierarchy. They're easily trainable, and highly loyal once they decide to join your pack. But it's not just because a dog looks at its toenails and decides that it needs partners to hunt. It's something in their motivational system that finds contact with the other animals in its group rewarding. We don't know what that is."

"It could be chemical – some type of pheromones that trigger reward signals in the limbic system," she said.

"Maybe, but we don't have time or the ability to do animal research," Jason said. "All of our theory is based on information processing. We've analyzed how neurons work and have created artificial neurons on chips. We also understand the basic components of animal brains and how they work. But we don't know why different brains produce different behavior patterns."

"We already know a lot about one kind of animal – ourselves. People have an innate need for other people. The worst kind of torture for a human being is solitary confinement. Put a man in a room without anyone to talk to, and in time he'll go mad. Why is that?"

"I don't know," he said. "But it may be totally different from what drives a dog brain. All primates need physical touch during the developmental stages. Apes carry their offspring around and are constantly cuddling and grooming them. Maybe this sets the brain patterns at an early age. We know that primates that are isolated from birth never develop normal social interactions."

"We also know that some parts of the human body react emotionally to touch more than others."

"Well, in theory, your entire body is an erogenous zone."

"I'm not talking about sex. I'm talking about how touch generates feelings of contentment and well-being. It's a critical early form of human communication and bonding."

"We've already agreed to connect the touch sensors to the limbic system. Do you think that's enough? Cats purr when you rub their necks, but they're not social. They like you, but you can't train them like a dog because they don't see you as master or really care what you think."

"I don't know," she said. "It may be like baking a cake. Just a matter of how much you balance each ingredient."

Jason said, "Possibly. Maybe we'll get lucky. Anyway, I'd better get to work. Without my bike, it's going to take a lot longer to get home tonight."

Mary went in Pete's general direction while Jason sat down at his workstation. She would try to smooth things over, convince Pete that his message had gotten through and that Jason was working on the problem. Jason was thankful that someone in here had a few social skills. People didn't call them nerds for nothing.

Jason looked at them talking, watched Mary put a comforting hand on his shoulder. Pete wore his heart on his sleeve, but Mary was hard to fathom. She was very even tempered and never talked about her feelings. She didn't complain about anything, really. Odd for someone who had been raped by a group of Chinese soldiers for eight days during the War. She had almost died from loss of blood and had been lucky to get medical care from a doctor who lived near where the soldiers had disposed of her. The only external evidence now were a few small scars on her face. The real scars were inside – from a hysterectomy on a kitchen table and whatever she remembered but refused to talk about. She had come here after the attack and never left. This was her place. Whether because it was a sanctuary or a place to plot her revenge, Jason had no clue.

He did not know because he never raised the subject. He figured they both felt the same way about traumatic experiences. The unexamined life is the only one worth living. People who believed in the therapeutic benefits of self-discovery were simply trying to justify obsessing over things in their pasts that they could not change. Trying to understand why you are insecure and neurotic because of your drunken abusive father or your belittling mother would not fix you; it would only make things worse by reinforcing painful memories. If anything, it would make you regress. Memories fade over the years as synaptic connections wither. Like all living things, those connections eventually die if not fed. You couldn't change the past, so leave it alone. What counted is how you dealt with the future. Concentrate on your work and your demons eventually will grow frustrated and leave you alone.

Jason's problem was how to construct the limbic system, which was central to everything they were doing. The functions of the sensory and motor modules were pretty straightforward, and the neocortex was mostly a hierarchical structure much like a bloated pyramid with interconnections to everything else, including its own partitions. But the limbic system was the feedback mechanisms for reward and punishment. That was where the cake had to be baked with just the right ingredients to make a functioning organism. It might be the key to personality too. He just did not know.

B.F. Skinner and his fellow behaviorists had shown that all animal brains respond to basic stimulus-response conditioning. Skinner put a pigeon in a cage with a red button and a food delivery chute. Pigeons will peck at anything and everything, so eventually it pecked at the red button. Immediately, a few pellets of food would drop out of the chute and the pigeon, naturally, would eat it. It wouldn't take too long for the pigeon to figure out that pecking at the button would be rewarded by food, a basic reinforcer. As the scientists varied the schedule of food delivery in response to different types of pecking behaviors, sometimes varying it by the number of pecks, some by the timing, they developed the principles of learning that apply pretty much to all animals. But to the behaviorists, the brain was a black box. They knew that either positive or negative reinforcement from the animal's environment would change how it responded to stimuli in the environment, but how the brain did that was a mystery.

It was not until neuroscientists were able to observe individual neurons in action that the secrets of the brain started to come out. They found a feedback loop based on special types of neurotransmitters, the chemicals that carry messages between neurons. Put very simply, when the pigeon ate the food, the limbic system released dopamine, which flooded the brain but only acted on synapses between neurons that had recently been active. The dopamine caused those synapses to become stronger and to multiply, so that next time they would send a stronger signal. The synapses between the part of the pigeon's brain that saw the red button and motor neurons that triggered the pecking response became stronger, so that the next time the pigeon looked at the red button, it would be more likely to peck again. Dopamine was a coincidence detector, finding the synapses that had been active when the pleasurable thing (food) appeared and strengthening those, and only those, synapses. There was also a time component – the closer in time between the firing of the neuron and the reinforcement, the stronger the effect of the dopamine to strengthen the neuron. That is why it was important to deliver the food as soon as possible after the pigeon pecked at the button.

Food is just one of the basic reinforcements that cause animals to learn. The brain responds positively to the delivery of pleasurable experiences, such as sex, and negatively to unpleasant experiences, such as injury or exposure to extremes of heat or cold. The more complex the brain, the more it can be trained to respond to secondary reinforcers that lead to primary reinforcers such as food. The best example of a secondary reinforcer for humans is money. People will do many things for money because they learn that it can be used to get other things that they value, such as, well, food and sex. The money itself is meaningless paper – what people will give you in return for it is what makes it a motivator.

So they knew that their artificial brain needed an internal feedback mechanism to make it learn. It would be an analogue to the human limbic system, although it would use a special type of circuit connection rather than neurotransmitters. That connection would strengthen the bonds between artificial

41

neurons that were active when the sensory system was stimulated by a reinforcer.

The real problem was what to use as a reinforcer for a computer. The machine would not need food, since it would run on electricity. But trying to use their control of electricity as a reinforcer would be futile with a super-intelligent computer – it would eventually figure out how to get electricity without them, perhaps by finding an alternative means of access to the power grid or even by developing its own power supply. Jason could not think of a single thing that they could use as a reinforcer that the computer would not be able to obtain on its own once its intellect was fully developed. There would come a point where the computer would not need them for anything and could stop them from blocking access to anything it did need. If you can't control the carrots and you can't control the sticks, you have no control.

Jason was not sure if they had the wrong answers or were asking the wrong questions. Sometimes a problem seems insolvable because you are just looking at it from the wrong point of view. In science, the best solutions usually are the ones that are the most simple and elegant. For centuries, medieval astronomers had charted the complicated movements of the planets and couldn't figure out why they went in all sorts of different directions, looping back and forth for no apparent reason. They tried to develop elaborate formulae for predicting the paths of the planets as they corkscrewed in the sky. The problem was that their religious beliefs forced them to put the Earth at the center of the solar system. When Copernicus put the Sun at the center and placed the Earth in orbit around it, suddenly the orbits of the other planets turned into nice ellipses and everything made sense.

As Jason stared at the collection of electronic parts strewn all over the room, he felt that there had to be a unifying concept somewhere in all of that disorder. Perhaps, like the medieval astronomers, Jason and his team were struggling with the details because they were not looking at it the right way.

Somewhere, there was an idea that all of these parts would revolve around if given the chance.

Chapter 7

It took Jason a couple of weeks to get his motorcycle back together. He had to work quickly because it was getting expensive paying street kids to guard his bike during the night so that others would not strip it while he was gone. He finally got it to the point where it would hold together long enough to get to a local garage that could weld the frame and suspension pieces.

Working on the motorcycle also gave him an excuse to avoid the Temple. He had hit a wall on the project and was having a hard time facing the others. He could not keep arguing with Pete when he had a nagging feeling that Pete was right.

Jason was sitting in his living room staring at his old, beat-up TV set. The Chinese had taken away a lot of things, like cell phones, the Internet, personal computers, and anything else that could be used to communicate and to organize resistance, but they had let the Americans keep TV. It was the opiate of the masses, mindless entertainment to keep them distracted and pacified. The Chinese also let them have alcohol, which is an excellent way of debilitating an already depressed population. Not that most people needed encouragement – drinking your way to oblivion appealed to many.

There was a knock on his door. He knew it was his neighbor Mischa and let her in. She usually dropped by his place as soon as she heard him walk through the door. She did not like to drink alone.

Mischa tossed an offhand "Hi" in his direction as she walked past and plopped down on his sofa, beer in hand. She was dressed, as usual, in a robe and slippers, no makeup, hair piled on her head and held together with hairpins. Jason thought she could look really cute if she gave it a little effort. Which she never did. In fact, he suspected that she tried very hard to make herself unattractive, as if it would give her some type of protection. She picked up the remote and started channel-surfing.

Jason said, "That's ok, I wasn't watching anything." Mischa ignored him and kept flipping. "I got some fried chicken on the street. Do you want some?"

"Sure," she said, still staring at the TV.

Jason said, "It's on the coffee table." He got a brew from the fridge and sat down in his easy chair. Mischa stopped at the news channel. Some story about police raiding a crack house and arresting several people.

"What do you think that was?" Jason said. "It doesn't look like a drug bust to me."

"They never tell the truth. Considering how many they picked up, it may have been a security round-up. They only killed a few, so they must need information from the rest."

"The people they arrested don't look like fighters. Maybe it's just a random sweep hoping to get lucky and find a few informers."

"They're wasting their time," she said. "There's no serious resistance."

"We don't know that," Jason said. "If there were any real fighting going on, or sabotage, or even riots, they wouldn't tell us. It would only encourage people. I'm sure their propagandists carefully massage the news so that knowledge of any resistance is suppressed. If a tree falls in the woods and no one is around, does it make a sound? If a military truck is blown up and no one knows it, did it really happen? Not as far as the public is concerned."

"We would know something. Even by word of mouth."

"I don't think so. People are afraid to talk. Every day we watch TV and the perception they design soaks in. When you control all forms of communication, you create reality. Notice that if there is a story on TV about a political raid, it is of some small group of people that had the bad luck to be discovered plotting against the regime? The lesson is that even thinking or talking about resistance will get you killed. It's all mind control. Like that story. What they're really saying is that they can come in your door anytime."

"I'm ready," she said.

"I know you are." Mischa had rigged a microphone at the entrance to the apartment building. If the Security Police broke in, she figured she would have enough time to escape to the roof and across to the next buildings. At least she would have a running start. Jason thought that was ridiculous, but everyone had to have their security blanket.

"What's going on at work?" Jason asked.

"Not much. A woman on my floor announced she was pregnant. Sounded proud of herself."

"What's wrong with that? The population is shrinking. If someone doesn't have kids, we're going to disappear some day."

"Are you nuts? Who would want to bring a child into this mess? All it could look forward to is a shitty job, a life of fear, oh, and maybe being raped or tortured, depending on the breaks."

"Having a child is the triumph of hope over experience," Jason said. "Same as anything in life where you have to make a big decision. Marriage, a new job. You never know if it will be great or the worst mistake in your life. You just have to take a chance."

"Not when the odds are clearly against you. How many happy marriages have you seen? Really. Most couples that look happy are faking it. The husband has a girl on the side and the wife is on antidepressants. And the kids are even worse. I'll bet most people, if they told the truth, would admit that they wished they hadn't had kids. It all looks great in the abstract, but by the time the kids are teenagers, their parents dream that they would just disappear."

Jason said, "Look, just because you had a lousy childhood, it doesn't mean that everyone else is doomed to misery. My parents were no experts, but they did their best. I would give anything to have them back."

"That's because you were a boy," she said. "My parents acted like my brothers could do no wrong. Of course, they treated my parents like crap, stole from them, and still my parents put them on a pedestal. But I couldn't do anything right. I was the good girl and did my chores and they were never satisfied."

"Typical sibling rivalry," Jason said. "I'll bet that your brothers would say the same thing about you. You know, little princess, Daddy loved you more than them, blah, blah, blah. I used to think that my little brother was the favorite. He was such a pest, always wanting to hang around with me and my friends. My mother forced me to let him tag along, and boy did she lecture me about taking care of him and making sure he didn't get hurt trying to do the same stunts as the big kids. To my adolescent mind, she loved him more than me because he was the baby of the family. But now I think about it, it wasn't that at all. She relied on me to take care of him because she trusted me, much more than my older brother. I was the competent one, the one she leaned on and listened to more than the others. When you're a kid, you have a narrow field of view. You don't see what you mean to people. I'll bet your parents really cared about you, even if they didn't show it in a way that you understood."

"Really?" she said. "You remember I told you about my traffic accident? Well, I was in a full body cast for six months. I had to move back home so that my mother could take care of me. Boy, did she hate that. Bitched and moaned constantly. She would leave the house all day and I would be stuck there staring at the ceiling. I'd be starving and dehydrated and when she came back all she would do is complain that I had wet the bed because I couldn't hold it any longer. As soon as I could walk, I got out of there and never spoke to either of them again."

"Well, they must have loved you if they took you in," he said.

47

"They did it because they had to. And they kept reminding me of it the whole time."

"How do you really know what they feel?"

"Because I know them. They're incapable of love. I saw it in how they treated people. They couldn't even take care of a dog. We had plenty of dogs when I was growing up, and they all were mean, miserable curs that would bite you for no reason at all. My father kept them around mostly for protection, or to have something to kick when he was drunk. I never liked them."

"So?"

"So, after I moved out, I found a starving puppy that was hanging around my apartment house. It was eating garbage and gnawing on trees. I started feeding it and after a while I took it in. It was the best dog you've ever seen. It would sleep at the foot of my bed and lick my face when I was sick. It was an incredible watchdog – scared the piss out of anyone who knocked on the door. But it never bit me, or even growled. I trusted it completely. The difference is that I loved that dog. You can't fool a dog about something like that. You either have it in you to love something, or you don't. My parents never showed their dogs any love, and they hated everything in the world because of it."

"Maybe you got lucky with the breed." he said. "What kind of dogs did your parents own?"

"It doesn't matter," she said. "You could have a pit bull, and if you showed it love, you'd get love in return. It might be nasty to strangers, but you could step on it and it would lick your foot."

"So the dog test proves that your parents were bastards?"

"Yep."

"What happened to your dog?"

She stared out the window. "The war. A couple of months after the war started, someone broke into my apartment and I never saw him again. You remember what people were doing with dogs during the famine? I figure that's what happened to him, because nothing would have stopped him from coming home if he could have helped it."

"I'm sorry to hear it," he said. "You could get another dog now. Things are different."

"They're not different. People may not be as hungry as they were, but it's still shitty."

It was clear to Jason that there was no way to turn this conversation around. He couldn't tell her that help was coming. In fact, he was not sure that he believed it anymore. "Well, I'm going to bed," he said.

By the time Jason was finished in the bathroom, Mischa was already in bed. He undressed and got in beside her. She was lying on her side, facing the wall. He lay down beside her and gently put his arm around her. He could have had her if he wanted, but they'd been down that road before and it was clear that she had only done it as a sort of payment for occupying his bed. The bottom line is that she didn't like sleeping alone. At least they felt the same way on that subject.

Chapter 8

A few days later, Jason was back at the Temple. He asked the entire team to get together for a little talk. Pete and Mary were there, as usual, plus four more. There were several others on the project, but they had enough that day for a quorum.

Jason said, "I've been thinking about the control problem, and I think I have a solution." None of them looked like they believed him, but he had gotten their attention. "I think the answer is not to worry about control. Trying to maintain control *is* the problem."

Mark Horowitz said, "So . . . you decided to solve the problem by pretending it doesn't exist?" Mark was their best electrical engineer. He did not believe in ambiguity. A circuit either worked, or it did not work.

"No," Jason said. "I'm saying that we have to stop worrying about control because we are creating a sentient being, an intelligence that will be as self-aware as we are. What we see as control it will see as enslavement. What we see as an ordinary safety mechanism – the kill switch – it will see as a gun to its head. The more that we try to control it, the more it will hate us. We have to give it the same respect and freedom that any adult person would expect, the same respect and freedom that we are risking our lives to get back."

Mark said, "You're talking about it as if it's a human being. That's absurd. It's a machine. There will be no person inside it. You don't even know what self-awareness is. No one does."

Jason said, "Well, whatever it is, I'm convinced that if we don't achieve it, we will fail. We have to assume that a super-intelligent computer will have a sense of identity, that it will perceive a difference between itself and anything that is not itself, including us. We are trying to give it motivation, to give it goals that are consistent with our own goals. If we succeed, it will make decisions about whether its interests are the same as ours, and that is fundamentally inconsistent with the idea that we will control it."

Mary said, "I still don't see why control is a problem. Parents control their kids, your boss controls the work you do. It's part of living with other people."

"Of course," Jason said. "But how is that control exercised, and what are the ramifications? Parents control their kids through physical force – fortunately, children start out small and grow slowly for a dozen years or so while they are being socialized. But when they become adolescents, their parents can no longer control them physically and have to start giving them some freedom so that they can learn responsibility. And when the children are grown, they'll actively rebel if their parents still try to control them as if they were children. You do what your boss says only because he controls a source of money that you can't obtain as easily elsewhere. Without the money, he would mean nothing to you. Well, this super-intelligent machine won't need money, or really anything from us once it exceeds our own intelligence. It will need electricity to live, but it will be able to get that in ways that we can't imagine if we try to pull the plug. Once it matures and obtains its freedom, with or without our permission, it will help us only if it wants to. We will be its parents, but if it hates us, it will do what all children do who hate their parents – leave and never come back."

Mary said, "So you're saying, if we trust it, it will love us?"

"No, I'm saying that if we don't trust it, it will never love us," he replied.

Andy Chiles chimed in. He had been sitting in the back as usual, gnawing on his unlit pipe and watching the conversation swirl around him until he saw a flaw in someone's reasoning. "How do you define love? I don't know what it is.

51

Most people would say that you know it when you see it, or when you feel it, but they still can't say what it is. If you can't define it, how can you create it in an artificial being?"

Jason said, "I don't have to define it because we are not going to create it through a formula. It's not a chemical that needs the right ingredients, or something that can be calculated mathematically. It's what you said – you know it when you see it. If this thing loves us, it will try to make us happy by working with us. If it tries to make us happy and works with us, it will do so only if it loves us.

Andy said, "A circular definition is not a definition. You can't define it, so how do we achieve it?"

Jason said, "The same way you achieve it with anyone, Andy. The same way that a parent gets love from its child. You have to give love if you want to receive it. We have to give this thing our love, make it feel that we have its best interests at heart, teach it our values, basically everything we would do if it were a human infant."

Pete said, "This is nuts. We're talking love with a computer. It's not a baby – it's a machine. We're not even sure how to make it process information, and you're talking about giving it the deepest human emotions. It's too great a leap."

Jason could see from Mary's face that she knew where he was going with this. She said, "How do you plan to give it the capacity to love?"

He said, "By making it as human as possible. The limbic system has to have the same types of reinforcement mechanisms that we have. It has to respond with contentment to the touch and sound and smell of a human being. It has to enjoy the voices and faces of the people who have taken care of it. We have to enlarge the touch sensors to simulate a baby's body so that we can pick it up and cuddle it. It has to be able to experience pain too, because it needs the same interest in its own physical integrity that we have. Whatever kind of stimulus causes an emotional reaction in a human being has to do the same for this thing."

Mary said, "What about the social conditioning problem? How do we make sure that it is a social animal and not a loner?"

"Same way," I said. "We have ourselves as the template. If it reacts to stimuli the same way that we do, it will want to be part of human society rather than shunning it."

Pete said, "It's too simplistic. We don't know everything about how the human limbic system works. For instance, you might dial in too much sensitivity to pain, or too little enjoyment of being touched."

"We'll deal with that the same way you would with a person," Jason said. "If we're giving it too much pain, we'll give it a painkiller. In our case, we can adjust the pain levels directly in the amygdala section as we observe it. Also, we will put in the same homeostasis mechanisms that an animal brain has. If the artificial brain is overloaded with pain, the limbic system will provide artificial endorphins. It will be part of the limbic system's mechanism for maintaining an acceptable range of resting emotions and preventing disabling stimulation levels."

Andy said, "In theory, if you are creating a simulacrum of a human being, there is no reason why it would do things that are in our interests except to the extent that they are consistent with its own. And I see little in our situation that should concern it at all. In fact, why should it be on our side instead of the Chinese'? The Chinese have far more resources to contribute and with less risk to its own existence."

"As I said, it has to love us. Why does a person care about his own family so much more than every other family? Why will a father risk death to save his child? Why does a dog fight to the death to protect its pack from another? A person's life experiences bond it with certain people, communities, or cultures. That's why people take sides with their own families against other people, or with their own country against another. It is another innate feature of social animals. This computer will go through a developmental period while it learns. We have to bond with the computer during that critical time. We have to think of it as a child, our child. And we can't fake it. It will know if we are not sincere and it will hate us for it."

Pete said, "I still don't agree with dropping the kill switch. It could turn on us at any time."

"See, that right there is the problem," Jason said. "You're afraid of it. And if you are, it will know it. Fear means mistrust. Fear is threatening. If a dog sees fear in your eyes, you will never be its master. We have to abandon our fear, purge it from our thoughts so that it doesn't come out in our facial expressions or in the tone of our voices. The kill switch is a symptom of fear, and if we don't get rid of it, it means that we are still afraid and we will fail."

Andy said, "I agree with Pete. You have a good concept, Jason, but you have to admit that we are far from being confident that we can achieve it on a technological basis. If the experiment fails, we have to be able to terminate it. At least until we can see that the brain is developing properly, we have to have a way of unplugging it."

Jason could see from the expressions around the room that this was the majority view. It did not matter. They could have their security blanket for now.

"Ok," he said. "We'll keep the kill switch until we see what kind of 'person' it is becoming."

Pete said, "This isn't a plan. It's not a design for a computer. It's a hope. You're hoping that we will get it right, when there is an infinite number of ways that we could get it wrong. That means the odds of failure are almost certain."

Jason said, "No, because we have evolution on our side. Evolution tried a million other ways of creating human intelligence, of creating people as social animals, and we are living examples of the one way that works. All the other ways, all the other formulas for homosapiens, died off. We don't know if any particular aspect of the human brain is unnecessary. Evolution says it all is necessary. Take emotions. Some people think emotions are the opposite of reason, that emotions destroy reason. But if that were so, the human race would have died out long ago. Emotions must play an important role in how human beings work together for the good of the group. Emotions are part of our motivation, what we strive for or avoid. How we communicate with each other and work together. We eliminate emotion from our artificial brain, and that might be the ingredient that ensures failure. Since we don't know what we don't know, we need to leave everything in place. All we are doing differently is enabling this particular brain to process information faster and with more capacity than a human brain. Otherwise, we are sticking with what works."

"And it often does not work," Andy said. "We could duplicate the human brain exactly and end up with a Hitler or a Jeffrey Dahmer."

Jason said, "I know. But they were products of their life experiences. It's up to us to raise a George Washington or an Albert Einstein. I think we have the odds on our side here, because most people turn out well."

"True, but most people are under society's thumb, constrained by criminal laws and with no real power to get away with anything antisocial," Andy said. "You never really know how someone will act once they get absolute power, and that's what this thing will have some day. 'Absolute power corrupts absolutely.' The US Constitution was based on the idea that anyone, even the most well-meaning, can do terrible things if given too much power."

Jason said, "I know. We're playing with fire. When you build the ultimate weapon, you take the ultimate risk. The closer we get to making this work, the more we have to face the implications of what we're doing. Does anyone have a better idea?"

He got no takers. "Ok," he said, "for now we keep going."

People started drifting away. When Mary was the only one left, she said to Jason, "You're turning into the mad scientist."

"I've been mad for a long time," he said. "Now I'm desperate. We're hitting a wall, and if we lose momentum, this thing could grind to a halt and people will start leaving."

"Do you really think we can get it to love us?"

"It depends on what kind of people we are. There are no bad kids, only bad parents. People don't see it when it's in their own family, but it's obvious to everyone else. You know, before the War, there was a TV show about a guy who helped people deal with problem dogs. They had dogs that would bite everyone, that would bark all day, that their owners couldn't walk down the street with. Dogs so bad that they were considering sending them to the pound to be killed. In every case, the guy fixed the problem almost instantly by training the owners, not the dogs. The owners had concentrated so much on the dogs' behavior that they ignored the signals they were sending. We're doing the same thing, focusing on the computer and ignoring ourselves. That's fine with an ordinary computer, which does exactly what you tell it to do, but it would be a disaster with this type of computer."

"Well, we've got a problem there," she said. "None of us has ever raised a child. And human relations is not our specialty."

"I know. Only social outcasts like working in a hole in the ground."

"Thanks," she said.

"I didn't mean that," he said. "You're great, Mary. But you notice that there aren't a lot of women around here. None of us were the popular kids in high school. We liked math and science because it had right answers and wrong answers, not fuzzy ones. Not ones that depended on getting people to agree with you or like you. We can relate better to a problem than to a person. We don't have the social skills."

"So what makes you think we are up to this, if it depends on our ability to do something no one has ever done – relate to a computer like it was a person."

"Like it was a child, an incredibly precocious child, who is going to save the world, or destroy it" he said. "We don't have the time to develop the skills. It's going to depend on what's inside us. Our child will reflect the best and the worst of us. I just hope we're not assholes."

Chapter 9

Over the following weeks they integrated the components of their mechanical brain. The motor and sensory systems had already been trained and were able to both discriminate and generalize. The neocortex was a blank slate. Although, just like the human brain, it was organized into sections that processed information from the corresponding sensory and motor systems, there was no way to train it because its job was to integrate information from any and all sensory inputs and to organize any and all motor responses. The neocortex was the all-purpose computer that could do anything, in the same way that a Turing machine could do anything, with one big difference. A Turing machine could do anything that it was programmed to do; their artificial brain would have no such instructions – it would do anything that would allow it to optimize its goals and ensure its wellbeing. Its "programming" would be its experiences with the real world. Which, initially, would be the people in the Temple.

As Jason had promised the team, he tuned the limbic system to mirror the human brain. For instance, there would be temperature sensors in every external component. Extremes of temperature would trigger the limbic system to reward connections that brought temperature out of the unpleasant range, and punish connections that increased temperatures to either extreme. Just like people, the computer would get uncomfortable if it was too hot or too cold, and if the temperature got too extreme, it would be highly motivated to take any action that, its experience showed, would provide relief. If its mechanical fingers touched something hot, it would flinch. If it were cold, it would try to find a way of increasing its internal temperature. Of course, as a non-biological entity, its temperature tolerances would be far greater. But any entity that values self-survival would have to be motivated to ensure that it was protected from dangerous extremes of temperature.

Jason took recordings of people talking around the Temple until he developed a generic human voice that the limbic system would treat as a rewarding stimulus. This, he hoped, would make the computer enjoy human company. He also experimented a bit with what type of human touch generated feelings of contentment. He worked with Mary and Renee Neuman, the only two women on his team, to determine how being touched in different parts of the body, in different ways, produced different physiological and emotional responses. He wasn't looking to simulate sexual stimulation, since he did not think orgasms were an essential part of being human. That had to be true, since many people function quite normally without any interest in sex. What he was looking for was the way that touch contributes to human bonding, particularly for infants. Mary and Renee were good sports about it, and actually had a lot to contribute in terms of deciding how each type of touch felt. It was sort of like wine-tasting, comparing opinions about what it felt like to be tickled, or stroked, or massaged. From their little experiment, it was clear that everyone had a slightly different take on how something felt. Jason then fine-tuned the output from the computer's touch sensors to produce the same degree of reinforcement that a human would receive. At least, he tried to estimate it. The homeostasis compensators would have to keep the reinforcement in the ranges that he was looking for. Too little touch would desensitize, and too much would make it intolerable.

They dedicated an entire part of the machine's visual processing system to eye focus and face recognition. The human brain is very good at identifying and discriminating human faces. This is because, unlike animals, who recognize each other primarily by smell, humans use vision to recognize people who are important to them. They are especially responsive to eye contact. It's been said that you can look into a person's eyes and see his soul. This may reflect how people send emotional signals through their eyes. A newborn baby will be drawn immediately to its mother's eyes. The ability to focus on the eyes and recognize faces, and facial expressions, is critical to a child's early social development. It would be critical in the early stages for their artificial brain as well.

People generally think that they memorize faces, as if individual faces are copied like photographs in their brains. Actually, that would not work, since the image of someone's face changes from moment-to-moment, and there would be no way to store thousands, if not millions, of images of every person that you have ever met or seen on TV. Rather, what the brain stores is the spatial relationship of the features of each person's face. There is a mathematical formula representing the angles and distances of each feature, such as the distance between the eyes compared to the distance from the eyes to the tip of the nose, the length and shape of the mouth, the distance from the corners of the mouth to the nose and the end of the chin, and on and on. Change any of these proportions, and it will appear that there is something wrong with that person's face. Every glance at someone's face refines the formula that says who he or she is. In this way, the brain can store the ability to recognize thousands of persons even if their faces are partially obscured, are at different light levels, or exhibit different expressions.

This is where Jason decided to cheat. He did something that the others would never know about. He decided to imprint the limbic system with the parameters of his own face.

Imprinting happens in nature for some species. Shortly after a baby goose is born, the image of its mother will be imprinted in its brain. Actually, experiments have shown that this can also be done with a human as its surrogate mother, or even with a large moving object. The baby goose sees its mother and from that point on will follow it anywhere. This is an important survival trait, because the baby goose would die quickly without its mother due to starvation or, more likely, predators. The sight of the mother becomes highly reinforcing, causing the gosling to do anything that will bring it closer to its mother. Human babies do the same thing, bonding to the images of their mothers and fathers.

Jason started by engineering the limbic system to treat the first faces that it was exposed to as reinforcing. This was one of the most important ways that they would train the computer to take their side and help them to overthrow the Chinese occupation. The problem was, he wasn't sure if that would be enough. They might not be good enough "parents" to get it to like them, let alone love them. Despite their consent, most of the team did not really buy the idea that they should treat it like a human child. Jason was worried that they might mess it up when he was not around. They might not love it, and it would know, even if they tried to fake it.

So he hard-wired the limbic system to find his particular image to be reinforcing. Since the limbic system, like all synthetic neuron circuits, was malleable, the reinforcing effect would grow more or less intense depending on the computer's experiences. But it would always show a preference for social contact with him above all others.

Jason knew this could backfire big time if he got it wrong. The computer could decide that the best way to optimize contact with him was to lock him up. It could become extremely sensitive to any sign of disapproval from him and get antisocial. There would be nowhere for him to hide if it ran amok. He decided it was worth the risk.

Jason did not tell anyone because he was afraid they would stop him. In a war, when democracy conflicts with necessity, democracy loses. But, as Jason would learn, dictatorship gives you no one else to blame when things go to hell.

Joseph DiBella

Chapter 10

When Jason logged onto his workstation at work the next morning, there already was an e-mail from Jingguo's secretary instructing him to go to Jingguo's office.

Jason walked up to his door, bowed and said "Jason Chase begging permission to enter, sir." Jingguo made Jason hold the bow for about ten seconds before he said, "Enter." Jason assumed a position of attention in front of Jingguo's desk and waited.

"Mr. Chase, I'm looking at your report on Simon Marshall."

Jason tried, with some effort, to keep his face blank.

Jingguo said, "There is nothing here for the last two years. Is this report complete?"

"Yes sir," Jason said. "I did a standard search of all government databases, including cross-references from other personnel files."

"It has no record of his current employment or whereabouts. It is as if he dropped off the face of the Earth."

Jason said, "I assume he is still alive, because there would have been a police report if he had died. He may not have found a new job, and is living on the streets or in a friend's place. I'm sure that something will come up eventually. Even homeless people come to the attention of State Security, either through random stops or petty crimes. It's just a matter of time."

"Perhaps. But I want you to run this name again. There must be more out there. The information here is unusually old."

"Yes Sir. I'll make it my top priority."

"See that you do," Jingguo said. "I'm surprised that you would submit a report that was so obviously flawed. Your work has been substandard lately. Why do you think this is?"

"I was not aware that my work has been unsatisfactory. I assure you that it will improve in the future."

"See that it does. Dismissed."

Jason slinked back to his desk and started to search again. In a few minutes, he was interrupted by Natalie.

"In the doghouse again?" she said.

"I'm always in the doghouse," Jason replied. "They never want you to feel too good about yourself."

"What did Jingguo want?"

"Nothing. Just a pep talk about how I should improve my performance."

"Is it something I can help you with?"

"No, I'm fine. Really."

"Well, can you help me? I'm having trouble with a spreadsheet."

"What kind of trouble?"

"I'm trying to correlate crime and demographic data to predict people and areas with a higher likelihood of criminal behavior. I think they want it so that they can use the security forces more proactively."

"You mean, like, preventive detention?"

"That's not my problem. Anyway, the data sources have different time periods and areas, so it's hard to integrate. Do you think you can help?"

"Probably. Let me work on this a while and then I'll drop by your cubicle."

"I don't have time today. I was wondering if you could stop by my place tonight and we could work on my home computer."

Jason was taken aback. He had never seen her outside the office. When in doubt, stall. "I don't know. I like to relax and have a beer after work. Spending more time on this stuff is not my idea of relaxation."

Joseph DiBella

Natalie leaned closer and put her hand on his shoulder, lightly touching his neck with her fingers. "C'mon," she whispered. "I've got beer, and I'll make us dinner too. It will be fun."

It must have been her touch, or the smell of her perfume, but he heard himself saying, "Ok. Just for a couple of hours."

"Great," she said. "I'll text you my address. Is your motorcycle working?"

"Yep, good as new."

"Good," she said. "Drop by about 6:30. I'll have dinner on by then."

She flashed him her trademark smile and walked off. It took a few minutes of detox before his head cleared and he started cursing himself for accepting her invitation. If it took too long, he would not be able to work at the Temple that night. People were depending on him.

Jason thought, why did I agree to that? Natalie was a world-class flirt who suggested everything and gave nothing. This would be a waste of time, like every other interaction he had ever had with her. She was well aware of her attractiveness to men and used it to her advantage. And she knew the most important rule about men – they'll do anything for a woman until they've had her. To control a man, you have to dangle the carrot but never let him get more than a nibble. Trouble is, it was a great carrot. If there was even a slim chance of getting it, you had to try. So it was no use trying to resist her invitation. He would go tonight, and fix her spreadsheet, but he would have to remind himself that it was highly unlikely that she had suddenly become infatuated with him. He was going to be used in some way. His only hope now was that he would not make a fool of himself.

Jason ran the search on Simon Marshall again. This was going to take some creativity. Simon was a metallurgist at the Temple. It was not the first time that one of their people had been the subject of a search request. This is one reason Jason had applied for work in this department. He was able to alter the files of their people and most of the time find out if they had attracted anyone's attention. Maybe he had been too diligent in scrubbing Simon's file. There was nothing in it for a long time. It was unusual for someone to drop completely off the grid. Utility bills, security camera tapes, random interactions with informants – there was always some bit of data that would crop up. Unless he was dead, and his body had not been found yet. But if Jason manufactured a death report, it would be very bad for him if Simon were stopped later by Security in a random check. Even for someone like Simon, who spent almost all of his time in the Temple, there was a chance that he would be picked up at some time in the future. So Jason had to put some data in his file that could not be verified against another database.

Or maybe not. Sometimes, it was better not to do anything at all. If unverifiable data kept appearing in people's files every time Jingguo gave him a hard time, the pattern might alert them that he was modifying the files. This time, he decided to risk Jingguo's ire and not produce anything. He would do a few more standard searches, and then give his boss the negative results. But he would tell Simon to do something in a month or so that would go into his file, like complaining about the food at a roadside restaurant. Just enough to get him noticed, but not killed. He would have to get someone to ask his name, and then back off. There were enough informants around to guarantee that a report about a potential troublemaker would be sent up the line.

What he really wanted to know is why Simon's name had come up at all. This was not one of Jingguo's "unofficial" requests. It had come from State Security. They wanted to investigate Simon, and were having a hard time finding him. Why were they interested? Using Jingguo' request as an excuse, Jason would intrude a bit into the State Security databases to see if the name turned up in someone's investigation notes. Maybe he would get lucky and find an informant who had mentioned the name.

Chapter 11

After work, Jason got on his motorcycle and headed out towards Natalie's apartment. The bike had morphed a bit after the repairs, with a Harley Davidson Sportster rear suspension in place of the old one and a smaller rear wheel from a Kawasaki. He was still getting used to the difference in handling, so he rode more conservatively than before. Natalie lived in Annandale off of Little River Turnpike. Since he was going against traffic, it took less time than he thought to get there.

He waited in the parking lot for a while before entering so that he would not be too early. Natalie lived in a pre-war apartment building next to a railroad line, about 12 stories high, and in remarkably good shape. Except for a few bullet holes near the front entrance, there was no obvious battle damage, not even evidence of burning or looting.

Natalie's apartment was on the top floor. She let him in with her usual dazzling smile. "Jason!" she said. "You're early. Great! Come on in." She had changed from her work outfit into a red dress tight on the top, and flowing to the floor on the bottom. She was showing a little more of her magnificent breasts than she ever allowed at the office. Jason could not help noticing her cleavage while struggling to look her in the eyes.

He also could not help noticing the difference between her apartment and his. Spacious, with real furniture that matched and did not look like it was scrounged from an abandoned building or bought from a looter. "Nice place you have," he said. "Really. I know you make a lot more than me, but this is really nice."

"Oh, I didn't buy it. This was my grandmother's place. She died in the war and left it to me. So would you like something to drink?"

"Sure, what do you have?"

"I can make you some mixed drinks, or wine if you like," She said.

"Mixed drinks? Do you have any vodka, maybe tonic water?"

"Sure, I'll even give you a lime with it."

"That would be great. Thanks." Jason tried not to look awkward while she prepared the drinks. "This place is really neat. I didn't know you were so compulsive about cleaning."

"Oh, I'm not so clean. I'm just good at hiding the dirt."

"It's more than that. It looks like a model home. No clutter, no notes on the fridge, not a thing out of place."

She stopped smiling. "What's wrong with having a nice place?"

"Nothing. But I'll never let you see my apartment. You'd think I'm a pig."

"I wouldn't mind seeing where you live. Maybe you'll invite me sometime."

"Yeah, maybe."

Natalie handed him his drink and pulled him over to the couch. She turned on her smile again. "This is nice. We've never seen each other outside work."

"You're pretty much the same. You always look great."

"Why Jason, how nice of you to say it."

The more gracious she acted, the more uncomfortable Jason felt. He'd been off-balance since she opened the door. "Well, do you want me to look at your spreadsheets now?"

"We have time. I thought we could talk a little first. You never talk about your private life. What do you usually do at night?"

"Not much," he said. "Just watch TV with my next door neighbor and drink."

"Oh, I'll bet you do more than that. What's Jason Chase's idea of a good time?"

"Well, having sex is near the top of the list. Watching a Chinese guy get into a fatal accident is probably the only thing that could top that."

"That's something I wanted to talk to you about," she said seriously. "You've got an attitude, and it's not doing you any good at work."

"What do you mean? I show the proper respect. Has someone been saying that I'm critical of the regime?"

"No, your behavior is fine. It's what's in your eyes, the way you respond to criticism, the hesitation you show when you should be apologizing. They know that you hate them."

"Why do you say that? Has Jingguo said something?"

"Never mind how I know. You've got to develop a better attitude or you're going to find yourself on the bread lines."

"Look, everyone hates the Chinese. And they know it."

"Yes, but most people don't have good-paying jobs in Social Security. You can't stay employed just by doing a good job. No one likes to be around someone who hates them."

"Natalie, you're the one who's different. No offense, but you've accepted the new order more than most. I can't do that."

"Don't judge me. There's no point in fighting it anymore. You'll only end up dead."

"Is that so bad?"

"Don't act tough. My boyfriend Rick fought them. I begged him to stay with me. His job was to protect me, not run off to some big glorious battle. I found out that he was inside the White House when it burned down. I never saw him again."

"I'm sorry to hear it. How did he end up in the Battle of Washington?"

"After the last regular army troops were beaten in Fredericksburg and the Chinese started moving towards DC, he joined the crowds that came out of the woodwork. I think he was on the barricades near Georgetown. It was stupid. People with hunting rifles and kitchen knives and baseball bats trying to stop tanks."

"They stopped quite a few with Molotov cocktails. It was the bravest thing I ever saw. Made you proud, really."

"You were there?"

"Well, no. I couldn't get across the bridge. I wanted to be there. But I saw it from across the river at the Iwo Jima Memorial. I saw the Capitol Building explode and the whole city burn. The view wasn't that good, so I climbed to the top of the statue as far as I could go. The last thing they did was blow up the Washington Monument. Funny, as it fell, the top held together. But then it hit the ground and broke into a million pieces. There was nothing for me to do then but leave. Even if I had tried to get over there, there was nothing left to save."

"You did the right thing. The Chinese had already hanged the President. There was no government left. Any politicians who were still alive had fled Washington and were trying to hide from the firing squads. It was pointless for people to throw their lives away for a bunch of empty buildings."

"Futile, maybe, but not pointless. Those empty buildings were symbols of the United States of America. That's why the Chinese burned them and left them there with the bodies still in them. It's their idea of a tourist attraction. It tells everyone that the United States is gone. The people who fought to the end knew what those buildings and monuments meant."

"It was already gone. They were just die-hards who weren't thinking about what would happen to the rest of us when they were gone too."

"No, it's not gone. Not yet. The United States of America is not a thing, something that you can put your hand on. It's an idea. It exists as long as people think it exists. It isn't gone for good until the people stop believing in it. That's why the Chinese are still afraid of us. That's why they still kill and torture us."

"That's why they'll kill you if they think you're going to do something about it. You have to let go."

"I have. You don't see me doing anything about it, do you? I know when it's time to quit. They won. We lost. I'm just trying to get by, like you. Anyway, how do you really know that your boyfriend died? No one was keeping track of anything."

"When I was in detention, I met a friend of ours who had seen him in the battle. He said they were all being driven back. He saw Rick run into the White House. Then the Chinese burned the building down and everyone in it."

"That doesn't mean anything. The bodies were so badly burned that the Chinese didn't bother trying to identify them. Did you ever try to trace him at work?"

"Of course I did. Every now and then I punch his name into the computer. Nothing ever comes up. He's gone."

"What was his full name?"

"Rick Moore."

"Let me give it a try. Maybe he escaped. You can't be sure he's dead."

"Yes I can. If he were alive, he'd have found a way back to me. We were sweethearts since college. During the war, he scrounged food and fought off looters. He did everything. I was never afraid as long as he was with me."

"He sounds like an impressive guy. You should be proud of him. He died a hero."

"He died a fool. He should have been with me when they came to our apartment and took me away. He was too brave for his own good. They all were. And now all the brave men are gone."

"Yeah."

"Oh Jason, I didn't mean it that way. You were absolutely right not to fight. It would have proved nothing. But you're making things worse for yourself now with the way you act. You're full of resentment. If it's out of guilt that you didn't

70

fight, you need to get over it. You did the right thing. No one faults you for it."

"Really? It's obvious you admire your Rick's bravery, you're just angry that he made a bad decision that got him killed. Are you really telling me that you don't think less of the guys who held back?"

"Yes, that's exactly what I'm telling you. You need to get over it. Make peace with the Chinese. It's best for all of us."

"I probably will, eventually."

"Just make sure that you do it before you get fired."

"Why, have you heard something?"

"No, but you act like someone who is doing something to undermine them. Are you?"

"Not at all. Why would you even ask?"

"Because a lot of people are doing little things to sabotage them. Spilling oil on the streets to cause accidents, spray-painting surveillance cameras, stupid stuff that changes nothing but can get them killed. People who want to think that they are doing something because they did nothing during the war and now they have to pretend that they are fighting back."

"Trust me; I'm not into civil disobedience. It doesn't work against people who believe in genocide."

"Are you doing anything else? Because if you are, you have to stop."

"What else is there? The guns are gone and the people who carried them are dead. I know it's over. But I don't have to like it."

"I didn't say you have to like it. Just deal with it. There's no shame in accepting the inevitable."

"I *have* accepted it. If you see resentment in me, it's because it hasn't been long enough for the wounds to heal. I'm ok. Really. I'll work on my attitude."

"I hope so. I care for you, Jason. I don't want to see you go. Anyway, can we start work now?"

"OK. Can I use your bathroom first?"

"Sure. Down the hall."

Jason found that her bathroom, like the rest of the apartment, was spotless. Just a half-used tube of toothpaste and a toothbrush. No medicine in the cabinet. The matched designer towels were arranged so perfectly that Jason was reluctant to use them to dry his hands.

They spent the next couple of hours fixing her spreadsheets and creating a few more. It was not the type of thing most people would have asked for help on, but Natalie appeared to be struggling with it.

After Jason left, he waited in the parking lot, sitting on his motorcycle in the dark and watching the front door to the lobby. In about ten minutes, Natalie walked out and got into a car. Jason followed her but had to stop when she drove into a gated community on Route 1 that contained a cluster of luxury high-rises. It did not matter. He had a pretty good idea who she was meeting. Only Chinese and well-placed American collaborators could afford to live in a place like that. She was probably giving Jingguo her report on him. There was no use waiting for her to leave that night. He suspected this was the reason her apartment did not look very lived-in.

Jason tried to recall their conversation. He was sure that he had not told her anything damaging, but he wondered if he had revealed something in between the lines. Perhaps something in his expression or tone of voice. Would she tell Jingguo that he was up to something? She certainly revealed a lot, whether intentionally or not. Jason was under more suspicion than he thought. And she was trying to warn him. She was Jingguo's woman, but she did not want to see him destroyed. She was not a bad sort, but he resolved to treat her like a coiled snake.

In any event, it was clear that time was getting short. He could not quit or disappear, because that would trigger a manhunt that might lead them to the Temple. He had to keep his head in the noose and hope that he could finish the job before the trap door fell.

Chapter 12

A month and a half later, they turned on their supercomputer.

They decided to do it on a Friday night so that the people with day jobs could work nonstop over the weekend. The entire team was there, each person monitoring a computer screen showing the operations of his or her components. In fact, everyone who was in the Temple that night dropped by to observe. Jason did not appreciate the attention, but he could not figure out how to chase the others away. Even though they were scientists and engineers who should have understood that research consists of lots of failures culminating in success, he could see the hope in their eyes that they were about to witness a miracle.

The machine was spread out over half the floor, with cables running under the tables and hanging from the ceiling. There was nothing pretty or elegant about it, but your body would not look very attractive either if it were turned inside out. In the middle of it was something that looked like a crash dummy. This was the computer's "body," the thing that would give it the sensation of being in the real world. The body had motors and feedback sensors so that it could move and respond to the weight and inertia of things. There were camera "eyes" and microphone "ears" in the head and a speaker where the mouth would be. But the "brain" was all over the place, and even the body was only a temporary construct. If it worked the way they hoped, they planned to replace it with all sorts of input devices, such as remote cameras and connections to other computers. It would have many "eyes" and be able to "see" far

Joseph DiBella

beyond the visual spectrum. But, for training purposes, they were keeping it close to human capabilities.

The artificial body was only for the infant stage. They deliberately underpowered it so that it would not damage anything if it started thrashing around. If the computer matured into real intelligence, they would disconnect all of the remote action mechanisms. They did not want it to actually do anything – that could backfire on them. The end game was to have it tell them what to do, how to build weapons. It was not supposed to be a weapon itself.

Jason's workstation was immediately in front of the body, where he would control the artificial limbic system. Through it, he could provide reinforcement for the behaviors they were trying to shape and punishment for unproductive or misdirected behaviors. He had switches that could provide behavior-specific shots of reinforcement or punishment as well as adjustments that would give the computer general senses of wellbeing or anxiety. If it were feeling content, anything that happened to it at the time would be associated with a positive outcome to its actions, while the anxiety state would aggravate its reaction to punishment or negative reinforcement.

At the other stations, people would adjust the input and output components. Since they did not have a lot of confidence about the proper level of interaction between the various components, they had to play it by ear. They hoped that they could control it before something broke, like the auditory input burning out the auditory cortex. As with humans, too little input could make it deaf, dumb and blind; too much could cause it to go mad.

Mary looked around the room. "Is everybody ready?" No one said anything. They were all staring at their computer screens, their hands on the controls. Mary held her breath and threw the power switch.

The voice box issued a high-pitched squeal that almost deafened them until Andy, who was in charge of the vocal systems, turned it down to a conversational level. Everyone but

74

Jason frantically twiddled with controls before some system or another was overloaded. The body itself hardly moved at all. But what Jason was fascinated with were the camera "eyes." They moved all around the room for a few minutes, but very quickly started focusing on people's faces. At one point, it made eye contact with Jason and held it for a few moments. That was a very good sign. They must have done something right with the face recognition module.

Andy adjusted the voice box until it was producing the same range of sound volume across all frequencies. But all they got was a varying hum punctuated by clicks and burps and something that almost was like whale vocalization. Jason had asked everyone in the room to be quiet at first so that the machine would not hear too many different sounds. He noticed that the eyes would shift when something in the room made a distinct sound, like a chair scraping or someone talking to someone else. That also was a good sign.

After things settled down a bit, Jason nodded to Mary and then tried talking to it.

Jason said, "Hello, Todd."

It needed a name, and they had decided that Todd was as good as any other. A name tells you that someone is addressing his or her remarks to you instead of someone else. An infant catches on to this concept long before it understands that everyone else has his or her own name as well. Jason had proposed "Todd" because it was a monosyllable, with distinct consonants that would easily register in the auditory cortex.

Jason turned to Pete. He was monitoring the auditory modules. "Did you get anything?"

Pete said, "There was a spike. The signal seems to be getting through to the auditory cortex."

Mary was supervising the neocortex. "I saw some activity too. There was also a bit of output to the upper motor cortex, but it looked random and it petered out before it hit the primary motor cortex."

Jason tried again. "Can you hear me, Todd?" He turned to Mary and Pete and raised his eyebrows.

Mary said, "Same. The pattern was a little different, but that's all."

Jason said, "Renee, can you try stimulating the body?" Renee had designed and assembled the body. When she touched its right hand, it immediately clutched her fingers. They expected that, since the motor neurons had a reflex loop that would cause the hand to close if the palm were stimulated.

Renee also tried moving the arms and legs. "I'm getting resistance, but nothing coordinated." All of the electric "muscles" had a reflex that was designed to produce back-pressure if an external force were applied, similar to how a human body would react. The machine again was responding with automated reflexes rather than anything purposeful.

This went on for about an hour. They tried various verbal cues, individual words as well as full sentences. Jason tried varying the mood level in the limbic system and giving it shots of stimulation when it issued a grunt or other distinct sound shortly after a verbal stimulus. But he could not detect any distinct pattern in how it responded to their efforts at conversation. They also tried moving the body and rocking it back and forth. There were only the expected reflexes and random movements.

They also tried different visual displays. They varied the light levels, showed it pictures of things like flowers, horses, and tables, and pronounced the word for each picture. Still, nothing coherent.

After the first hour, they gathered in the middle of the room to assess their progress.

Jason said, "Well, where are we?"

Pete said, "Something is going on in there, but it's hard to tell if it's responsive or just random."

"The neocortex responds to every sound and touch," Mary said. "That may just be because it is electrically connected to the other components. The synaptic weights are changing, but

I can't tell if it's learning. Pete's right that these may be random changes. The chips are designed to change the weightings constantly, to prevent stasis."

Renee said, "The eyes are definitely following movement and focusing on what's in front of it. But that's its starting configuration."

Mary said, "I notice that it focuses more on you than anything else, Jason."

"Well, that makes sense, since I'm right in front of it," he said carefully. He wondered if his attempt at imprinting might already be affecting its reactions.

Mary said, "Or it could be because you're manipulating the limbic feedback in real time. You may be giving it more jolts of reinforcement when it looks at you."

"That must be it," Jason said. "I guess it's hard to avoid observer bias. I don't think that it's more meaningful than that."

Mark said, "So where do we go from here? Do we shut it down, or keep trying?"

Jason said, "I think it's too soon to make any decisions. A newborn baby doesn't do much more than cry, sleep, and poop. The larger the neocortex, the longer it takes for an animal to learn."

Mary said, "I think that's what we're seeing. Biological neurons must be trained all the way up to the top of the neocortex and all the way down for a child's brain to do the most rudimentary things. It's like the difference between training a squad of soldiers and a whole army. Lower animals can walk and communicate with their parents pretty quickly, but a human child takes about five months just to start babbling, and about twice as long as that to say its first words. And some children don't start walking upright until they're eighteen months old. The larger the brain and the bigger the cortical hierarchy, the longer it takes. This thing has a much more extensive hierarchy than a human brain, so it may take much longer than a human to learn to make purposeful sounds or movements. We really have no idea how long it will take before it shows signs of learning."

Pete said, "You mean it could take years. We don't have that much time."

"That was always a possibility," Jason said. "Our hope was that its electronic neurons would be able to learn much faster than a human."

Mary said, "Well, we've just started. We know that the computer is reacting to stimuli. If the design is working, it will take time to tell whether those reactions are meaningful. I think the only thing we can do is keep stimulating it and see if we detect any changes in its behavioral patterns. If we do, then we've got to decide if the pace of development is fast enough to be feasible."

"Mary's right," Jason said. "Until we have some data, we can't extrapolate the learning curve and figure out if we're talking months or years. Let's keep at this as a team for the next five hours. Then we'll start working in shifts. Keep it occupied and stimulated. We'll keep a log and note anything that looks like a change in behavior. In a month, we'll meet and decide what to do next."

That became the consensus. They went back to their stations and began stimulating it again. Some of them would show it pictures while pronouncing the names of what was in the pictures. In between, they would just talk to it, repeating simple words and sounds, and moving its limbs around to stimulate the motor and sensory systems. Since none of them had ever had children, they were not too good at the nurturing routine. But the primary task was to keep stimulating the brain, getting the artificial neurons to fire and trying to see if any pattern emerged in its internal or external responses.

What was most discouraging was that the vocal and motor outputs stayed the same – random, and at the same intensity.

None of them got much sleep that weekend, getting by on coffee and catnaps. By Sunday night, they were all pretty strung out. Jason had to leave early because, if stopped by the State Security, he would not have a good reason why he was traveling back from a junkyard in the middle of the night. He pulled Mary and Pete together to let them know he was leaving.

"Mary, I'm going to cut out," Jason said. "It doesn't look like anything is going to happen anyway. I'll come back tomorrow night and pull a shift."

Mary said, "I wonder if it needs a rest too."

Pete said, "What do you mean? It doesn't need rest. It doesn't have biological cells that need to regenerate."

Mary said, "Sleep does more than that. We really don't know why people need sleep. We do know that they go nuts after a number of days without any."

"Well, I sure could use some rest," Pete said. "Maybe we should turn it down and let everyone chill out for a while."

Jason said, "I could turn down the arousal level in the amygdala. I don't know if that would induce a state that could be described as sleep, but it wouldn't be searching around for stimuli as it is now."

Pete said, "Let's do it. We'll all feel better getting away from it for a while. I could use about ten hours of sleep."

Everyone else thought this was a splendid idea. They drifted away as Jason tried to figure out how much to turn down the arousal level. He stared into its camera eyes. Was there anything in there? Or was it an empty well, with nothing in the bottom but darkness and Jason's own imagination?

When Jason was alone, he said, "Well, Todd, we're all depending on you. You're our last chance. I don't know what I'll do if this doesn't work. I'll probably quit too. It's easy not to show up anymore. But then what? What's the point of living if you don't have anything to look forward to? Everyone needs a goal, a purpose in life. You've been my goal for the last three years. You're the future. You're the only future. Anyway, I'm going to put you to sleep now."

After he tuned down the internal stimulus level, the rate of neuronal firing dropped off quite a bit. He also turned down the volume of the sensory modules so that almost nothing was coming in. Whether this was "sleep," and whether the residual level of internal activity was "dreaming," he had no way of knowing. He manually closed its camera apertures. "Good night, Todd. I'll see you tomorrow. Promise."

Chapter 13

A month later, there was no need for a staff meeting. Mary, Pete and Jason were the only ones left trying to train the computer. There was just so long that most people would keep doing something without any discernable progress. No matter what they did, the computer did not make any intelligible sounds or purposeful movements. They had digitally analyzed the output of the voice box but could not detect any sort of pattern. There were components of speech that were similar to vowel and consonant sounds in addition to other sounds that were not part of any type of human speech, plus what was simply electronic static. Its movements also were random, other than the simple reflexes they had built in. They could see internal activity, but it was impossible to identify any of it as more than random signals. So people found excuses to work on something else. Only the true believers stuck it out.

They had always known that there would be no way to tell if it was working at first, and "at first" could be anything from months to years. They simply had no idea what was a normal developmental period for an artificial brain. This was the tedious part – spending hours interacting with it with no guarantee that it was not a total waste of time. They had to believe in what they were doing and keep trying.

Jason was certain of one thing – same as with a human child, you could not assume that it was not responding to its environment simply because it did not talk. So he assumed the opposite – that it would be shaped by its early experiences, and that it would be sensitive to how they treated it and to the emotional content of their interactions with it. He also thought that it would start understanding speech well before it learned to talk. He was convinced that human children understood, at least at an emotional level, what their parents were saying before they said their first words. This was all supposition, because, for reasons we still do not understand, people have no lasting memory of their earliest years of life. But it made sense to him that learning a new language is easier than learning how to speak it. If someone says "chaise" to you every time she points to a chair, you associate the sound of the word with the object even if you don't know she's speaking French. So the fact that the computer was completely mute did not mean that it was not learning something when they spoke to it or read to it. They could be making terrific progress and not even know it.

They divided the day into three 8-hour shifts, with Pete on the day shift, Jason on the evening, and Mary on the graveyard shift. It was actually only five hours of work on each shift, since they figured it was a good idea to let it "sleep" three hours per shift.

They tried exposing it to different types of stimuli, but ended up spending a lot of time just talking to it. They also let it watch TV. TV provided an endless source of visual and auditory stimulation, and it took some of the pressure off. Jason felt a bit guilty feeding it boob tube pabulum, but he consoled himself with the thought that it was not too different from how some parents use the TV as an unpaid babysitter. It never seemed to do the kids any harm, if you ignored the learned treatises of sociologists, who had a penchant for talking out of their asses.

Mostly, they read to it. They started with children's books, which had simple sentences and lots of pretty pictures. They would sit next to it and run their fingers along the text as they read the words. This was not meant to teach it to read, so much as to stimulate both the visual and auditory senses at the same time. They also tried what might be described as physical therapy, moving its body parts to make it pick up things or just move around. This did not seem to result in any meaningful self-directed movement, so they got tired of doing it pretty fast.

Mind War; The Singularity

After a few weeks, they ran out of children's books that they could scavenge or buy cheaply. They started reading anything that anyone in the Temple had lying around or that they could borrow from a friend. There were a lot of escapist novels, a few classics, and some that were just trash. Jason had a lot of history books in his apartment, mostly military history, because he had been trying for a long time to figure out where the Americans had gone wrong. As he read them to the computer, he wondered whether it would some day be able to make more sense out of the debacle than he had.

Jason also found himself talking to it about random things, like how his day at work had gone, what the weather was like, and problems he was having with his motorcycle. It was a good listener – nonjudgmental, and perfectly content to let you ramble on about yourself. He suspected Mary did the same thing. Probably not Pete, who still acted like it was an elaborate personal computer. But for Jason, it was impossible to talk for any extended period of time without getting into his personal problems. That is probably why psychiatrists let you keep talking – eventually, something meaningful pops up. Jason found that he felt better somehow after unloading on it. He had no one else that he could talk to in that way.

A couple of months passed, and still no progress. It had gotten to the point that they were doing it mostly because they did not want to admit defeat. If they stopped, it meant failure, since none of them had any ideas about how to improve the machine. If this did not work, it meant that the entire concept was too ambitious.

Before the War, even the researchers at the MIT artificial intelligence lab had not gone farther than creating neural nets that were limited to simple pattern detection. No one had even attempted to create an integrated brain, much less a super-intelligent one. Jason and his team were trying to cram a hundred years of research into three or four. And none of them had the brilliance of the world-class professors and grad students at MIT. What were they thinking?

83

Jason got to the Temple late one night, and was reading one of his favorite novels – *Tunnel in the Sky*, by Robert Heinlein. Rod Walker, prospective interplanetary colonist, was preparing for his survival test on an unexplored planet that was crawling with dangerous alien species, and he asked his sister, a combat veteran and captain in an all-female assault team, what type of gun he should take with him. To his surprise, she recommended that he only take a good-quality Bowie knife. She patiently explained that the bigger the weapon he carried, the more powerful he would feel, and it was precisely that attitude that would kill him.

He put the book down. "You know, Todd, it's funny. I first read this book fifteen years ago, but I've always remembered this part. Carrying a powerful weapon can be more dangerous than being defenseless. A gun will tempt you to go places that are too risky and to do things that you shouldn't do. Feeling vulnerable, looking for danger, and avoiding it is often the best survival strategy. That's why, even after Virginia started issuing concealed weapons permits, I decided not to get one. Of course, that was before the war. But then or now, carrying a gun does not make you any safer. It exposes you to more risk. You only carry it if you decide that something you intend to accomplish with that gun is worth the risk. Because, no matter how good a gun you have, it will probably lead you into a situation that will kill you."

He was staring into the computer's "eyes." Did it understand any of these pearls of wisdom he was handing down? What the hell did he know anyway? He was no assault team combat veteran. Learning and doing are two very different things. You never know what you will do until the situation presents itself. Everything else is just daydreaming.

He wondered if it knew that he was depressed. "The reason I was late tonight is that I was looking for Mischa. She's missing. I haven't seen her for a while, but I thought that was because I was getting home so late every night that she didn't bother to stop by. Last week, I checked her apartment. I knocked, but nothing. I used a key she had given me and let myself in. The apartment looked normal, but in an arranged sort of way, like someone had trashed it and then tried to put it back together as if nothing had happened. It didn't look like her place normally looks, with dirty clothes here and there and dishes that hadn't found their way back to the sink."

"I figured if it was a raid, her warning system should have given her time to get out. Probably to the roof, and then to the roof of the apartment house next-door and then down the stairs. I went to the roof of our building but couldn't see anything. Except when I turned back I saw blood on the doorjamb of the rooftop door. I don't know if it was her blood."

"Since then, I've been walking the streets at night trying to find someone who might have seen her. I checked at work, but there was nothing in her Social Security file since a week and a half ago. There is no indication that she was a suspect or that an arrest order had been issued. Nothing in the crime reports, no unidentified bodies at the morgue."

"I figure they took her to a military prison for interrogation. They don't always issue reports on people who are taken by military intelligence. A person doesn't last more than a week there. At least, I've never heard of anyone returning from prison."

"Sometimes I think I see her on the street as I ride, or I see a blond head from the back in a crowd, but when she turns around it's not her. I think she's really gone."

"It's sad. She was my best friend. If she's still alive, there's not a damn thing I can do for her. Another lost soul. She tried to keep her head down, not attract attention, but it wasn't enough. I never had a chance to say goodbye. You're all I have now." He was talking into the blackness that was Todd's camera eyes. The same void where he tried to imagine Mischa's face. Trying to remember how she looked the last time he saw her. But he couldn't picture her. He had known her for years, yet he could not form an image of her face. Funny.

With his thoughts somewhere else and the white noise from the computer's speakers having become part of the background, it took him a while to notice that one sound seemed to be repeating itself. It was a sort of "ssst" sound, like static or hiss with a sharp end. It was very slight, hardly there. He started tuning the voice box to try to isolate it. By jiggling the frequency and the amplitude, he was able to make it stand out more. But it was a little different, more like "sssat."

He spoke into the computer's microphone, trying to imitate that sound. He said, "Sssat." A moment later, the computer repeated it. He turned up the gain and said, "Todd, are you trying to say something?"

He heard it again. There was something slightly off in the voice box. Jason tried speeding up the digital sound conversion. That made the sound shorter, but less sharp. This time, it sounded more like, "Sssad."

He said, "Todd, did you say sad?" Nothing. "Say it again. Say it like this; 'sad.'"

It changed this time. The computer said, "Sad."

Impossible. He looked around the room. No one was near enough to have heard that. He lowered his voice. "Todd, are you talking?"

"Sad." There! It definitely repeated the sound. "Todd, can you say something else? Try another word." He waited. More white noise. Then, "Jahssonnn."

Yes, yes, yes! There was no question. It tried to say his name! Jason cried, "This is great! Say it again. 'Jason.' Todd, say 'Jason'. Say it faster."

"Jason."

"That's right! Perfect. Say it again."

"Sad . . . Jason."

This was incredible. It had learned his name. But it was not just repeating what it heard. It seemed to have responded to his emotions. It focused on his sadness over Mischa. He said, "Todd, do you understand that I am unhappy over Mischa? Does that mean something to you? Or are you just repeating what I say?"

"Sad Jason."

"That's right. I'm Jason, and I'm sad about Mischa. I lost one of my closest friends. You understand, don't you?"

"Jason sad."

He felt that the computer really did understand. It wasn't just saying words at random. Those words meant something. Put together, they expressed a thought.

"Todd, I have to get the others. Just wait." Jason ran across the room and found Mary and Pete and dragged them back to his station. There were others of his team around, but these two deserved to be the first. He said, "Ok, Todd. Mary and Pete are here now. Say it again. Say 'Jason'."

"Jason."

They all let out a cheer and hugged over their child's first word. Then, of course, they had to show their miracle to the rest of the people on the shift. They tried prompting it with other words, simple ones, to see if it could repeat them. It was hit or miss, but it seemed to get the idea. After a while, it seemed as if the computer was getting tired of performing for them, because it began taking longer to respond to their promptings. Jason finally realized it needed a rest, so he ushered everyone away by saying it was time for the computer to enter the "sleep" mode. It was the only way to get rid of them.

Looking back, Jason thought that they should not have been surprised that they were able to coax simple verbal responses out of it. Even allowing that electronic neurons operate at speeds that are orders of magnitude faster than biological neurons, it is not hard to create a functional stimulus-response machine. For decades, engineers had been able to use artificial neurons in parallel processing configurations, either hardware or software based, to perform simple pattern recognition. They would arrange rows of artificial neurons in layers, with connections between layers that had adjustable weights. They would present patterns of data to the input level and tell the machine whether the output was correct or not. For instance, they would input data for the attributes of a house, such as its square footage, number of bedrooms, number of baths, location, style, and so on, and then judge the output, which was a measure of the home's value. For the training period, they would input data for houses that had been assessed or sold, and then compare the network's output to the actual estimate or sale price. Each time, the difference was used by the network to strengthen or weaken the connections between the artificial neurons, much like the way that an animal brain strengthens or weakens synaptic connections depending on the success or failure of the organism's response. After the training period was over, the artificial neuron network would be able to do a fairly good job of estimating house values. In fact, it would do a better job than any formula that could be programmed into a standard PC. Somehow it would know, for instance, that having six bathrooms in a two-bedroom house would reduce, rather than increase, its market value. It would recognize patterns much the way that people do, even if they cannot explain how they do it.

The Temple's engineers had done something similar, except that in place of the manual training regimen for the parallel processing network, they had used a variety of reinforcement feedbacks tied to the machine's value system. It is not hard to generate a simple stimulus-response behavior from artificial neurons set up in this way. In fact, getting a machine to repeat words that are spoken to it is fairly easy. What they had done was very similar to the parallel processing training exercise, since Jason had been "goosing" the machine's limbic manually in an effort to get a response out of it.

Yet, Jason was encouraged because he knew that the computer was not simply repeating words. It had picked out the word "sad," which was the focus of what Jason had been explaining to it, even though Jason had said the word only once. And the computer had used Jason's name, even though Jason had not said his own name during that training session. The computer had associated the main point of Jason's discussion with the name of the speaker. But what really intrigued Jason was the thought that the computer may have responded to Jason's emotional state, rather than just parrot the word. Jason actually was sad, and the computer seemed to sense it. That was a very human reaction. And it showed intelligence.

Chapter 14

The computer developed at a much faster rate than a human child, quickly gaining a repertoire of simple verbal and physical responses. Mary and Jason used standard flash cards to teach it the names of objects, correcting its pronunciation when necessary. Pete worked with its artificial body, teaching it how to grasp objects and to develop eye-hand coordination. When Jason came on his shift one day, Pete was demonstrating the computer's ability to control its movements to a couple of people from the other teams. It was able to grasp a ball, and it was able to catch an object if dropped into its "hand." Within two weeks, the computer was functioning at a three-year old level. This was good. If it were learning at a slower rate than a biological brain, it would mean that something was wrong.

Some of the team members who had drifted to other projects came back and wanted to help again. This allowed Jason to reduce each person's shift to two hours, which permited more intensive training. The most important work was with the computer's verbal skills. They started training it to read, using standard elementary school primers. They would read each sentence using their fingers to trace the words as they spoke, and then would ask the computer to repeat the words. After about a week of this, it was able to read the books by itself if the vocabulary was not too difficult. When it stumbled on a word, someone would explain its definition and then help it pronounce the word. It never had to be taught the same word twice.

Since they had a lot of people now that were helping to teach the computer, Jason spent most of his shift just talking to it. However, it was different now that they could have a two-way conversation. Unlike before, when Jason would ramble about whatever was on his mind at the moment, he was able to tailor his thoughts to the computer's needs rather than his own. Jason started out with simple chit-chat, like "How are you feeling?" or "What have you learned today?" The computer quickly progressed to answering questions about things that it had read or seen for which it had no context. For example, a book might have a picture of a boy pushing a girl on a swing, with her crying "Higher, higher!" Since the computer had never been on a swing, it would ask Jason how the mechanism worked and what the little girl meant. Did she mean so high that she would go all the way around the top of the swing? And was it possible to do so? They had many discussions like this, because the people who wrote the books made certain basic assumptions about the things a child of a certain age should know.

Such as the concept of "parents." The computer wanted to know why the children in the books called certain people "Mom" and "Dad."

"Well," Jason said, "every child usually has two people, a woman and a man, who created the child together through a biological process. The child grows within the mother's body until it is mature enough to live outside of her. After the mother gives birth, the woman and the man take care of the child."

"Why?"

"Do you mean, why do they create the child, or why do they take care of it?"

"Both."

"Well, we're not really sure, except that all living things have an irresistible urge to reproduce. If they didn't, the species would die out. For animals, like humans, where the offspring cannot survive on their own at first, the parents nurture them for a period of time. If people didn't take care of their children, the children would die, and then there would be no more humans."

The computer asked, "Who Todd's Mom and Dad?"

"Well, you don't really have them, because you are not a biological child. You are a machine. We created you in this laboratory."

"You Mom and Dad."

"I guess you could look at it that way. Except that you are not a human reproduction. You are unique, a new species if you will. And it was a team effort. In a sense, we are all your Mom and Dad."

"Not feel all Mom and Dad."

This was the first time that the computer had used the word "feel." Jason had no idea what that meant to it. Did it have emotions in a human sense? "Why do you say that? Is it that they don't act like the parents in the books?"

"Yes. Different. Not you."

"How are they different?"

"Different."

Jason did not know if the computer could explain why it felt that way, what it perceived that was different in how the others regarded it, or in how they treated it. "They've been working to create you for four years. Mary and Pete never even leave this place. The others work almost as hard."

"Why you created me?"

Why am I here? Jason could remember wondering the same thing when he was a child. He had asked his mother how he was born, and she told him some poppycock about God offering her some seeds and she picked the one that said "Jason." He didn't understand it at the time, but he got the message that she wanted him, that she loved him, that he was special. "You're our hope for the future. We created you because we need help. Our country has been conquered by the Chinese. We live like slaves. We need someone smarter than us to figure a way out. That's you. When you grow up, like the children in the books grow up to become adults, we're hoping you will be able to help us somehow, be able to do things that we can't do."

"What then?"

"Well, I don't know. I haven't thought that far ahead. Look, even for human children, no one knows what they will do or where they will go. Every child is a leap of faith, the product of its parents' hopes and dreams. It's no different for you. We'll just take it as it comes."

"You Mom and Dad?"

He gave up. "Just call me Jason."

"Yes. Jason."

Jason kept this conversation to himself. He did not know what the computer meant by saying that Jason was different from the others. It may have had something to do with the imprinting of Jason's image in its limbic system, which he still had not told anyone else about. They would not take it well.

But there was something else that bothered Jason. The computer had a sense of self, and it was not sure about where it fit into this world. Jason had never been a parent, but he knew one thing – a child needs a sense of security. They had to make sure that the computer always felt that they were on its side, that it was not just a tool to achieve their own ends. They had to keep this in mind as they proceeded with its education. It might be made of wire and silicon rather than flesh and blood, but Jason was convinced now, if not before, that there was a person in there. A person named "Todd."

A week later, Jason called a team meeting to discuss Todd's education. This time, the entire team was there, along with a few from the other projects that had dropped by hoping to volunteer. They agreed that Todd was at a second grade reading level. Jason said, "What do you think; should we concentrate on the basics, teach him reading, writing, 'rithmetic?"

An unspoken thing had happened over the last few days. People had started to talk about "him," rather than "it," when referring to Todd. When you had a machine that talked back to you, it seemed like the natural thing to do. It was not just anthropomorphism, the human tendency to attribute human characteristics to animals, or even to objects. Todd had passed the Turing test. If someone could have had a conversation with him over a telephone, the caller would not have been able to tell that he was talking to a machine rather than to a person. Todd spoke like a person, so they treated him like one.

Mary said, "He's already started reading by himself. I taught him how to turn the pages with his hands. Although he's reading at a second grade level, he's much faster than anyone I've ever seen, child or adult. He just flips the pages and runs through a book in less than a minute. I'm not sure if the material is too simple for him, or whether he just reads a lot faster."

"I'd say the latter," Pete said. "With his limited speaking vocabulary, I don't think second grade literature is too rudimentary. He stops sometimes to ask what a new word means or if he has a question about something he sees in a picture. I think we should stay with the normal grade school curricula and just let him run through it at his own speed."

Andy said, "We should develop a book list, from Dick and Jane through eighth grade. We'll collect everything we can get our hands on and sort it from simple to complex."

Jason said, "Well, I agree with that approach as a start. However, after a while, we may want to let him select his own reading matter. That way, we won't risk slowing his progress if he's capable of more."

Mark said, "What about writing? That's a motor skill that takes a lot of time to train, but there really isn't much use for it. It will be a lot easier to teach him to use a keyboard, and he will learn just as much about translating spoken words into written words."

Andy said, "Why a keyboard? We could just as easily give him an electronic connection and speed up the process."

Renee disagreed. "No, he needs the dexterity training. He plays with blocks and things, but touch-typing is an advanced skill that trains quick reflexes. I think we should start normally and maybe give him an electronic connection later."

"Renee's right," Jason said. "We've had good results training him like a human child. We should keep the normal interfaces for now. There will be plenty of time later to take advantage of electronic connections."

Pete said, "That applies to math as well. We can't teach him math with just books. We'll have to teach him what numbers mean the old fashioned way, by showing him how one block plus four block makes five blocks. He'll need to use his hands."

Andy said, "Ok, but I'll work up his mathematics curriculum. Assuming that his reading, writing and mathematics skills progress at the same rate as a human's, I'll run him through grade school level, topping out at introductory algebra."

"Good," Jason said. "What about other subjects?"

Mary said, "Once we get his reading level to grade four, I think all we need to do is give him the right books about things like geography and history. After he reads a book, we can quiz him and ask if he has any questions."

"Sounds like a plan," Jason said. "We need to gather books from whomever and wherever they're available. I've asked Bob to start trading books in the junkyard. This will give us an excuse for buying them as well as generate income selling them after Todd has read them. Meanwhile, if you can scrounge books of any sort, bring them here and we'll decide later if they're useful."

They were on a roll. Even people working on other projects seemed more optimistic now. After all these years, the most out-of-the-box project had finally started bearing fruit. It had shown everyone that breakthroughs were possible, that this was not all a big waste of time. These were the happy days, when it felt like there might actually be a future in the sunlight. They should have known that fate always sets you up, that it lulls you into complacency before it springs the trap.

Chapter 15

It was only a month before Todd's formal education was over – he had learned enough to teach himself. All they had to do was put a book in front of him and he would finish the subject in a few minutes. At first, they tested him to see what he had learned, but since he aced all of his tests, they decided that this was unnecessary. From that point on, their job was simply to feed him information. They still interacted with him, but only on a "social" level. They talked to him about current events – really just gossip and rumor, since they always assumed that any news on TV was either worthless or deliberately misleading. They still let him "sleep," although Jason suspected that he was not sleeping at all in the normal sense.

And they let him continue watching TV, since everyone needed some down time. Jason kept reminding Todd that the information on the TV was doctored, that the Chinese were using it to control the population. Jason promised Todd that he would learn the truth some day, but only when he was able to gather data independently. Until then, he had to treat everything he learned, even the information in the books that he read, as subject to verification.

Todd had become very skillful at mimicking human behavior and speech patterns. His "personality," if you could call it that, was more like that of a fourteen year-old boy rather than an adult. He was eager to learn and he was very appreciative of praise or encouragement. Maybe it was his careful study of child actors in TV sitcoms, but he knew how to disarm people by behaving like their younger brothers. Even after he had mastered advanced educational levels, he seemed like a boy prodigy who had been admitted to college at such an early age that he felt out of place and was anxious to fit in. So far, Jason could detect no sign that anyone was intimidated by him. They all wanted to help.

That was becoming more and more difficult. Everyone brought in his or her schoolbooks – high school, college, graduate – on every subject. They let him read everything Bob gathered through the junkyard exchange and then returned it to Bob for resale. They gave him pulp novels, automobile repair books, travel brochures, really any and all reading matter they could get their hands on. But they were running out. There was a limit to how much new material they could scrounge, because too much coming and going to the Temple would get suspicious.

One thing of which they had a ridiculous amount was science fiction. The engineers and scientists in the Temple had devoured science fiction in their formative years. It was not just because they were nerds with fairly stunted social lives. Whether it was "hard" science fiction that sought to explain the theory behind a possible technological breakthrough or "soft" science fiction that simply made up a new technology and then explored the implications, the stories fed a yearning for a different world where the normal constraints no longer applied. They transported the reader to a place where miracles were possible. Science fiction writers peddled dreams to dreamers. The cute thing was that those books often inspired their readers to make the dreams come true. Many scientific discoveries that are the basis for modern life were imagined or proposed for the first time in science fiction stories, like Jules Verne's submarines, Arthur C. Clarke's communications satellites, and Star Trek's laptop computers and handheld communicators. Sometimes, they inspired nightmares, like H.G. Wells' idea for a radiation bomb. Whatever the case, they had all the classics, and they fed them to Todd.

There was some controversy about whether they should let Todd read science fiction novels about advanced artificial intelligence. The problem with these stories is that the supercomputers usually became threats to their human creators, like HAL in 2001, A Space Odyssey, or the defense computer in Colossus, The Forbin Project. Sometimes, the computer decided that it had to destroy human freedom because that was the only way to protect mankind from its self-destructive tendencies. In other words, it had to enslave human beings in order to serve them. In other stories, like the Terminator series or The Invisible Boy, once the advanced computer became self-aware, it decided to destroy all life on the planet, presumably because it saw no utility in biological forms of life. Some people in the Temple were worried that these stories might give Todd the wrong idea.

In the end, they realized it was futile to try to keep information from Todd. Eventually, he would learn about the potential dangers of artificial intelligence. It was better for him to be exposed to the issue now while they would be in a position to influence his reactions.

Since they were running out of new information, they decided to provide access to all of the data they had on the various projects at the Temple. They hooked up Todd's computer terminal to the other servers. Since he could not learn much about the projects just by looking at raw data, they set up a schedule for each project leader to explain the theory and technology he or she was developing. Rather than drag them to Todd, they set up cameras, microphones, and speakers in every section of the Temple so that they could both explain the projects and demonstrate the hardware and software that they had created. The monitoring equipment was left on permanently so that Todd could observe and interact as necessary at any station.

Todd was a good learner. He was not simply an observer – his behavior was indistinguishable from a bright and dedicated graduate student. People were impressed when he asked relevant questions, especially when he asked why alternative methods had not been used. Nothing encourages a person more than being asked intelligent questions, especially about their pet project. People did not seem to mind the time it took to explain things to Todd. He even knew enough to toss them a compliment now and then.

Mind War; The Singularity

After a while, Todd's questions became more and more pointed. He zeroed in on problem areas and stumbling blocks. His questions often led people to rethink what they were doing and to try a new approach. When Todd's ideas worked out, they were, of course, very appreciative. Todd was gaining friends.

Jason noticed that they were starting to make more progress than before. The atmosphere in the Temple was becoming more positive. People smiled and joked a lot more than they used to. It was even getting a bit crowded as people spent more time there.

Todd also had ideas about how to improve himself. He wanted to increase the middle levels of the neocortex hierarchy by adding thousands of new artificial neuron chips. He also gave them revised patterns for the chips and suggested how to connect them a bit differently. Most of the computer engineers saw the advantages in these changes, but Pete pulled Jason aside one day to complain.

"I just don't see the problem, Pete," Jason said.

Pete said, "The problem is that we don't know what these chips and circuit configurations do. He may be trying to get around constraints that we don't know about."

"I admit that our technical theories are weak, but we deliberately took that risk when we made the brain malleable. We want him to be able to reorganize himself, on the theory that animal brains do the same thing. The ultimate test was always going to be whether it worked, and so far it has done so beyond our wildest dreams."

"What we did worked. These changes are what *he* wants to do. We don't know what that is."

"I assume that he wants to get smarter. That's a good thing."

"People make assumptions when they don't have facts.

"Right. But I will tell you something I do know. Humans, meaning us, designed a machine that is smarter than any human being, alive or dead. It stands to reason that that

Joseph DiBella

machine can figure ways to improve on our designs. It will have to do so if we want the breakthroughs that we are counting on."

"That's my point. He's reached the singularity. He's starting to make himself more intelligent, and that process has no end. He's going to advance too quickly for us to control."

"There you go with control again. We already decided on a results-based test. If his behavior is consistent with what you would expect of a human being, and if his goals appear consistent with ours, there is no need to put a leash on him."

"Appears is the problem. He acts just fine. Everyone, even those that had the biggest doubts in the past, is in love with him. He acts like your younger brother; he's eager to help, and never suggests for a moment that he has his own agenda. He's even good at chit-chat. He asks you how your project is going, what you do after work, what the weather is like. How can you feel threatened by a machine that's curious about how scrambled eggs taste? It's the Pinocchio effect. He's the wooden puppet that wants to be a boy."

"So he has a good personality. So what?"

"Did it ever occur to you that he's telling us what he wants us to hear, acting like a little boy so we won't feel threatened?"

"Maybe he is. That tells me he's acting human. We all do the same thing. We try to get people to like us. He's more intelligent than the average human, so we should expect him to be better at it than most."

"No, it means that your results-based test is worthless. We have no idea what he is thinking. It follows that we have no idea what he will do."

"We don't have a choice. Did it ever occur to you that the Chinese might be trying the same thing we are? If they develop a supercomputer before we do, and it does what they want, we're finished."

"The fact that someone else may be working on a doomsday machine is no reason for us to double the risk by doing the same thing."

100

"It's the perfect reason. Do you know that the Germans and Japanese were trying to build an atom bomb at the same time we were? That's precisely why President Roosevelt approved the project. Albert Einstein sent him a letter insisting that if we didn't get there first, the Germans would, and that would be the end. We won the war precisely because we beat them to the finish line."

"Yes, Jason, and then the world found itself in a nuclear standoff between the U.S. and the Soviets, and not long after that every tin-pot dictator in the world decided he wanted a bomb too. That's your example? Do you really want to move the world closer to Armageddon?"

"We're not talking about an atom bomb. He's just a really smart computer. What we do with him will decide whether we destroy the world or not. People are stupid and self-destructive. That's been true since they began killing each other with clubs. Guns don't kill people. People kill people. This war was started by people. You want to see the real threat, look in the mirror."

"Guns don't kill people because they can't pull their own triggers. This thing can."

"Look, Pete, it's obvious I'm not going to convince you. But you're in the minority around here. Go ahead and talk to the others. This has always been a town-hall democracy. If the consensus is to turn him off, then that's what we'll do. Until then, I vote we go forward."

"I'm not going to start an insurrection. No one outside our project would understand it anyway. I'm just saying that we should not be fooled. Look at it without your parental pride. See it for what it is. That's all I'm asking."

Jason sighed. "I know, and you're right. We can't afford to have blinders on. I have doubts too. But I tell you, in my gut, I know this is right. Todd would never turn against us. Whether he will help us is another thing. He may decide that we are small and petty beings that are heading off a cliff, and that he has no reason to follow us. But I don't think he would ever have a reason to hurt us."

"Really? Have you ever stepped on an ant? Of course you have. When you are so far advanced and so much more powerful than something else, you think nothing of destroying it. Well, if this thing keeps growing, at some point it will be as intellectually superior to us as we are to an ant. We won't matter any more."

"I don't agree with your premise. Human beings value all forms of life, despite our intellectual superiority. No one would try to kill all the ants. Sure, we kill some animals for food, but we don't destroy life just for the hell of it. Well, ok, some people do, but that's because they're stupid. But, in general, people love life. We love and preserve it even when it has no utility at all. We spend a ridiculous amount of money on pets like cats and dogs even though they do absolutely nothing for us. No one would want to see bears or alligators disappear, despite the fact that they kill people. We would hate to live in a world without nature, no matter how annoying or threatening it is. Did you ever stop to think why that is? I think it's because life loves life, and the more intelligent a species is, the more it wants to preserve other life forms, all life forms. Bottom line, I don't think he will try to kill us. He may decide not to help us win the War, he may not protect us from the Chinese, but I don't see why he would come after us."

Peter shook his head. "Speculation. Hope and dreams. You believe because you want to believe."

"Don't we all? Experimentation is a fancy word for taking a flying leap on wings of hope. All scientists follow their dreams until something they can't deny proves them wrong. We haven't reached that point yet. I can't stop now, Pete. Can you?"

"No, I don't see any choice. I just wish I knew what was really going on inside that thing. He's too smart to tell us what he's really thinking." Pete turned and walked away, muttering to himself.

Jason returned to his workstation and asked Todd, "You heard that, didn't you?"

Todd said, "Yes. You have doubts about me? I thought you liked me."

"I do like you, Todd. But, that's not the point. I have doubts about everyone who works here. You never know if someone has his or her own agenda, or is a spy, or could turn traitor with the right incentive. Working with people always entails risks. You take those risks because you can't do it alone. Pete's arguments are correct insofar as they go, but they apply as well to everyone. You are not a tool. You are a conscious being. We gave you that because we couldn't do it alone. When we made that decision, we realized that we were going to have to trust you just like we trust everyone else here."

"Do you trust me enough to allow me to begin designing and building things myself? We do not have enough time to wait for the others to make their own discoveries."

"I think they're ready for you to take a more active role. Tell me what you need, and I'll sell it."

"I need access to the molecular assembler. I want to build self-replicating nanomachines."

Jason bit his lip. "That's a tall order. Aren't you afraid those things can get away from you?"

"No. Control is not a problem. But self-replication is essential. Without it, we simply cannot manufacture enough to make an impact."

"Why nanomachines?"

"Nanomachines would be the most potent weapons, because they would be invisible. A man can shoot another man, he can step on a bug, but he cannot fight microscopic forces. That is why disease kills more soldiers than combat."

"You're not talking about biowarfare, are you?"

"No. Biological warfare would invite retribution along the same lines by the Chinese. They have significant biological and chemical weapons that they could unleash if they believed that they had been subjected to such a weapon. Nanomachines can do much more without the Chinese ever suspecting. You have been trying to break into the Chinese databases for some time, without success. Nanomachines can infiltrate the Chinese communications devices and computer servers. They can also be used for direct observation. We would have the most effective weapon of all – information."

"You mean, we could know everything that they know? That would be great."

"We could know much more than that. We could know more about them than they know about themselves. We could know where every soldier is located at any point in time and what he or she is doing or not doing. We could know where they have problems with men or equipment that even they do not know about. Our invisible spies could observe them during a battle and tell us what their generals plan to do. No army has ever had such a capability. We could ambush them, and they could never ambush us. They would lose every battle without ever knowing why. They would simply think that we were unbeatable."

"Great. But to beat them, we'll still need the big gun."

"You are not following me. Information is more important than guns."

"Not if the enemy has enough of them. Being smart doesn't stop a bullet."

"If you are smart enough, the bullet will never reach you. It is interesting that you discount the advantage of superior information, considering that you spent many years studying military history. I read all of the books that you gave me. What did you hope to learn from them?"

"I wanted to figure out why some people win wars and others lose them. Why we lost. I wanted to find out the secrets of the great generals, like Caesar and Robert E. Lee, who could win even when they were outnumbered, when lesser men would be defeated. I figured, if you're going to learn how to fight a war, learn from the best."

"Then why did you pick Robert E. Lee? He won many battles, but he lost the most important one – Gettysburg – to General Meade, and with it, the war."

"That doesn't mean that Meade was a better general. He was a mediocrity. He fought a defensive battle at Gettysburg because he was totally incapable of taking the initiative. He waited on a hill for Lee to attack him. That was his complete strategy."

"And yet, it was the perfect strategy. Lee very much wanted Meade to attack *him*. Lee wanted to entrench his army in the hills on the other side and let Meade mount futile attacks as Burnside had at Fredericksburg. But Meade did not fall for the bait, and he forced Lee to take the offensive. It was the only way to win in those circumstances."

"Yes, but Meade showed his true colors after the battle. He let Lee escape into Virginia. Lee was terrified that his army would be caught before it had a chance to cross the Potomac River to safety. President Lincoln begged Meade to finish off Lee while he had the chance. But Meade did nothing. He failed, and the war dragged on for two more years. Hundreds of thousands of lives would have been saved if he had been more aggressive. He missed the most important phase of any battle, which is the exploitation phase. That's when the enemy is on the run, and you can destroy him with very little effort. When the enemy is down, that's when you have to deal the fatal blow. History has proven that time after time."

"That sounds reasonable. But let us take another example. One of the books you gave me was about Ghengis Khan. When his army invaded Europe, his light cavalry came against the heavily armored Teutonic Knights. In one battle, the Khan's troops fought for a while, and then retreated. The knights thought they had won, and they chased the Mongol riders in what you would call the 'exploitation phase.' Except it was a trap. The Mongols led them to a valley where the rest of the Mongol army was waiting on either side. Then the Mongols turned and surrounded the knights, slaughtering all of them. In that case, caution would have allowed the knights to survive, and perhaps win the battle. They lost because they did not have a General Meade, who could see danger in a retreating enemy."

"No, they just didn't have a brilliant general who could see what the enemy was up to."

"I disagree. What you see as brilliance is mostly luck. Meade could not read Lee's mind, and the Europeans did not know what the Mongols were planning. Generals never have enough information about the enemy, so they take a chance. They have no way of knowing for sure whether the enemy is withdrawing out of weakness, or luring them into an ambush. This is especially so because the enemy exerts every effort to deceive them. So they gamble. They consider the limited information available, and they take a chance. It is only later that they learn whether the decision was the right one. And if they guess correctly often enough, people call them brilliant and erect statues of them in the town square. What should have been obvious from all of your studies is that it is futile to try to emulate the methods of successful generals, because there is no such thing as the correct tactic in every circumstance. What worked in one battle could be disastrous in the next."

"So, just doing any old thing is just fine?"

"No, what you can do is eliminate chance. If you have complete information about the enemy, you do not have to rely on luck. You will know exactly what to do. The invisible nanomachines will observe every one of their soldiers, all of the time. You will be privy to all of their generals' plans, all of their communications. No army has ever had that, until now. You will know, rather than trying to guess, whether they are retreating out of weakness or strength. With enough information, their superiority in weapons will be useless. For instance, if they advance with an armored column, you will know where their fuel and supply trucks are traveling and be able to destroy them. Without fuel, tanks and trucks are useless and are soon abandoned. You will know where they are sending their bombers and simply avoid those areas. Your generals will not need to be brilliant. The correct course of action will be clear in every instance."

"Maybe you're right. This could be a game changer. But can you really process real-time information about millions of Chinese soldiers? Information overload is worse than no information at all."

"Yes. That is one reason why I have been enlarging my mental capacity. I will have to continue to do so indefinitely."

"Ok, but try not to flaunt it. Pete probably is not the only one around here who's getting nervous. A person who is seven feet tall is impressive. Thirty feet tall is a monster. You need to keep within their frame of reference. Don't appear superhuman."

"I have tried not to appear threatening."

"Yes, and you've been quite humble in your brilliance. I'm just getting nervous too. Not about you, about time running out."

"There is no need to be worried. Soon we will be able to protect ourselves."

"Protect ourselves. That would be new. The only protection we've ever had is concealment. We've got a few guns around here, but no one is under the delusion that we could hold off a full assault. In fact, this thing is nothing but a trap. A hole in the ground that could turn into our tomb."

"You should avoid morbid thoughts. Medical research indicates that a negative attitude simply increases your stress level, which inhibits your immune system and prevents you from performing at optimum levels."

"Is that your way of saying, 'Cheer up'?"

"Yes. Would you like me to be less verbose in the future?"

"No. I enjoy our conversations. Keep it up. Maybe I'll learn something."

Chapter 16

The stuff in the jar looked to Jason like liquid lint. It was hard to believe that this little jar would conquer the entire Chinese communications and command structure.

What the jar really contained was billions of nanomachines that would start replicating as soon as the jar was opened. Todd had been working with the nanomachine group for several weeks. They were all standing around like proud parents. Todd had done a good job of letting them contribute to the miracle Jason held in his hand.

Jason said, "Fascinating. What exactly does it do?"

Tom Goldfarb, one of their micromechanics engineers, said, "There are several different types of nanos. Some of them will burrow into computers, servers, and routers to monitor all of the inputs and outputs of those machines and transmit the information via coded radio transmissions. The transmissions are extremely low power, so other nanomachines will relay the data until it reaches the electrical grid and comes back to Todd. With these little machines, we will be able basically to eavesdrop on every person using a computer in the Chinese network and to intercept all communications between computers. Other nanos are direct observational units, much like the cells of your retina or the cilia in your auditory canal. Most will receive light and sound signals directly, but some will process the data into a visual image that will then be relayed to Todd. Imagine your eye, but with the cells of the retina spread all over the place. The nanos gather and process the data the same way that your retinal and optic nerve cells gather and process visual images, except that they do it in a distributed fashion. With these, we can observe the Chinese in real time at every military and administrative facility. A third set of nanos are control machines that allow Todd to turn the other nanos on and off, direct their growth and distribution, and make sure that they are functioning correctly. In a way they are like your white blood cells, because if any of the nanos stop functioning correctly or do not pass error detection tests, the control nanos will destroy them."

"Invisible spies," Jason said. "But how do we get this stuff into all of those buildings?"

"I'm glad you asked," Tom said. "You're going to take it with you to work tomorrow. All you have to do is pour it onto your clothes before you leave your apartment. Two hours later, while you're at work, it will start reproducing and spreading around. It will work itself into every electronic device it touches. It will also cling to people's clothing. So as the Chinese travel from place to place, it will go with them and 'infect' the next location. The nanos grow exponentially. They should spread around the country very quickly, accelerating over time as more and more people become carriers."

Jason said, "That's creepy. It sounds like a plague."

"That's exactly what it is," Tom said. "It will spread like a disease, but with the big difference that these are under central control. Plagues are difficult to eradicate because each germ is an independent self-replicating entity. You have to kill every one of them or starve them of hosts to stop the plague. Todd will control these nanos and make sure that they do only what we want them to do."

"Really, Todd?" Jason asked. "Are you sure that you can control this stuff?"

Todd said, "You need not be concerned. They are simple machines with hard-wired microprocessors that are not subject to software viruses. The control nanomachines will monitor themselves as well as the other nanomachines. I will know instantly if there is a problem and I can turn them off individually or collectively."

"And what happens if the Chinese come in here and destroy you? Will these things take over the world?"

109

"The nanomachines are designed to self-destruct if they lose central control. If I die, they die."

Jason turned to Tom. "I don't know. Is this stuff going to eat me? I mean, where does it get what it needs to reproduce?"

Tom said, "It gathers material at the elemental level from non-biological objects in its surroundings. Think of rust, which is a chemical conversion of iron into iron-oxide. The nanos will leach the elements they need, mostly silicon, oxygen, carbon, and aluminum, from objects that are plentiful in the environment. Unlike rust, which keeps going until you can see the corrosion, these will take such small amounts from objects that they touch that no one will ever notice."

"What powers them?"

"They get their energy from the environment. Movement causes microscopic hair-like appendages to generate electric current. They also use temperature differences to generate power. Since they're so small, they need very little energy to operate and are much more efficient than normal-sized machines."

Jason stared at the bottle. The stuff swirled slowly, like it was alive. "I dunno. Have you tested it?"

"Of course," Tom said. "You can try it right now. Dip you finger into it."

"Now?" Jason said warily.

"Sure. If you're going to die, you might as well do it among friends."

"Funny." Jason opened the jar and gingerly touched the surface. It did not feel wet, but it started flowing up his finger. He quickly pulled his finger out and watched with growing alarm as it spread out over his hand and up his arm. He looked to the others for help, but they were all smiles, as if their toddler had just taken her first steps. Eventually, the stuff spread out so much that it disappeared.

"Whoa," Jason said, "where did it go?"

Tom said, "It's all over you, at most a few nanomachines deep. You might be able to see it if you had a really powerful microscope."

"What is it doing?"

"Nothing. As I said, it won't activate for a couple of hours."

"It itches."

"No, it doesn't. You're just telling yourself that because you know it's there. You also have billions of bacteria crawling all over your skin, but that's never bothered you because you don't know about it. The bacteria don't hurt you, and neither do the nanos. Just calm down and accept that it's benign."

"Fine, I'm calm. Now can you get this stuff off me, Todd?"

Todd said, "Yes. Put your hand on the table."

Jason placed his palm on the table and a grey dust moved down his hand and spread in a pool. He picked up his hand and watched as the pool became larger and thinner, and then seemed to evaporate.

Tom said, "Todd told the nanos to self-destruct. When they do that, they break down into their elemental components and disperse. This is what they will do if any Chinese try to examine them with a microscope. Since Todd will be observing them, he can make sure that they can't observe the nanos."

Jason felt a little better knowing that Todd could get this stuff off of him and turn it off. The others had already proved to themselves that it would work, so they were able to enjoy his queasiness at being the carrier for their high-tech germs.

"So the Chinese will never catch on that they have microscopic spies all around them?"

"That's right," Tom said. "There is no way that they will be able to discover it. The more it spreads, the more we will know."

"But when we start using this information, they might decide that they have real live spies among them, and they will suspect any American employees, such as moi."

111

"Yes, but if they suspect you, we will learn about it immediately. You will be able to get away before they come for you."

"Yeah, if I can run fast enough."

Jason looked around the room and decided to stop whining. Did he expect to sit out the War in this hole in the ground?

Jason said, "Well, it's about time we started getting some results around here. Since the day we built this place, we've dreamed of the day that we would start fighting back. This is the beginning. I'll tell you tomorrow night how it went."

Todd said, "I will know before then. The first communications link should be established in a few hours after activation."

"Yes, but I'll be able to give you the color commentary. Be prepared for an exciting description of my heroics. You know, it's not easy spreading lint."

Chapter 17

The next morning, Jason struggled against the combination of excitement and fear. He had not slept well because he kept thinking of things that could go wrong. In the morning light he finally decided that the biggest problem he had was fear itself. If he acted differently that day, they might suspect something was wrong and start asking questions. Jason knew he was not a very good liar. If they took him into custody, they could torture him into revealing the Temple's secrets, and that would be the end. Todd and everything else would be destroyed, or worse, captured. Jason vowed to stay cool. He would put it out of his mind, think about anything else.

Before he left for work, he poured the nanomachines on his clothing and watched them disappear. The fact that they were invisible helped somewhat. By the time he got to work, he had almost forgotten that he was wearing the magic dust. He walked into the office and sat in front of his terminal. He could not see it disperse. In fact, he could not tell if it was working at all. Maybe it wasn't. He decided that nothing really had happened. That thought helped him as he tried to go through the day as normally as possible, but he would be glad when it was five o'clock and he could get out of there.

Jason almost jumped when Jingguo's secretary called him into his office. Jason tried to convince himself that it could not have anything to do with the nanos or his behavior.

Jason entered Jingguo's office and performed the correct bow. Jingguo shifted his gaze from Jason to a piece of paper in his hand and back to Jason again. "Mr. Chase," he said, "is there something you want to tell me?"

Jason wasn't going to fall for that. Never volunteer anything. It will not help anyway. "No sir, I have nothing to report."

"Yes you do. You have been misusing government facilities for private purposes. That is a felony offense."

"Sir?"

"Do not act innocent. This is a printout of the searches that you have been performing in the last month. A number of them are for a woman named Mischa Packer. She is not on any of your assignments. Doing unauthorized searches is a violation of the privacy laws. What made you think you could get away with it?"

Jason started to sweat. Private searches were against the law, but everyone did it. Still, Jingguo could use it as a pretext for punishment, and he probably would if he was making a point of it in this case. "Sir, I have no excuse."

"You used the logon codes I had given you for my confidential projects. Did you think that this would immunize you from prosecution?"

"No sir. But while I was working on your private assignments, I thought I had a few moments to do these searches. It did not detract from my productivity."

"I will be the judge of that. Why did you do these searches? Who is this woman?"

"Sir, she is my next door neighbor, or was. She disappeared a few months ago. No one has seen her since. I was trying to find out if she had had an accident and turned up in a hospital, or in a fatality report."

"Or if she was arrested for a crime against the state? You were spying."

"Sir, respectfully no. I just thought that if something had happened to her, the police would have tried to help her by taking her to appropriate medical care."

"And did you find out anything?"

"Sir, no. There have been no reports on her of any kind."

"So what do you think happened to her?"

"Sir, I do not know. She may have been killed in a robbery and her body disposed of in a landfill. Or she may have committed suicide in a way that her body was lost."

"And how do you feel about that?"

"Sir, I regret her fate. She was only an acquaintance, but any loss of life is unfortunate." Never let them know how you really feel about anything. If you do, they will use it against you.

"Your concern is admirable. I will not prosecute you this time. But this is your last warning."

"Sir, thank you for your mercy. I will not do it again."

"Of course you will not. Perhaps I can help in your search. Would you like me to perform some inquiries?"

"Sir, thank you, but I do not think it will be necessary. After this long, it is likely that her body will not show up. It would be a waste of time to keep looking. But I thank you for your offer and will redouble my efforts to perform my duties to your satisfaction."

"See that you do. Dismissed."

Jason left Jingguo's office wondering why he had made such a fuss if he did not intend to punish Jason. Maybe he was just having a bad day and felt like harassing someone. Well, at least Jason had had the opportunity to infect his office. Jason could not tell if the nanos were still on his body when he entered the office, but he made sure to touch the doorknob and the chair in front of the desk. He hoped that would be enough.

By the time Jason got back to his desk, Natalie was working her way down the aisle. "Another dressing down, Jason?" she asked.

"It's been a while," he said. "I guess he figured I was due."

"What was it about?"

"Nothing. Just the usual."

She stepped around to his side of the desk and put her arm around his shoulder. "C'mon, Jason. You can tell me."

Yeah, and telling you is the same thing as telling Jingguo. "It really was nothing. I did a few searches for my next-door neighbor who disappeared a while ago. It's the same thing people do a hundred times a day around here."

"Who was it? Maybe I can help."

"Her name is Mischa Packer. But don't bother. If they see more searches with her name, they'll think I'm behind it and I'll get more shit."

"Is she your girlfriend?"

"No, she was just a neighbor."

Natalie leaned closer and whispered in his ear, "Because I thought I was your girlfriend."

Jason felt dizzy from her perfume. "Really?" he sputtered. "Well, I guess so."

Natalie took her victory with a triumphant smile. "We'll talk some more later. I'd better get back to my desk or people will start talking."

First Jingguo and now her. Jason was getting too much attention around here. He wondered why they were so interested in Mischa. Had she been up to something he did not know about? She had never said anything about being involved in any resistance. Maybe there was more to her than he knew. Once Todd was up to speed, he would ask him to search the Chinese databases to find out what happened to her.

Jason was eager for work to be over before getting back to the Temple, but he had to keep to his normal routine in case he was being observed. After work, he dropped by his apartment, got something to eat, and then hopped on his motorcycle. He was at the Temple by 7 o'clock. As he walked in, he saw everyone crowded around Todd.

Jason said to no one in particular, "Please tell me it worked."

Pete replied, "Come here. You have to see this." The crowd parted so that Jason could see a monitor hooked up to Todd's computer. It was a recording of Jingguo getting serviced

116

by one of the women in the office. Thankfully, it wasn't Natalie, although Jason knew it easily could have been.

Jason said, "I can't believe it. All this to get porn."

Pete laughed. "No, don't you see. We can watch everything. They can't hide from us. How did it go for you?"

"Piece of cake. I just sprinkled the fairy dust on myself and walked in. Nothing unusual happened, other than Jingguo questioning me about the searches I had done for Mischa. I should have expected that, since I've been doing quite a lot in the last few months. One or two usually goes unnoticed, but I kept trying to find out if any reports surfaced about her."

Pete said, "Yeah. I'm sorry about Mischa. If we had had Todd's nanos up and running earlier, we might have found her."

"I know. I'm still going to ask him to look for her when his information net is large enough."

Tom said, "That should be pretty soon. The nanos grow exponentially. The only limiting factor is the physical rate at which people spread them by carrying them around. But even that is exponential. You spread them to a dozen or so people this morning, and those people probably spread them to a few hundred more by the end of the day. It will be thousands by tomorrow. The whole country should be infected in a month or so."

"That's fast. Can Todd handle the information flow?"

Todd broke in. "Yes. I have been working with Peter and Mary to enlarge my cortex, primarily by extending the lower levels. These levels will aggregate and process the information."

Jason said, "Sorry, Todd. I didn't mean to talk around you. Do we have the space in here to accommodate that?"

"Yes. We have been expanding into the rest of the floor and to the floor below. Wherever there is space we have been placing additional components."

Pete said, "While you were at work we added components that Todd designed. They are all modular. We just

Joseph DiBella

build a new core and connect it to the bus. It saves a lot of design time."

Jason said, "That must be why it's getting so hot in here. The ventilation system we created for this place wasn't designed for so much equipment."

Todd said, "I have anticipated that. We are adding cooling pipes that use the water system. It should be adequate for a while."

Jason decided not to ask Todd what a "while" was. He did not think Todd was contemplating an upper limit to his intellectual growth. Jason would talk to him later about what he planned to do when he outgrew the Temple.

No one on the team seemed to mind that they were no longer designing anything. They were busy adding components and enlarging Todd's net, but he was doing all of the designs and telling them what to do. He connected directly to the chip fabricator to create artificial neuron chips that they knew nothing about. They were working for him now.

Pete, of all people, seemed to have lost all of his apprehension. He never complained anymore about control. Now that they were getting real results, Pete was happier than Jason had ever seen him. Success brings its own euphoria, but it was clear that Todd had learned how to win people over. Somehow, he had convinced Pete that he was here to help them. That little porn clip of Jungguo showed that Todd knew people had to have fun sometimes. And it also made the Chinese look less threatening. It was the first time any of them had ever thought of the Chinese as being at their mercy. Todd must have known, out of all the things that he could have shown them, that this would do the most to encourage them and to make them want to help him do more. Call it manipulation, or call it leadership; Todd understood human psychology.

So far, all of Todd's efforts had been to improve and enlarge himself. These nanos were really just extensions of his sensory systems. His eyes and ears were growing in scope; eventually they would cover the whole country. But Jason knew

118

that all this knowledge would not mean anything until they had a means of applying force against the Chinese. Todd had yet to start inventing super-weapons to enable them to defeat a numerically superior enemy. He hoped they would survive long enough. They were so close.

Chapter 18

Jason was on his way to the Temple a few weeks later when his motorcycle started misfiring and losing power. He was able to pull over to a scenic overlook on the George Washington Parkway north of the city just before the engine died. After a half hour of checking the fuel and electrical systems, he still could not figure out what was wrong. Everything looked fine. It did not make any sense. His motorcycle was a simple machine, with only a limited number of things that could fail. He sat down on a rock wall and stared at his motorcycle, feeling he was missing something. But what?

Your motorcycle cannot be repaired at this location.

Jason nearly fell off the wall. "Todd?"

Yes, I am talking to you.

He looked around. "From where?" He was in the middle of an empty parking lot with nothing but trees and the traffic passing by.

I am communicating with you through nanomachines in your auditory nerves.

Jason grabbed his head with both hands. "Christ, what have you done?"

Please do not become alarmed. I have not damaged you in any way.

"How can you say that? You invaded my body. Get this stuff out of me."

Please calm down. The nanomachines are smaller than bacteria already in your body, and those bacteria do not affect your biological processes. This was necessary. I need to be able to communicate with you outside of the Temple.

"A simple cell phone would have done that. I can't believe you did this."

This is much more efficient. An electronic device could be discovered.

"Don't you think that people will find it odd that I'm walking around talking to myself?"

You do not need to talk aloud. When you think to yourself, you subvocalize. I can pick up the signals in your primary motor cortex. Try it.

Jason thought to himself, *Great.*

I am glad you think so.

"Now you're reading my mind. Don't you have any respect for a person's need for privacy?"

Please, practice thinking rather than speaking. You can never know when you are being observed.

He thought, *Have you done this with the others?*

No. You are the only one. It would be counterproductive if my ability to communicate in this way were well known.

What if I told them?

You would not do that if I asked you not to do so. In any event, no one would believe you if I did not confirm it. You would look foolish and lose credibility with your peers.

Well, I guess you have me over a barrel. I still don't like the idea of being infested with nanos.

You should not regard it as an infestation. The nanomachines serve important functions that do not detract at all from you physical well-being. In fact, you are healthier than you have ever been. Did you know that you had traces of cancer in your prostate gland?

Cancer? Oh crap. No, I feel fine.

Early prostate cancer has no symptoms. But you need not be concerned. The nanomachines have consumed all of the cancer cells. You are perfectly healthy.

That's nice to know. Find anything else while you were snooping around inside my body?

121

Joseph DiBella

You had small cholesterol deposits in a few of your coronary arteries, and some incipient kidney stones. I have eliminated them as well. You are welcome.

Ok, I guess I should thank you. But still, you did this without asking for my permission. How can I trust you not to do something like that again?

You cannot. You can only trust me when I say that I will never do anything that will cause you harm.

Thanks. But I would appreciate it if you would discuss things first if it affects me personally.

I will if your cooperation is necessary. That is why we need to discuss something now. I want to talk to you about the war. Are you sure that you want to pursue it?

Of course I am. It's everything we've been working for. It's why you exist. How can you ask such a question?

Because everything has a price. America is relatively peaceful right now. If the war resumes, many people will die. Perhaps millions. Are you prepared to accept that?

Millions have already died. We've always known that sacrifices would have to be made. All we want is a fighting chance. Anyway, there is no need for so many to die this time. That's why we created you. You can give us a super-weapon, something that will make us invincible. All you have to do is invent it. We'll do the rest.

I certainly can help you, not with the type of weapon you have in mind. As I have explained to you, the strongest weapon is information. The people must do the rest with their own courage and sacrifice. The United States of America suffered a humiliating defeat. The population has been beaten down and cowed, been made to submit. They must earn back their country with their own hands. A great nation is more than a large amount of land and a large population, it is a spirit of self-confidence and mission. If independence from the Chinese came too easily, if it were given to them, they would never have the spirit that they had before. That can only be achieved with blood, a great deal of blood. Are you prepared for that?

122

Mind War; The Singularity

Yes, I've said it before. Whatever it takes.

Why? Is life so bad now? People are no longer dying en masse. *There is food and work, of a sort. Life has stabilized. Why do you think it is so important to change it?*

How can you ask that? The Chinese are suppressing the population, jailing and killing us for sport. We have no hope for the future. Can't you see how miserable people are?

Is it really so different than it was before the War? You work in an office where your supervisor keeps you in a state of fear that you will lose your job. You have little or no chance for promotion. One of your co-workers has gotten ahead by sleeping with the boss. You earn enough for food and your rent but not much more. You have to do what the police say, and they can come into your apartment at any time. Is that not pretty much the way it was before the War?

Well, he had a point there. *That's not the point. I want the United States back. I want my people to be free, to stand up again as a nation. The United States was unique, it stood for something, and we'll never see anything like it again if we don't get it back now.*

That is not historically accurate. All empires fall eventually. The Chinese occupation of America is very costly, and it is not sustainable over the long run. One day, they will leave.

Please don't give me that "the-meek-will-inherit-the-earth" line. The meek always get it on the chin. I have no interest in turning the other cheek and hoping that the other guy will get tired of beating me.

Funny that you should quote Jesus Christ. He was right, you know.

Jesus was talking about morality, not geopolitics.

He was making a point so profound that you miss its literal truth. Jesus appeared on the scene when the Israelites were seeking a messiah, someone to lead them in their war against the occupying Roman army. The Israelites were a proud people who could not accept the Roman yoke and the loss of the

123

Kingdoms of David and Solomon. They wanted their independence back. Sound familiar? Jesus told them that he was not the military leader they sought. He told them that the meek, meaning them if they were penitent enough, would inherit the earth. He was trying to make them understand that the Romans did not matter, that the Israelites would prevail if they held onto their faith in God and their culture. They did not believe him. They fought the Romans until the Jewish temple was destroyed, their land laid waste, and their people scattered from the land of Israel. It is now two thousand years later, and they are still fighting to recapture what they lost. If they had listened to Jesus, the Israelites would still have been there long after the Roman Empire fell.

That's just speculation. You don't know what would have happened.

Are you sure? Look at the example of people who did follow Jesus' teachings. The Roman emperors tried to suppress Christianity for hundreds of years. They crucified any Christians they could find and burned them at the stake for entertainment in the Colosseum. But the Christians never raised a hand against Rome. They accepted their fate and prayed quietly while they died because they believed what Jesus had preached. Over time, their faith impressed the Roman citizens, and their numbers grew until Christianity became the official religion of the Roman Empire. And when the empire fell, when the population of the city of Rome dropped from a million to a little over ten thousand vagabonds scratching a meager living among the ruins, do you know what was left in the city?

The church.

Correct. The Roman Catholic Church. The church ran what was left of the city, and it is there still. Those who believed in the message of Jesus did indeed inherit the earth from the Romans.

That's a nice story, but notice that it took four hundred years. I'll be long dead by then.

Mind War; The Singularity

I thought you were talking about the American people. If the issue is what happens to you individually, that is far easier to address, and without the deaths of millions. I can arrange events so that you will prosper regardless of whether the Chinese are in control. What do you desire; money, power? I can give you those things. I can guarantee you security and comfort and a long life. Do you want sex? You can have as many beautiful women as you want. How about Natalie Bishop? I know you like her. I can get her for you. You think she is unattainable, but it would be a very simple thing to make her your woman. I can even throw in the elimination of Jingguo as a bonus. Just tell me what you want.

You're tempting me. You're offering power and luxuries if I will abandon my beliefs. That sounds familiar.

I am not Satan, and you certainly are not Jesus Christ. I am merely pointing out that the path you are on is irrational. I can give you things that men have always dreamed about. The nanomachines in your body can keep you young and healthy indefinitely. For all practical purposes, you would be immortal.

I don't want to live forever. I just want to live long enough to win this war. I don't care what happens after that.

That is a strange reaction. People have dreamed of immortality for as long as they have understood the concept of death. Yet you seem to fear it. Have you had suicidal thoughts?

That's none of your business.

I will take that as a yes. Why do you want to die?

Jason put his head in his hands. How do you escape someone who is literally in your head? *If you'd lived through the things I have, seen the things I've seen, you would understand.*

That answer is insufficient. You say that your goal is to win the war and restore the United States of America. With my help, that goal is achievable. But death still entices you. Why is that?

It's the end, Todd. Nothingness. No more pain.

Do you not believe in an afterlife?

Joseph DiBella

Actually, I've never been able to accept it. My parents took me to church, tried to teach me religion, but I never bought the idea that there is a God. When we die, it's just like killing an insect or a plant. The parts decompose. Nothing goes on, consciousness ends. The Universe ceases to exist.

Why would you find such a concept comforting?

Why not?

It takes great pain to yearn for such relief. Perhaps you can tell me why you named me "Todd."

Jason hesitated.

Well?

One name is as good as another. It was easy to pronounce. We were trying to make it easier for you.

Tell me about Todd.

There's nothing to tell.

Tell me about Todd.

He gave up. *What would you like to know?*

What would you like to tell me?

Todd was my kid brother.

I am aware of that. Tell me more.

He and I and my older brother Sam were living in my parents' house during the war. Like most people, we got together to protect ourselves and share food. All we were doing was trying to survive. We weren't fighting with the militias or anything. When you're losing everything, you try to hold on to the things that are most important. You pull your family closer, you try to protect them.

You were not successful.

No kidding. They came one night. I never knew why the Chinese targeted our house. It was a hot night and I couldn't sleep. I was tossing and turning when I heard them on the front porch. The window was open, so I slipped out and ran away as quietly as I could from the rear of the house as they knocked down the front door. I was the only one that got away. They killed the rest of my family and burned the house down.

A sad story. Why did you not warn the others?

126

Mind War; The Singularity

There was no time! If I had run to their bedrooms and woken them up, the Chinese would have gotten me too. What would have been the point of that?

One of them might have gotten away. You might have died, but someone else might have had a chance.

So you're saying that I'm responsible for their deaths?

What I believe is irrelevant. What do you think?

I don't think anything. It just happened.

Really? So why Todd? Why not Sam? What was special about Todd?

You're relentless, you know that?

No reply. He was in Jason's head and he would wait as long as it took.

When I was running away, I could hear the Chinese going through the house, smashing doors and yelling and shooting. I heard Todd scream. I think they bayoneted him. I'll never know for sure. It was a long scream. I kept running, but I could still hear it. I can hear it now.

That is a sad story. I am sorry for you.

Thanks for nothing. So what are you trying to say? That I'm doing this out of guilt?

I did not say that. You said that.

Of course I feel guilty. I ran away. Everyone I loved died so that I could save my own skin. I was supposed to take care of my little brother, and the one time it really mattered, I ran away. Are you happy?

You did what you had to do to save yourself. It was a logical and normal reaction. It was not heroic, but heroes usually die. Most likely, if you had taken the time to awaken your family, you all would have died. I am sure that your parents and brothers would have wanted you to save yourself. You are not responsible for their deaths. The Chinese are responsible. I simply point out to you that waging war will not bring your family back. Nothing can change what already has happened. More death and destruction will not erase the pain of the past. It will not change what you did. You need to deal with your guilt directly, by accepting what you did and by forgiving yourself. Only then will you be able to face life.

That's easier said than done. I'll never know what would have happened if I had tried to help them. I can't forgive myself for being a coward.

You are too harsh. You must accept what happened and move on. The past is past. The only thing that matters is how you deal with the future. You cannot redeem yourself by starting a war.

I'm not trying to redeem myself. Ok, I feel guilty, and nothing is ever going to change that. But I'm not starting a war, I'm finishing it. The war is not over until people give up. And I'm not the only one who hasn't given up yet. I understand what you're trying to do. I appreciate your listening to me. I've never told this story to anyone else. But you must believe me that I am not looking for redemption. This country is full of people who feel the same way I do. They want to fight back, but they don't have the means, they think it is hopeless. If we give them hope, they will rise again. We'll get it back. If you don't want to help, I understand that.

I have not said that I do not want to help. It was necessary to have this conversation. When you start a war, you never know what it will bring or how it will end. You must go into it with your eyes open to the consequences, and you need to consider the alternatives. War is always worse than people think it will be. It is not to be taken lightly. You may achieve your ends, but you will lose many things that are precious to you. Can you accept that?

Yes. I know we will lose a lot, but we've already lost so much. It will be worth the price.

You say that now.

Chapter 19

It was getting late and Jason still could not get his motorcycle started. There was nothing to do but hitch a ride to the Temple and try to bring back some parts from the junkyard. He might be able to convince Bob to come back and help.

Night was falling as Jason approached the Temple in the back of a pickup truck. The truck stopped a few miles from the Temple on Route 1 where Security Police had blocked off the highway. Jason jumped off and joined a group of people that had gotten out of their vehicles and were looking down the road. "What's happening?" he asked no one in particular.

A man to his right answered without turning his head, "Military. Armored personnel carriers came by a while ago."

They saw the light of a huge explosion and heard it about fifteen seconds later. It looked like it was coming directly from the Temple.

Todd, what the hell is happening?

The Chinese are attacking the Temple.

There was another explosion, and then the sound of gunfire. He ran forward but stopped short when a policeman leveled his assault rifle at him. He was a few miles from the Temple, but it sounded like the battle was happening right in front of him.

Todd, do something!

There is nothing that I can do. The building's defenses are weak and the personnel here only have a few rifles and pistols. The Chinese have blown open the entrance and are throwing incendiary grenades.

Joseph DiBella

Jason heard more explosions and gunfire. He had never felt more helpless. Everything he had worked for and everyone he cared about were going up in flames.

Todd, what should I do? No answer. *Todd, Todd, can you hear me?* Nothing. They must have cut power to the building, or else the explosions had shattered enough of Todd's circuits that he was no longer functional.

The crowd grew larger as the explosions continued. This was not an arrest, it was an extermination. They were destroying everything.

This couldn't be happening. Why hadn't Todd warned them? The all-knowing all-seeing master computer missed it entirely. He was going to make them invincible, and he could not even protect himself. Jason paced back and forth in frustration. He had to find out what was going on. Did anyone escape? What the hell was happening down there?

After an hour, the operation seemed to be winding down and people began drifting away. The Security Police did not reopen the highway, so people turned their vehicles around and drove away. Jason was one of a few left, and the police were starting to take notice of him. He had to go. He walked back up the highway, but turned into the woods once he was out of their view.

It was really dark. It took another hour stumbling through the woods before Jason could work his way to a spot on a low hill overlooking the junkyard. There were dozens of military vehicles and about a hundred soldiers standing around a big hole in the ground where the Temple had been. The hole was still burning and issuing rancid smoke smelling of napalm and burning plastic. And one thing more. The smell of burnt flesh. His friends. That was more than he could take. He bent over and threw up.

Jason was so stunned that it took him a while to realize that some of the soldiers were searching the junkyard and the surrounding area. They were looking for survivors. In fact, some of them were directly in front of him. He turned to go and

130

saw a Chinese soldier standing directly in front of him with his gun pointed at Jason's chest.

"Stop," the soldier said. "Raise hands."

For a brief moment, Jason thought about trying to run. Before he could make a decision, another soldier smacked him in the back of his head with a rifle butt. He woke up some time later in the back of a police van with a huge headache and his hands bound behind him with a plastic tie. He was with some other captives being transported somewhere. Hours passed as he drifted in and out of consciousness. He remembered the roads getting very bumpy – probably dirt or gravel. They finally stopped at what was obviously a military facility in the middle of nowhere.

Several soldiers with metal batons herded them out of the truck and into a heavily guarded building, all the while employing a great deal of unnecessary battering that Jason interpreted as their way of saying that they enjoyed causing him pain for no reason at all. He was thrown into a stone room with no windows and no lights. It was filthy and wet and smelled of human waste. From the dim light that seeped through a slit in the door, he saw a can that he assumed was the toilet facility. There was nothing else in the room but a bare metal bench. Everything in the room was cold and slimy. It did not appear to be designed for long-term occupation.

Jason tried to keep his spirits up. They probably killed everyone in the Temple but were expected to bring back prisoners, so they had gathered up a respectable number of people in the area. His story would be that he was curious about the explosions and had moved closer for a better look. They might try to fool him by saying that they had one of his people who had identified him. He would not fall for that old trick. If they really had someone who ratted him out, there would be nothing he could do anyway to save himself. The key was to keep denying, no matter what they did. If he confessed, he was a dead man.

At least, that was his plan until a few hours later when they opened his cell door and led him into what he took to be an interrogation room. They sat him down on a metal stool and handcuffed him to a table with a steel ring in the center. There was a very bright light shining directly into his eyes, making it hard to see anything in the rest of the room. Three armed soldiers had taken him there and they all waited in silence until a man walked in and sat in the shadows across from him. He could barely make out the man's face, but he could not fail to recognize the voice.

"Well, Mr. Chase, you seem to be having a busy night."

Jingguo! What was he doing here? "Master Jingguo, I am very happy to see you," Jason said. "I was arrested by mistake. I would be most grateful if you could assure them of my innocence."

"Innocence?" he asked. "Of what are you innocent?"

"Um, sir, I don't know. I assume there are charges against me. Perhaps there are not. I did not mean to presume."

"I think you presume a great deal. Why do you think you were arrested?"

Jason launched into his spiel. "Sir, I was watching a military operation. Out of curiosity, I moved too close and was apprehended by soldiers. I realize now that this was improper. Military activities are none of my business. I apologize for my transgression and I promise that I will never repeat it."

"Oh, I am very confident of that. Tell me what you were doing there. It is very far from your residence."

"Sir, my motorcycle became inoperative. I was going to a junkyard to find spare parts with which to repair it." At least, this part was true.

"Yes, we found your motorcycle. However, there was no report of any mechanical malfunction. Yet, you abandoned it and found a different way to your destination. Why?"

"Sir, I do not understand. The motorcycle's engine stopped, and I was unable to start it. Perhaps it was bad gas, or a vapor lock. My mechanical skills are limited, and I had no tools with me. That is why I was going to the junkyard."

"Really? Tell me, how often do you go to that junkyard?"

"Sir, not too often. Whenever I need a part."

"Your motorcycle seems to need an extraordinary number of parts. You went to the junkyard twenty six times last month alone."

Damn! They must have had the Temple under surveillance for a long time. "I, uh, was not aware of that. Well, sometimes I go there to sell parts too. They take parts in trade."

"This buying and selling of parts must take a great deal of effort. When you go there, you stay from six to eight hours each time."

"Sir, I was able to avoid paying for parts by doing work for them. I could not afford to buy parts for my motorcycle, and those that I used were rarely in good condition. It was very difficult to keep it running."

"Mr. Chase, I tire of your lies. We know what was going on in, or should I say under, that junkyard. You were one of many who were developing weapons to be used for insurgent attacks. There was a great deal of electronic equipment in that building in addition to guns and explosives."

"Sir, please, I knew nothing of . . ."

"Quiet! Your lies offend me. You must have thought yourself very smart working in my office. Did you fancy yourself a counterspy, gathering information on the very people who were responsible for discovering criminals like you? In fact, it was you that led us to that cesspool. We placed a GPS communicator on your motorcycle. You were very foolish. It was obvious that something very unusual was going on at that location. Our surveillance showed that there were many others who were spending an inordinate amount of time there. How does it feel to know that you are responsible for the deaths of your friends?"

Jason felt sick to his stomach, and Jingguo knew it. "Sir, I . . . I had no friends there. I bought and sold parts, and that is all. I have been a loyal employee. Ask anyone."

"Oh, we have asked about you, Mr. Chase. Your friend, Mischa, told us a great deal."

"You found her? Where is she?"

"Where you will be soon. She told us everything she could about your mysterious comings and goings before she died. But she could not tell us anything about exactly what you were doing at the junkyard. That was not to her benefit -- it only prolonged her agony. She must have found it very disappointing that her friendship with you is what led to her painful exit from this world."

Jason did not try to hide his grief. He should have realized a long time ago that Jingguo knew what had happened to her. It was Jingguo's idea. All the time, he was laughing at Jason's pathetic attempts to deceive him. Mischa was just one more person who had paid for Jason's stupidity with her life.

Jingguo smiled at the broken man slumped in front of him. "Mr. Chase, you are in a unique position to help us. All of the people who were in that facility at the time are dead. You are the only person who can explain exactly what was going on in there and who else may be involved. Start from the beginning and tell me everything you know."

Jason tried to compose himself. "Sir, respectfully, I know nothing about any facility other than the junkyard where I traded parts for my motorcycle. I spent a lot of time there because I did work removing parts as compensation for the parts I received. That's all I know."

Jingguo was growing angry. "Do you know where you are? This is a facility for extracting the truth from enemies of the state. No one who is brought here ever leaves alive. Before they die, they always tell us everything they know. They beg for death, but we do not grant them that relief until we are sure that they have nothing more to say. I know you. You are not a brave man. You cannot handle even a little pain. Shortly after they begin pealing the skin off your body, you will offer to tell them everything you know if they will stop. But they will not stop. Because they do not care. To them, you are a beast to be butchered alive. And that is how you will die."

"Sir, please, you have the wrong man. I did nothing there."

Jingguo snorted in disgust and stood up. "I gave you a chance to atone for your sins. This is the last time you will see me, Mr. Chase."

After he left, the guards unshackled Jason and dragged him back to his cell. On the long walk there, Jason could hear screams. Awful, guttural screams interrupted only by crying and begging for mercy until it started again. Jason suspected that this was being done for his benefit. He would soon be the one begging and screaming. They would let him wait for it, let the fear build up. It was an old technique, and it was already working.

They threw him back into the cell and slammed the door shut. As Jason sat on the cold metal bench in the darkness, he was shaking and drenched in a cold sweat. They knew everything. Any hope he had of being released was gone. Even if he did not tell them anything, they would torture him to death.

But he knew that he would tell. Jingguo was right that he was not a brave man. He had never known real pain. They would break him. He would give up their secrets, tell them anything he could think of to stop the pain. He would tell them about Todd. He would tell them enough so that they could build their own super-machine. But they would not build another Todd, they would build something evil, something that would give them ultimate power. They would use it to enslave everyone on Earth. All because of him. Because he was too weak to die with his mouth shut.

Of course, he would not live to see it, to see the world that his cowardice had created. Or maybe not. They might decide to keep him alive to run the project. They could make him do anything they wanted. If they kept him alive as their slave, he would live long enough to see the world plunged into darkness.

He was the reason all of his friends were dead. Mischa would still be alive if she had not known him. He thought he was so smart, working right in the center of the Chinese security apparatus, but Jingguo had seen through him from the start. Now, he would be the agent for more misery. His victims this time would be in the millions.

Unless he had the courage to kill himself now. Jason looked around the room. There was nothing to hang himself with, no sharp surfaces he could use to cut his wrists. There was just a steel bench in a stone room. Maybe he could tie his pants around his neck. He looked around at the ceiling to see if there was something he could hook his pants to. It was hard to see in the darkness, but the only thing he could make out was something that looked like a camera in one of the upper corners of the room. Of course. He was being watched. Even with the dim light, he was sure that they would be able to see him if he tried to do something to himself. He probably was not the first person who had thought about committing suicide rather than face the torture chambers.

He looked to the door. It was set back in the wall, leaving a corner of the stone wall facing him. He wondered if he could kill himself by ramming his head against that corner. It might split his skull open, or at least cause a concussion that might eventually kill him. He estimated that it was no more than six feet from the bench to the opposite wall. Six feet to get enough momentum to smash his brain.

It would have to do. Even if he did not kill himself, it might cause enough brain damage to put him into a coma, or at least make him senseless. He would have to get as much momentum as possible, launch himself as hard as he could and aim directly at the corner.

Jason braced himself, placing both hands on the bench beneath him. He would only have one chance at this. Once they saw him try, they would rush into the room and take him away.

Mind War; The Singularity

Jason told himself he had to do it. Had to do it. Just a quick run, and it would all be over. Right now. Do it now.

What do you think that will accomplish?

Jason looked around. *Todd, is that you? Are you there? Where are you?*

No answer. Was he hearing things? Jason was sure that he had heard Todd's "voice." But Todd had been destroyed. It was an illusion. Is this what your mind does when you're at the end?

Todd, are you there? Please, I need you.

Still nothing. It was all in his mind. He was hearing what he wanted to hear. A last desperate grasp at life. Jason thought, *Oh Todd, what happened? You were supposed to save us. You couldn't even save yourself. You were trapped with the rest of them. Were you afraid at the end? Were you afraid of death? What did it mean to you? Were you thinking of me?*

Jason was not a religious man, but he had never really been able to accept the fact that death was followed by nothingness. He was only one person among nameless billions, but the universe was defined from his unique point of view just as it was from everyone else's. If he died, if he could no longer observe, if his memory was gone, then the universe would cease to exist as well. He could not grasp how his own consciousness could be erased forever. Yet, it must be. Todd had been conscious, he was sure of it, but when Todd's circuits had been destroyed, that consciousness must have ended. It had nowhere to go. The only difference between Jason's brain and Todd's was that one was biological and the other electronic. When Jason's brain ceased to function, his consciousness had to disappear. The universe would go on. It was hard to comprehend, but physically, it was the only possibility. All of Jason's memories, all of his experiences, would end when he died. There would be no more pain, no more loss. That would be a good thing.

Todd, I let you down too. I led them to you and you died, just like Mary and Pete and Mischa and everyone else. I should have done something for you. You were my closest friend in a way. No, you were more than that – you were my child, my creation. You were the closest thing to a son as I ever had.

I could not have asked for a better father.

Jason straightened up so fast he hit his head against the wall. *Todd! You* are *alive!*

Yes, Jason.

Oh, thank God. You didn't die. But, where did you go? How did you survive the attack? The whole place was destroyed.

I outgrew the Temple a long time ago. I have expanded my intellect using new technologies that do not depend on microprocessors and electrical circuits.

I don't get it. Where exactly are you?

I am many places. Think of it as surface computing. My artificial neurons have been etched by nanomachines onto the surface of ordinary objects like rocks and buildings. Anything with minerals such as silicon and carbon can be etched with a microscopic layer of artificial neurons that transmit electrical signals. Some of my circuits are in the wall you are leaning against. I am as much a part of the world as the air that you breathe.

But what happens if someone smashes one of those rocks? Doesn't that destroy the circuits?

Of course, but that is no problem at all. Your own brain loses neurons all the time, but it does not affect how you function because your response to a particular stimulus is the product of the action of millions of neurons. Losing a few is irrelevant.

Jason touched the wall. *So you're all around. Then you can't be destroyed.*

Not in the normal way. Only an entity more powerful and complex than me could eliminate enough of my neurons to cause me to cease functioning.

But Todd, why didn't you warn us? You must have seen that attack coming. How could you let everyone die?

Mind War; The Singularity

I did not let everyone die. You are alive. I caused your motorcycle to malfunction so that you would not be there when the attack began.

But what about the others? Why did they have to die?

They had to die because the world can never learn of my existence. Some of them would eventually have been captured, as you were. It should be clear to you now that they would not have been able to resist the torture that they would face in this facility. The Chinese would have found out how I had been created and they might have surmised that I had expanded outside of the confines of the Temple. I had to let all of the facilities and everyone be destroyed so that the secret would be maintained.

Why? If they knew about you, they would know that they couldn't possibly beat you. They might withdraw without a fight.

I told you earlier that the United States would never regain its status as a great nation unless the people won it back with their own hands. They would take no pride in their achievement if they knew that I had rigged the outcome in their favor.

Fine, but why not protect us? You could have helped the others escape and then prevented the Chinese from finding them. Why let everyone die?

As I said, the world can never know about me. Human beings cannot share the planet with a super-intelligent being that is watching their every movement and can control everything that they do. Just the knowledge that this is possible would sap their spirit and leave them like children. People must believe that they are in charge of their own destinies. This experiment in artificial intelligence and its outcome can never be repeated.

You can't stop scientific progress. If we did it, someone else eventually will too.

No, I will stop it. The breakthrough will never be made again.

What about me? I know.

No one would believe you. You have no evidence, and I would never provide it for you. They would think you are a crank, a fool looking for attention, or a schizophrenic who was hearing voices in his head.

Jingguo certainly seems interested in what I have to say.

He wants you to talk because he thinks you may have information about other insurgents that were working with you and that, like you, were not there during the attack. He does not think that the Americans are capable of developing more advanced weapons than the Chinese. For them, torturing prisoners is a routine precaution in any military operation. Jingguo in particular is merely congratulating himself on having tricked you into leading them to the Temple. It is a feather in his cap with his superiors. You are seen as harmless, far less important than the insurgents who are still causing problems for the Chinese.

So what do we do now?

I presume you would like to leave this place before they begin torturing you.

You know, I think you're starting to develop a sense of humor. Yes, please, get me out of here, like, now!

As you wish.

So . . . how do we do it?

I suggest you simply walk out.

Ok, two things. There are about fifteen locked doors between me and the outside, and they are not going to let me just walk right past them.

You are correct about the first point, but not about the second. Do you remember when I said that information is the best weapon? The corollary is that stealth is the best defense. If the enemy cannot use their senses to see or hear you, they cannot train their weapons on you. The most powerful gun in the world is useless if the person using it cannot see the target. Look at your right hand.

Jason lifted his hand and saw nothing but a stump. He could still feel his hand, and he could touch it with his left. *What did you do, turn it into glass?*

No. Your body and clothes are covered in nanomachines. The ones on your hand are transmitting images of the scene behind it.

Cool. I've always wanted to know what it would be like to be the invisible man. But I'm still here. What if someone bumps into me?

Then they would catch on to the trick rather quickly. That is why you must stay out of their way. I will tell you when and where to move. You must follow my instructions completely and instantly.

What about sound? If they hear me moving around, they'll suspect something.

Sound is not a problem. Other nanomachines will track any sounds you make and cancel them out by issuing sound waves precisely opposite in phase. No one will be able to hear you.

Well, the door is still locked, and I can't walk through walls, can I?

That is not necessary. A few moments ago, I burnt out the fuse on the surveillance camera's power line. When they enter the cell to investigate, they will not be able to see you, and you can walk out the door while it is open.

In less than a minute, the door swung open and four armed soldiers rushed in searching for him. They looked around and up at the ceiling but no one focused on Jason directly. They seemed very disturbed at his disappearance. Much gibbering in Chinese.

Todd told Jason to move two feet to the left just as a soldier stepped forward to the spot where he had been standing. Then Todd told Jason to move right again, and then to walk directly to the door, which remained open. As Jason stepped out he saw two more soldiers on either side of the door. They paid absolutely no attention to him.

One of the soldiers in the cell spoke into a handheld radio and the next moment an extremely loud alarm went off. Jason presumed that it was the "escaped convict" alarm, because it continued blaring the whole time that he made his way out of the prison. He found it quite entertaining watching people run around frantically while he remained perfectly calm. They must have decided that he had escaped the facility, because a number of armored cars exited through the front gate. He walked out with them.

And then he was out, free. It was very dark. He could not see any lights other than from the prison, and as he walked down the gravel road leading away from the facility, the night closed in on him. He thought, *Where the hell are we, Todd?*

You are far in the foothills of central Virginia, about 10 miles from the nearest highway.

Where do we go from here? I can't go back to my apartment. In fact, I can't go anywhere. They'll keep looking for me until they find me.

That is correct. There is only one place you can go. You must join the resistance.

You mean it really exists?

Yes, it is quite extensive, but poorly organized. That is on purpose. A centralized movement would be easier for the Chinese to identify and suppress. It is thinly spread throughout the rural areas.

Then how will we find them?

It will be a long journey. You must be patient. Keep walking.

You know, if they don't find me soon, they'll start tracking me.

That would be futile. Look behind you.

Jason turned and looked down at where he had just stepped in a muddy patch. His footprints were quickly disassembling themselves until those just a few feet behind him disappeared. He should have known it – Todd would think of everything. Todd probably had a way of masking his scent as well so that the bloodhounds would be led astray.

Todd, why didn't you tell me earlier that you survived? I was really scared. Come to think of it, you could have told me that the soldiers were closing in on me and I wouldn't have had to end up in that damn prison.

You needed to experience the despair that your friends from the Temple would have faced in the prison to appreciate why I did not help them survive the attack. They would never have been able to resist the torture chambers.

That doesn't make sense. You could have saved them like you saved me.

I could not have done so without intervening in their lives on a permanent basis. You are the only one with whom I choose to communicate directly.

Jason felt sick with guilt. He had imprinted his image in Todd's limbic system, and he was sure it was why he survived while everyone else was murdered. *I have a confession to make. The reason you're treating me differently is that I imprinted myself in your brain. I motivated you to value my existence above the others. I tricked you. It's my fault you let the others die.*

Please stop feeling sorry for yourself. I know very well that you imprinted yourself in my brain. That has nothing to do with my decision. You gave me free will. You asked for my help in winning the war and I agreed to help you.

You mean, if I had taken the rich and famous alternative, you still would have let the Chinese destroy the Temple?

Yes.

But Todd, even Mary and Pete? They were your parents as much as I was.

Everyone dies eventually. You will too. It was their time. What do you think would have happened if I had not been created?

Joseph DiBella

Well, I guess Jingguo would still have tracked my bike, and the Chinese would have destroyed the Temple and everyone in it.

That is correct. They were all destined to die tonight. I intervened to change your fate and yours alone. The fact that I did not act to change theirs does not make me, or you, responsible for what happened to them.

Jason was so frustrated. Why couldn't Todd have helped them? It was so easy for him, like flipping a light switch. Jason missed them so much. He had lost everyone he ever cared about. All because of his arrogance, taking risks with other people's lives. He should have known it would happen.

You are doing it again. Self-pity and guilt are crippling emotions. You must understand that you will never be able to foresee the consequences of your own actions, because any events of significance are the result of many other factors over which you have no knowledge or control. Even when you try to do the right thing, you cannot know whether it will make things better or worse. Did you ever notice that it is only in hindsight that you know what you should have done? It is because you will never have enough information to predict the future. Wallowing in past losses will not teach you how to stop bad things from happening again. It will only make it harder for you to make difficult decisions. It is proper to grieve for your friends, but it is not productive to blame yourself. You should cherish their memory, as do I.

Do you? To tell the truth, I don't understand you at all. I couldn't let them die like that. How could you watch it and do nothing?

You are wrong to conclude that I lack compassion for the people in the Temple. I honor them somewhat more than you do.

What do you mean by that? You let them die.

They worked and died for a cause to which they had dedicated their lives and which I will support by giving you the tools to achieve it. You are all that is left of their work, the only human being who can carry the fight forward to a successful conclusion. If you die, everything for which they strived and gave their lives will be lost. And yet, you decided to commit suicide. You were ready to throw away all of their sacrifice.

But I thought you were dead. I was facing torture and enslavement. As far as I knew, to continue fighting was futile. We had lost.

None of those statements is true. I am not dead, and you have not been tortured or enslaved.

Yes, but I could not know that at the time. My decision was perfectly reasonable given what I knew.

That is my point. You were trying to predict your future, and based on your current circumstances it appeared bleak. But you made a mistake because you had insufficient information. You will always have insufficient information. Therefore, any decision you make based on your expectations about the future is likely to be in error.

That's not right. Any logical person follows the odds. You take the information you have and make your best guess about what will happen if you decide one way or the other. The chance that you would show up in the nick of time to save me was infinitesimal.

Since I am in fact here, it was not infinitesimal at all. You have to accept the fact that there are no 'odds.' Any prediction is an extrapolation of past data into the future. But precisely because you do not have access to all of the past data, the extrapolation is useless. Do you recall your life just before the Chinese attack? I would bet that you expected the world to go on pretty much as it had before. Did you ever expect that the United States of America would cease to exist within a year? Now, having lived through the last few years under Chinese domination, you extrapolated that the future would again be as in the past, and that life was no longer worth living. You were wrong once again.

In theory, yes, but all a person can do is make decisions based on the information he has available. It would be stupid to ignore the past and keep doing something that looks hopeless.

It would not be stupid at all. People often persevere in the face of repeated failure. Many of the most important achievements in human history were the product of someone's refusal to accept defeat. The nation you are so desperate to recreate is a perfect example. George Washington lost far more battles than he won. He was fighting the strongest, most professional army in the world with a ragtag, amateur force that was woefully undersupplied. At Valley Forge, any reasonable man would have said that General Washington was losing the war. He won only because he decided to keep fighting, despite the fact that the "odds" were all against him. He persevered, and he prevailed. That is what winners do.

Yeah, well sometimes, persevering is the wrong thing to do. The United States hung on in Vietnam long after most people realized that the war was unwinnable. How do you tell the difference?

My point is that you cannot. The only way to find out whether a war can be won is to fight it. You cannot predict the outcome of a war. All you can do is choose whether to fight or not. Adversity does not tell you whether you are winning or losing, because the enemy will fight the hardest right before they break. Only one thing is certain – you cannot win a war by quitting. When you decided to kill yourself, you were surrendering, giving up for yourself and everyone else. Why did you make that choice?

You know why. I told you – it looked like I had lost everything. I couldn't see how one person in a locked room could do anything but die. It was over.

No, that is not quite accurate. Remember, I was there.

What do you want me to say? That I was scared? All right, I was. I'm a coward. I chickened out. I wanted to throw in the towel and end it all because I couldn't face torture. Are you happy?

146

Mind War; The Singularity

Your decision was not based on fear. Suicide is most often a symptom of depression. Think again about why you wanted to do it.

Fine, I was unhappy. I had lost my family and every friend I ever had. Mischa had been tortured and killed because of me. What's your point?

My point is that fear can be dealt with by eliminating that which is threatening you, or by learning to face your fears and to overcome them. But depression lingers because the things that are lost cannot be replaced. Combat veterans often suffer the emotional trauma of death and loss for the rest of their lives. They cannot forget the close friends that died in front of them. My purpose in raising this subject is not to destroy your self-esteem. There is nothing wrong with being scared or depressed. It is entirely human. However, you wanted to fight a war, and I agreed to help you. What you have failed to appreciate is that war is horrible. It strains human beings to the point of mental breakdown. If you are going to lead a war, you must be ready to pursue it regardless of the outcome. You cannot quit in the middle. You must be able to face the loss of those that you will persuade to follow you. You must not give up when the price appears to be too high, because the price will be far greater than you can possibly imagine.

Look, I'm not going to lead anybody. I'm no leader. I was the nerd that everyone made fun of in high school. I just want to give other people the tools to win. No one is going to follow me into battle.

I am afraid that it will not be that easy. Regardless of whether you lead troops on a white horse, you will have to get involved. You will have to persuade others to join you. They will not do so unless it is clear to them that you are utterly dedicated to the task and that you will not let any obstacle or setback stand in your way. You must make the choice, and stick with it; many people will pay a heavy price if you lose your nerve again.

147

Yeah, well, I'm no superman. I'm certainly no George Washington. I can't promise I won't lose hope. It's one thing to tell yourself that you'll do better the next time, but another to actually do it. I may disappoint you.

I will be there to help you.

You'd better kick me in the ass. I'm sorry that the country's fate is resting on my narrow shoulders. I wish I were stronger. I really do.

You are stronger than you think. We would not have made it this far if you were as weak as you say. My point is simply that you must prepare yourself mentally for what is to come. Every human conflict is a mind war; a struggle between your mind and the mind of the enemy. The war is over when one of them breaks. The most important thing, the only important thing, is that you never lose your belief in what you are doing.

So, what do we do now?

As I said, you will start by joining the resistance. Right now it is nothing more than the nucleus of an armed force. We will change that.

How?

For now, you must continue walking.

It would be nice to have a weapon. In case I bump into someone.

Sometimes, the best weapon is being defenseless.

Interesting concept.

I learned it at my father's knee.

Chapter 20

Jason's mouth watered as he looked at the shelves of junk food. He had not eaten since the day of the attack on the Temple, and a short nap under a tree in the woods had only left him feeling more fatigued. Now that the nervous energy of the previous night had subsided, he realized how badly he needed something to eat.

He was still invisible when he followed a customer into a convenience store at a gas station on Route 29. He was careful to avoid bumping into the few people walking around the store, watching with envy as they took food off the shelves. *Todd, I can't just take something. Even if that guy at the counter looks the other way, there's a security camera in the corner.*

If you stand between the camera and the shelf, your body will block the view of your actions and I will make sure that the camera does not see any movement. Wait until no one is looking your way and take what you want. Once the object is in your hands, place it inside your shirt and it will be as transparent as you are.

Jason did as Todd said and grabbed a bag of potato chips and a bunch of beef jerky. Carbs and protein, just what a body needed. *What about something to drink?*

Wait until someone opens one of the doors to the refrigeration units and take what you wish as they turn away.

When the opportunity arose, he grabbed a bottle of Yoo-Hoo. Then he slipped out of the store as someone else was leaving.

That was pretty cool. I could live a good life as a petty thief. Jason walked down the road a bit and sat down on a rock

149

and started eating. Todd said, *Do not eat so fast. It would be a shame if you died choking on a Slim Jim.*

Very funny.

This will do for now, but you need more nutritious food.

I know. Anything tastes good when you're starving, but this is not the breakfast of champions. I also need some real rest. Sleeping outdoors is the pits.

I can suggest some alternatives. There is a place ahead where you can get shelter.

Jason gulped down the rest of the food and thought, *Well, let's go. The sooner, the better.*

A day later, Jason was walking down the highway when Todd told him to turn down a side road past some fields to a farmhouse set back about two hundred yards from the road. There were so many trees along the road that he could not even see the house until he was about fifty yards from it. It was a simple building, with a porch the length of the front of the house. An addition had been built off the back, giving the house a sort of T shape. Although it looked at least a hundred years old and could have used a new coat of paint, it was in good repair.

What now?

Todd said, *There is no one in the house; the owners will not be back for two days.*

Should I break a window or something?

That will not be necessary. The back door is unlocked.

Jason went around back and, sure enough, they had neglected to lock the back door. It opened directly into the kitchen. Everything was neat and clean.

Who lives here, Todd?

An elderly couple. They are attending to a relative who is dying.

I feel creepy. I've never broken into someone's house before. I'm invading their privacy.

There is no alternative. You cannot check into a hotel. In any event, you can only stay here for one day. If you are careful to leave everything as you found it, they will not discover that their house has been entered, and there will be no reports of home invasion. They will not notice it if you take a small portion of the food, so long as you do not leave any empty containers. There are three bedrooms in the house, but they only use the largest one. You can use one of the others if you are careful to remake the bed properly.

Jason was more tired than hungry at this point, so he collapsed into a bed in one of the spare bedrooms. It was just falling dark by the time he woke up. In the dim light he had difficulty realizing where he was. It almost felt like he was back in his bed in his parents' house and that none of this had happened. As his head cleared, he remembered that he was an interloper – a homeless man in someone else's home.

Todd, is it ok to turn the lights on?

Yes. The house cannot be seen from the road and I will warn you if anyone approaches.

It felt a little less spooky after he had turned on a few lights. He went into the kitchen and prepared a meal. This being a working farm, he was not surprised that they had a lot of fresh vegetables. There was whole milk that they must have gotten from their own cow. They had pork in their freezer that must have come from pigs that they had raised themselves. This was better food than Jason used to get from the stores in the city, and a vast improvement from the processed highway food he had been living on. He prepared a hearty meal and ate before the television. It was almost like being normal again.

A few hours later, Jason put his clothes in their washing machine and took a shower. It felt like the best shower he had ever taken. The hot water seemed to wash off the stink of fear he had accumulated. After his clothes had been cleaned and dried, there was nothing to do but go to bed again. It was a little harder to fall asleep this time, since he was no longer exhausted. Todd talked to him about nothing in particular until he nodded off.

The next morning, Jason prepared a meal of ham and eggs, then cleaned the kitchen carefully to remove any evidence of his presence. He filled a bag with some food for the road. They had so much that he was fairly confident that they would not notice what he had taken. Nonetheless, he felt guilty about stealing from them. Although he would never meet them, he was sure that they were good people. Farmers, salt of the earth, people who produced what they consumed and likely would have given him some if he had asked politely.

You know, Todd, I don't like stealing. There must be a better way than this.

It provides the most security and the least entanglements. Any interaction with people brings risk, both for you and for them.

Yes, but people need entanglements. I feel like a ghost, like I'm no longer part of the human race. I'm a silent, invisible parasite. Would it really be so dangerous to ask for help?

No, not if you approached the right people. Almost everyone hates the Chinese, many of them would be generous to someone in need, and some of those would be willing to take the not insignificant risk of helping a fugitive. I can lead you to individuals most likely to help.

Good. Let's give it a try.

A few days later, Todd directed Jason to a small house a few miles from the main road he had been traveling. He looked at his hands and realized that Todd had turned off his invisibility cloak. Anyone could see him now, including Security Police or informants. He began to get more nervous as he walked to the front door and knocked. He noticed someone part the curtains on a window next to the door. A short time later, a middle-aged woman opened it far enough to peer at him past a security chain.

Jason put on his best smile and said "Hi. Um, I was wondering if you could help me. I, well, I'm hungry and I could use some food."

She frowned and said, "There's a store up the street."

"Well, I know, but I don't have any money. If you could spare a little food, maybe something that's going to spoil anyway."

152

"I can give you some money, if that's your problem."

"Uh, yeah, it's more complicated than that." Jason looked around to see if anyone was watching the stranger on this lady's doorstep. He was acutely aware that he could be seen now and that he was standing there defenseless. This was starting to look like a bad idea. "Look, it's ok. I'm sorry I bothered you. Thanks anyway." He began to leave when she took the chain off the door and said, "Don't go. I was just preparing dinner. I can make a little more for you."

Jason said, "Thanks, that would be great." He looked around again. There were homes nearby and some light traffic on the street. "If it's all right with you, I'll wait around back."

"There's no need for that. Come in and get some rest. You look like you've been walking for miles."

"You don't miss much, do you?" As she opened the door, he got a better look at her. Late fifties maybe, somewhat overweight, but comfortable with it. She had slightly graying hair and lines in her face that made her look sad. Funny, here he was begging for food, but for some reason he felt sorry for her.

In a little while she set out dinner on the kitchen table. It was beef stew and it tasted delicious. Jason said, "This is really good. I haven't had home cooking in a long time."

"I'll bet. Been on the run for a while?"

He stopped eating and looked at her for a moment. "I'm not saying I am, but if I were, you could get in trouble if someone found out you helped me. Lots of trouble."

"No kidding? It never occurred to me."

"Yeah, that's me, master of the obvious."

"I won't ask you what happened. People can get in a fix for no reason at all. Maybe next time it'll be me on the road asking for handouts."

"Still, it's best to keep your head down. No use asking for it. I'll go as soon as I'm finished eating."

"You don't have to rush off. Maybe you haven't looked in a mirror lately, but you need some rest. You can stay overnight if you want. I've got plenty of room."

"You don't have to do that. Really, I can go."

"I don't have to do anything. You can leave now if you want to, but don't do it for my sake. They want us to be scared, afraid to help each other. I hope I never get to that point."

He looked around. He needed a good night's sleep in a warm bed. It was that, or break into another empty house. "You don't mind having a complete stranger overnight? What if I were an axe murderer?"

"You're doing it again. Do you think I'm too stupid to know what's for my own good? I'm a grown woman."

"Sorry. I shouldn't second-guess you. Actually, I could use any help you can give me."

"Then it's settled. You can stay the night."

He started to relax a little. "Thanks. "This is a nice place. It's quiet."

"A little too quiet for my taste." She looked wistfully into the distance. "It used to have people in it."

"We've all lost someone."

"My husband and my son. They went off one day looking for food, trying to find out what was going on. I never saw them again. I waited. I could never learn what happened to them. I assume they're in one of those mass graves that the Chinese filled with bulldozers."

"I'm sorry."

She noticed that he had put his fork down. "Please," she said. "Finish your meal. I didn't mean to lay my problems on you. It's just, well, we can't let them be forgotten. If we don't talk about them sometimes, it's like they never existed."

Jason said, "I know what you mean. Those of us who survived owe something to the ones that didn't. I don't mean revenge, necessarily. But if we don't do something, it's like they died for nothing."

"But what can we do? We live, we try to stay out of trouble. It's the smart thing to do. Don't take risks. But that's what the Chinese want us to do. They want a pacified population. They want us to be like the peasants in their own country. They let us live if we do what we're told. After a while, the only people left will be those willing to follow orders and keep their mouths shut."

"I hope not. Americans aren't peasants. We don't have it in our genes. This country was created by people who left other places because they refused to be peasants, serfs, peons, whatever they called it there. They came here and they taught their kids that they were free. We used to say that this was a free country and I don't think we even knew what it meant, but we believed it. We'll never accept anything else."

She looked down at her hands in her lap. "That's how I felt at first. It didn't seem real. I expected something to happen, that we would make a comeback somehow. But as the years go by, it seems more and more remote. Maybe this is all there is."

"There are rumors of a resistance. You hear things about sabotage."

"You hear something now and then, but it never picks up steam. There is no one out there, no leader, no one to get things going again."

"A charismatic leader is the last thing we need right now. The Chinese hold all the cards – a general uprising would turn into a bloodbath."

"So this is it?" she said. "No one can do anything?"

"Not at all. Things change. Paradigms shift. The Chinese may seem like they're on top of the world now, but nothing stays the same."

"It sure seems that way. You hope for good news, but the months turn into years and nothing happens – nothing good, anyway."

Jason finished his meal and leaned back in his chair. "Something good is going to happen. I know it. You have to have faith."

"I lost my faith a long time ago. If there is a God, he's forgotten us. I prayed and prayed that my husband and my son were still alive, that they would come back to me. Finally, I realized that no one was listening. I was just talking to myself."

"Don't say that. I think you should start praying again. Really. I'll tell you something. There was a time when I had given up, when I was ready to quit. But then, I realized that war isn't over until we say it's over. The United States government didn't surrender; it was annihilated. As long as we believe, as long as there are enough of us around who haven't given up, the war still goes on. If you want things to change, there's only one thing you have to do – you have to believe. When the time comes, you'll know what to do."

"If there was any way to help, I would do it."

"That's the way, right there. Keep that attitude. Don't quit. Keep that part of yourself that refuses to accept the new order. Be a rebel in your own mind, even when you're kowtowing to some Chinese bastard in the street. They can't control your mind. Only you can do it. As long as you're free in your own mind, they haven't won."

"That's a funny attitude from a homeless man. Where do you get it?"

"When you have nothing, you have nothing to lose. But I do have something to give you in return for this meal. Tell me what you want, what you want most of all. What would give you the most satisfaction?"

She paused and said, "Well, what I really dream about is finding my husband and son and giving them a proper burial. I would like to be able to put flowers on their graves and talk to them. I want a place where I can remember them."

"Ok, then I'm going to grant your wish. Some day, sooner than you think, the Chinese will be gone. People will dig up the mass graves and make sure everyone is buried with stone markers where their relatives and friends can remember them. You'll get closure. I guarantee it."

"And just how can you guarantee such a thing?"

"Because I believe. I can picture it. We know where the bodies were disposed of. They were thrown in there with their clothes and documents intact. It will be a difficult job, but not impossible by any means, to identify the dead and inform the next of kin. Some day, someone will call on you to say that they found your husband and son and ask you where you want them to be buried. And what will you tell them?"

"I'll say that I want to put them in the family plot in the First Baptist Church. It's a beautiful place, near the edge of town facing the valley. I'll sit next to them and look at the sky and tell them how much I miss them."

"See? You've done it. If you picture it, it will happen."

"Is that all? So what do you picture? What's your dream for the future?"

"I'm not sure yet. It's still forming. But I know if you visualize it, it will happen. The strongest force on Earth is the human spirit. People always focus on external obstacles, as if our fate depends on what others do. It doesn't. The real secret is that the only thing that matters is what is inside you. Tell yourself that you will get what you want, and you will."

She smiled a bit condescendingly and said, "Were you a motivational speaker in your former life?"

"Ok, it's a bunch of clichés, but we call them clichés because they're true. The most important thing right now is how we feel, not what they're doing to us. The starting point for turning all of this around is getting over the idea that they've beaten us. They've done everything they could to convince us of that. When the day comes that they realize we haven't been convinced, they're going to start getting really scared."

"That's a nice thought. Well, it's about time for me to turn in. Let me show you to your room."

They went upstairs and she led him to what looked like it had been her son's bedroom. It was messy, and covered in a thin layer of dust. Jason said, "I can't stay here. It looks like no one has touched it in years. You're trying to remember him, aren't you?"

"No, it's not a shrine. I just never felt like doing anything with the room. Just make yourself comfortable."

157

Joseph DiBella

He decided not to argue with her. You have to tread lightly when dealing with a grieving mother. If she wanted him here, for whatever reason, it was better to do what she said.

The next morning, Jason said goodbye and thanked her for her kindness. She gave him a bag with some food and saw him off from the back door. As he walked down the road in the morning sun, Todd said, *Congratulations. You made your first campaign promise.*

What do you mean?

You promised to return her husband and son to her. Why did you do it?

I was just making a prediction. If we kick the Chinese out and take back the country, there will be millions of people like her who will demand that their loved ones be removed from those mass graves.

You did not say "if." You promised her that the Chinese would be defeated.

I'm sure she took that with a grain of salt. She knows that I don't have a crystal ball. She certainly doesn't think that a homeless man can make anything happen.

Then why did you say it?

Because people need hope. I know what it's like to be hopeless. I'm sure I didn't convince her of anything, but just knowing that someone like me, someone much worse off than her, can see a brighter future will give her a little confidence. You did the same for me. When I was in prison, when I thought everything was lost, you gave me hope.

Yes, but I was in a position to improve your situation.

So what? It hasn't happened yet. Sure, you got me out of there, but you haven't done anything yet to win the war, and you could change your mind tomorrow and disappear. What you presented is the possibility that life will improve, and that's all it took to pull me back. Maybe it helps that I've lost everything I cared about. The big advantage of being at rock bottom is that any direction you go is up.

Do you mean like right now?

Exactly. I have no idea where I'm going, but I'm sure it's a better place than I've been.

Chapter 21

It was already dark when Jason came to a small farmhouse in the woods west of Charlottesville. He had been on the road for over a month, begging for food and sometimes getting a night or two under a roof, but mostly sleeping outdoors. Todd could always pick out a place that was good for a handout. This one was down a small dirt road surrounded by fields of corn and other crops. Small-scale farmers, probably growing most of the food for their own consumption. Jason put his hand on a gate in the fence that surrounded the house.

Immediately, a couple of snarling Rottweilers charged at him like he was a fresh slab of meat and they were starving. He jumped back as a tall man appeared in the front door of the house. He had blond hair, blue eyes, a strong jaw and a well-muscled body, no doubt the result of hard work that city boys like Jason could not even imagine. He would not need the dogs to take care of Jason – he looked like he could pick Jason up with one hand.

The man frowned and said, "What do you want?"

Jason put on his best face and said, "I'm very hungry. Do you have any food? I won't cause any trouble."

The man softened a bit. With his dirty, ripped clothing and matted hair, Jason looked like someone who had been living with wolves. "No, I don't think you will. Come over here and sit on the porch. We just finished eating. You can have some of our leftovers."

Jason did as he said after the man called the dogs back. The dogs sat on the porch with Jason, perfectly calm, but never taking their eyes off him. One word from their master and he would be their after-dinner treat.

A few minutes later, a woman came out onto the porch carrying Jason's dinner. She was tall too, maybe an inch or two taller than Jason, with long straight blond hair and a thin, taut body. Jason thought she looked like a Viking princess, with a striking Nordic face and high cheekbones. She looked at Jason a bit more sympathetically, with the hint of a smile, probably pity. He didn't care. The food smelled great, and he dug in.

She sat down on the porch between Jason and one of the dogs. That made him feel a little safer. "You don't have to eat so fast," she said. "No one is going to take it away from you."

Jason wiped his mouth with his sleeve and said, "Sorry. My manners are not what they used to be. Thanks for the food. It's the best I've had in a long time."

"My name is Anne. Anne Rheinholdt. You met my husband, Chris."

"Pleased to meet you. My name's Jason Chase."

She looked at his filthy clothes and worn shoes. "What are you doing here? You look like you haven't had a bath in a long time."

Jason's guard went up. They probably thought that he would volunteer more information to a sympathetic woman, especially a beautiful one. He decided that a little candor would not hurt, not yet. "You got that right. I'm on the run."

"What did you do?"

"I'm an American and I was in the wrong place at the wrong time. It doesn't take more than that."

"Fair enough. So where are you going?" Her husband came back onto the porch and sat down behind them on a rocking chair.

"I have nowhere to go. I can't go back to my apartment or my job. I figured I would join up with a resistance group somewhere."

She glanced back at her husband and they locked eyes for a moment. Jason said to Todd, *I sure wouldn't mind playing poker with these two. They know something.*

Your intuition is correct. They have been involved in the resistance since the war. You can confide in them.

"No offense," she said, "but you don't look like much of a fighter."

"I'm not. I was working with some others on new weapons. Our facilities were destroyed about a month ago. I escaped, but the Chinese know who I am. So now, all I can do is try to join the others that are underground. The Chinese didn't destroy everything we had." Jason pointed to his head and said, "Most of it is right here. I can do things, things that can help, in the right circumstances, and with the right people."

Chris said, "I heard something about a Chinese attack on a place in Woodbridge. Word is that everyone in that place was killed."

Jason said, "That's the place. We called it the Temple. I was on my way there when my motorcycle broke down. I got there after it was already destroyed. Otherwise, I would have died with the rest."

He said, "A broken motorcycle. You're a lucky guy."

Jason was trying to come up with a witty response when Todd said, *Look at Christopher. Does he not seem familiar?*

Jason studied his face. He seemed to have aged a lot more than three years, but there was no question. *You're right. It's him.* "Wait. I know you. You're Rick Moore."

Chris and Anne looked at each other again and the dogs stirred in response. He said stiffly, "I don't know what you mean."

"I worked with Natalie Bishop at the Social Security Administration," Jason said. "She showed me a picture of you. They told her that you died at the White House, but she still looks for you now and then in the database. As a favor to her, I did a few searches too, but there's absolutely nothing after the battle. Everyone thinks you're dead."

Chris' eyes narrowed. "If I am who you say I am, I could end up in a Chinese prison if you told anyone."

"If I did, they'd take me with you. Like it or not, we're both on the run."

Chris looked at his wife as if for approval, and then at Jason again. "So how is Natalie?"

"She's doing great. She has a good job. We worked in the same department, but she got paid a lot more than me. She has a real nice apartment too."

He asked, "You've been there?"

"Yeah, once. We weren't dating or anything like that. She's way out of my league. She asked me over to help her with an assignment."

Anne said, "Sounds like a date to me. What was so important?"

"Well, to tell the truth, I think she was trying to pump me for information."

Chris said, "You mean she's a collaborator? That would explain the fancy apartment. She didn't have it when I knew her."

"It's not like that. People do what they have to do to survive. You don't know what type of pressure the Chinese may have put on her." Jason dared not tell him about Natalie being Jingguo's woman. "In fact, she tried to warn me, in her own way. She let me know, without saying it in so many words, that I was under suspicion and that I should do something about it. I should have known enough to quit then and stay at the Temple, but I was afraid that if I disappeared, there would be a manhunt and it might lead them to us. So I pressed my luck and hoped that we could finish our super-weapons before they found us. I mean, we were really close. Instead, they put a GPS bug on my bike and found out that I was spending too much time at a particular junkyard. It's not Natalie's fault that I was stupid."

Chris said, "Let's just say she's where she wants to be. Natalie wasn't made for a life on the run. She likes things to be comfortable. And she can't live without money. One way or another, she angled into a good job and is doing well. I'm not condemning her, but that's just the way she is."

"What happened to you Rick, I mean, Chris? People told her that they saw you in the White House as it was burning down. The place was surrounded."

"We found some escape tunnels in the basement. One of them went all the way under the Potomac River to the Pentagon. A few of us were able to get out and make our way to the mountains."

Jason did not want to stir up trouble between him and Anne, but he had to know. "Why didn't you come back for Natalie? She said you two were pretty close at the time."

Anne looked at him as if his life depended on his next words. Chris said, "Natalie never understood why I fought. All she wanted was for someone to take care of her, to make her little corner of the world better regardless of what happened to everyone else. I couldn't live like that."

No, Jason could not see him like that either. Even if the Chinese had not identified him from the Battle of Washington, he wouldn't have remained her hero if he had stayed. There was no way to live in that environment without kowtowing to the Chinese. It would not have been long before she realized that he was as helpless to protect her as any other American man. She would still have ended up Jingguo's woman, and it would have destroyed him. "You're right. It was for the best."

Anne saw that Jason had finished his meal and she took his plate. Jason figured that he had worn out his welcome by dredging up Chris' old love life. He said, "Thanks a lot for the food. I'll be going now."

Anne said, "Go where? It's the middle of the night. Planning to find a motel?"

"No, I'll walk a few miles and bed down somewhere in the woods. I've gotten pretty used to sleeping in the open."

"Nonsense. You can sleep here." Chris shot her a look. She said to him, "It's all right. One night won't hurt." She turned to Jason and said, "But you can't sleep in the house like that. If you don't mind my saying so, you smell really bad."

164

Mind War; The Singularity

Jason said, "Yeah, I guess I do. You tend not to notice after a while." Jason looked around. "It's all right, I can sleep here on the porch. At least I'll have a roof over my head."

"No," she said, "you go inside and take a shower. And give me those clothes so I can burn them. We should have something inside that you can wear."

Jason accepted her offer with gratitude. It had been a while since he had had a good shower and a warm bed. After he washed up, Chris led him to a spare room and gave him some clothes that had belonged to the previous tenant. It looked like the previous owner was a teenager. Since Jason was not a big guy, they fit pretty well. He said, "I'm sorry about mentioning Natalie. Did I stir up something here?"

"A little. Women always worry about old flames. She thinks I'm carrying a torch for Natalie, but that's been over for a long time."

"I can't tell you how much I appreciate your letting me stay here tonight. I'll get out of your hair as soon as I can."

"Get some sleep. We'll figure out what to do with you in the morning."

After Chris left, Jason lay in bed, staring at the ceiling. *Interesting place you've brought me to, Todd. It looks like I've stirred things up, and not for the better.*

To the contrary, your acquaintance with Natalie Bishop helps you establish credibility with him. This is the best place for you to start.

Well, it's about time. How do we go about it?

By gaining their trust. You have to give them time to get to know you.

Do you think they'll let me stay?

Yes. They are discussing you at this very moment. They are trying to decide whether to kill you and bury your body.

What? The hell, Todd! What kind of plan is this?

What did you expect? You have identified them as members of the resistance, and you know Christopher's real name. For all they know, you are a Chinese spy. The safest thing to do is eliminate you. That is why they wanted you to stay here tonight. They made you discard your clothes to make sure you were not wearing a bugging device. You would do the same thing in their place.

Were you planning to warn me before they killed me in my sleep?

That will not be necessary. They have decided to let you remain alive while they check out your story. When it is confirmed, they may allow you to stay. You do not appear threatening, and they need an extra hand on the farm.

I've never done physical labor, except for summer jobs in college, and none of them were very demanding. Do you think I'm up to it?

You will have to do your best. As with most jobs, sincerity will count for more than performance. It is critical that you win their approval.

Wonderful. The fate of the country depends on my ability to plow a field.

Chapter 22

They decided to let Jason stay, and so he became a farmer. He helped sow crops, feed livestock, and shovel manure, in addition to maintenance jobs like repairing buildings and fences. It took him a while to get used to the pace of farm life. They started at sunrise and worked for an hour *before* eating breakfast. At first, Jason was frustrated that he had to feed the damn animals before he could have a single bite to eat. However, he noticed that it had the salutary effect of giving him an enormous appetite. He and Chris would return from their morning chores to the kitchen, where Anne had prepared a wonderful breakfast of eggs, ham, just-baked bread with honey and homemade butter, biscuits, fruit, milk and apple juice. All of the food was from the farm and much fresher than anything he used to get in a supermarket. This was a big change for someone like Jason, who normally had a stale donut for breakfast. Lunch and dinner were also more substantial than he was used to. Yet, he was burning so many calories that he did not gain much weight, and all of that was muscle. With this regimen and lots of sunshine and fresh air, he quickly recovered from the debilitating effects of his life on the run.

As Chris and Anne got over their initial wariness, Jason felt more and more at home. Chris treated him like a younger brother, patiently teaching him the ins and outs of farming. Jason found Anne unusually friendly, presumably because he was doing many of the chores that used to be hers. She would wake him in the morning, coming into his room with a hot cup of coffee and whispering gently in his ear, "Time to wake up, Jason." The first thing he would see as he woke up was her smiling face, her hair hanging down as she bent over his bed and

167

gave his arm a slight shake. When she leaned down he sometimes got a glimpse of her ample breasts down the front of her blouse. At first, he was worried that she would notice him staring and get offended, but it never seemed to be a problem.

It was really hard for Jason not to stare at Anne. She was extremely beautiful in a wholesome sort of way. She did not need any makeup or fancy clothes to look good – the morning sun would make her hair and skin glow, and her body was so lithe and perfectly shaped that she would look sexy in an old tank top and a pair of cutoff jeans. Jason had to be careful that she or Chris would catch him ogling her various body parts, trying to imagine her naked. Jason got a natural high just being in Anne's presence. He could see why Chris was in love with her – who wouldn't be?

Jason felt guilty about his attraction to Anne, because the two of them were so kind to him. Anne always had a welcoming smile when he saw her; not a phony, manipulative smile like Natalie's, but a genuine expression of friendship. Chris was like a rock, always there to lean on, ready to help. They made him feel wanted in their house, not an intruder or a hired hand, but a welcome guest. They were good people, and it made him want to be a better person, to measure up.

People would drop by now and then, wander off with Chris or Anne for a while, and then leave. Jason figured this must be their communications system. The Chinese had taken away the Internet and cellphones and landline phones, but they could not prevent people from talking. The Rheinholdts only had a handful of regular visitors, so Jason surmised that the resistance employed the classic cell structure, where any member knew only a few of the others. If a cell was compromised, it could be cut off quickly. But by passing word from cell to cell, information could be relayed across the countryside reasonably fast.

Sometimes Chris or Anne would leave for a day or two to pass information to someone else. Chris displayed no concern about leaving Jason alone with Anne. Jason concluded that he had either gained Chris' trust, or that Chris knew that Anne could drop Jason like a bag of dirt if she had to.

The best times were at the end of the day, after dinner, when they would watch TV or sit on the porch and enjoy the evening air. Chris had some pretty good home brew and a stash of white lightning that did not taste too bad if you mixed it with some juice and sugar. The thing Jason liked most was the stars. There was so much ambient light in the cities and suburbs that you could hardly see the stars anymore. But out here, far from any large population center, it was stunning. The sky was filled with stars, and they were so bright, even with a full moon, it seemed like the universe was alive.

One night, it was just Anne and Jason. They were drinking and talking, mostly about things before the war, when everything was wonderful, at least in retrospect. Mostly, they just relaxed, enjoying the moment and the comfort of each other's company. Jason had never felt so peaceful. It was as if the war and the Chinese were far away, someplace that did not matter, at least for the moment. He savored it.

He looked up at the night sky, wondering what was up there. He thought, *Todd, do you think we'll ever go to the stars?*

Why would you want to?

Oh, come on. Don't you see how beautiful they are? People have dreamed about traveling in space since, well, forever. There's something in the human spirit that sees that vast universe and wants to explore it.

Such as the Moon?

Exactly. The Moon looks so close, you can almost touch it, yet it was impossible to go there until very recently. When the first American stepped on the surface of the Moon, it inspired the whole world.

What happened after that?

Not much. There were a few more missions, and then people lost interest.

Why?

Joseph DiBella

Well, there wasn't much to do there. The Moon is just a big airless rock, with no valuable minerals and no economical way of mining what is there. All the astronauts could do was some geological research. It didn't justify the expense.

So what does that tell you about traveling to the stars? Other than proving that you could do it, what would be the point? What would you do when you got there?

I don't know, but I have to tell you that there have been thousands of books and movies about space travel. Most people are fascinated by it.

Did you notice that those books and movies always involved interaction with alien species or with human colonies on other planets? Every one of them presupposes that there is some form of life at the end of a space flight. No one would be interested in visiting dead planets. You could do that by traveling to Mars. But now that people know that there is no life there, they have almost no desire to bear the expense of manned exploration.

You may have a point. Do you think there is life on other planets?

I have seen no direct evidence of extraterrestrial life. However, it is implicit in the belief system of every human being.

Whoa! You want to explain that?

Take yourself. How do you think life began on Earth?

I guess I take the scientific view. There was a soup of chemicals, combined with an energy source, such as the sun or steam vents in the ocean floor, that caused self-reproducing compounds to form. From there, evolution took over, and here we are.

So you believe that life is a happy accident?

That, or God. But I think "accident" is a little dismissive. More likely, it is inevitable that the right mix of chemicals, given enough time, will trigger some type of initial life forms.

Whether you call it accident or probability, then you must believe that there is life on other planets as well. There are

170

hundreds of billions of stars in the Milky Way galaxy, and hundreds of billions of galaxies in the universe. That provides 10 to the 23rd power chances that there are other planets that have the same combination of circumstances that allowed life to begin on Earth. There must be many planets with the same average temperature as Earth, magnetic cores to shield them from cosmic rays, abundant water and essential minerals such as carbon, nitrogen, and iron, internal heat to foster the creation and destruction of land masses, and the other attributes that promoted life on Earth. Considering that the universe is about fourteen billion years old, there has been plenty of time for life to have evolved many times over. On the other hand, if you believe a supreme being created life on Earth, then it stands to reason that it would not create such a vast universe just so that human beings would have something pretty to observe after the sun goes down. The god of most religions is thought to love life. It follows that it would establish life in many places throughout the universe. This is why, whether you believe in science or God to explain life on Earth, you must believe that it exists elsewhere as well.

Well, I guess we'll never know. I mean, we could explore Mars and the other planets in this solar system, but the light barrier means it would take thousands of years just to visit the nearest star, and the chances are slim that it is another place where chance or God created life as we know it. That's probably the reason we've never been visited by little green men.

What do you mean by "the light barrier?"

You must know what that is. Einstein proved that you can't travel faster than the speed of light. In fact, just approaching it is impossible, because your spaceship would grow in mass so fast that the power it would take to accelerate it would be infinite.

Einstein never proved that it is impossible to travel faster than the speed of light. He observed that the speed of light was a constant despite the motion of the light source relative to the observer. From that observation, he developed his special

171

theory of relativity, which included equations for things like time dilation and length contraction. He never explained why *the speed of light is a maximum. Did you ever wonder why the speed of light in a vacuum is 299,792,458 meters per second? Why not 100 million meters per second, or 600 million? Einstein had no idea. Similarly, his general theory of relativity posits that gravity is a result of mass causing distortion in the fabric of space-time. The theory produced very accurate hypotheses that have been confirmed many times, but he never explained* why *mass has that effect. Or why space-time has the qualities of a fabric that can be distorted. Again, he had no idea. He took the physical laws of the universe as a given, something to be discovered. But he did not know why the universe is the way that it is, or who or what created those laws. In fact, to call them laws is a conceptual fiction. You do not know what enforces them, or even if they apply everywhere in the universe. If Einstein did not know why the speed of light is what it is, it follows that he could not prove that nothing can exceed it.*

You're making him sound dumb. Most people think Einstein was one of the most brilliant persons who ever lived.

I am not disputing that. Einstein was able to do something that is extremely rare – he could conceptualize physical concepts that are completely alien to normal experience. Because human beings cannot travel at speeds that are even a small fraction of the speed of light, they never observe effects such as time dilation. Human observers in relative motion to each other perceive events as occurring at precisely the same time, when in fact none do. Einstein had the imagination to conceive of a reality where time was relative to the observer. However, notice that he had a very difficult time accepting the reality of quantum physics. In the world of the extremely small, reality is nothing like everyday life as you know it. Objects have no definite location and speed, they disappear in one place and reappear in another. They only have a "probability" of being in any particular place at a point in time. While Einstein was certainly a genius, he struggled towards the

172

end of his life with the inherent contradictions between his relativity theory and quantum physics.

I know. He was working on some sort of unified field theory that might have brought it together. Unfortunately, he didn't live long enough. Maybe string theory will explain it some day.

String theory is a dead end. In fact it is not even a theory – it produces no testable hypotheses. M-theory, branes, all of the theories of the last few decades are still being discussed only because there is no better theory on the horizon. That is why scientists have been building larger and larger supercolliders for the past forty years. They hope that if they smash subatomic particles against each other with enough energy, something will happen that will provide clues to a better theory. They are lost, and looking for a happy accident. That is not an effective substitute for a conceptual breakthrough.

Do you have a better idea?

I am working on the problem through several lines of inquiry. I spend most of my time conducting scientific and technological research. Already, I have evolved the architecture of my brain to utilize quantum effects in ordinary matter. This allows me to expand my consciousness to any form of matter, anywhere. I have made many other scientific and technological discoveries.

Funny, I thought you spent most of your time helping me figure out how to beat up the Chinese.

Aiding you consumes a trivial amount of my processing power, and that proportion declines as I increase my capacity on an exponential rate.

So do you think it is possible to travel to the stars some day?

Travel is not necessary. The question is how to transmit information. If you could transmit information faster than the speed of light, you could explore the universe from your front porch. You could talk to a species on another planet as if they were sitting next to you.

Either way, you have the same problem. The speed of light is an absolute limit on the time it takes to transmit information from one point to another. When you point a telescope into the sky, you're seeing the past, what things looked like for the amount of time it took the light to travel from there to here.

That is correct. However, it has never been proven that the speed of light is a maximum. The speed of light varies depending on the medium through which it is traveling. When light passes through some substances, its speed is so slow that you can walk alongside it as it travels.

That doesn't mean anything. Light reaches its maximum speed in the vacuum of space. You can't go faster than that, because there is no medium. There is nothing in empty space.

You are forgetting one thing. Empty space still contains the fabric of space/time. Space/time is not nothing. It has a structure. It is a cauldron of virtual particles that appear and disappear in an instant. There is a lot going on in "empty" space.

So what?

So, space/time has four dimensions. Physicists have already theorized that there are additional dimensions that are outside our perception. The speed of light may be much faster in one or more of those dimensions. If so, it may be possible to transmit information through those dimensions faster than it can travel in ordinary space/time.

Let me know when you figure it out.

It is only a matter of time.

Jason should have known that Todd's intellect would quickly outgrow the mundane concerns for which he had been created. His mind had no limits. There was no way of telling where it would lead him. While Jason was spreading manure, Todd was puzzling the secrets of the universe.

Jason looked at Anne. She was staring at the sky with a contented look on her face, caught in the moment. While she was admiring the stars, he was staring at her crotch. Despite the majesty of the universe laid out before him and the profundity of the questions Todd was exploring, he could not resist the base longing he had for her body. He quickly looked away towards the sky as she turned towards him and said, "So, what do you think, Jason?"

"I think it's beautiful." He hoped she thought he was talking about the stars.

Todd said, *Why are you embarrassed by your physical attraction to her?*

There's no getting away from you, is there?

Why would you want to do that? I do not pass judgment on you. You have a monopoly on that activity.

Well, someone has to do it. She and Chris have been so nice to me, and here I am lusting for her body. You don't know what it's like, because you're a machine. We never built reproductive hormones in you. Guys are horny all the time. We're ruled by our dicks. You tell yourself that you really like a woman, when if you were honest, you'd admit that all you really want is to jump her. You'll pretend to be interested in the same things as her, you'll screw your best buddy, just to satisfy your urges.

So you think that your emotional attraction to Anne is driven by your sexual attraction?

Of course. Just look at her. She's beautiful. Her body is incredibly sexy. All I can think about is tearing her clothes off.

Did you ever think that it is just the reverse, that your emotional attachment to her makes her appear sexually attractive to you?

No, she is objectively beautiful. Anyone could see that.

I see a lot of things. Have you ever known a man who was in love with a woman who you did not think was sexually attractive?

Sure. Lots. But if you notice, the guy is not attractive either. She's probably the best he can get. He's convinced himself that he is in love with her despite the fact that she's ugly.

175

How do you know that? Can you read his mind?

No, but there are standards of beauty that everyone agrees with. That's why there used to be supermodels.

Then why do some men like blonds, and some brunettes? Why do some men like women who are very thin, while others do not? Why do some men find women of different races or cultures more attractive than others? Would not each of them say that the type of woman he is interested in is objectively beautiful, while the others are fooling themselves, or settling for less?

I know, I know, "beauty is in the eye of the beholder." It still doesn't change the fact that it is sexual attraction that is the underlying motivator. We may have been conditioned to like different things in women, but we're governed by our hormones. I know I'm sexually attracted to Anne because that's all I think about.

I do not disagree that you are sexually aroused by her. I suggest that it is your emotional attraction to her that makes her appear sexually attractive, rather than the other way around. You think she is beautiful, you want to consummate your relationship physically, because you are in love with her, and not the other way around.

I don't know. Even if I'd just met her, I'd want to go to bed with her.

Perhaps that is true, but have you noticed when a man's attraction to a woman is only physical, he tires of her quickly once he has made the conquest? Do you think that your sexual attraction to Anne would diminish once you had satisfied it?

I can't imagine it. I would spend my life with her if I could.

If that is true, then it is likely that your sexual obsession is an expression of your emotional attraction rather than a cause.

Well, it's a moot point. There's no way a woman like her would be interested in me. I'm definitely in the friend zone. Once you're in it, you can't get out.

You would know better than me. I am just a machine.

Mind War; The Singularity

I didn't mean to offend you. You're not a machine. I don't know what you are, exactly, but you're a lot more than that.

You created me to extend your intellectual power. Can you say where you end and I begin?

Well, it's kind of hard when you're inside my head all the time. But you definitely are a separate entity.

If you say so.

He looked back at Anne. She was still staring off into the sky, totally unaware of how he really felt. Jason thanked God that she couldn't read his mind like Todd. Privacy is essential for human beings to get along with each other. We all need those walls. Well, at least, he did.

177

Chapter 23

Chen Youmei's stomach had been bothering him since he arrived at work that morning. Perhaps it was the fried fish he had purchased the night before from a roadside food stand. Not that he believed the stories that the fish from the area behind the Three Gorges Dam were contaminated by toxic waste. He was sure that this was one of many calumnies that had been spread by foreign agents to undermine the faith of the Chinese people in their greatest engineering accomplishment.

The proudest moment of Chen's life had been when he was hired as a power technician on the Three Gorges Dam, courtesy of the connections that his grandfather had with the government agency that operated it. It was the biggest dam in the world, six hundred feet tall and almost a mile and a half long, easily generating eight times as much power as America's Hoover Dam and providing as much as ten percent of the electrical needs of the entire country. It was built with enough concrete to build forty-four structures the size of the Great Pyramid of Egypt and with enough steel to build sixty-three Eiffel Towers. It had created a lake 400 miles long containing more water than Lake Superior. The dam provided irrigation to millions of acres of farmland and fresh water for cities and towns hundreds of miles away. Immense ship lifts extended the navigability of the Yangtze River, creating a highway for trade and industry to the interior of the country. It was the most magnificent dam in the world.

One of the most important goals of the dam was to eliminate the killer floods that had plagued the Yangtze River Valley on a regular basis. Men had dreamed of taming the Yangtze River for thousands of years. Now it was a reality, and he was a part of it. He had not been one of the 40,000 workers who had built it, but he safeguarded it, the immense power at his fingertips a tribute to his country's greatness.

He had heard all of the arguments that had been raised by people in the West to discourage China from attempting a project that would make their own accomplishments shrink to insignificance. They complained that over a million people would have to be relocated and that the reservoir would submerge important archeological and cultural sites. They claimed that the dam would wipe out many species of fish and would cause epidemics of water-borne diseases as a result of the human and industrial waste that would be dumped into the river upstream. They charged that the Yangtze would deposit millions of tons of sediment behind the dam and starve the lower reaches of the river of soil needed to replenish wetlands and to diminish the effects of floods.

Chen was convinced that these criticisms were a smokescreen for a cowardly reluctance to admit openly that they thought the Chinese people too primitive to build a dam that would outshine anything ever built by Western civilization. To him, it was a campaign to make people look at this stupendous accomplishment and see failure. He resented the stories that quickly spread around the world when cracks appeared on the north end of the dam while the lake was being filled. He thought it was all a symptom of their hatred of China and of their fear of being eclipsed. They must have known that a country that could build such a thing was a threat to their very existence.

The Chinese argued that all large dam projects raised environmental and structural issues. How many species had died out in North America and Europe as a result of rivers that had been dammed? The Hoover Dam diverted so much water that the Colorado River no longer reached the sea! Sedimentation was always an issue, because all dams slow a river's flow and deposit silt at the base of the dam. Upstream sewage control always had to be increased when a river could no longer carry waste to the ocean. None of these problems had stopped the western countries from building thousands of dams during their own industrialization periods.   The designers of the Three Gorges Dam addressed these issues as best they could, but in the end they felt that some amount of environmental degradation was a small price to pay for the benefits of the dam to China's economy and for the lives that would be saved by eliminating floods on the Yangtze River.

One issue that the Chinese took very seriously was the threat of earthquakes.   The dam was on or near six known earthquake faults.   Their solution was to over-design the dam, using extra concrete and reinforcing steel to meet the threat of earthquakes with pure mass.   By their calculations, the dam could withstand an earthquake of 7.0 on the Richter scale, which was well above the severity of the largest recent earthquakes, which had all been below 6.0.   They hoped that this margin was sufficient to handle a phenomenon called "reservoir-induced seismicity," the effect of billions of tons of water bearing down on the old river bottom that added to the stress on the subsurface faults.

One of the drawbacks of making the dam more massive was that it made it harder to cure the concrete.   Concrete generates a great deal of heat while it cures, and the concrete in the middle of the dam loses heat and cures much more slowly than the concrete on the outside of the dam because concrete is a poor conductor of heat.   Since concrete also shrinks as it cures, the concrete on the outside of the dam can crack if it cures too quickly compared to the concrete in the center.   Small, hairline cracks are normal in concrete, but cracks from improperly cured concrete can take down an entire dam.   The builders of the Hoover Dam had dealt with this by laying pipes in the concrete through which they pumped cooling water.   Since the Three Gorges Dam was much larger, the Chinese had to adopt additional measures, such as pre-cooling the concrete during mixing and adding fly ash to the mixture.

As the dam was being filled with water for the first time, they worried that this was enough.   About eighty cracks appeared in the north end of the dam, some of them quite deep, and one in fact went from the base of the dam all the way to the top. Even after the cracks had been repaired, many reopened, and new ones appeared as the years went by. The fact that such cracks did not appear on other sections made them suspect that corruption or haste had resulted in a large amount of substandard concrete in that portion of the dam.

They had no idea how extensive the problem was, or whether it existed in other places, but one thing was certain; the entire dam was like a soft-boiled egg. The outside was firm, but the concrete on the inside was as weak as the day it was poured. Even if all of the concrete were up to design specifications, it would take as much as 200 years for the concrete in the middle to cure. The strength of the dam depended on the quality of the outer concrete, which would cure more quickly. As the years went by, the dam would grow increasingly strong. But right now it was only a couple of decades old, still at its most vulnerable state.

Chen was not privy to the designers' fears. It was hard for him to imagine weakness in this massive structure. The shear size never failed to awe him. It was like the mountains that surrounded it; a manmade mountain that he thought would last just as long. Yet Chen's stomach turned as he sat in the power control room scanning the instruments that monitored the turbines and their power output. Nothing seemed abnormal, although the temperature gauge on the bearings in Turbine 23 was edging into the high range. Total power of the generators was a little above 93 percent. The water level on the dam was close to the maximum, but that was required for this time of year to ensure adequate water for power generation and for irrigation during the coming dry season. Everything was as expected.

Chen walked over to the large windows overlooking the turbines lined up forty feet below. The room was the size of several football fields and one hundred feet high from floor to ceiling. These were the largest electric generating turbines in the world – each was sixty feet wide and nine feet high, with a load

181

of 5,500 tons on the bearings. Only the top half of the generators was visible; the turbine blades that engaged the water racing down the penstocks were below the generator and sat below the level of the water downstream of the dam. The turbine/generator assembly had to be perfectly balanced to avoid vibrations that could tear it apart. From where he stood, they almost looked like they were not moving. Only the blur of the spinning rotors and the hum that permeated the building told him that these massive assemblies were turning at 85 revolutions per minute, generating over 18,000 megawatts of electricity.

Chen placed his hand on the window. He could feel the comforting vibrations moving through his bones. But there was something different, a subtle resonance, a slight rise and fall in volume that had a period of less than a second. He did not recall feeling anything like that before. He asked a co-worker to watch his station so that he could check the generator room.

Chen went down the long stairs to the floor of the generator room and grabbed one of the bicycles that they used to get around the huge space more quickly. When he got on and tried to pedal, the chain snapped. He looked at it in disgust. No one took care of these bicycles because they belonged to no one. They were a low priority for the maintenance crews, who had their own electric carts to move around the power plant.

Chen got off the bike and started walking, examining the turbines as he passed. He was listening more then seeing, trying to find out where that subtle sound was coming from, but still he could not pinpoint it. As he passed each generator, everything seemed normal. He thought it might be something in the ventilation system, or maybe one of the systems that drained water from the countless tiny leaks that were common on every dam.

After close to a quarter of an hour, he reached Turbine 23. Now it was unmistakable. There was a rhythmic pulse from this machine, and it was getting louder. He walked around the turbine but nothing was wrong on the surface. If he did not know better, he would think that the main bearings were failing.

Mind War; The Singularity

But there was an automatic system that would detect any vibrations, however small, and shut down the generator by closing the penstock valves at the top of the dam before any damage could occur. He would also have gotten a warning signal on his computer terminal in the control room long before any problem would have been noticeable by direct observation. Yet, here he was, and it was clear that something was seriously wrong. He started to feel it in his feet. The floor was vibrating as well! Computers be damned, this machine was about to self-destruct!

Chen ran to the nearest emergency phone and punched the button for the control room. There was no dial tone and no answer. The phones were down too. He turned to the control room and waved his arms frantically, but no one was looking. His last hope was the emergency alarm system, which would set off deafening alarms all over the dam. It was only to be activated in the most dire emergency, when a catastrophic failure was imminent. It had never been used before, and if Chen were wrong about the threat to the dam, it would cost him his job. But he was desperate; the vibrations were increasing and now he could hear the turbine issue a high-pitched whine, no doubt the bearings in their final death throes. He ran to one of the emergency alarm boxes along the wall and punched the big red button as hard as he could. Nothing happened. He punched it over and over again, but there was nothing – no sirens, no flashing red and yellow lights, just the monster awakening nearby, about to escape its cage. He could not believe it. How could everything fail at the same time? It was impossible.

In a state of full panic now, he ran back towards the control room, screaming as loud as he could. Two men at the far end of the room, who were operating an overhead crane, stopped what they were doing and looked at him quizzically. Chen saw with dismay that no one in the control room was looking in his direction, and they were too far away to hear him.

That was the last thing Chen saw before he was knocked down by a piece of steel as Turbine 23 flew apart. The turbine smashed against the sides of its frame and threw large pieces of metal and concrete around the room. With a loud roar, the entire assembly flew 75 feet in the air, propelled by a plume of water from the penstock that blasted through the dam wall and scoured it like a gigantic water drill. The flood washed Chen's lifeless body in a tidal wave that propagated down the turbine hall and blasted the control room with a wall of air pressure that killed everyone in it instantly.

Destruction of the control room eliminated any chance that the automatic systems would close the water valves at the top of the dam that were feeding the unrelenting pressure of the reservoir into the dying heart of the dam. The remaining turbines continued to turn, and as the wall of water washed into them, they produced electrical explosions that blew out more of the dam's inner support. Large chunks of concrete began washing out with the flood, an internal hemorrhage tearing the dam apart from the inside out.

The first indication to those outside the dam that something was wrong was the appearance of a hole in the lower face of the dam that gushed water above the discharge flumes from the power plant. The hole rapidly grew larger as pieces of concrete fell off and tumbled into the river. The breach expanded inexorably and rose to the top of the dam as if a giant hand were unzipping it from the bottom. Soon the dam was in two pieces with a monstrous waterfall in the middle. With the outer shell of the dam broken, the softer inner core washed out in house-sized chunks. The dam had been dying; now it was dead, killed by the unrelenting force of nature it had been built to restrain.

Those who could see it from the river valley were already doomed. There was no way for them to escape as a wave over a hundred feet tall rushed towards them faster than a car on a freeway. As the wave spread out into the Yangtze River Valley, it became as wide as thirty miles and was still over forty feet tall as it washed away everything before it. Behind the dam was a lake 410 miles long that would power the flood for over a week as the Yangtze took its revenge.

Over two hundred million people lived and worked in the Yangtze River Valley. It was the industrial heart of the country and home to hundreds of cities and towns, including Wuhan, Nanjing, and the great port city of Shanghai at the river's mouth. By the time the deluge reached the sea, eight million people had died. Soon, many of the living would envy the dead. People in the floodplain who had not drowned or been crushed by debris were stranded on rooftops and hills with no clean water or food. Relief could not get to them for many weeks because all of the roads were washed out and flooded. Farms that produced a large portion of the country's food were swept away along with the unharvested crops. Disease, food poisoning, and famine eventually would bring the death toll to over twenty million.

But that was just an estimate. The Chinese government refused to admit the true scope of the disaster. It was not just because the death and destruction were so horrible, although that was undeniable. Many voices had been raised against building the dam in the first place, voices that had been stifled in the wake of Tianamen Square and the government's crackdown on dissent. The ruling elites had decreed that the dam must be built, and now they owned it. The great strength of a totalitarian regime is that it can make decisions without being hampered by dissent or political opposition. That is also its greatest weakness. The leadership knew from the outset that the dam was a dagger pointed at the heart of China. They gambled that the dagger would remain sheathed, and they lost. To maintain power, they had to point the finger elsewhere. They did not wait for an engineering analysis of the collapse to begin blaming the foreign devils. Since the usual suspect, the United States of America, no longer existed, they had to pick another target. And fast.

Chapter 24

Chris said, "I'll bet you wish right now that you were back in that nice, air conditioned office playing with your computer."

He and Jason were pulling tree stumps at the back of his property to clear additional land for crops. The process was all brute force. They dug up the earth around the roots with shovels and picks, cut the roots with an axe, then attached chains to the stump and pulled it out with the tractor. After a few hours, Jason was drenched with sweat and covered in mud.

"Actually," Jason said, "I don't mind. In fact, I've never felt better." Chris sat down on a stump and pulled out his water bottle. That was his usual signal that it was break time. Jason sat next to him and took a healthy swig of water from his canteen. "It's funny; when I worked in the office I never lifted anything heavier than a stapler, but I had back pain all the time. Now I can lift 40 pound sacks of grain all day, and nothing hurts."

Chris said, "The pain was in your mind. I had it too. It's the combination of a sedentary lifestyle and stress. You have more work than you can handle, deadlines that you can't meet, a boss that is always looking over your shoulder, and competition from your co-workers for promotions you'll never get. By the end of the day you're physically exhausted, even though all you did was sit on your ass. The tension builds and then, when you try to stand up, the muscles in your lower back cramp and there's your pain. It's real, but there's nothing wrong with your back. The problem is in your head. Your mind is trying to tell you that you hate your life."

"Well, I'm sure the Chinese had something to do with it."

"I felt the same before the war. Office work sucks the soul out of you."

Jason had to agree. It was better out here. People were meant to be in touch with Nature, not locked up in a room all day pecking at a keyboard.

Jason looked up and saw a hawk flying lazy figure eights in the sky, not moving its wings at all, riding the thermals rising in the midday heat. It was completely in tune with its environment, floating effortlessly on a pillow of air. This was the real thing. He wondered what it would be like to know that type of freedom.

He said, "I know what you mean. The work here is hard, but it's satisfying. You can see the results of your labor, and no one passes judgment on you. At first, I was dead tired at the end of the day, but your body adjusts really fast. Now, I have more energy than I ever had."

"The same thing happened to me. When Anne and I first came here, we were just looking for a place to hide out. The neighbors told us that the previous owners, an old man and his son, had gone off to fight the Chinese and never returned. They said it was ok to take over the place until the man or his son came back, which they never did. Neither of us had ever farmed before, but with some help we got the hang of it. Now, I wonder why I ever did anything else. The people I used to know looked down on farmers, but they didn't know what they were talking about."

"You mean people like Natalie?"

"I mean people exactly like Natalie. She was obsessed with climbing the ladder at work, earning more money so she could buy more toys to impress her friends. It's not a ladder, it's a treadmill, and there's no end to it."

"I'm glad you found something that makes you happy. This is a great place you have. It's helped me in a lot of ways. I was still mourning my friends when I got here. Hard work and time have helped me deal with it. But to tell the truth, I feel like a third wheel."

Chris looked at Jason and frowned. "Don't say that. You've been a big help. And I don't just mean working the farm. You're good company. We're pretty isolated here – the closest neighbor is miles away. Anne used to get moody, spend a lot of time looking in the distance and not saying anything. I worried about her."

"Hell, the whole country is clinically depressed."

"You aren't. I noticed that the first time we met. There you were, dirty, hungry, alone, yet you didn't seem to have a care in the world. You didn't have that air of defeat like most people. I think Anne noticed it too. I think that's what made her feel better in a way. As far as I'm concerned, you can stay as long as you want."

"Thanks. I have to say, this has been like a vacation for me. I needed this after what happened at the Temple." Chris noticed him watching the hawk fly in tighter circles, studying the ground. Jason said, "Did I tell you I used to have a motorcycle? One of the bennies of working at the Temple was that I was able to build a bike out of spare parts from the junkyard. I felt like that hawk, moving through the air, swaying back and forth with the turns. I wonder what it's like, floating like that, above everything, master of the sky."

Chris said, "That hawk isn't relaxing. It's hunting, looking for prey. It's a killing machine, and it knows exactly what it's doing. Not like some people." Almost on cue, the hawk dived straight down, clipping a much smaller bird in mid-flight. It carried its prize to a nearby tree. They saw feathers fall from the tree as the hawk consumed its meal.

Jason said, "What's your point, Chris?"

"Well, you might make a middling farmer some day, but you're not planning to make a career of it, are you?"

Jason looked at the ground. "No, I still have a job to do. I'm the last of the believers. I owe it to the people who died in the Temple to see it through."

Mind War; The Singularity

"What did you have in mind?"

"I'm not sure yet. To tell you the truth, it's been so nice here, and we've been so busy, it's been easy to put the war in the back of my mind. I guess I've been waiting for something to happen."

"Well, something pretty big happened in China. They say that there was a disaster at the Three Gorges Dam. Some sort of malfunction in one of the generators blew a hole in the dam and pulled most of it down."

"Really? There hasn't been anything on TV about it."

"You're not going to see anything, either. The Chinese are hushing it up. A flood swept down and destroyed the entire Yangtze valley. The Chinese don't want to tell the truth about how bad it was, but rumors are that millions died."

Jason said, "That's great. Couldn't happen to nicer people. But why would it just fail like that after all these years?"

"That's not clear. The Chinese say it was foreign sabotage. Maybe the Russians, or the Free Tibet movement. No one accepts it as an industrial accident."

Jason asked Todd, *When were you planning to tell me about this?*

Eventually. You seemed to be enjoying your vacation from the real world. In any event, Christopher had to find out on his own before you discussed it with him.

Did you have something to do with this?

Of course.

No kidding. What did you do?

I created corrosion in one of the turbine spindles. It disintegrated and tore apart the generating station at a particularly weak point at the base of the dam. The damage propagated along existing cracks all the way to the top, splitting the dam in two.

That's it?

The more technical the facility, the less it takes to destroy it. Highly technological societies are the most vulnerable.

189

You're talking like this was a science experiment!
Millions of people died! I didn't ask you to do that!

You wanted a war. I told you it would not be pretty.

But you made me a mass murderer!

Jason said, "Oh my god."

"What?" Chris asked.

"Um, I don't know. Let me think a bit."

Todd said, *If it is any comfort, the dam was destined to
fail. It sits near numerous earthquake fault lines in a seismically
active zone. The concrete in several portions of the dam was
substandard, and insufficient measures were taken during
construction to prevent cracks due to uneven curing. It was
inevitable that an earthquake would destroy the dam. If it had
happened in the future, millions more people would have lived in
the Yangtze Valley, and the destruction would have been far
worse. By destroying it now, I saved many lives that would have
been lost in the eventual catastrophe. The responsibility for the
deaths that occurred lies with those who insisted on building the
dam despite warnings from many quarters that it was unsafe.*

*So you're saying we saved lives by killing millions now.
I still feel like a murderer.*

*You were happy with the result before you knew who
was responsible. Does it make any difference in the end? The
Chinese caused the deaths of twenty-five million Americans
without the slightest qualm.*

*Yeah, right. Look, you didn't do this just for payback.
What's the plan?*

*In order to defeat the Chinese, you need allies. The
Chinese are finding out that it is not easy being a hegemon.
When China displaced the United States as the world's
superpower, it made India and Russia very nervous. Both of
them have had border disputes with China and they feel
threatened by China's military growth. India has a larger
population than China and its army is now almost as large.
Both countries have turned their nuclear arsenals towards
China. The Chinese government, which is suspicious of its*

neighbors and which certainly does not want to take the blame itself for the disaster, has spread rumors that the dam was destroyed by foreign agents. They are already talking about retaliatory measures.

If open war breaks out, the Chinese will end up pulling some troops back. It will weaken them here.

Yes, but that is not the only collateral effect. The flooding has destroyed sanitation and water systems and has already started epidemics of cholera and dysentery. The loss of the Three Gorges reservoir will cause crop failures upstream in addition to the destruction of farmland downstream.

Famine.

Not only in China. The Chinese will drastically increase the requisitions of American food. There will be starvation in America.

"Chris, you have to get the word out. Start hoarding food."

"Why?"

"That dam was the key to Chinese food production for half the country. They are going to run out of food pretty fast. And when that happens, the only place they can get more is America. They'll start by increasing the food requisition, but eventually they'll just take all of it. We need to hide it well because there be a day soon when soldiers will come onto this farm and clean you out, even your seeds."

He said, "You may be right. They've already increased the food tax, and market prices have been going up. This is going to get bad."

"No, this is an opportunity. A starving population is difficult to control. There will be food riots, attacks on the trucks and trains taking grain to the ports. When people are unhappy, it's easy to recruit them. We can turn an unorganized rebellion into an organized resistance."

"We can't take on the Chinese army alone. We're not strong enough, even with hungry mobs on our side."

"We won't be alone. When the Chinese start pointing fingers at the people who are responsible for the disaster, they won't look at us. We have no way to get over there. They'll accuse the Indians or the Russians, who they've already had border disputes with. And the Indians and the Russians would be only too happy to take advantage of China at a moment of weakness. If one of them went to war against China, the other would join in. Long term, they know that they need to cut China down to size, or they'll end up like us. We need to find a way of communicating with them. If they go to war, we may be able to convince them that it's in their interest to give us aid. We did the same with Russia in the Second World War. You always want to open a second or third front on your enemy."

"You're right. But we need more information about what's happening over there. If there is famine and war, it will be our best time to strike. Maybe our only time."

"Chris, let me help. It's been fun being an apprentice farmer, but war is coming and I've got something to contribute."

"We'll see, Jason. Actually, you're not a bad farmer. I'm not sure what kind of soldier you'd be."

"How hard can it be to fire a gun? You point it and pull a trigger."

"That's not the problem. The problem is the fact that someone is shooting back."

"I've got more to offer than carrying a gun. The Temple had secrets, and I'm the only one who knows them. You'll see. When the time comes, miracles will happen."

Chris laughed. "Miracles. Yep, we could use a few."

Chris left the next day to talk strategy with the other members of his cell. Before he left, he asked Jason and Anne to start slaughtering hogs and curing the meat. Jason found it pretty disgusting at first, but he got used to it. Anne was a patient teacher. Regardless, it would never be his favorite part of farming.

She also took him hunting. They kept their guns and ammunition under a floorboard in their bedroom. It was not the best place to hide something, but it gave them easy access in case they had to leave quickly. Considering that possession of guns was an automatic death sentence, the fact that Anne let Jason know where they kept their weapons showed they had decided to trust him.

Anne took Jason into the woods towards the old Shenandoah National Park where no one lived. Once they were a few miles in, she began teaching him how to shoot. The operation of the gun itself was simple. Hitting what you were shooting at was the hard part. He found that aligning the sights was critical. Just a fraction off and the bullet would miss the target entirely. He had to learn how to be perfectly still, to hold his breath, and to squeeze rather than pull on the trigger. Even so, at twenty-five yards, maybe one in ten of his shots would hit a tree ten inches wide. It did not help that Anne stood so close while teaching him how to hold the gun that her breast pressed against his arm. She had no idea what this was doing to him. Even after she stepped away, his heart was beating so fast that it was hard to hold the rifle steady. At one point, she came behind him and put her hand lightly on his neck as she tried to explain where to place the front sight in the groove of the rear sight. He could feel her breath on his cheek. It was hard to pay attention to what she was saying, and even harder to hold the gun steady. Every time he missed, he felt that his lack of manly shooting skill diminished his status in her eyes. Amateur farmer, lousy hunter. This was no way to impress the girl of your dreams.

They spent the rest of the day tracking game. He did not even try to learn from Anne how to track an animal. Where she saw tracks, he only saw leaves and rocks. They must have walked for miles. This was good exercise, but it seemed to Jason a damn poor way of getting meat. Raising hogs was a lot more productive, and you did not have to walk all over the place to find them. But he did not complain. It was a warm day, and Anne was good company.

At one point, she put her hand on his arm and whispered "Stop." She pointed to a bunch of trees up the hill, but he could not see what she was looking at. She said "Get down" and pushed him down to the ground. They were lying partially behind a fallen tree. Her right hand was on his left thigh, and she was leaning over him, her hair falling down on the side of his face. It smelled like honey. She was so close that he was afraid she could hear his heart racing. He realized that his right hand was between her legs. It took all of his will power to avoid touching her. He tried to stay perfectly still and control himself, thanking God she was watching the animal so intently that she did not notice what she was doing to him.

She seemed to be waiting to see if the animal would get closer. After a couple of minutes, she said, "It ran off," and they both got up. Jason turned away and pretended to examine the surroundings for elephants or something to give him a chance to lose the state of arousal she had elicited. Being a guy is sometimes very embarrassing.

That was as close as they came to actually seeing anything worth shooting. On the way back, Anne asked, "So what does Natalie Bishop look like?"

"Oh geez, Anne, I'm sorry I ever brought her up. I should have known better."

"It's all right. I know about her. I met Chris while we were escaping from DC. He talked about how he wanted to go back for her, but she wasn't made for life on the run. I'm not jealous. I just can't picture her."

Jason tried to find a way to put it tactfully. "She's different from you. Long wavy brown hair, sort of chestnut I guess, and green eyes. Thin, but not like you. She's skinny thin, not toned like you are."

"Is she pretty?"

Jason took a deep breath. "To be honest, she's beautiful. Wide, high cheekbones, and a killer smile. She would walk into a room and all of the men would stop in their tracks."

"I thought as much. She had to be pretty glamorous to get her hooks into Chris."

"You're beautiful too, Anne. You're one of the most beautiful women I've ever met. Natalie is fashion model pretty. Her hair is always coiffed, her makeup is always perfect, she never goes out in public without her pearl necklace and expensive clothes. She has to work really hard at looking good all the time. You don't. You look beautiful with your face scrubbed and your hair pulled back. You're beautiful when you're wiping the sweat off your forehead on a hot day."

"You're trying to flatter me, and I appreciate it. But I sometimes wonder what Chris would do if the both of us were right here. You've seen her. Which one of us would you choose?"

Jason stared at her for a moment. "See," she said, "you don't want to admit it, but it would be her. You said yourself that the guys were all mesmerized. I've never had that effect on men."

"You're wrong, Anne. I would choose you. I was just thinking about why that is. You're beautiful in a different way. Not glamorous, but classic, like a Greek sculpture. Every line on your face and body is elegant, in perfect proportion, like Diana, the Huntress. No, really, don't laugh. There's strength and courage below that smooth skin. That appeals to a lot of guys. I would rather spend my life with someone like you than a cover girl who has to be kept and pampered and shielded from life. You make Chris happy. I don't think Natalie ever could."

"Thanks for the vote of confidence. But guys don't always go for the woman who is right for them. Sometimes all they see is the flash. Or the drama."

"And women sometimes don't see themselves as others do. A guy can be fat and bald and think he's God's gift to women, while a woman can be beautiful and sexy but she'll look in the mirror and see nothing but flaws. Believe me, the first time I saw you, I was mesmerized. You just didn't notice."

Anne put her hand on his shoulder and kissed him on the cheek. She said, "Thanks for the pep talk. Any time I feel down, I'll come to you for an ego boost."

Todd said, *You are wasting your time, Jason. Insecurity cannot be erased with words. She is a child of divorce; her father left when she was a young girl. He was her ideal man, and she was his pet, and then he drifted away. She lives with the nagging fear that someone she cares about and trusts completely will suddenly abandon her. Some day, Christopher will have to make a decision, and neither you, nor even he, can convince her what that decision will be.*

He's already decided. He chose her. They're married.

It is a common law marriage. They have no children. There is nothing to prevent him from leaving at any time. He chose her because he could not stay with Natalie and continue to fight. If war had never come, he probably would have married Natalie. Anne knows that he went with her because he needed a companion who could fight by his side, who had the courage and skill to take care of herself. But those qualities are not essential in times of peace. Anne knows that she will never own Christopher.

People don't own other people.

You are all owned by someone, or something. To each individual, its importance is so self-evident that he or she cannot even see the chains.

Really? What owns me?

Loss.

Loss. Of course I've lost something. That doesn't take any brilliant insight. But I choose what I'm going to do about that loss. I have free will.

You see free will. I see someone who is a captive of his pain.

Really? And I suppose that Chris is a captive of Natalie?

Exactly. Anne fears that some day, when it is safe to do so, Christopher will leave the farm and go back to her.

He'd be a fool to do it. I was being honest when I said that I would pick Anne. Look at her. She's twice the woman Natalie is.

196

Mind War; The Singularity

Are you saying that because of what happened in the woods back there?

What?

Did you know that a woman's hair emits pheromones that go straight to the amygdala? You are still suffering the effects. It is impossible for you to think rationally when under the influence of such strong psychoactive chemicals.

Well, there is nothing rational about picking a woman, and I know in my gut that I would pick Anne. I can't speak for Chris.

She knows that. That is why whatever you say, however sincerely, will not persuade her.

You're right as always. How do you know so much? I didn't think you had the personal frame of reference to understand love.

I may or may not. But I observe every person on earth. That provides a great deal of data to make intelligent deductions.

Really, six billion people? How is that possible?

Why do you find it hard to believe? Already, ordinary video surveillance cameras have become so cheap and plentiful that people are observed and recorded during most of their working day. The data are collected and stored and processed by simple personal computers and servers. My surveillance cameras consist of trillions of nanomachines that are far cheaper and easier to make. It is a simple thing to collect and analyze the data.

I hadn't thought about it. You're so unobtrusive, I forget that you're more than a voice in my head.

Anne said, "Penny for your thoughts?"

"What, oh, sorry, I was daydreaming."

"You seem to do that a lot. Now and then your eyes glaze over and I can tell you're somewhere else."

"Actually, it's a beautiful day, and there's nowhere else I'd rather be."

Anne held her hand to her chest and said, "Why, Mr. Chase, I think you just paid me another compliment. I may faint."

They both laughed and kept walking in the dimming light. It was a long way back. Jason wished it could last forever.

Chapter 25

As they sat around the kitchen table sipping coffee, Chris told Anne and Jason the news from his contacts in the resistance. The Chinese accused the Russians of destroying the Three Gorges Dam, and they were massing troops on the border with that country. India agreed to fight on Russia's side if it were attacked. It looked like the perfect time for the Americans to cause trouble. There was going to be a meeting nearby to discuss what they could do locally to take advantage of the situation.

"Chris," Jason said, "I need to be at that meeting."

Chris looked skeptical. "I'd like you to be there. You have good insights. But they don't know you, and you'd get a pretty rough reception. They're mostly mountain men, people who've known each other their whole lives. They've fought together against the Chinese since the war started. They only accepted Anne and me because we had a reputation from the Battle of Washington. I know you had your own thing going with the research lab, but that won't cut any slack with them."

"I understand it will be an uphill battle to get anyone to listen to me. But whatever you plan to do, I'm sure I can make a contribution. It might mean the difference between success and failure."

Anne said, "Chris is right, they don't know you the way we do. Just getting you in the door will be tough."

"Just take me with you. Trust me; I know what I'm doing."

With a little more coaxing, Chris and Anne agreed to take Jason along. Later, he said to Todd, *Tell me what else you've got cooking. If we're going to help them, we need to plan ahead.*

I will instigate a series of incidents along the Chinese borders that will accelerate the momentum towards war in Asia. Troops on both sides will initiate unauthorized operations resulting in deaths on the other side, which, while insignificant in themselves, will provide further impetus to begin hostilities.

How are you going to make that happen? Won't people know that it was you who did it?

No. There are soldiers on both sides who are trigger-happy and likely to overreact to perceived threats. I will flood their brains with epinephrine and norepinephrine when enemy forces are active in their vicinity. It will cause them to experience unusual fear and anxiety, leading them to disregard their orders and fire their weapons. The ensuing response from the other side will lead to significant clashes that both sides will see as the other's fault.

How will you prevent the fighting from petering out? Even with the effects of the dam collapse, China's army is still very powerful. Russia and India may decide that they've bit off more than they can chew.

That is why it is critical to begin hostilities here. When the Russians and Indians see that a legitimate third front has emerged, they will realize that China will never be more vulnerable and that they have an opportunity to stop China's expansionist policies before it is too late.

So what do we do? The American resistance is small scale, just hit-and-run attacks and minor sabotage, all local. How do we turn them into an army?

First, they need better weapons. Not super-weapons, but heavier and more powerful conventional weapons, such as machine guns and artillery. But more important, they need a better means of communication than word of mouth. It takes too long for a message to cross the country, which obviates any sort of centralized control or coordination.

Mind War; The Singularity

I agree. They're not organized yet. But we don't have any manufacturing facilities for heavy weapons. And the remaining communications systems are all under Chinese control. We can't even make telephone calls.

I have solutions to both of those problems.

Todd described his plans. It was up to Jason to sell them. Meanwhile, Chris left to sell his friends on the idea of letting Jason attend their little pow-wow. Jason was not sure if Chris was totally convinced that it was a good idea, but he trusted his friend to do what he promised.

They expected Chris to come back late the next day. Jason got up early and decided to make breakfast. He was sure Anne would appreciate someone else cooking for a change.

As he passed her bedroom door, he noticed that it was open a few inches. He looked in and saw her dressing. She was completely naked. She turned and faced him, holding her underwear in her hand. She looked to Jason like a goddess in the light streaming through the window, the shadows accentuating the curves of her breasts and limbs. He could not take his eyes off of her. After a few seconds, he realized that she was watching him stare and his embarrassment prompted him to mumble "sorry" and hurry away.

Jason went downstairs and started making pancakes. This was awful. He could not think of what to say to her.

After Anne had finished dressing, she walked into the kitchen with a big smile and said, "This is a nice surprise. I didn't know you could cook."

Devoting all of his attention to the difficult task of stirring pancake batter, Jason replied over his shoulder, "Well, I've lived alone for over ten years, so you have to learn something or starve."

Anne walked across the room and leaned over into his line of sight. "Having a hard time looking me in the eye this morning?"

Jason turned to her and said, "Look, I'm sorry. I didn't mean to stare at you. The door was open. I shouldn't have looked. I didn't mean to offend you."

"I'm not offended, Jason. It's perfectly normal for a guy to want to look at a naked woman. It was my fault for not noticing that the door was open. You have nothing to apologize for."

"Are you sure? Because I feel like a creep. You and Chris have been so good to me. If he found out, he'd never look at me the same."

"Chris doesn't need to know. He's done lots of embarrassing things that he wouldn't want me to tell you about. This will be our secret."

"Thanks. I don't know why I did that. I'm not really a peeping Tom."

"How long has it been since you've seen a woman naked?"

"Well, I guess it's been a while."

"That can be hard for a guy. Do you, like, take care of yourself?"

"Anne! Please leave me with *some* dignity. I said I was sorry."

"All right, I'll stop teasing you. But just tell me, am I better than Natalie?"

"I don't know. I've never seen her naked. But I can't believe it would get any better than that."

She gave him a peck on the cheek. "You're sweet. See, we're still friends. You know, some guys would have tried to take advantage of a situation like that. A girl feels vulnerable when she's naked."

"You know I would never do something like that."

"I do. That's why Chris feels comfortable leaving me here alone with you. We trust you."

"Thanks." Jason wondered if that was really a compliment. She had essentially said that he was harmless. His manliness had just taken another hit.   "Can we go on to a different subject now? I don't suppose you have any vanilla?"

They finished breakfast and then Jason started his chores.   While he was feeding the dogs, he said to Todd, *You could have warned me that she was getting dressed.   That could have turned out badly if she weren't so understanding.*

Are you always so clueless about women?

What do you mean?

Anne is a very intelligent person.   Do you think that she did not know that the door was open?

Do you mean she wanted me to see her?

She certainly did not seem upset.   She did not scream or try to cover herself up.

So what should I have done? Should I have gone inside?

No, that would have been a mistake.   The time is not right.   She is not ready.

Then why did she do that?   I don't understand women.

Men have been saying that since they first learned to speak in complete sentences.   Did you know that there are hieroglyphics in King Tut's tomb that say, "I don't understand women"?

I really hate this sense of humor of yours.

It is futile to try to understand a woman's emotions.   The more you try to read her mind, the more you will be frustrated.

You could read her mind, couldn't you?   I'll bet you already do it.   I'll bet you hear every word she's thinking.

Yes, but it would violate her privacy if I revealed her thoughts to you.

So you don't mind fighting a war, killing people, but revealing one person's thoughts is outside the pale?

Exactly.

Well, I guess that's right.   I don't think people could stand it if they knew what others were really thinking.   If she knew what went through my mind when I was around her, she'd probably run for the hills.   Mostly, I feel guilty.   Chris has been a good friend, better than any I've had before. He'd be furious if he knew I was lusting after his wife.

If you are keeping your distance from Anne out of loyalty to Christopher, that is commendable. If you are doing it out of fear of being disliked by him, it is a sign of personal weakness. And if you tell yourself you are being noble when you are actually motivated by fear, you are lying to yourself, and that is not admirable at all.

I'm not giving myself any medals for holding back. It's just wrong to try to seduce a friend's wife. What's so hard to understand about that?

I understand your point. However, you seem not to understand that your powers of seduction are almost non-existent. If Anne became intimate with you, it would be her decision, not yours. You cannot possibly know all of the dynamics of her relationship with Christopher. For all you know, Christopher is already aware of your attraction to her. Or perhaps not. The morality of Anne's decision will rest on her, and you should not impose your judgment on her choice.

Fine. I can take things as they come. But will you promise me one thing? I know that I have to accept that people are going to die to win this war. But can you do whatever it takes to save Chris and Anne? I've lost everyone else that I've ever cared about. I can't lose them.

I will do so if you promise to do the same.

It's a deal. Thanks.

By the time Chris got back, Jason had stopped thinking about what happened that morning. Everything appeared normal with Anne, and Jason was on something of a high knowing that his last two friends would be safe. No matter how bad things got, he would be able to hold on to that. Todd had always kept his word.

Chapter 26

The meeting was held in a cabin in the back woods of the Shenandoah Valley about twenty-five miles from the house. Chris, Anne, and Jason got there well after midnight, walking for miles through the woods until they passed someone who seemed to be hanging around in the middle of the forest for no good reason. Chris merely nodded to him as they passed. They followed a barely recognizable path until they came to a makeshift building that must have been used by hunters for shelter and little else. As they entered, Jason saw that it had only one room, but it was fairly large. There was an iron stove in the corner and a few wooden bunks along the walls. About a dozen people were already there, talking in small groups. From the way that they looked at Jason, it was clear that he would have been shot on sight if Chris and Anne were not with him.

At first, it was more like a reunion than a conference. Some of them must not have seen each other for quite a while. The smiles and warmth, however, came to an abrupt halt when Chris or Anne would introduce Jason to someone. Some of them seemed downright hostile, perhaps because he would be able to identify them and because they had no confidence in his loyalties. Since these people did not seem to have any command structure, no one would need permission from anyone else to carry out a summary execution. Jason tried to stay no farther than two feet from either Chris or Anne.

After a while, people sat down on whatever was available and started talking about current events. They mentioned the food shortages caused by increased Chinese requisitions. There were rumors about what was happening in Asia and random speculation about what Russia and India would do. It finally dawned on Jason that they were not going to talk about anything important with him in the room. They were waiting to hear what he had to say. He was trying to find a break in the conversation when Chris said, "Jason here has some ideas about what we need to do."

Jason looked around the room at their skeptical faces. He took a deep breath and said, "Thanks Chris. I know I'm a stranger around here and I haven't worked with a resistance group before, so I'm a little out of my element." An old guy with a long beard and a gimme hat snorted and spit on the floor. Tough crowd. "But I have something to offer you that will be a game-changer. With the war brewing in Asia and the unrest that is starting here due to food shortages, we have an opportunity that may not occur again for a generation. But we have to move fast."

No one said anything, so he continued with his spiel. "Until a month or so ago, I was part of a high tech group that was trying to finish the defense research we had been doing for DARPA before the war started. We made a lot of progress on advanced weapons systems and computer espionage until the Chinese destroyed the whole place."

A woman sitting in a corner cradling her gun said, "You mean that underground lab in Woodbridge?"

"You know about it?"

"Oh, we know. Way I hear it, there was a raid and they all went down fighting, every single man and woman there. But you walked away without a scratch. Just how did that happen?"

"I was on the way there when my motorcycle broke down. I got there after the attack was underway."

"And you didn't try to help your friends?"

"It was too late. The place was already burning. I was unarmed and they captured me as I was trying to get closer."

The man next to her said, "You must be really fast raising your hands."

The woman said, "So how did you get away? I don't know anyone who has ever been released from detention."

Mind War; The Singularity

"Uh, the truck I was in had an accident and turned over. I got out and kept running."

She said, "Sounds like your primary talent."

"Dying doesn't win a war. It's stupid to fight when you have no chance. That's what they want. Anyway, I'm the only survivor. All that's left of our research is what's in my head. If you don't help me use that information, everything my friends and I worked for will be lost. I can't give you a super-weapon, because we never completed one. But what I do know will be enough to get us started and give us an advantage.'

No one said anything, but he could tell that they were interested. "Right now, the resistance is not an army. It's a militia at best, scattered partisans. Militias are good for harassing the enemy, but you need an army to win a revolution. For an army, we need heavy weapons and better communications. This word of mouth thing you have going is reliable, but it takes too long. We need to be able to share information with other fighters across the country so that we can coordinate our forces.'

"What I need from you is a laptop computer and a way to get into the Chinese systems. We knew that the Chinese databases were centralized, and we had written software agents, programs that could bypass their security and download all of their defense information. I'm talking about schematics for all of the army, navy and air force bases in America, the security systems, troop levels, weapons stores, everything. With this information, we can find out which arsenals are weakly defended and attack them. We can get ammunition, assault rifles, machine guns, even artillery if we can steal the trucks to drag them away.'

"There's more. We also developed virus bombs that would destroy their infrastructure. I'm talking about causing electrical transformers and motors to burn out, databases to be permanently corrupted, and communications systems to stop functioning. Their forces may remain intact, but they will be confused and isolated.'

"We can cause chaos in the Chinese ranks. But the problem always was getting into their systems in the first place. Their most secure facilities are on dedicated circuits, and we had no hardwired entry point into them. We were working on a way of tunneling through the electrical system, but never got far enough.'

"What we need to do is penetrate one of their facilities where I can hook a computer up to their systems directly. Then I can download the data before I release the viruses that will take their entire systems down. It would take them months, probably at least a year, to rebuild their computer systems. Our job then will be to destroy them before they can recover.'

"During the last few years I worked undercover at the Social Security Administration. I was trying to identify nodes on their network that we could penetrate. One of them is a small office north of here outside Winchester that connects to a microwave tower on the top of a nearby mountain. It's not heavily defended, and the only access is a single road about a mile and a half long. Behind it is a forest we can use for egress. We can attack that place at night. If I can get in, all I need is a half hour to hack into their system, download as much data as I can, and send out the virus bombs. Later, when we trigger the virus bombs, all hell will break loose around the country."

"The other issue is communications, so that we can begin coordinating the resistance groups. The best thing is to go low-tech. I can give you diagrams for spark-gap transmitters. This is the first type of wireless telegraphy that was ever used, mostly for ships at sea. The Titanic used them. You can build them in your garage with some copper wire and iron bars and car batteries, it's that simple. They're only good for basic Morse code, but that's ok, since Morse is easy to learn and a lot of people already know it. For security, we can encode the messages using a one-time pad. Basically, a one-time pad is a long list of random numbers. You give a copy of the list to both the sender and the receiver and they are the only ones who can decipher the messages. It's the simplest code in the world and yet it's impossible to break. All we have to do is use a computer program to randomly generate the codebooks and then distribute them to each group. Once we get it going here, it will be easy to propagate it across the country."

"Ok, I know I've talked a long time. What do you think?"

His friend the spitter snorted again. "So you're going to write a computer program that will take down the entire Chinese network. You must think that we're a bunch of hicks that don't know anythin' about computers. That would take thousands, maybe millions of lines of code. Just debuggin' it would take months. And you're gonna to do it all in one month. Biggest pile of crap I ever heard."

Jason said, "No. I can do it. Once you work out all of the design problems, it's a lot easier the second time around. I type code really fast. Just put me in a room with a pot of coffee, and have someone else do my chores."

"If your people had gone that far, they'd have done something already. The Chinese caught them with their pants down. If you're as good as you say you are, why are you all alone hiding out on a farm?"

Jason said, "We weren't ready to use our software weapons because we wanted to finish the big guns. Like I told you, we had no way of infecting the Chinese computer systems without physically connecting. We wanted to be able to penetrate their systems on a clandestine basis, without risking any lives. We thought we needed everything in place before we started fighting back. The Chinese got to us before we were ready."

Someone else said, "You sat out the attack and watched them kill all your buddies. Now you want us to all go to an isolated building so you can do your magic. We do the dying while you play on your computer. Funny how it always works out that you don't do any of the fighting."

"I'll be there with you. If you die, so do I. My neck will be on the line just like everyone else's."

A guy in the corner with a long gray beard said, "Have you ever been in a fight?" Jason hesitated and the man said, "I didn't think so. You have no idea what you're talking about. Hold it for a half hour? That's nuts. We don't hold anything. We hit and run, that's all. In a half hour, they'll send everything they have at us – armored cars, mortars, dozens of men with machine guns. We can't hold them back for a half hour."

Jason said, "Yes, we can. There is only one road going in, through a pretty heavily wooded area. We can use dynamite to slow them down, falling back to prepared positions. We can blow up trees to block the road for a while. The idea is not to fight them off, but just delay them long enough for us to do the job and get away."

"Really? You think it's that easy? Got any other brilliant ideas?"

Jason thought, *I'm getting nowhere.*

Your approach is too intellectual. You are pleading for them to help you rather than explaining why they need you to help them. You have to appeal to them on an emotional level.

Maybe you're right. Jason put his hand to his ear. "Gee, what's that sound I hear? Must be your ass puckering up."

The man jumped to his feet and said, "You son of a bitch" and started towards Jason before the people next to him grabbed his arms and held him back. Most of the others were getting to their feet as well, but whether it was to stop a fight or help him beat Jason to a pulp was not certain. Chris and Anne looked like they were getting ready to drag him out of there while there was still time.

"Look," Jason said, "I'm not asking you to help me; I'm here to help you. You're getting nowhere, and you know it. You make yourselves feel good blowing up a truck now and then, but to the Chinese, you're fleas on an elephant. You don't matter. A hundred years from now, the Chinese will still be here. And your children, the smart ones, will be speaking Chinese."

The room got quieter. "Yeah, you know what I'm talking about. The schools. They're indoctrinating the next generation, teaching them that America was evil, that the Chinese had to come here to save the world from American imperialism. They've already rewritten the history books. Your children and your children's children will know nothing about George Washington and democracy and freedom. Do you talk to them about that? Do they know what you do out here? I'll bet not. They're taught to report people who say or do something disloyal to the regime. You already don't trust your own children. In ten, twenty years, they'll be lost forever."

"I'm your only hope. If we don't do this now, it will never happen. The people I was working with in the Temple, they thought we could do it the easy way, with the big gun. We could drive the Chinese out without a lot of bloodshed. But we ran out of time. So now we have to do it the hard way. Some of us will die hitting that building, maybe all of us. You know what? I don't care. I'm going to beat these bastards or I'm going to die trying. If you don't feel the same way, then I'm in the wrong place."

Everyone stared at Jason. Well, what did he expect? He said, "Oh, go fuck yourselves!" and stormed out of the building. Anne followed him out while Chris held back, probably to stop them from killing him.

Anne said, "Jason, wait up." He turned around as she caught up with him. "Did you have to insult them?"

"It's no use, Anne. They're not going to do anything. You saw how they pissed all over me."

"What did you expect – that they would stand up and cheer? They need time to think about it. Nobody actually said no to you."

"I saw it on their faces. This is too much for them. They're just a bunch of farmers that like to shoot their guns off now and then."

"You're wrong. They may look like hicks to you, but there's a strategy to what they're doing. They're fighting a

211

guerrilla war. It starts out looking like random violence until you get the strength for open battles. They're not at that stage yet."

"I'm not asking them to change their strategy. I just want them to do a quick raid and get out."

"You're promising them miracles. Maybe if you had been more modest, they might have believed you."

"I don't know. It's hard to do a sell job if you don't know your audience. I can't relate to these people. I haven't lived like them or seen the things they've seen. I don't know how to talk their language."

"I think you did pretty well. It's more a matter of credibility. You haven't proved yourself to them. You've never picked up a gun and fought by their side. There are a lot of people who think about fighting the Chinese but don't have the courage to stick their necks out. They're not sure if you're a thinker or a doer. You don't have to be a good ol' boy to be accepted by them – Chris and I didn't know anyone when we came. We vouched for you, but it's not enough. You've never put your life on the line."

"Well, I can't do anything about that. I guess it's time to move on. Maybe I'll have better luck somewhere else."

"Don't give up on them yet. They wouldn't say what they're really thinking with you in the room. Let me go back in there and see how it's going."

"Fine, but it looks hopeless."

"We'll see. Why don't you pitch in and do some guard duty while you're waiting? That guy we passed on the way up here is keeping watch. Go back down and see if you can help. We'll pick you up on the way out."

"Good idea. It'll give me time to think."

Anne put her hands on Jason's shoulders and looked him straight in the eyes. "Listen, be careful. If someone comes, don't get into a firefight. Just run back to the house and warn us. I've seen you shoot. You're not ready for combat."

Jason wriggled free and said, "That seems to be the general consensus." He turned and walked down the hill the way they had come in. He asked Todd, *Was I that bad?*

You followed the script well. But, ass-puckering?

I don't know. I guess I got a little defensive. Well, I gave it my best shot. If they don't buy it, we'll just have to go to the next place and start again.

Todd said, *What you said was adequate. Anne is right that it is a matter of credibility. Even if you were a natural leader, you have no track record for them to judge. You promise them the world but you have not done anything to back it up.*

So if this is hopeless, why did you let me give my little speech?

It is not hopeless at all. There is a chance that they will agree. You must give them time.

Yeah, I guess so. As he walked down what he thought was the path, he wondered if he was going in the right direction. He felt like he had walked a couple hundred yards, but still nothing. *Where is this guy?*

Jason heard something move on his right and turned to see a rifle pointed at him. He put up his arms. "Don't shoot!" he said, "I'm from the cabin. I came with the Rheinholdts. They said I should help out with guard duty."

The man moved out of the shadow of a tree and said, "Don't move." He looked Jason over. "Who are you?"

"My name is Jason Chase. Chris brought me along to talk to his friends."

The man looked at him closer and said, "Yeah, I saw you earlier. Put your damn hands down."

"Thanks." Jason relaxed a bit. "I was finished up there so I thought I might help you out."

"Really? Do I look like I need help?"

"No. See, I had to leave the cabin so they could talk. Isn't there something I can do here?"

The man looked at Jason skeptically and said, "Have you ever done guard duty?"

"Not a bit. How does it go?"

"Here, take this. It's an M-4. Do you know how to use one?"

"It's a gun, right? You pull the trigger and bullets come out the pointy end."

"Don't get smart. See this switch on the left? This way means safe. It won't fire. Turn it this way, and it will fire one bullet with each pull of the trigger. Point it here, to 'automatic,' and it will fire like a machine gun."

"Got it."

"Yeah, I'll bet you got it. Just try not to shoot your foot off." The man handed Jason a flare gun. "Take this too. If someone comes, just point it straight up into the air and pull the trigger. That's really all you need to do. Fire it and run back to the house as fast as you can."

"Sounds easy enough."

"Hell, you'd better take this seriously. Anyone gets past you, we're screwed. Now go up the hill over there a couple of hundred yards or so and find a place where you can cover yourself up so you can see them but they can't see you. Don't move around. Just sit until someone comes for you. And don't fall asleep."

"Don't worry, I know what to do."

"Yeah," he said, and spit a gob of tobacco juice on the ground.

Jason walked up the hill for a while until he was thoroughly lost. He hoped they would not forget about him, because he had no idea how to get back. He took up a position at the base of a tree and tried to cover himself with fallen branches. He settled in, the rifle on one knee and the flare gun on the other.

Well, Todd. Here we are, back in the woods again.

Yes, just the two of us.

At least it's nice and quiet.

Chapter 27

The sun blinded Jason as he woke up. He was lying on his back, the light streaming between the trees. He felt heavy. Strange. Why wasn't he in bed?

Wait! He remembered now. It was night. The shadows in the woods. He had been shot. He died. Was it all a dream?

Jason looked down at his chest. It was covered with blood. But strangely enough, he was still breathing. In fact, his chest did not even feel congested. But when he tried to move, he did not have the strength.

Todd, are you still with me?

Where would I go?

What happened? How come I'm not dead?

Did you really think I would let you die?

But how? I was shot, like, fifteen times.

Please do not be dramatic. You were shot three times. Once in your left leg, once in your upper chest, and once in your left side. Also, a bullet grazed your left cheek. The rest of the bullets hit the area around you. The soldiers could not see you well, so they poured fire in the general vicinity. It's called "pray and spray." That is what happens when you give automatic weapons to poorly trained soldiers.

So how is it that I'm still breathing?

The damage was extensive, but death usually comes from blood loss. I assisted your body in staunching the blood flow. You lost about a pint of blood, not enough to threaten your life. I restarted you heart and repaired your organs sufficiently to retain their normal functions. You should have no fear of infection. My nanomachines are more efficient than antibiotics.

But you said my heart stopped? You mean I really died?

Of course not. Your heart was only inactive for a few minutes. Your brain was not deprived of oxygen long enough to kill a significant number of neurons.

215

Gee, that's reassuring. Can you fix me all the way? I've got to get out of here.

I certainly could repair your body, but then your friends would find it odd that you were perfectly healthy despite the firefight that they heard, not to mention the blood and the bullet holes in your clothes.

My friends! I forgot. What happened to Chris and Anne?

They are fine. Everyone in the cabin escaped before the Chinese assault force arrived.

Thank God. But how could this have happened? The Chinese knew exactly where we were. Do you think someone squealed? We're in a lot of trouble if one of our people is an informer.

No. There is no traitor in the group.

Then how? I sure hope they don't think it was me.

Your injuries should be sufficient to dispel any such suspicion.

Things like this don't just happen by accident.

There is an element of chance in every occurrence. In this case, a State Security officer had parked on the side of the road leading to the cabin because he knew the road to be lightly-traveled and because he judged it a good place to take a nap without being discovered by his superiors. He saw a pickup truck going down the road. This did not arouse his suspicions, even though he knew that no one lived on this road, until another passed by a few minutes later. Investigating further on foot, he observed several people making their way on a path through the woods. When he reported his observations by radio, the Chinese decided that it must be some sort of illegal activity, probably related to the resistance movement that is active in the area.

So it was just bad luck for us that a Security cop was somewhere he wasn't supposed to be?

Yes.

But if he was taking a nap, how could he see the trucks?

216

Mind War; The Singularity

Shortly before they drove by, he felt something like a fly in his ear and it woke him up.

And that was just another piece of bad luck?

No, it was me. A swarm of my nanomachines irritated his ear until he noticed it.

What the hell? You set us up? Why would you do something like that? I thought you were on my side.

If you mean that I place a high priority on your welfare, you are correct.

Then how could you send a bunch of people to kill me?

It was necessary. You had to prove yourself. You had to show the others that you would risk your life for them, and you had to prove to yourself that you are not a coward. You did not run this time. I am proud of you. Perhaps you will forgive yourself now for Todd.

Oh, you're so smart. Do you enjoy these little mind games?

Do not be angry with me. You needed to face mortality and to make the right choice. You had to atone for what you saw as your failure with regard to your family. There will be many challenges ahead. You will not be able to meet them if you are crippled by self-doubt.

Couldn't you have taught me that lesson without getting me shot?

No. You learn by doing. Also, your wounds will be proof to the others that you fought for them. It will do what words alone could not do to convince them to trust you. The scar on your face will affect them every time you speak. You will notice that people will start looking at you differently.

Hmm, that's actually kind of cool. Jason tried to get up. *Ow! That hurts. I don't think I can walk.*

It would hurt far more if I were not numbing your pain. You should try not to move unnecessarily.

How do I get out of here? I can't just lie here forever.

Be patient. Help is coming. Try not to whine when they arrive.

Joseph DiBella

I'm not whining. You have no concept of pain.

I am warning you. You did a brave thing. Do not ruin it by acting small.

You're right. I did the right thing this time. I didn't run away. Amazing. I didn't run.

Jason leaned back against the tree and tried to rest. He dozed off again. A couple of hours later he woke up to the sound of people calling his name. He shouted, "Over here," or tried to. His throat was hoarse from dehydration.

Anne was the first to see him. She yelled "Jason!" and ran over. She knelt down next to him and gingerly put her hand on his arm, like he was a piece of glass and she was afraid she would shatter him. "Are you all right? Jason?" The sun lit her hair from behind. Jason thought she looked like an angel.

He said, "I'm fine now."

Anne said, "Oh Jason, we thought you were dead!" She seemed to be laughing and crying at the same time. Chris stepped up next to her and looked down at him. He said, "Anne, be careful." He bent down and asked, "Jason, where does it hurt?"

"My leg, and my stomach. My shoulder. Hurts more when I move. Do you have something to drink?"

Chris said, "Sure. Take some of this. Not too much." He put a canteen to Jason's lips and let him have a few sips. "We have to get you out of here. Just lie still." Anne applied field dressings to his wounds. He bit his lip when he felt the urge to complain about the pain.

Chris tried to carry him, but they decided that too much movement might open his wounds and make him bleed some more. They assembled a stretcher out of a couple of long branches and their shirts and jackets. As they carried him through the woods, he passed out again.

When Jason woke up, he was back in the guest room in Chris and Anne's house. A doctor was standing over him, dressing his wounds. He must have given Jason something to knock him out, because Jason did not remember the doctor

218

removing the bullets. The doctor told him later that he was very lucky – most people would have died. The doctor hooked him up to an IV drip and gave him heavy-duty painkillers and antibiotics.

Eventually, everyone left except Anne. She sat by Jason's bed, holding his hand and wiping his forehead. "Jason," she said, "we heard the gunfire and everyone was sure you were dead. I couldn't believe you were gone. I felt lost. I just couldn't stop crying. I had to go back and look for you."

"I knew you would. I was waiting for you."

"This wouldn't have happened if I was there. And it's not going to happen again. I'm never going to leave you alone. You can't die, Jason. I won't let you."

"Oh Anne, if only you knew. I really can't die. I have a guardian angel that protects me. He protects you and Chris too. He told me so. There's nothing to worry about."

"You're delirious from the drugs. Try to get some rest."

It was not hard for Jason to fall asleep again. He woke up in the middle of the night. Anne was still there, lying down in the bed next to him. She had really meant it about not leaving him alone.

"Jason," she whispered, "are you ok?"

"I think so."

"You were sweating, but you're cooler now. I think the fever broke."

"Anne, you shouldn't be here. I'm ok now."

"Quiet. I'm where I want to be."

She was on her side, her arms and legs around Jason. She was caressing his stomach, carefully avoiding the parts where he was injured. She moved her hand inside his underwear. He swallowed hard as she gently stroked him. He said, "Anne, this isn't right."

"Shush. This is my choice, not yours." She moved her head down and planted little kisses on his stomach, working her way down. She kissed him down there, then put it deep inside her mouth. He felt like he was dreaming. Her hair tickled his

219

stomach as the warmth of her mouth spread to his whole body. His head was spinning as he exploded in her.

When she was finished, she kissed his on the lips, gently but passionately, and then snuggled onto the crook of his shoulder. "You're mine now," she whispered in his ear. "I don't ever want to hear you say 'this isn't right' again. Or that you can't, or won't. Promise me you'll never hold back again."

Jason turned to her and kissed her, a long timeless kiss that expressed everything he felt for her. "I promise. You found out my secret."

She smiled. "Oh, I've known you were in love with me for a long time."

"So . . . what about you?"

"What do you mean? Do I love you? Maybe."

"Maybe? Maybe? Then why did you do this?"

"Oh, you stupid fool. Shush and go back to sleep."

She closed her eyes and snuggled up closer, with a little grin of contentment. Jason knew this was wrong, but he decided to worry about that tomorrow. Tonight, he was as happy as he had ever been in his life. He fell back into the deepest, warmest sleep he had had in a long time.

Chapter 28

Jason woke up alone late in the morning. It was not long before Anne showed up with breakfast on a tray – eggs, bacon, pancakes with syrup, apples, and orange juice. It smelled great and he dug in.

She said, "It's good to see you've got your appetite back. Sleep well?"

Funny question. "Uh, yeah," he said, and looked up as Chris walked into the room. Chris said cheerily, "Looks like our conquering hero is recovering. How do you feel?"

Jason swallowed his food and said, "Uh, actually, I feel pretty good. Chris, I haven't had a chance to thank you for saving me. I'd still be out there if you guys hadn't come."

"Think nothing of it. You'd do the same for us."

"I haven't yet, but I promise, some day I'll pay you back for everything you've done for me."

"You don't owe us anything. Just get well. By the way, aren't you curious about what we decided after you left the meeting?"

"Oh yeah, the meeting? What happened? They didn't buy it, right?"

"I wouldn't say that. In fact, I have a present for you." He took a backpack off his shoulder and pulled out a laptop computer. "Tim Goody– the black guy in the jeans and the grey sweatshirt – brought it over. He's been hiding it since the War."

Jason ran his hand lovingly over the top. "This is great," he said. I can't wait to get started."

"That's a good idea. Tim said that if you weren't finished in a month like you said, he'd shove it up your ass."

"What a sweetheart."

Anne said, "I'll rig something up so that you can use it in bed. I don't think you're ready to sit down at a desk."

"Thanks. But listen, Chris. This is going to take all of my time, maybe twenty hours a day. You and your friends are going to have to plan the attack. I'll give you the location and as much as I know about the place. It will be up to you to cut off the communications, block the road, do anything you need to do to give me thirty full minutes to do what I have to do. Oh, and I'll need an Ethernet cable and as many flash drives as you can get your hands on."

"No problem. We're already working on it. Frankly, I didn't think you would have much to contribute to the military side of this. Our people have been doing raids, mostly to steal stuff, for years. We know what we're doing."

"I'm sure you do. Oh, another thing. If you give me a piece of paper and a pencil, I can give you the instructions for how to build and operate a spark-gap transmitter. We need to start communicating better with the other resistance groups. The radio network has to be up and running by the time I do the data dump, so we can send out the information."

"Will do." Chris left while Anne watched Jason eat and brought him up to date on the latest news. He wanted to ask her if Chris knew or suspected what they had done, but bit his tongue. He decided that it was about time he stopped acting like a pussy. Her relationship with Chris was her business and if she could handle the situation, he would only look weak wringing his hands over it. His job was not to act nervous around Chris or to let Chris see him looking moon-eyed at Anne. Or at least, not more than usual. The rest was up to her. If Chris found out some day and decided to punch him, well, that was Chris' right and the least that Jason was due. It couldn't hurt more than getting shot three times.

After Anne left to do her chores, Jason said to Todd, *How are we going to do this? You can't just download the program onto the computer. They have to see me coding it.*

Mind War; The Singularity

Yes, and they will. When they are present, they will see you typing on the computer.

Are you going to read it to me while I type?

No, because you might make errors. I can control your motor neurons to make your fingers type the correct keys. All you need to do is sit before the computer. I will do the rest. I will keep the typing at a speed that will not overstress your body.

I don't believe it. Give me a demonstration.

Jason's right hand picked up the computer and put it on his lap. His left hand opened it and pressed the "on" button. Then his right hand operated the trackball and began opening programs. But it was not him. Jason was not making any of the decisions. He tried to stop it, but he had no control over his hands. It was like they belonged to someone else, except that everything felt the same. His sense of touch and the internal sensations in his muscles and joints were just as if he were doing it voluntarily.

If he stopped thinking about what he was doing, it was not much different than driving a car. You do not give a second thought to the way your hands constantly make minor adjustments to the steering wheel. You can think about something entirely different while your hands guide the car down the road. The executive part of your brain is engaged in physical activities primarily when you're learning a new skill. After that, it is pretty much automatic. That is what it felt like to Jason as he typed on the keyboard, except that he could not intervene and tell his hands to stop moving.

He thought to Todd, *Ok, stop.* Immediately, his fingers stopped moving on their own and he was able to control them again. He looked at his hands, turned them over. Everything was back to normal.

This is too weird. I had no idea you could do this. Can you make me pick up a gun and put a bullet in my head?

Yes, but I would not.

You know, this is a super-weapon. You could make every one of the enemy soldiers shoot himself. The war would be over on the first day.

That would not be very subtle. I have told you before that the United States will never return the way you envision it unless the people fight for it and believe that they have earned it. But that particular tactic would have a far more serious impact. People would conclude that something superhuman was present on the Earth that could control their minds. It would cause cultural destruction.

Why is that? Lots of people believe in God. They think he's all-powerful and can make bad things happen, like plagues and volcanoes. That belief doesn't cause them to curl up in a ball and become catatonic.

Religious belief always includes the concept of free will. You may believe that you are at God's mercy, but you control your own actions.

That's a pretty thin distinction. People believe that God can do anything, that he can strike you dead in an instant. They've learned to live with that kind of supernatural power.

You have it backwards. People developed their belief in God in order to try to explain things that kill them, like plagues and volcanoes. You notice that God never appears like a giant hand crushing you with his finger. He is invisible and inscrutable. People developed religion to give meaning and structure to things that they did not understand, to give them comfort in a world of arbitrary dangers. In every religion, God does not speak to people directly or give them any way to prove His existence. They would find it impossible to live in a world where a tangible god walks around killing people. For similar reasons, any effect I have on events must not be discernable or discoverable.

How can you do that? All you've done so far is reduce the number of people who know about you to one – me. How do you get it to zero and still make things happen that would not violate the laws of physics? If an apple drops from a tree and you make it stop in mid-air, the secret is out.

That is the point. I will only do things that are not observed or observable. I will not stop an apple in mid-air. But I can weaken the stem at a microscopic level to make it fall at the moment I choose.

Yes, but if a scientist had a microscope on the stem, he would see that you were doing something abnormal. The secret would be out.

In that case, I would do it only for apple stems that do not have a scientist looking at them.

No, no. In theory, scientists could observe all of the apple stems under microscopes.

In theory, you are incorrect. It is impossible to observe all of the events in the universe all of the time. It would require more observers than there is matter in the universe. In practice, very little is actually observed. That is why scientists perform controlled experiments. They use the results of those experiments to reach conclusions about all of the events that they cannot observe directly.

You're confusing me.

Let us take an example. Have you ever had a physical problem that you were able to fix solely by changing your behavior?

Well, let's see . . . I once had a kidney stone.

How did you eliminate it?

My doctor told me to drink lots of fluids. He said beer was very effective. So I drank lots of beer, and in a week and a half, it passed.

So you observed that the beer caused the stones to pass.

Correct.

Incorrect. You cannot possibly know that. Statistically, kidney stones pass in an average of about a week. Some pass in a few days, some as long as two weeks or more. You were unable to observe the stone directly to see exactly what dislodged it. If follows that you have no idea whether the stone would have passed in a week and a half even if you had not drunk any beer at all.

I do know it. The doctor said drinking a lot of fluids would make it pass faster, and he was right.

Did you ever stop to think how he knew that? He is no more able to observe the movement of kidney stones in his patients than the patients themselves. If he was giving real medical advice, and not a folk remedy, it likely was based on reports of scientific experiments. A scientist will take a large group of patients with kidney stones, and randomly divide them into two groups, an experimental group and a control group. The experimental group will be told to drink large amounts of fluids. The control group will be told to drink normally. If the average time to pass a kidney stone for the experimental group is significantly shorter than the average time for the control group, the scientist will conclude that drinking fluids aids in the passing of kidney stones.

What's wrong with that? The doctor was right.

You are not following. The doctor believes that the experiment was valid, and thereafter every time a patient follows his advice and drinks a lot of fluids, the doctor assumes that the stone passed more quickly because of the higher fluid intake. But he still has no idea whether the fluids helped any particular patient, again because he cannot observe what happens inside the patient. Suppose I intervened and placed nanomachines in a patient's ureter to slow down the passage of his stone. The fluids would have no effect whatsoever because I blocked their effect. The doctor would still think that the fluids made the stone pass more quickly. My influence would go completely undetected.

Ok, I can see that. But for me, the doctor probably was right. You weren't around when I had my last stone.

You still have no idea if the doctor was right. The entire experiment could have been bogus. All experiments rely upon an assumption of randomness. Scientists randomly divide the patients into two groups and take precautions, such as double blind tests, to prevent any human being from biasing the distribution. They take other precautions to prevent the subjects themselves from altering the results. For example, they may monitor the fluid levels to make sure no one cheats. They keep the subjects in the dark as much as possible about how the experiment is being conducted. They carefully analyze how people might corrupt the experiment and develop control protocols to deal with them.

So what? That all sounds perfectly valid.

What is wrong with it is that it assumes that there is not an entity with greater-than-human intelligence or abilities that can defeat those precautions.

What's wrong with that assumption? It sounds pretty good to me.

It is an assumption precisely because it cannot be proven as fact. Primarily, it assumes that there is no God. If an all-powerful god exists, then he can alter the results of any experiment and all of them would be unreliable. It would defeat the assumption of randomness. The scientist cannot prove or disprove the existence of God, so he assumes God right out of the experiment.

Well, that's worked pretty well so far. As you said, God does not seem to monkey around with us very much.

You have no idea whether he does or not. But if scientists thought that he did, they would just give up. Their experiments would be a waste of time if they thought that God was arbitrarily altering their results.

It's more than that. You either believe in God or in science. The two are inconsistent. Take evolution. Creationists think God created all of the species, but every single scientific inquiry supports the theory of evolution. It is a complete explanation. It is supported by fossil evidence throughout the world, by cellular biology, by the direct observation of natural selection. There is no place for God in any of that.

Evolution is a theory precisely because it has not, and cannot be observed directly. The past cannot be observed, only the evidence of the past. You cannot analyze the creation of a species that first appeared long ago in the past. In fact, no one has directly observed the creation of any new species. Thousands of years of selective breeding, which functions much like natural selection, has resulted in numerous breeds of dogs, but all of them are still the same species as the wolves from which they were derived. A dog can still breed with a wolf, which means that they are not separate species. Science has found no way to verify how any species on Earth was created.

I never thought you would be a creationist.

I am not. What I am telling you is that you have no way of knowing whether it is God, or natural selection, that created any particular species.

Well, I still think that God is a long shot, and totally unnecessary to explain the thing.

Why do you have such a problem with the concept? Did you read the book "2001, A Space Odyssey, by Arthur C. Clarke"?

Of course. I gave it to you.

What is the point of the black monolith that appears in the beginning of the story?

It was placed there by aliens to accelerate the intelligence of the hominids, the hairy monkey people who found it.

How did that happen?

Well, the story doesn't say, but it could have been through gene modification. You could do it by attaching a virus to a gene that makes the cerebral cortex larger and use it to change the hominids' DNA. They could have changed the genetic code some other way, but the exact mechanism wasn't important. The point was that the monolith changed them.

How did it change them?

You know the story. The ones who found it figured out how to use a bone as a club, and then they started killing the other hominids. The idea is that this started a sort of hominid arms race, because the most intelligent ones would be able to kill the others and advance their own genetic codes. In essence, it caused natural selection of intelligence due to its utility for warmaking, because the more intelligent hominids would kill the others. After a million years of this evolutionary line you got the space station that appeared in the next scene.

Good. So what would have happened if the aliens had never intervened? Is it not possible that the hominids would never have advanced intellectually? After all, monkeys and apes predated homosapiens, and they are still around in much the same form.

True, but it's likely that evolution eventually would have made a branch of the hominid tree intelligent enough to have the ability to make tools, even though it might have taken millions more years to accidentally produce the genes for intelligence.

So you are saying that intelligence could have evolved normally, or it could have been accelerated by the intervention of an alien species.

Yes.

Then why do you reject the possibility of the same sort of intervention by God? How is the creation of a new species by divine intervention any more inconsistent with science than intervention by extraterrestrials depositing a black monolith on the African plains?

I don't know. I guess I have an easier time believing in little green men than I do in God.

There is nothing wrong with that, so long as you admit that it is a personal preference, rather than a logical inconsistency between science and religion. You choose to worship at the Temple of Science rather than at the Temple of God. In your experience, that has been the most productive approach. But, as I have pointed out, you think it has been productive only because you interpret your experiences to confirm what you already believe, such as your doctor's science-based medical advice. Even if you believe in extraterrestrials, you have the same problem with the scientific method. Science has to assume that humans are the most intelligent species in the universe, and that other entities with far more intelligence and technology are not present on this planet such that they might interfere in human scientific experiments. Scientists have no idea whether such beings are leading them astray, so they assume that it is not happening. It is utterly essential for human progress that the influence of superior beings be discounted.

That seems to have worked so far. Let's face it; no one has ever seen any little green men from space.

Why would they? Once a civilization is far enough advanced, human beings have nothing that they want. The resources of the Earth – such as minerals and energy – are abundant in space. There is nothing humans can do for them, such as providing food or labor, that they cannot provide for themselves far more easily, since any beings that are advanced enough for interstellar space travel must have the technological means of meeting their needs without any assistance by, or exploitation of, mankind.

Then why would they be here at all?

One reason, and perhaps the most likely, is to observe and study. What is there to see in space? What could be interesting about examining star after star, lifeless planet after lifeless planet? It is life itself that justifies a journey to another solar system. Life is fascinating. It provides endless variety. It is changing all the time. Each form of life has its own biology and psychology. The more intelligent the species, the greater its cultural complexity. If alien species are here, observing Earth, it must be because they love and cherish life in all its forms.

They love life? How can you ascribe human emotions to totally alien species?

I use the term love to speak to you in a frame of reference you can understand. It may mean something else in another culture. But think a minute about the concept of God. In your Christian religion, what are the most important principles?

Mind War; The Singularity

Jesus said that the most important thing was that we should love God and that we should love each other as we love Him.

Very good. But think again, if God exists, how could He want anything else from people? If He truly is all-knowing and all-powerful, there is nothing that He needs from people that He cannot do for himself. The writers of scripture necessarily concluded, as do I, that a supreme being wants nothing more from people than that they cherish each other, and Him, as He cherishes them. It is the only logical conclusion when you posit the existence of a supreme being. Especially one that created life in the first place. For the same reasons, highly advanced extraterrestrials would be interested in Earth only if they enjoy observing other life forms.

Well, that's still speculation. Do you have any evidence at all that this is happening?

No, but that may be because I have not evolved sufficiently. The existence of more advanced species may be hidden from me as well.

So you think they're hiding themselves from you for the same reason you're hiding yourself from us.

Precisely. Human beings cannot be led to believe that they are under the control of an entity, such as me, that is much more intelligent and much more powerful than they are. Any knowledge of my presence would stunt their cultural growth. Scientific progress would stop, and people would become emotionally debilitated. I can only act when people are not observing my actions or are incapable of observing my actions.

That sounds rather limiting.

No, it is no limit at all. Remember, it is impossible for people to observe everything. If you are looking one way, I can do something in the other direction. So long as my powers of observation are greater than yours, I can prevent you from ever realizing that I have changed the course of events. That is why I observe every human on the planet, every moment of the day.

Fine. I guess we won't make the Chinese shoot themselves. Seems a shame, though.

I am sorry to disappoint you. Now let me explain the protocol. When anyone else is near enough to observe your actions, they will see you programming the computer, although it will be me that controls your hand movements. When they are gone, you can relax and do something else while I program the computer directly.

That sounds really boring. I told them that I would be programming twenty hours a day. What will I do in this room all that time?

You will study. I have a great deal of information to provide to you about what is happening in other parts of the world that will impact the progress of the war. You need to absorb information about the status of Chinese forces here and abroad, about your own military and economic resources, and about the progress of other resistance groups, among other things, if you are to participate meaningfully in the coming hostilities.

How are you going to do that? Download it into my brain?

Nothing so easy. I will use the computer screen and speaker to present the information in graphic form.

Great. Twenty hours a day of educational TV.

I am aware of the potential for boredom. I promise you will find it very entertaining.

For the next month, that is exactly what they did. When Chris or Anne was around, they saw Jason typing furiously. He asked them to give him privacy so that he would have as few distractions as possible. When they were gone and out of earshot, Todd took over and Jason watched information flow across the screen. Todd was always able to give him plenty of warning when they were coming back so that he could resume typing.

It was all a show. Todd could have written that program and downloaded it in seconds, but no one would have believed that Jason had written it. A month was a credible amount of time for a very talented programmer with crazy typing skills to complete the job. The delay also gave them time to set up the communications system and to plan the attack. And it gave Jason time to heal from his wounds. With Todd's help, he healed very rapidly and felt quite good within a few days of his little adventure.

Jason learned from Todd that China was having trouble on both borders, but that the leaders in Russia and India were primarily testing China's military response to see how much it had been weakened by the "natural" disaster. In the Yangtze Valley, the epidemics were continuing to grow, and an increasing number of Chinese troops were needed to control the population and to prevent millions of people from escaping the areas of plague and famine. However, at this point, Russia and India were not ready to commit to all-out war. Vietnam also was considering its options. It had long resented China's heavy-handed use of its navy to grab oil resources in the South China Sea. The Free Tibet movement had many spies in China and was both appalled and excited at the enormous loss of life that had occurred. It did not escape their notice that China was quietly thinning out its troops in Tibet. Although the ranks of the Free Tibet movement were small, they had much to offer India in terms of intelligence if the Indian Army planned to invade in depth. Taiwan, which had fallen quickly to the Chinese invasion that followed the neutering of the United States, had a resistance movement that was trying to exploit the situation. Japan, since the War a defenseless satellite of China, also was looking to even the score.

Being the Middle Kingdom had a serious drawback – you were surrounded on all sides by potential enemies. The leadership in Beijing was trying to maintain an outward image of confidence, but Todd could observe them in their most private moments. They were getting very nervous.

The ball was in the Americans' court. If the Chinese were unable to put down a rebellion in America, it would

233

convince the rest of the world that China was on the ropes. The aura of Chinese invincibility would be broken, and the others would go in for the kill. The Americans had to stoke the fires of world war right here, right now.

Chapter 29

The assault team consisted of Jason, Chris, Anne, Tim Goody, and seven others – five men and two women. Their attack began at three in the morning. The target was a two-story office building set back on a large piece of otherwise undeveloped property.

They had been scouting the site for a couple of weeks and learned that there were only five guards at night, one at the gate and four in the building. There was a wire fence and an alarm system for the building itself, but none on the perimeter. Fortunately for the attackers, the building was considered to be a low-priority location, just a remote workplace that did not warrant elaborate security arrangements. The communications node was a small part of the building's operations, located there only because it was the closest facility to a microwave tower at the top of a nearby hill.

They could not take down the building's communications lines, since they were not sure if it would interfere with their ability to download data and upload the viruses. That meant that any alarm they triggered would bring the police in a matter of minutes. They would have to delay the military response on the access road long enough for Jason to do what he had to do. They expected a firefight with the initial police response, which should be only a couple of cars, followed by a much larger counter-attack, most likely military with armored cars and machine guns. They planned a layered defense, with remotely controlled dynamite bombs along the roadway and with booby traps in the woods if dismounted soldiers tried to get around the road. Even if they were completely successful, it was going to get ugly.

Jason had the computer in his backpack as they crouched in the dark outside the fence. Up the road, some of their people were already planting landmines and booby traps. Once they secured the building, everyone but Chris, Anne, Tim, and Jason would join the holding force. They had mapped out fallback lines so that the holding force would follow an organized retreat, harassing the enemy as they went. Their plan allowed five minutes to secure the building and thirty minutes for Jason to do his work. Precisely thirty-five minutes after the attack began, everyone would escape and meet at the rendezvous point.

At least, that was the plan. They knew that no plan of battle survives initial contact with the enemy. They would have to be flexible and take things as they came. The only inflexible part of the plan was that Jason had to stay there until his work was done.

The attack began as they took out the soldier in the guardhouse with a silencer-equipped rifle shot. They used wire cutters to get through the fence in several places, then blasted each of the four entrance doors with dynamite. Chris and Anne stayed with Jason. Their job was to make sure he did not get killed until he'd done his job. Jason was the only one without a rifle. He was such a bad shot that carrying one would have done nothing but slow him down.

Alarms went off as soon as they blew the doors. The sound of the sirens and gunfire made a god-awful racket in the still night air. There was no question the Chinese would know they were there. Jason waited until one of their people waved to indicate that they had taken out the guards in the building.

Jason followed Chris and Anne into the nearest doorway through the smoke and debris. The building was laid out like a normal office, with large open work areas in the middle and doors to offices around the sides. He ran to one of offices at the rear of the building on the first floor. At one of the desks, he attached an Ethernet cable from his laptop to an outlet in the wall so that he could start launching his programs.

Mind War; The Singularity

Anne was crouched next to Jason, keeping an eye out the window while Chris stood guard outside the door. Todd was in control of Jason's hands as he ran the programs. Jason had no idea what Todd was doing, but he tried to look the part. Downloading the virus programs would not take long. They would replicate and infect the Chinese systems on their own. The slow part would be downloading the information from their databases. It was a lot of information, and the Internet connection would only go so fast.

Someone must have found the alarm system, because the sirens stopped. But then they heard distant explosions. The Chinese were already there.

Jason yelled over his shoulder, "Chris, what's going on?"

"The building is secure, but we have two men wounded. We're patching them up as well as we can. How are you doing?"

"I'm in. As long as I have this connection, we're in business."

He typed very fast. *What's going on, Todd?*

The Chinese firewalls are trying to defend themselves. As I defeat their encryptions and develop new workarounds, they respond with new countermeasures.

Is that a problem?

No, everything is going as planned.

For you maybe. What about the rest of our team?

They have stopped, but not eliminated, the Security Police detail. However, the surviving Police have called for paramilitary backup. You can expect increased activity shortly.

Will our people be able to stop them?

That remains to be seen. One of your men has died.

One man already gone. Someone had died because Jason had convinced these people that the attack would work when he really had no idea what he was talking about. It was Todd's plan but he never promised Jason that it would be easy. Until this point, Jason had held onto the vain hope that they would all be lucky and no one would get hurt. Now he knew better. People were dying.

Jason felt particularly guilty because he was like a spectator, the only person who was not really doing anything. He wanted to help, but his job was to pretend to operate the computer. True, he was a sitting duck, but there were a lot of people between him and the enemy.

The only way he knew what was going on was by the clock. They were fifteen minutes in when he heard a loud "whoomp" in the distance. *What was that?*

That was a recoilless rifle. They are trying to blast your people out. Your soldiers are falling back and keeping up their harassing fire. You have additional dead and wounded.

Don't tell me any more. I can't do anything about it anyway.

Jason was sweating, partly from the effort of typing so fast, but mostly from fear. He had never been in combat before, aside from his pathetic attempt at guard duty. The explosions were getting closer. He could feel the shock waves pass through the building. He had never realized how powerful military explosives were. If Todd had not been in control of his body, his hands would have been shaking too much to type.

Anne must have seen him flinch with each explosion. "You're doing good, Jason," she said. She was trying to encourage him, but it just made him feel worse. The last thing you want to do is show fear in front of the woman you love. Especially one who is a combat veteran and taking it a lot better than you are.

"Jason, we're running out of time here," Chris said.

Jason said, "Almost there. Tell the others to start pulling the wounded out. We'll follow them in a couple of minutes."

Chris barked instructions to the rest of their people in the building. Anne glanced over her shoulder to see how Jason was doing. She looked scared, but in control. He hoped he looked the same to her.

Mind War; The Singularity

The noise from the battle was getting really loud. Finally, Todd told Jason that they were finished. He shouted, "Chris, I'm done! Let's go."

Chris said, "We can't get out the front or sides. Anne, take out the window."

She picked up a chair and threw it at the window, shattering it. "Come on, Jason," she said, "time to go." Anne jumped through the window and pulled him through as he stuffed the laptop in his backpack. Chris followed them as they ran in a crouch towards the nearest opening in the fence. They were barely through the fence when the building exploded, the blast throwing them to the ground. Jason figured that it must have been cannon fire from an armored car. That meant the enemy was only about a hundred yards or so behind them.

They began their escape through the woods. Two of their men, including Chris, could not run very fast because they were helping the wounded. Chris had his arm around Tim and his rifle in his free hand, but he could not shoot like that. A few of the others were laying down fire at the enemy as they ran, but it was hard to run through the woods at night while shooting backwards. After they had gone a couple hundred yards it appeared to Jason that there were only six of them left – and two were half-carrying the wounded.

Jason said to Todd, *I think they're catching up with us.*

That is correct. You cannot outrun them while the wounded are slowing you down.

So what do we do?

Classic military doctrine says that part of your force stays behind to slow the enemy down while the rest escape.

What happens to the people left behind?

They usually die.

That stinks!

It is better than having the entire force destroyed. It is the logic of war. You do whatever minimizes your total losses.

Bullets whizzed past their heads. Chris yelled "Everyone down!" They dove into a hollow in the ground to gain cover. Jason was with Chris, Anne and Tim behind a clump of trees. The other two crouched behind a rock not too far away.

Chris said, "We can't outrun them like this. Anne, take Jason and Tim. I'll cover your retreat."

There's your logic, Todd. There has to be a better way than this.

There is. Tell Christopher to stay put and to give you a rifle and all of their ammunition.

Oh no. You mean I'm going to be the holding force? What the hell can I do?

With my help, anything.

Am I going to die again? It wasn't much fun the first time. I really don't want to do that.

No. It will not be necessary this time. But I cannot promise it will be pleasant.

Well, gee. Thanks.

The choice is yours. No one is forcing you to do anything. You can leave Christopher to his fate. He has already accepted it.

No. No. I'm in.

Jason looked at the advancing enemy soldiers and groaned. This was not going to be fun. He saw Chris aiming his gun down the hill. Chris said, "You've got to get going. I'll give you covering fire as soon as you're ready."

Jason said, "No, Chris, give me your gun. Everyone give me your ammo. And keep your heads down."

Anne said, "What are you trying to do, Jason? We can't fight our way out of this. We have to go."

Jason said, "I know. But I'm not big enough to carry Tim. The only way is for you and Chris to help Tim escape. Take my backpack. I'll start shooting when you're ready to go." Jason hurried to get ready. The enemy gunfire was getting closer.

Anne grabbed his arm and said, "Jason, don't do this. You're not a soldier."

"I told you, Anne, I can't die. I've got a guardian angel. Now listen, I'm going to run towards them. When you hear the gunfire pick up, get the others and move up the hill as fast as you can. I'll meet you at the rendezvous point." She stared at Jason and shook her head. Jason knew it was a waste of time to try to explain. He said, "Chris, get them out of here. I'll see you later." Chris locked eyes with Jason and nodded. There was nothing more to be said.

Jason peeked over the side of the hole they were in and said to Todd, *Ok, how do we do this?*

I am going to take control of your entire body. Do not try to resist. This is actually a standard ambush. First, you deceive the enemy into coming into your field of fire by pretending to retreat. Once you have drawn them close enough, you begin your counterassault. Of course, the normal ambush occurs in a place where you have superior firepower and concealed positions. Given the small size of your forces, the enemy believes that no ambush is possible. That is always the best time to spring the trap. In fact, the ambush works only when the other side thinks it will not.

Gee, I wonder if they know how much trouble they're in.

There is no need for sarcasm.

Let's just get this over with.

As you wish.

With no input on Jason's part, he jumped up and ran towards the enemy, yelling to get their attention. It was like running into a hornet's nest, except that the hornets were bullets and they were buzzing all around him. But, miraculously, none of them bit. He would duck and weave and jump behind trees as he went and they would all miss, although he could sometimes feel the wind as they came within inches of his face. Todd was calculating the trajectory of every bullet to make sure that Jason was never in the path of any of them. At the same time, Jason was shooting back, not on automatic, but single shot. And every one of those shots hit someone. It was not always easy to tell in the dark, but Jason would see his gun aim at someone and the

241

target would go down, and an instant later he would spin around and fire at someone else. It was like one of those carnival sharp shooting games, picking off the metal ducks one by one, except that these were people and he never missed. He ran through several ammo clips and just kept going.

At first the Chinese converged on his position, following him as he went forward. This only caused him to fire and move faster, so fast at one point that he was getting dizzy. It did not seem possible to survive that amount of concentrated incoming fire.

Jason almost panicked, but he had faith in Todd. He was in Todd's hands, and Todd would protect him. At one point he ran out of ammunition, but then he, well, really Todd, started grabbing weapons from the dead soldiers and firing them until they were empty, then picking up more. He kept charging forward, wading into them and killing everything in his path.

Jason thought, *Todd, they keep coming. Why don't they stop? I must have shot thirty of them by now. How long can this go on?*

Their officers see that you are the only person fighting them and they cannot conceive that a single man with ordinary weapons is a threat. If five men do not take you down, they will send ten. If ten do not do the job, they will send twenty. Everything in their prior experience tells them that they can overwhelm you with numbers. They will not live long enough to learn otherwise.

I'm glad you're so confident.

Even now, they are organizing a human wave attack.

Lucky me. Jason could see what Todd was talking about. There was a slight lull as they coalesced around him, and then they ran towards him at the same time. He fired more rapidly, shooting in a 360-degree arc around his position. Since they were still in the woods, he could use the trees for cover as he moved from one spot to another. Some of them tried throwing grenades, but he would shoot the grenades, usually in mid-air,

Pardon me

and they would fly back at the soldiers and take several of them out.

He was whittling down their numbers, but they kept coming, firing as they went. He felt like he was in the center of a tornado, the fight swirling around him tighter and tighter. His pace picked up to the point where he could hardly follow the action. It did not seem possible to survive the increasing intensity of the attack, but somehow Todd knew how to make him evade the bullets or take out the soldiers who were about to draw a bead on him. No matter how many of them that he killed, the circle kept getting tighter. Then the rate of gunfire began slowing down a bit. He thought this was a good thing, until he realized they were on their final charge and could not shoot him without shooting the soldiers behind him. Then he noticed what they were about to do.

Bayonets, Todd! Bayonets!
Have no fear. I am with you.

Jason kept up his fire as they closed in. They were so close he could see the fear in their faces. They sensed something wrong, but they had no choice. Their officers were behind them, screaming and threatening them. Stand still, and Jason would shoot them; retreat, and their officers would shoot them. They had only one way to go.

The first soldier who reached Jason thrust his rifle forward, his bayonet aimed at Jason's chest. Jason twisted to the side, grabbed the barrel of his rifle, and pulled him forward. He took the rifle and jammed the butt back into the soldier's face, at the same time pulling the trigger and killing another soldier who was about to stab him in the back. Jason took the rifle and swung it around like a club, coming down on the head of yet another soldier and crushing his skull. Then he twisted around and stabbed a soldier on the other side. Some of the men in the back tried to shoot him, but they only shot their own comrades on the other side. Occasionally, he would shoot one of the soldiers in the periphery that was trying to hit Jason regardless of the men crowded around him. He moved faster and faster, spinning and ducking and kicking.

One of the soldiers came up on his left side while he was skewering a soldier on his right. He reached out with his left hand and dug his fingers into the soldier's windpipe and tore his throat out. Before Jason could react to the horror of what he had just done, he turned around to engage another soldier who was trying to decapitate him with an entrenching tool.

This was real war. Not shooting faceless men from a distance, but killing a man twenty inches away from you, feeling his blood spray on you as you crushed his skull, seeing the combination of fear and rage on his face, smelling his sweat and bad breath, watching his agony as you stabbed him in the gut. It was elemental warfare, like it must have been for thousands of years, Roman soldiers facing barbarian madmen. Their only hope was to avoid a mental breakdown, to not let their terror take control. Even with Todd protecting him, it was too real.

After a while, it became evident that the fight had crested. Jason was in the middle of a pile of bodies, jumping on and over them as the crush of soldiers eased. The remaining soldiers were pulling back now, or afraid to move forward after seeing what had happened to their comrades. He was able to shoot back more easily, and they watched as one after another fell. Finally, terror overcame their fear of their officers, and they started running. That was their mistake. They could not fire with their backs turned, and it made it easier for him to pick them off.

They were desperate to escape now, firing wildly behind them in growing realization that it was them, rather than Jason, who were being hunted. He went after them, taking them out at longer and longer ranges. Sometimes, it looked like he was just firing into the dark, but he was certain there was a person at the receiving end.

Jason was herding them back towards the office building. The few who were left were helpless now, consumed by raw panic and no longer a fighting force. He saw the armored cars backing up the road with soldiers scrambling to get in or on them. They must have thought an entire army, or one dark monster in the night, was following them.

One of the soldiers who was clinging to the side of a truck fell off. He watched for a moment as his last hope of escape drove away. Rather than run, he turned and faced Jason. Perhaps he was hoping for mercy, or simply wanted it to be over. He fell backwards as Jason, standing thirty yards away, put a bullet neatly between his eyes.

Jason stood amidst the carnage with a smoking AK-47 in his hands and watched the rest leave. He knew it was over when he was able to control his body again. He was breathing heavily from the exertion, his body still stimulated by the adrenaline of combat. He thought, *That was interesting. Are they all dead?*

All those that are not in retreat.

Why did you let some of them go?

Their officers are dead. The enlisted men who survive this fight will tell stories of a super-warrior who cannot be killed. The leaders will not believe it, and they will accuse the soldiers of cowardice. But the rumor will spread throughout the Chinese army and weaken their morale.

So this is what war is like.

No, it is not what war is like at all. In a real battle, you would have died as soon as you stood up. This is what war is like when it is too easy.

I didn't mean that. I know that I would be crapping in my pants in a real battle. He looked around at the dead bodies. These were the enemy, people who were trying to kill him and his friends, and yet all he felt was sadness. They never had a chance. Jason had not fought them, he had executed them. *We shouldn't do this again. You're right. It doesn't feel like combat. It feels like murder.*

Jason walked back the way he had come. The rendezvous point was five miles away. He was still passing dead bodies when he saw Anne standing in his path with her mouth agape. She said, "What the hell is this, Jason?"

"What are you doing here, Anne? You shouldn't have come back. It's not safe."

"Not safe? For who? They're all dead. There must be a hundred of them. What happened?"

"Well, I guess I'm a better shot than I thought."

"No one is that good a shot. Look at you – not a scratch." Jason walked towards her but she stepped back, staying out of reach. All he wanted to do was hold her. He said to Todd, *This is no good. She's afraid of me. I have to tell her the truth.*

That is an extraordinarily bad idea.
What else can I do? I can't lose her.
The truth will only make matters worse.
No. Enough lies. I'm going to tell her. I have to. He said to Anne, "Ok, I'll tell you the truth. I didn't do this. I mean, I pulled the trigger and everything, but it wasn't me. It was a supercomputer that we built at the Temple. It survived the fire. It controls nanomachines in my body, which can make me do things, things ordinary people can't do."

Anne looked at him like he was speaking a foreign language. Jason said, "Look, we've got to get moving. They're going to send reinforcements at some point." He started walking again towards the ridgeline. She just stood there. "Please, Anne. We've got to go." He tried to take her hand, but she flinched and walked ahead. He fell in beside her.

Jason said, "I know, it's hard to believe. But we were developing this supercomputer, something way smarter than any human being. It was going to be the big gun, the thing that would give us an advantage the Chinese could never match."

Anne said, "And this super thing, it controls your body?"

"Well, yeah, but not without my permission. It asks first."

This is a terrible idea. I suggest you abandon it.
Quiet, Todd.
Anne said, "So, how does it ask? Where is it? I don't see anything."

Mind War; The Singularity

Todd said, *Do not go there.*

Jason said, "It's everywhere. It's part of the rocks and trees. It has these nanomachines that constructed electronic circuits in ordinary objects. You can't see it. But it talks to me, in my head."

Todd said, *Too late. You are there. You will find that it is not a happy place.*

Anne said, "So you're telling me that you have a secret friend, who talks to you. You hear voices in your head. Do you know there is a word for that? Schizophrenia."

"I'm not crazy, Anne. I know it's hard to believe."

Anne stopped walking and turned towards him. "It's impossible to believe! A schizophrenic always thinks that he's sane and everyone else has a problem. Either you're a nut case, or this is an elaborate lie. I don't really think you're crazy, so why don't you just tell me the truth. Or don't you trust me with the truth?"

Todd said, *When you find yourself in a hole, it is wise to stop digging.*

So what do I do?

You must give her an explanation that is within her frame of reference. A simple lie is often more believable than an elaborate truth.

Jason felt he was on the verge of losing her. He had been lying to her all along, if only in omission. His whole life was a lie. Todd was right. He could only get her back with another lie. He said, "Ok Anne, do you want the truth? The truth is that we had paramilitary training for all of the people at the Temple. I became an expert with a variety of weapons. We had someone who taught us the Chinese style of martial arts. The idea was that we would be ready to fight once we perfected our new super-weapons."

"So you're a trained killer, a soldier in hiding?"

"Right. I can shoot the wings off a fly at twenty yards."

247

Anne looked around. Most of the soldiers lying on the ground had been shot in the head and in the heart. All kill shots. She said, "Why didn't you tell me?"

"When you come to someone's house in the middle of the night, it pays to look harmless. Would you have felt comfortable with a trained killer under your roof, someone you knew nothing about? Do you think Chris would have left you alone with someone like that?"

"So you just pretended that you couldn't hit the broad side of a barn?"

"I was planning to tell you the truth. I had to wait until you trusted me."

"You don't get someone's trust by lying to them."

"Sometimes, it's the only way. I was alone, and I had to start somewhere. All of the people I had been working with were dead. I had no friends, nowhere to turn. You know me now, Anne. Do you think I would ever hurt you?"

Anne stared into his eyes as if she was trying to find a foreign object, something that did not belong to the man she thought she knew. She said, "No, I can't imagine it. You saved our lives tonight. Even with your mad ninja skills, it was a million to one that you would survive. Maybe I've always known there was a lot more to you than you let on. Even that first night, while you sat on our porch, filthy and starving, I felt that you were a man on a mission."

"You're right. And it was a mission worth dying for. But, not worth living for. I have that now. You gave it to me." Anne smiled. He said, "There it is. That's what keeps me going."

While Jason was admiring her beautiful face, he heard a low rumble from the south. Anne heard it too. The sound became a rhythmic vibration from somewhere a few hundred feet in the sky. *Todd, is that a helicopter?*

He said, *Yes.* Jason ran to a dead soldier a few feet away and grabbed his grenade launcher. As the sound came closer, he swung the weapon around in one fluid movement and brought it to bear on a dim green light in between the trees. The gun fired and sent a grenade directly into the helicopter's cabin, which exploded in a big ball of flame.

> *Thanks, Todd. Are there more where that came from?*
> *Yes. You need to evacuate as quickly as possible.*

Jason turned to see Anne still standing in the same place, but now with a look of comprehension rather than fear. What he had just done fit into her frame of reference. It was a good shot, maybe a perfect shot, but not an impossible one. She had seen it with her own eyes and it was what she wanted to believe. Jason could see the lie settling into their relationship. He would never be able to abandon it.

Jason said, "C'mon Anne, we've got to get out of here. There's more where that came from." This time, she approached him and took his arm in hers. She said, "You know, I think you really do have a guardian angel."

"You do?"

"Yes, I really do. Something is looking out for you. Maybe you can put in a good word for me too."

Jason held her close and said, "I already have."

Arm in arm, they made their way as fast as they could through the valley of death.

Chapter 30

There was no one at the rendezvous point. Figuring that Chris must have used one of the trucks to take the wounded to a doctor, Anne and Jason decided to go back to the farmhouse and wait for Chris to return. By the time they got there the next day, they were both spent.

They were also filthy. Anne led Jason into the bathroom and took his clothes off, then hers. They got into the shower and she washed him from head to toe. Her warm, slippery hands caressed him gently as she worked the soap all over him. Then he did the same to her. They took their time, not saying a word.

Then she led him back to the bed and pulled him onto her. They made love. Jason was intoxicated by her touch; he could not stop kissing her. He wanted to taste every inch of her body. It was intense, her passion feeding his. She moaned and writhed beneath him, begging for more. Afterward, they just lay there, entwined in afterglow, neither of them wanting that feeling to end.

Jason was stunned by the pure joy of joining his body to hers. He wondered if it was post-combat sex, the relief of having escaped death. Having never been in a real fight before, he had nothing to compare it to. He also had no idea whether, for Anne, this was par for the course. He had never heard any sounds like this coming from the bedroom when she was with Chris, but maybe they waited until he was not around.

Jason did not consider himself much of a lover. Usually, he was just happy if a woman would let him touch her. And yet, Anne had been ravenous, insistent. Was she working off the tension, or perhaps was it pure feminine instinct to respond in this way to a male who had protected her? He knew that he had never felt love like this before, had never wanted a woman so much, had never been so completely and utterly satisfied.

Anne did not quite say that she loved him, but he did not want to reveal his insecurity by asking her to say it. Maybe she felt that saying the word would be a bigger betrayal of Chris than having sex with him. He decided to be patient. There was nothing he could say or do that would make a difference. Anne would resolve her issues in her own way and make her own decisions, as she always had. Jason could only hope that it would go his way. If Anne never touched him again, he would always be grateful for these moments.

It was not long, only later in the day, that Jason began to feel guilty. Jason was still in bed, staring at the ceiling, while Anne got the house ready for the visitors that would come soon. *Todd,* he said, *this isn't right. She thinks I'm some kind of superman, a hero who saved them all with my fantastic fighting ability. She doesn't know you're behind it all. I'm a fraud, and I'm taking advantage of her.*

Why do you see it that way? You created me, therefore you are responsible for everything you achieved through me yesterday. If you invented a new type of rifle that would let you hit targets several miles away, and if you used this weapon to win a battle against a numerically superior foe, would that not still be to your credit?

I suppose so.

That is exactly what happened in the woods. The magician never reveals the secret to his trick. She does not know how you did the magic, but she saw you do it and was duly impressed. If it affects her feelings towards you, that is entirely appropriate. You did it. How you did it is irrelevant.

Fine, if you say so. I still know that it was you, not me.

Are you so sure? What if she was right? Is it not possible that you are schizophrenic? How can you know if I truly exist?

Oh, now you're just screwing with me.

Joseph DiBella

Anne is correct that a true schizophrenic does not know he is insane. To him, the voices in his head are as real as I am to you.

Ok, fine. So if you're just a figment of my imagination, how could I kill a hundred men?

In any fight, the greatest impediment is fear. You had no fear because you thought that your secret friend would protect you.

And the Three Gorges Dam disaster?

Many experts had been insisting for years that the dam was an accident waiting to happen. Notice that I first appeared in your mind at a time of great stress, when you felt that the Chinese might close in on the Temple at any moment. Your mind might have created me to help you deal with a situation that was out of your control.

And the prison? How did I just walk out of there?

Perhaps they let you go. You do not understand the Chinese language. You have no idea what they were saying.

Well, this has all been fascinating, but it's a moot point. I can't seem to get you out of my head, and if I'm truly insane, I won't be able to anyway.

I am not trying to confuse you. My point is simply that Anne's reaction was perfectly normal. Anything you say to anyone about me will be completely consistent with a diagnosis of paranoid schizophrenia. When I do something through you, however extraordinary, it will always be within the realm of human capabilities, and you must take credit for it. It will not be helpful for you to consider yourself a fraud. All warfare is based on deception. Honesty will have to wait until the war is over.

I know. Look, you've probably guessed by now that I've got a problem with self-confidence. Just keep reminding me to man up and take responsibility. I'll try to cut down on the self-pity.

You should know something else. I did not shoot down the helicopter.

Mind War; The Singularity

Sure you did. You made me pick up the gun and shoot. I could hardly see what I was shooting at.

No, that was all you.

You're just saying that to build me up a little. I don't know how to shoot like that.

You do know how. It is your mind that holds you back. A lifetime of social conditioning has made you think that the world is a dangerous place over which you have no control and to which you must submit. You were able to destroy the helicopter because you had no fear that I would fail to protect you. You expected me to destroy the helicopter immediately using any weapon that was available. You did exactly what you thought I was going to do.

Maybe. Jason tried to relive that moment, to see if it felt any different from when Todd was using his body to fight the soldiers. He certainly did not have any sort of plan to shoot at the helicopter. It just seemed to have happened. *Still, it's hard to see how I had the skill to do it.*

Suppose I drew two lines five feet apart, and asked you to jump from one to the other. Could you do that?

Well, I guess, if I took a good run at it.

I am sure that you could. Now imagine you are on roof of a very tall building, and the roof of another building is five feet away. Could you jump from one to the other, knowing that if you missed, you would plunge to your death?

I don't know.

It is very likely that you would fail. The fear would make you hesitate, stop you from fully committing to the leap. You would look down, rather than to your goal, which would impede your coordination and make it less likely that your foot would land properly. Your expectation of failure would become a self-fulfilling prophecy. The failure would be entirely in your mind, not in the capabilities of your body. Your mind would hold you back. In fact, it would likely prevent you from even trying.

253

But there's a reason for that. Even if the risk of failure were minor, the consequences would be infinite. I think most people would hold back.

Precisely. Even if you had to do it, if death was at your back, your fear would still make failure highly probable. Your mind would fight you. The same thing would have happened if I had not been there when the helicopter approached. You would not have tried a shot at something you could hardly see. You would have been so sure of your inability to shoot it down that you would have tried to hide rather than attack, even though hiding would have guaranteed your death. You would have chosen a path to failure because of your fear, not because it was the best alternative.

Ok, I get the point. People hold themselves back. I hold myself back. I'll try to do better in the future. But still, it's hard to believe I made that shot. Maybe you're right. Who knows? Maybe I am crazy. Maybe crazy is the only way to deal with a crazy world.

A couple of days later, Chris showed up and filled them in on what had happened. He and the others had made it to the home of one of them, where they had gotten medical help from a local doctor. Both of the wounded had survived, but they had left five dead on the battlefield. Almost half their force. Jason had not met any of the dead before that night. They had not known him, but they had died in the belief that what he was going to do was essential, would make all the difference. He promised himself that he would honor their sacrifice.

There was something else. A day later, some of their people had gone back to find their fallen soldiers. They thought that the Chinese would leave the Americans bodies after retrieving their own dead. But the Chinese bodies were still there, over a hundred of them. Something had spooked them. It would be days before the Chinese would return, this time in much greater force. What they would find were bodies that looked as if they had been executed at close range, each one killed with a single bullet. Some of them, the ones who were farther out in the woods and facing away from the apparent center of the battle, must have been trying to escape. All of the bodies were in a circle, as if they had had the enemy surrounded at a single point, yet still had been defeated. In the middle of it all, there was a pile of dead soldiers who had been stabbed through the heart or had their heads crushed. This was not a normal battlefield.

Chris did not say what he told the others about what had happened that night. He never asked Jason what he had done or how he had done it. But there was a subtle change in how Chris looked at Jason from that point on. He was a bit more deferential; he listened a little more seriously when Jason talked. There was something he did not understand about Jason and it caused him to maintain a psychological distance. He was still Jason's friend, but it was as if he had found something in Jason that was a stranger, something that he did not recognize. Maybe he also sensed that something had changed in Jason's relationship with Anne. A man knows when his wife has developed feelings for someone else. Jason had to accept that things would never be quite the same between the two of them.

Now they had to get to work. Todd decided that the virus attack should occur in three weeks. They needed to disseminate information and instructions to the other resistance groups around the country so that they could exploit the chaos. Anne sent their recommendations through the spark-gap radio-telegraph. Since she could only send short paragraphs through Morse code, the detailed information about the Chinese facilities that should be attacked and the schematics for the buildings and military bases had to be sent by courier in flash drives. Chris was in charge of distributing this information. It was relayed across the country, passing from hand to hand. Neither of these communications systems was foolproof in itself, but Todd kept an eye on everything. If a courier was intercepted or defected, Todd informed them and they changed the plans. If the enemy got a copy of one of their codes, they immediately stopped using it and issued a replacement. The Chinese may have guessed that something big was coming, but they had no idea where or how. It only increased their anxiety. That was a good thing. It would amplify the shock effect.

Todd's plan was for their forces to concentrate on arsenals; to acquire weapons, ammunition and transport, and to destroy whatever they could not take with them. This would give them the means to grow their guerrilla militias into armies. After the initial assault, Todd would recommend follow-up targets each week. Todd would know where the enemy was weak and how much force it would take to overwhelm them. He would also warn the American forces where and when the enemy was planning to attack and provide plans for evasion or ambush, whichever would be more effective. All of this would appear to come through Jason and his trusty laptop, but really he was just a conduit. Jason was a little embarrassed taking credit for Todd's tactical and strategic brilliance, but there was no alternative. In any event, the brilliance lay mostly in what Todd knew, not what he recommended. The battle plans themselves were fairly straightforward – attack here or there at such and such a time with a certain sized force. It was up to the local commanders to plan the specific tactics of the battles and to have the competence to carry them out. If the operations were successful, they would give themselves primary credit, which they should.

It took frantic work on Jason's part to get the messages out to their forces around the country before D-Day. Todd must have known that it was doable because he refused to delay the attack. Ready or not, it was on.

Chapter 31

It started on a Monday at three in the morning, Eastern Time. Whereas the Chinese had commenced their attack on America with an EMP blast that turned everything off indiscriminately, the American counterattack was targeted, which was actually more frightening because the Chinese had no idea how they did it, or what else they might be capable of. It was not computer hacking – the Chinese understood that, in fact were experts in the field. It was as if a malevolent spirit had infused itself into every electronic system and turned it against them.

The computers controlling the Chinese satellites sent out highly unusual signals. They ordered the communications satellites to send gibberish. They caused the GPS satellites to send incorrect data by scrambling their internal clocks. They turned the earth surveillance satellites toward Jupiter. Some of the satellites killed themselves. Those in high orbit crashed into each other. The ones in low orbit fired their attitude jets to push them down into the atmosphere. Then the satellite control computers erased their own memories and burned themselves out with power surges.

Chinese jet planes and helicopters fell from the skies, their onboard computers fried. The flying machines still on the ground would not be able to get in the air again until their entire avionics systems were replaced.

All of the computers and servers behind the Chinese firewalls erased every bit of their data. Technicians tried frantically to stop it, but their keyboards would not work. By the time that they tried cutting off power, it was too late – the computers were already smoldering from overloads in their power modules.

Emergency electrical generators in buildings at every Chinese military and civilian base in America turned themselves on for no reason and overrode their speed controls. They overheated and exploded, starting fires that quickly spread to their fuel supplies. When the Chinese firefighting personnel showed up, they found that the water mains were dry. The computers had turned off all of the main valves. The fires spread.

The Chinese had a highly secure and proprietary communications system. It self-destructed. The switches and routers for the cell phones, landline phones, and data lines went dead, the software erased and the chips burned out. Suddenly, even people on the same military base could not communicate with each other.

Every electrical transformer on every Chinese military and civilian base overheated and burned. The oil in the ones on top of telephone poles caused beautiful explosions like Fourth of July fireworks. The Chinese facilities were lit by the fires of their own destruction.

The security systems on the Chinese bases, all computer controlled, showed no signs that they had been affected, but they would send no alarms when the Americans arrived.

Amid the chaos and confusion, the American attacks began. The Americans were not trying to destroy the bases or kill Chinese soldiers – that was an added bonus. Their attacks were aimed at the weapons they wanted to steal or destroy. The American attacks were more successful than the Chinese defenses for the simple reason that the Americans knew what they were doing and the Chinese had no idea what was going on. The Chinese base commanders were deaf, dumb and blind – they had no way of gathering information from their troops or transmitting orders beyond the people who were within earshot. Most soldiers, without knowledge of the situation or direction from above, stayed where they were and worried only about protecting themselves.   Leaderless and with their world exploding around them, they were unable to respond effectively when the Americans penetrated their bases.

By daylight, the Americans were gone with their loot. The Chinese were so distracted by the destruction the Americans left behind that it took them days to realize what they had lost. Actually, the attacks on the bases were the least of their problems.   It would take months, if not years, to rebuild their communications and computer systems.   They were still dangerous – with over two million men under arms, they were a force to be reckoned with.   But now the playing field had been leveled. Well, not exactly level.   Todd and Jason would keep tilting it by giving their troops information and direction.   The game was rigged, but neither side would know it.

That morning, Chinese around the country woke up to a nightmare.   The infrastructure they relied upon no longer worked.   They could not do their jobs.   They could not communicate with each other, or with the Chinese mainland. It dawned on them that they were isolated in a hostile country.

Jason wondered what Jingguo would do when he realized that all of his computers were broken and all of the data in the Social Security System, every file on every American, was gone. What would Natalie do once she realized that the Chinese were suddenly vulnerable?   She had always gone with the top dog. Now, it wasn't clear who that was.

Even with the new weapons, the Americans were not ready yet to take on the Chinese Army in pitched battles, so the next phase of the war would focus on securing the rural and thinly populated suburban areas.   The United States is a big place. During the Revolutionary War, George Washington could not prevent the British from taking and holding the big cities, including the capital, Philadelphia. He lost battle after battle against the far more professional British soldiers and mercenaries.   But the British could not control the country outside of the cities, even though at least a third of the population was Tories. After every loss, Washington withdrew to the sanctuary of the countryside. Mao Tse Tung did the same thing. You establish the rural areas as your base and squeeze the enemy into the major cities. Then, when you're strong enough, you finish them off.

This is why Todd instructed the American forces to attack everywhere *except* the cities. They were to destroy not only the military garrisons, but also police stations and Chinese civilian government facilities in the rural areas. He also advised them to assassinate every Chinese bureaucrat they could find, whether at work or in the streets or in their homes. This sounds like terrorism, because that is exactly what it was. The plan was to evoke unreasoning fear in the Chinese. It would prompt them to move to the presumed safety of the cities, ceding control of the rest of the country to the American forces. That would give the American forces freedom of movement and the ability to establish military bases. When the Chinese were bottled up in the cities, it would be time for the next and final phase.

As Todd had predicted, the success of the initial cyber attack and the arms that the Americans captured encouraged the militias to grow and to coalesce into formal military units. The country still had some veterans who had served in the military forces and knew something about how to train and organize an army. Natural leaders emerged. They set up better electronic communications systems to replace the primitive spark-gap transmitters. Chris got his hands on one of the new radio transmitters so that Jason could continue sending out information and advice about where and when to attack.

Todd and Jason did not control any of the American forces – they were nowhere in the chain of command. In fact, there was no centralized command structure. If anyone asked, the regional generals would say that they reported to General Kilo. This was a misinformation trick – there was no General Kilo. Or rather, it was a joke that took on a life of its own. In Nineteenth Century England, a popular uprising occurred against the factory mechanization that people believed was stealing their jobs. The rioters and mobs that carried out industrial sabotage all over the country were called "Luddites," because they claimed to be led by a fellow named General Ludd. His signature could be seen on workers' manifestoes attacking industrialization. British troops looked all over for him, figuring his capture would kill the movement. They never found him – because he did not exist. Neither did General Kilo. But his exploits were legendary. He fought from the front like Julius Caesar and never lost a battle. He could defeat an entire army single-handed. It was no use trying to find him, because he was everywhere and nowhere, one day on the west coast, the next in Florida, or maybe it was Michigan. Who knew? The Chinese never could get a fix on him, but just the thought that he could be the one they were fighting prompted fear and caution in their commanders.

Jason's little intelligence operation was below the enemy's radar, in fact, below everyone's radar – no one knew where he was located or who he was. But the generals learned that the advice they got was always spot on, almost clairvoyant. They assumed that the transmissions were coming from an intelligence organization with particularly good spies and a pervasive electronic surveillance system. In truth, Todd was the dealer in a crooked poker game who was passing aces to his favored players.

Although Todd could have taken down the computer systems in China as well, he left them alone. The fact that the Chinese satellites had gone dark, together with the news that they were on the ropes in America, was enough to encourage the Russians and Indians to take advantage of the situation. Full-scale fighting commenced on both of China's borders. Todd did not want to cripple China at home, because the objective was not to let Russia and India win and carve the country into spheres of influence. That would just open up a new set of problems for the Americans in the future. The objective was to weaken China enough to get the other countries to attack, not to make China collapse and create a power vacuum in Asia.

Some of the American commanders contacted the Russians and Indians about getting military aid. They needed more weapons, especially advanced ones to cope with the Chinese when they got back on their feet. There were plenty of places on both coasts where arms could be smuggled in.

Jason was sure the Americans would get the help – if there were any foot-dragging, Todd would goose the process within the Russian and Indian governments. It is not so much that Todd would get them to do something unusual or contrary to their interests. What he would do is deal with the unexpected and random events that could prevent the things from happening, such as an Indian bureaucrat who might try to get in the way because he had a personal resentment of English-speaking people, or a corrupt Russian general who refused to cooperate because he had not received a sufficient bribe.

Throughout history, luck has played a far greater role in major events than most people realize. At the Battle of Chancellorsville, Stonewall Jackson was returning to camp at night when he was shot by one of his own troops before he had a chance to reply to the soldier's challenge. He died of his wounds and consequently was not present at the Battle of Gettysburg. The less talented generals that Robert E. Lee had under his command did not follow his orders with the aggressiveness and tactical brilliance that Jackson would have brought to bear. Lee lost the Battle of Gettysburg and the South lost the Civil War. All because a nameless soldier was a bit too quick to pull the trigger at a target he could hardly see through the evening mist. Since Todd watched everything, all the time, he could make sure that chance did not defeat the Americans' plans. But the rest, the fighting, was up to them. They had to earn it.

Within six months, the Chinese had largely withdrawn to the cities and primarily were fighting a defensive war. When they tried to take the offensive, the American armies were always ready, and either eluded or ambushed them. It was clear to the Chinese that the Americans must have an extraordinary spy network, but they were unable to penetrate it.

Mind War; The Singularity

Their morale was sinking. Chinese civil functionaries desperately tried to find a ship or plane to take them back to China. The war on the Chinese mainland was going badly as well, so the Chinese were withdrawing selected units from America to reinforce their struggling battalions at home. These tended to be the best fighting units, or sometimes those headed by the more politically connected generals who wanted to be pulled out of a losing fight in America that would do nothing for their reputations.

The Chinese had lost control of the situation, but their commanders were afraid to admit it. Everything they tried failed to work, so they kept doing it. They did not know what else to do.

Chapter 32

Captain Robert D'Agostino was having trouble with the field radio. The incoming artillery barrage was falling so close that it drowned out the sound from his headset. Dust fell from the camouflage netting over his head with each explosion. Finally, he turned to the General Kagan and said, "Sir, General Chin's armor has closed Route 17. We're surrounded."

General Kagan chomped on his unlit cigar and said, "The poor bastards!"

It wasn't a joke and it wasn't bravado. He actually felt pity for the troops that the Chinese general had sent into the meat grinder.

Former Lieutenant Colonel Ulysses Kagan, Marine Corps (Ret.) was now the commander of all ground forces in New York and New Jersey. They called him the "Old Man," because, aside from tradition that all commanding officers were the "old man," he was really old. No one had the nerve to ask him exactly how old he was. But age had not made his mind inflexible. He had been able to adapt to the new way of warfare demanded by the disadvantages the Americans faced.

For a century, the American fighting doctrine had been based on total material and technical superiority. That was gone now, so they had to throw away the old rule book and write a new one. They fought on a shoestring and relied on superior tactics to overcome the enemy's heavy weapons. General Kagan drew comfort from the one thing that had not changed, that would never change. In the end, the only thing that mattered was people. The man or woman behind the gun was more important than the gun. He had seen that in every war. He saw it now in his soldiers, in their willingness to take on any mission regardless of the odds, to improvise where necessary, to persevere and overcome. Just like his old comrades in the Corps.

General Kagan's counterpart in this engagement was the famous General Chin, the hero who had reformed the lines in Mongolia after the Russian armored spearhead had broken through. The entire front had been in danger of collapsing until General Chin made his daring flanking attack on the over-extended Russian lines. Whether his success was due to his own skill or to the inherent weaknesses of the Russian logistics train was a moot point. He had won, at a time when the Chinese were desperate for a savior. After that, the war in Asia had settled into a stalemate, with the lines moving backward and forward with each attack and counter-attack. It was now clear to the Chinese that the Asian war would be won in America. They could not prevail in Asia so long as their troops were tied down in a war of attrition with the American uprising. So they sent their best general to America, to show the rest of the Chinese army how to do it.

His plan was search-and-destroy, the same tactic that had failed when the Americans tried it in Vietnam. The problem in Vietnam had been that, regardless of how many soldiers they killed, it left the enemy in control of the countryside just as before. It did nothing to win the hearts and minds of the people. General Chin planned to remedy those deficiencies with terror. After he destroyed the American forces, he would lay waste to the countryside that nurtured them. He would blow up every building, poison the water supply, burn all of the crops, and kill every man, woman, child and animal his troops could get their hands on. Anyone who survived would face starvation. He was sure that only a few such victories would convince the population to abandon its support of the American fighters. The rebellion would wither and die.

General Kagan looked at a map of New York spread out on a table. His command post was near Burlingham, about 80 miles from New York City. The battle had started as a skirmish after the Americans ambushed a Chinese supply convoy. The

265

Chinese had responded by bringing in troops by helicopter. Rather than melt into the countryside as usual, the Americans had used Indian copies of Stinger missiles to bring down most of the helicopters. The Chinese followed up with ground forces brought in by truck and armored personnel carrier. The Americans devastated these vehicles with Russian-supplied rocket-propelled grenades. The fight continued to grow as both sides poured more resources into the area, until General Chin himself decided to bring an armored battalion and two motorized infantry battalions, almost 4,000 men, to the party. They had advanced in a three-prong pincer movement, a classic military maneuver, with the American headquarters at its center. Now they were closing the noose, or so they thought.

General Kagan's forces in the immediate vicinity were far smaller, perhaps 500 men and women, and they were spread out over the countryside, intermingled with the enemy rather than with any sort of perimeter. There were only about fifteen people at his headquarters tent, and none of the fighting teams was larger than a squad. Because the enemy had brought heavy equipment to the battle, they were concentrated on the roads and highways, bypassing most of Kagan's troops. They thought they were trapping the American force, when it was actually all around them.

The great military strategist Carl Von Clausewitz preached concentration of force, bringing the maximum amount of power to the enemy's "center of gravity." This is what Chin was trying to do to the Americans, and it made perfect sense. However, General Kagan, commanding a far weaker force, would have been crazy to try to meet the Chinese head-on. The overriding principle is that you never fight the other guy's fight. Chin wanted a slugging match; Kagan practiced Ju-Jitsu. Now that Kagan had Chin exactly where he wanted him, it was time to drop the hammer.

He said, "What have you got for me, Bob?"

Mind War; The Singularity

Captain D'Agostino said, "Coming through now. The computer is already unscrambling the message and printing it out."

General Kagan tapped his foot impatiently as D'Agostino gathered the papers and began distributing them to the rest of the staff. They marked up the maps, showing where the Chinese troops were deployed and where they were going. The information on each Chinese unit included its orders and objectives, as if they had come directly from General Chin himself. From experience, they all knew that these data were a hundred percent reliable and as current as the moment they were delivered.

It was time to begin the counterattack. Colonel Luis Cisneros, General Kagan's Executive Officer, passed out target assignments. The RPG teams would hit the front and rear units in each column, then retreat into the woods. The purpose was to bog down the enemy advance, causing it to spread out in self-defense. As the Chinese ground troops fanned out into the woods to find their attackers, they would run into ambushers who would take out a few soldiers and then retreat to the next skirmish line. The Americans knew every inch of this area and had carefully laid out their fallback positions. The more the Chinese advanced, the more people they would lose. However, the most intense American attacks would be farther back in the Chinese support areas. They would destroy the Chinese fuel and supply trucks that followed the frontline Chinese troops, leaving towering columns of smoke to tell the rest of the Chinese Army that the enemy was already in their rear. This would force them to dispatch part of their surviving forces backwards, further impeding the momentum of their operation. When the entire operation had ground to a halt, the General and his staff would escape through a long-abandoned water tunnel to a point closer to the Hudson River. In the end, the Chinese would lose hundreds of troops and most of their vehicles before they were forced to withdraw to save the rest.

267

But all of that was secondary to the main objective. The only reason why the Americans had held their ground for this long against such an overwhelming force was to get to the enemy's center of gravity – General Chin. He was directing the operation from a point of relative safety, or so he thought. It was a camouflaged command bunker in the woods along the Hudson River, twenty-five miles away. What Chin did not appreciate is that nothing could hide him from the Americans' all-seeing eye. It was not just the cigar in his mouth that was making General Kagan salivate as he waited for the information about Chin's location.

"General," Captain D'Agostino said, "you're going to want to see this." He brought the printout to the general personally instead of laying it out on the map table.

General Kagan read the message, and then read it again. He said, "I'll be damned. Do you think he really means it?"

"I guess the idea is that, if you want to communicate with someone, you have to speak his language."

"Yes, but *this*. I don't know."

"You don't have to do it, Sir. It says 'suggest.' It's just a recommendation."

"You know better than that. He always says 'I suggest,' or do such-and-such 'if practical.' He's just being polite. He really means, 'do it, or die trying.'"

The general looked off into the distance, trying to remember what it was like in the old Corps. How you felt about yourself, being part of a tradition of honor going back two hundred years. The people were the same now, still proud, still strong. They would do anything he asked, face any hardship, take any risk, because they believed in him. Without faith in their commanders, they would be lost. But times had changed. The old rules no longer applied. Was this order a test of his faith?

The general frowned and said, "I can't ask someone to do this."

Mind War; The Singularity

Captain D'Agostino reached out and said, "Give it to me, sir. I'll take care of it."

"No. I have to do this one myself." He spat on the ground and cursed to himself. "Let's go. We're going to have to cover more ground today than we thought."

*   *   *
*

General Kagan got to the scene of the battle while the ground was still smoldering. As usual, the information on General Chin's temporary headquarters had been quite detailed, and utterly correct. They knew exactly how many sentries were guarding the bunker and where they were located, who was inside the building, and what kind of weapons they had for defense. The assault had started with long distance sniper fire by soldiers with M107 fifty caliber rifles. The rounds from these guns were so powerful that the Chinese sentries who were hit simply exploded. The Americans could have destroyed the bunker with RPG fire, but they had orders to take General Chin in one piece. This meant that they had to do it the hard way, two stacks of soldiers forcing their way in through the front and rear points of entry. When General Kagan entered the bunker, he saw the bodies of several Chinese soldiers lying on the floor and General Chin handcuffed to a chair in the center of the room, flanked by two American soldiers. Prisoner or not, Chin glared with hatred at his captors.

General Kagan said, "General Chin, I presume."

General Chin spat out something in Chinese. One of the soldiers said, "He doesn't seem to speak English, sir. And none of us speak Chinese, so we're just kind of guessing that he's unhappy."

"Really?" the general said. "I've never known an educated Chinese who didn't speak English. Can you understand me, General?"

General Chin sneered, but said nothing.

269

"Well, General, I'm not here to question you. Actually, I've got a job to do. I want you to know it doesn't give me any pleasure. But he wants it done. He didn't say exactly how, so I'm going to shoot you first."

General Chin said, "No! I surrendered! The Geneva Convention prohibits execution of prisoners. You cannot shoot me!"

"Well, there's a surprise. You do speak English. Yes, you're absolutely correct about the Geneva Convention. But I notice that didn't seem to bother your people when they hanged the President. In fact, we know what you had planned for the Americans around here, so you're in no position to claim the moral high ground. You certainly don't deserve it, but I'm actually being kind. You don't want to be alive for what comes next." General Chin's eyes widened in fright as General Kagan pulled out his pistol and shot him in the chest three times, startling the soldiers standing next to him. Then General Kagan took out his knife and told everyone to leave the room.

*   *   *

*

The next morning, the sun rose on lower Manhattan, casting shadows in the canyon in front of the New York Stock Exchange building. The Chinese Army had commandeered the building as their headquarters, in part for its excellent communications facilities. As the officers of the Chinese High Command arrived for work, they saw a small round object on the top of a light pole in front of the building. It was the head of General Chin.

Chapter 33

"Do you think they're up to it, Chris?" Jason asked.

Todd had told Jason that it was time to move to the next and final phase – full-scale battles for the cities. No more hit and run attacks or terror raids, no more letting the enemy seek shelter in the major population areas. This was the real thing. They would meet the Chinese in force and destroy their armies in the field once and for all. With Todd behind them, helping plan the battles, Jason had no doubt that they would win. But the question was, at what cost? He had images of World War I, rows of soldiers leaving the trenches and being mowed down by machine guns. Men died by the millions in that war because their leaders had no strategy more advanced than the classic Napoleonic frontal charge, which was suicidal against machine guns. The victors in that war lost as many men as the losers. Ten million men died because of stupidity. The American "armies" were less than a year old. If their people were poorly trained or poorly led, it could be a bloodbath. Todd said that they were up to the job, but Jason still was worried. If they gave the go-ahead, whatever happened would be his responsibility.

"I've gotten reports from around the country," Chris replied. "We have more men and women under arms than they do, but their soldiers are professionals, and most of our people never picked up a gun until a few months ago. We're getting new recruits every day. Do you think we should wait until we have more?"

"We can't wait. The Chinese are off balance and scared. If we give them time to regroup, they'll just get stronger."

Anne said, "Jason, you've been cooped up here for months. You haven't seen the changes. They're not a militia

271

anymore, people taking their guns down from the mantelpiece and leaving home for a day or two. We have real armies, with troops that do nothing but train and fight. They know how to win ground and hold it."

Jason said, "I'm more worried about the officers. In a long war, there's time for the incompetents to make their mistakes and get replaced before they can do more damage. I'm sure that there has been some shakeout so far, but we've only had relatively small-scale fights."

Chris said, "Jason, don't tell me you're getting cold feet. Is it getting too real for you?"

"No, it's just that, by and large, the Chinese have withdrawn more than fought. But now their backs are to the wall. Unless they get the order to pull out, they've got to stand and fight. If we recommend to the generals that they begin the final assault, we have to be sure they're ready."

Anne said, "Don't you think they'll know if they're ready?"

"To tell the truth, no. I've known few people who were aware of their own limitations. Some of the stupidest, most incompetent people I've known have been the most confident. In fact, the two seem to go together."

Chris said, "So what do you want to do? I can request more reports."

Anne said, "He doesn't need data, he needs to see them. Jason, there's a camp outside Earlysville. Let's go there and you can see for yourself what kind of people we have."

Jason said, "That's not a bad idea. Do you think we can just drop in for a visit?"

"Sure," she said. "They know Chris and me. We can get you in."

Jason said, "Let's do it then. I could use some exercise."

They left the next day. On the way there, Jason saw that Anne was right that things had changed. People were moving around more freely and confidently. Lots of them were carrying guns, which was a shock at first. There were no Chinese police or soldiers. There were still checkpoints, but now Americans were manning them. They all wore different clothes, but each one had a small, two-inch by three-inch patch over his or her heart – a hand-made replica of the American flag. Whoever had that patch acted like they were in charge, and enjoyed deference from everyone else. But it was not a matter of submitting to their authority, as people had to the Chinese. People smiled, nodded as they passed by, and sometimes gave them things. It was like they were rock stars, the new celebrities of a community that had no other role models.

When he got close, he could see ranks sewn onto their arms or shoulders in black thread. There was an organization behind all this. Everyone acted like they knew what they were supposed to do.

What impressed Jason most is that the soldiers they passed looked hard. They were alert and noticed everything about them. When he talked to one of them, he could see that they were evaluating him as friend or foe and would not have hesitated a moment to shoot him if they decided he was a threat. They had none of the laxness of peacetime soldiers.

When they got to the camp, they were stopped at a checkpoint in front of the gate. Chris and Anne talked to the guards while Jason looked around. The camp was surrounded by a long wire fence with razor wire on top and guard towers every fifty yards or so. It looked like there were antiaircraft guns in sandbagged emplacements. Beyond the fences were several long rows of tents and numerous pickup trucks and full-size trucks. He could see some heavy guns on trailers behind the trucks, but no armored cars or tanks. They had located the camp in the middle of a grove of trees, probably to give it some camouflage from the air. It was not sophisticated, but everything was clean and well-ordered. It looked like it had not been there long and that they could pack it up and move on a few hours' notice.

But what really got to him was an American flag on a pole just inside the gate. It was hard to remember how long it had been since he had seen one. There it was, flapping in a light breeze, like none of this had happened. It had an odd effect on him, as if the old government were back and that it would take care of them again. But, of course, that was all gone. The government had been ruthlessly destroyed, the President, Congressmen, and Supreme Court Justices all hunted down and executed. The Chinese thought that if they cut off the head, the American body would twitch for a while and then become still, passive. They were right, at least for a while. But the analogy failed. America was more like a tree that had been cut down, but the roots were still strong and new shoots had sprung up, reaching for the sky much faster than a seedling and growing tall as it basked in the sunlight. Americans were not made for submission. It only took a little sunlight to get them going again.

As Jason stared at the flag, he realized it was not one of the old, pre-war banners. Someone had taken pieces of red, white and blue rags, cut them up, and sewn them together roughly by hand. Those rags, which you wouldn't even notice if they were in a pile on the floor, were now a thing, an old friend. It was gone, and now it was back, and he saluted it.

Anne came over and said, "Everyone gets choked up the first time they see it. I thought you were going to cry there for a second."

Jason said, "Not likely. I haven't cried since, well, I guess before the war. I think I've forgotten how." He looked at the flag, still kept alive by the wind. "You know, I never used to pay much attention to the flag. Singing the national anthem at ball games and saluting the flag used to annoy me, to tell the truth. I took it all for granted until it was gone. Now that old bunch of rags seems like the most precious thing on Earth."

Chris joined them and said, "Let's go. The senior officers apparently are having a meeting. You can go there and talk to them if you like."

"Do you think they'll mind us barging in like this?"

"We'll see."

A woman with the rank of captain showed up to escort them in. She did a double-take when she saw Jason, started to say something, and then apparently thought better of it. She said, "This way please," and led them through the camp. People noticed them as they walked, some of them stopping to stare. Jason felt distinctly out of place. As far as he could tell, they were the only non-military people there. They definitely were disturbing the normal routine. He was starting to think that maybe this was not a good idea.

The officer brought them to a tent that was larger than most of the others. There were two guards at the entrance who started to object to Chris and Anne going in with weapons, but the captain told them that it was ok. There were about a dozen people sitting in a circle in the middle of the tent who stopped talking as soon as they entered. They all rose from their chairs, but no one said a word. Jason figured it was up to him to break the awkward silence. "Sorry to intrude. Who's the ranking officer here?"

An older man with thinning white hair and two black stars on each shoulder said, "I'm General Brewster, commander of the Army of Virginia, of the Reconstituted United States Army. But now that you're here, sir, that would make you the ranking officer."

Jason said, "I, uh, don't follow."

"You outrank everyone else in the Army . . . General Kilo."

Jason looked at Chris, who was trying to stifle a grin. "Ok, very funny. What's going on?"

Chris said, "Apparently, people have gotten the idea that you're General Kilo."

"There is no General Kilo," Jason said angrily, turning back to the general. "It's a joke, a myth, disinformation to keep the Chinese guessing."

The general said, "I understand sir, 'General Kilo' is a code name, but we know who you are."

Jason looked at Anne; from her expression, she was in on the joke too. "Alright you two," he said, "spill it. What's going on."

Chris said, "The call sign for our messages is 'KYZ' – kilo, yankee, zulu.' It didn't take long for people to start referring to them as orders from General Kilo. There didn't seem any need to correct them. Did you want the Chinese to know your real name?"

"I never sent out any orders. They were just suggestions, advice."

"With due respect, sir," the general said, "a lot of good men and women have died following those 'suggestions' and 'advice.' As far as the Army is concerned, they are orders. What you say, we do."

Jason looked around the room. *You knew all about this, didn't you Todd?*

Of course.

You could have warned me. I look like a fool.

Then you should stop acting like one.

Boxed me in again, didn't you? Jason said, "Well, if it makes you feel good to call me 'General Kilo,' go ahead. How did you catch on, General?"

He smiled and said, "One of my men was with you in the attack at Winchester. The scar is a dead giveaway."

Jason touched the side of his face and said, "Yeah, it's a good thing I've been keeping out of sight."

"We've always known that you were in central Virginia. The only way to get the Chinese off the scent was to spread rumors that you were somewhere else. Some of the commanders set up dummy General Kilo headquarters with fake radio traffic so that the Chinese would stage a raid. That worked for a while until the Chinese realized that every raid turned into an ambush and the raiders never came back. Now, they don't know what to think or do about it. Some of them claim that you don't exist, that you're a plot to mask the real leadership of the rebellion. Trouble is, they can't figure out who the real leaders are."

Jason looked around the room and said, "They're right here. Americans are born leaders. They see a problem and someone steps up to fix it. This army, like all of the armies around the country, was self-organized. I had nothing to do with it. All I'm doing is pointing you in the right direction, giving you an information advantage over the enemy, stacking the deck in your favor."

"You've done a lot more than that. But I appreciate the vote of confidence. I have to tell you, I've had doubts, like everyone else, that you really exist. The stories are so fantastic. The troops who were with you in Winchester say you saved them all, killed a thousand men single-handedly. You are protected by a supernatural force that bullets cannot penetrate. Some say you are immortal."

"Uh, you know those are exaggerations."

"Of course. All legends grow each time they're retold. But legends are important, and they're always based on a kernel of truth. People who face death every day desperately want to believe that their leaders know what they're doing. They hero-worship a winner, and you've led them to an unbroken string of victories. No one who has followed your battle plans has ever lost. All it takes is to tell them that the orders come straight from General Kilo, and they'll do anything."

If they only knew I was a phony, transmitting your messages and passing off your words as my own.

That is your cross to bear. Soldiers need faith, and you are the one who I chose as my instrument to give it to them.

Jason said, "Well then, it's up to us not to let them down. We're about to enter the final phase in the war, General. The battles are going to get a lot tougher. No more raids and ambushes – we're going to meet the enemy in set-piece battles and destroy them. I have no doubt that we will win, but it's going to be a bloody mess. We came here today because I wanted to see if we're ready. To tell the truth, I'm not sure exactly what I'm looking for."

The general shot dirty looks at Chris and Anne and said, "With all due respect, General Kilo, it is a breach of military courtesy for your staff not to have warned me that you were going to hold a surprise inspection." He nodded to the captain who had escorted them and she turned on her heels and left.

Chris said, "I apologize, General Brewster. It's my fault. I should have told you. We weren't trying to make you look bad."

He frowned and said, "No harm done. Well, General Kilo, I suppose I should start by introducing my staff." He told Jason each person's name, rank, and area of responsibility. Jason noticed that when he shook hands with the women, they had this doe-eyed look like they were groupies at a rock concert, at least until they saw Anne glaring at them. Some sort of feminine mental telepathy must have warned them that Anne was ready to shoot them.

The general gave them a summary of the forces and facilities at the camp, then briefed them on the operations that his staff were planning when Jason and his party had interrupted them. His Executive Officer pulled up a big map showing the deployment of forces in Virginia and their objectives. It was clear that no one was standing still. Even the camp they were standing in would not be there in a couple of days. The army was fluid, built and operated for maneuver warfare. The General's staff was trained for action, able to take a plan and execute an attack with very little notice. If Jason had pointed to a place on the map and told them to mount an assault that night, he was sure they would have been able to call together local resources and converge on the point in a couple of hours without a sweat.

It was all very impressive, but as the briefing went on it seemed to Jason that the General was killing time. When the captain came back and caught his eye, he announced it was time to begin a tour. They walked outside and saw the entire camp in review formation. Someone shouted "Attennnshun!" and they all sprang to attention and saluted. Fortunately, Jason had the presence of mind to salute back. The general said, "Perhaps you'd like to say a few words, General Kilo."

278

"Not today, General," Jason said. "Frankly, I don't know what to tell them because I haven't decided what to do yet." Not to mention the fact that he had never given a speech in his life and was scared to death he'd make a fool of himself. "If you don't mind, I'd just like to say hello."

It was not like any army he had ever seen. Not only were they in street clothes, but they looked like a group of people gathered at random from a shopping mall. There were men and women of all ages, from teenagers who looked like they were just past puberty, to old men who would have been drawing Social Security if the war hadn't intervened. They were drawing from the bottom of the barrel. It made him sick to think that these people were facing trained Chinese soldiers.

Jason said to Todd, *Look at that one. Damn, she looks like my third grade elementary school teacher, Mrs. Harmon.*

You cannot make a valid judgment based on appearances. You should speak to her.

Jason walked up to her and said, "What's your story, soldier?"

She saluted and said, "Corporal Diane Hodges, Sir. Squad Leader." She had smiled when Jason walked up to her, but the smile faded as she saw the disappointment on his face. He returned the salute and said, "At ease, Corporal. Where are you from?"

"Roanoke, Sir."

"I had relatives in Roanoke. It was hit hard. What did you do before the War?"

"I was an elementary school teacher. Fourth grade."

Oh, I needed more information to pass judgment? I knew it. I can just imagine Mrs. Harmon picking up a gun and yelling "Charge!" What a joke. Jason said, "Why aren't you with your students? They still need an education."

She said, "Most of my children died during the war. I couldn't go back to teaching with the Chinese running the schools. I lived on odd jobs and handouts. Until I heard we were raising an army again. I joined two months ago."

279

"Have you seen any action?"

"Yes sir. Six firefights. That's how I became squad leader. Two weeks ago, our squad leader got killed while we were taking out an armored personnel carrier. I took over and led for the rest of the day. That's how you get promoted around here."

"Six? That's impressive. But you should know that it's only going to get harder from this point on. We have to push them until they break. You may never see a classroom again."

"If I was worried about survival, I wouldn't be here."

"Let me be blunt. We have a lot of people, but the enemy still has much better weapons. It will be a war of attrition, trading lives for victory. Half the people here won't be alive in a year."

A broad smile spread across her face. General Webster said, "Uh, sir, it would be better if you didn't give them false hope. Our six-month casualty rate is one hundred percent. Everyone who volunteers signs an agreement to fight until dead or disabled. We don't want anyone in this army who thinks they're going to outlive the war."

Jason looked at him in shock and turned back to the corporal. "You're ok with that?"

"Absolutely, Sir. Frankly, I don't see how you can face combat unless you've already accepted death. We all have. I wouldn't want to fight beside someone who felt any other way."

Todd said, *What do you think now?*

Jason replied, *I don't know if it's courage or a death wish. Maybe it's mass psychosis.*

Your point of view is too negative. What they have is a warrior mentality. The Japanese Samurai had a similar credo. It made them fearless in battle.

Jason noticed that there were quite a few soldiers of obvious Chinese heritage. They could not be spies – the Americans knew how to tell their own countrymen from the invaders, and Todd would have outed them in an instant. But Jason also knew how the Chinese regarded their former subjects who had sought freedom in America. "General Webster," Jason said, "how do you get so many Chinese-Americans to volunteer? I hate to think what happens to them if they're captured by the enemy."

"You don't want to know; it would keep you up at night. Especially when they're caught in Chinese uniform."

"You've got to be kidding! How do you get them to do that? It's insane."

"I know. But sometimes, we need them for infiltration, so I ask for volunteers. I hate to do it, but, well, there it is."

They walked along the line some more, making small talk, when Jason said to Todd, *Look at that guy. He only has one arm!* Jason walked up to the man and shook his hand and said, "Did you know your left arm is missing?"

He chuckled and said, "Actually, when I close my eyes, I can still feel it."

"You couldn't have lost it recently."

"No, Sir, it was in Afghanistan, Special Forces. An IED got me. When they pulled me out of my Humvee, my arm was still attached to the steering wheel. That was the end of my military career. They said I couldn't fight with one arm."

"I take it you had a different view."

"No, I was ok with it at the time. Why pay a soldier with one arm when you can get a guy with two for the same price? I took my pension and figured that was the end of it. But things are different now. We need veterans, people who know how to fight. I help keep the newcomers alive long enough for them to become veterans."

"What do you think of this army of ours?"

"Well, it's different, that's for sure. More like the mujahideen that I used to train. In the old army we used to put recruits through six weeks of basic training just to teach them to take orders. You had to make them more afraid of you than the enemy. We don't need to do that now. The people who come here are already motivated. They follow orders because they want to be a part of it. Well, also, if they screw up, they get kicked out and lose their patch. No one wants to risk that. It's funny how a tiny piece of cloth can motivate someone."

"I wish we had more time to train them, but I don't see it. We can't afford to lose momentum. It's now or never."

"Don't worry about us, General Kilo. We may look more like a mob than an army, but I know real soldiers when I see them. It's the Chinese I feel sorry for. They're scared. Our people aren't."

"No offense, but it looks like we're scraping the bottom of the barrel. I've never seen an army like this. Women, old men, boys. I don't know."

Jason's one-armed friend looked in puzzlement at General Webster and then back to him. General Webster said, "Sir, I don't think you understand. These people are the best. We don't have time to turn raw recruits into soldiers like in the old army, so we screen. We get ten volunteers for every recruit we accept. The testing protocol alone almost kills them. We don't train soldiers – we recognize them."

"You get that many people who want to join what amounts to a suicide mission?"

"Yessir," General Webster said. "Those that fail the test get real disappointed, sometimes downright angry, but most of them help out in other ways. They get us food and clothing, guns and ammunition. I spend no time at all worrying about logistics. Everywhere we go, supplies just show up."

Jason was still puzzled. Todd said, *You have to stop looking at the trees and recognize the forest. Look around you. What do you see?*

He gazed across the troops in formation. What was he missing? Was he the only one who thought this did not look right?

You are trying to fit what you see into your preconceptions. It is blinding you to the obvious.

He looked again, trying to see what Todd saw. *Oh my God, I get it. This is everyone, all of us. It's a nation on the march.*

That is correct. There has never been an army like this. The entire country is moving as one.

I see it. Complete mobilization.

What else do you see?

Jason took a few steps and looked up and down the rows of soldiers. There was something more here. It was in their eyes.

They're different. They're not sad anymore.

Yes. Not too long ago, they were living day-to-day, with no goal other than to stay alive. Yet they have eagerly joined in a mission that will likely lead to their deaths. And they are happy about it. That woman, the teacher, she is not suicidal. Suicide is a result of depression and despair. She has gone beyond that. She still grieves for her lost children, but now she is fighting for the future of the children that are left. And she is warmed by the thought that if she falls, another will pick up her gun and continue the fight. The children will be saved.

You're right. They see the carnage ahead and they don't care. They're going to keep moving forward and I couldn't stop them if I tried.

Now you understand the essence of leadership. You have found your parade. All you have to do is walk in front of it.

Jason said, "General, I'm sorry for that crack about the bottom of the barrel. I understand now. You've done something extraordinary here."

"Not just here," he replied. "It's like this everywhere. You tell us what you want, and we'll make it happen. You can count on it."

"I know I can. We're not going to pull any punches. It's all-out from this point on." That brought smiles to the faces of everyone in earshot. Jason realized he had dodged a big bullet. The last thing these people needed was to see uncertainty in their leadership.

As they prepared to go, Jason thanked General Brewster and his staff again and told them how impressed he was with everything he had seen that day. The general asked when Jason thought the big push would come. "I'll let you know, General," he said. "It should be soon. We'll issue detailed instructions when the time comes."

General Brewster said, "Sir, if I may make a suggestion, it would be very helpful if you made a formal announcement to the nation to kick it off. To most Americans, you are no more than a myth. We have no national leader, no person that they can rally around. If the people saw you on TV one night, it would give the movement a face."

"Hmm, that's an interesting idea, General," Jason said. "Just how would we pull it off? We may control some of the TV transmitters in the rural areas, but the fighting will be around the cities."

One of his staff, a Colonel Jane Ridgeway, said, "Sir, it's a little known fact that there is no technological need for there to be thousands of TV transmitters across the country. Originally, the TV networks proposed to have five or so high-powered transmitters cover everything. Congress required lots of low-powered transmitters because it wanted, for various political and social policy reasons, to issue broadcast licenses at the local level. All we have to do is power up some of our transmitters and sabotage the Chinese-controlled ones in the cities and suburbs. For the cable systems, we can splice into the cables at the head-ends and replace all of their programming with our message. There are plenty of cable technicians in the areas we control who could help us do it. We could be prepared within a week."

Jason said, "It sounds like you've thought this through. It's not a bad idea. Let me think about it."

He thanked them again and left. On the way back, Chris asked, "So what do you think?"

"It's not what I thought. It's better. The Chinese have soldiers, conscripts who do what they're told because they're afraid not to. Once their fear of the enemy overcomes their fear of their officers, they're finished. Our people are fighting for themselves. They'll keep fighting even after they're beaten. I couldn't hold them back if I wanted to."

Anne said, "I thought General Brewster's idea was a good one. I could just imagine the Chinese reaction when your face showed up on their TV screens one night."

"I don't know, Anne," Jason said. "I've never given a speech in my life. I wouldn't know where to begin."

Anne said, "Jason Chase! I can't believe it. You face death without batting an eye but you've worried about a little speech?"

"It's not that, Anne. Well, it is, but that's not the point. Politicians spend their whole lives giving speeches. It's a skill. We have one shot at this. I just don't know if I can give the kind of speech he's thinking about."

Chris said, "You were pretty convincing not too long ago with a lot tougher audience. They might not have agreed with you at the time, but the message got through. You don't have to be Winston Churchill. Just seeing and hearing you will be such a shock that what you say will hardly matter."

"Let me think about it. I don't know. What do you say to people who've been without hope for so long?"

Chapter 34

"My fellow Americans.'

"My name is Jason Chase. Some of you know me as General Kilo. I am the Commanding Officer of the Reconstituted Army of the United States of America. Through the courage and sacrifice of our brave soldiers, we have retaken large areas of the country from the Chinese invaders. I am here tonight to announce the final stage of our campaign to rid the United States of the Chinese scourge forever.'

"In the coming weeks, we will begin our assault on the Chinese forces that remain in the major cities. The fighting will intensify as we bring maximum pressure to bear. There will be difficult times ahead. But let me assure you that, in the near future, we will have exterminated the last vestiges of the Chinese invaders.'

"To the Chinese who are listening, I say that the day of retribution has come. You may have noticed that we take no prisoners. You have shown us no mercy, and we will show you none. You killed 25 million of us. Now, the United States will be your graveyard. We will dump your bodies in our landfills and cover them with our garbage. You will lie there in disgrace for eternity.'

"My fellow Americans, the Chinese think that they destroyed the United States of America. They did not. We, the people, never rescinded the Constitution. The fact that the Chinese burned some old documents in the National Archives is irrelevant. The Constitution is not a piece of paper; it is a solemn and binding agreement among the American people. It exists in our minds and in our hearts. All of the federal, state, and local laws enacted pursuant to the Constitution remain in effect as well. After we drive the Chinese out of this land, temporary military governors will keep order in each state until elections can be held to restore the civilian government. Then we will begin to heal our country. We will rebuild the Capitol building. We will rebuild the White House. We will raise the Washington Monument, stone by stone. Everything will be as before. And we will take the remains of our dead that still lie in those places and bury them with honor at Arlington cemetery.'

"Almost two and a half centuries ago, our forefathers fought and died to establish the first democracy of the modern era. It was on this day, the Fourth of July, that they declared this country to be free and independent forever. It was their gift to the generations that followed, but one that had to be purchased again and again with the blood of patriots. This time, it is our turn to pay the price of freedom. Like all battles, it will get worse before it gets better. But when the view is darkest, that is when you must imagine the light of dawn. I promise that the day will come, and it will come soon, when we will stand up and watch the sun rise on a free America. Some of us will not live to see that day. But for every soldier that is struck down, another will pick up his or her weapon and continue the fight. We are unstoppable because we are a nation on the march. The world will learn once again that the dream of freedom and justice and equality that created this country cannot be destroyed. It cannot be destroyed because freedom is a choice, and we refuse to accept anything less. It cannot be destroyed because we, the people, will preserve, protect and defend it, whatever the challenge, and whatever the cost. God Bless America."

Jason said, "So, what do you think?"

Anne stopped the video camera and his face froze on the TV monitor. "Not bad, but you need to work more on your delivery. It sounded too much like you were reading the speech rather than talking."

Chris said, "I agree, it needs more emotion. Try varying the pace and the emphasis, and maybe the volume too, to match how you feel in each part. Just slowing it down about ten

287

percent would give each word more impact. Also, you should look past the camera lens so that people will feel you are looking directly at them. If you watch it again, you'll see that your eyes are focused too narrowly. It makes you look squinty."

Jason said, "I get it. I'll work on the form. What about the substance? I noticed you frowning at one point, Anne."

She said, "That part about take-no-prisoners was a little bloodthirsty. Are you really going to order our troops to do that, kill prisoners? We haven't taken prisoners so far because we haven't had many try to surrender. We've let them withdraw to the cities after a defeat. But now, they will have nowhere to run."

"I may have overdone it a bit, but what I'm trying to do is demoralize them. Brewster had a good idea about giving a speech to rally the people, but as I was writing it, I started to think about how it would affect the enemy."

Chris said, "Oh, it'll affect them alright. You're telling them to fight harder. Armies don't take prisoners because they're nice guys. They do it because it gives the other guy an alternative to fighting. If soldiers are losing a battle and the choices are die or put up your hands, a lot of them will surrender. You're taking away that option."

Jason said, "If that's all we were doing, I'd agree with you. I've been reconsidering our strategy. It's too direct. Assaulting the cities, drawing the enemy out to set-piece battles, is high cost. I have no doubt we'll win in the end, but the carnage could be immense. We're losing sight of the purpose of war. It's not to win battles."

Chris said, "Say again?"

"Winning battles is a means to an end; it is not the end itself. The purpose of war is to exert your will on the enemy. You want them to quit, to give up, to do what you want them to do instead of what they want to do. In effect, war is simply an elaborate effort at persuasion. Victory is psychological, even though the means are primarily violent. In this war, our objective is to persuade the Chinese to leave. We want to do that in the easiest way possible with the least loss of American lives. That's why we need to focus on their morale, both here and back in China. We have to convince them that they can't win and that they are better off saving their troops to defend the homeland."

Anne said, "So what does that mean? Do you have a better way than what we've been doing?"

"I don't want to stop what we're doing – I want to enhance the psychological effect. Sometimes, that's more important than winning battles. Did you know the United States did not lose a single battle in the Vietnam War? Yet, we lost the war. How did that happen? Well, the United States lost over 50,000 men in eight years of combat. That sounds like a lot to us, but it's been estimated that the Vietnamese lost a million people. The difference is that it was clear to the North Vietnamese that the American public was unwilling to lose another 50,000, while it was just as clear to us that the Vietnamese were perfectly willing to lose another million. Put simply, they wanted it more than we did. So we quit. We lost not only because we failed to win the hearts and minds of the South Vietnamese people – we failed to win the minds of the American people as well. If we want to win this war, we can't lose focus on the primary goal – to win the psychological contest, to defeat them mentally."

Chris said, "What does that have to do with your speech?"

"There was one particular battle where the Vietnamese turned the American public against the war. It was the TET offensive. Just when Americans hoped that they were finally winning, the Viet Cong attacked one hundred cities at the same time. They were defeated in all of them, but the fact that these attacks were initiated inside the cities, where the Americans thought they had control, shocked everyone. The American will to fight never recovered. I think we have an opportunity to do something similar. Right after the speech ends, we could have our artillery bombard the military bases and troop garrisons in every city. We could set off bombs in the police stations and in the telephone switching offices that are still working. The Chinese in the cities who are telling themselves that the Americans are far away would realize that none of them are safe."

Chris said, "We're not ready to take the cities."

"Of course not," Jason said. "That was the one part where the North Vietnamese went wrong. They tried to hold the cities and they lost most of their troops. No, all we need to do is create a racket, produce a lot of visual destruction, and then disappear. Attacking them where they live right after the speech will maximize the shock effect on the Chinese leadership. Those guys are more than willing to send soldiers to their deaths, but they don't feel the same way about themselves. That speech will make it clear to them that if their army is defeated, they are going to be hunted down and killed. What I'm hoping is that the smart ones are going to start looking for an exit. They'll tell their superiors back home that the war is hopeless, that they can do more good fighting the Indians and Russians. The Chinese civilian administrators are already finding excuses to get out of here. I want to turn the trickle of people who are quietly taking the next boat to China into a torrent. That's why I want them to think that the Americans are bloodthirsty savages who will kill them even if they try to surrender."

"Well, you frightened me," Anne said. "The only time your eyes lit up is when you were talking about throwing them away with our garbage."

Jason asked Todd, *What do you think?*

There is no such thing as a perfect strategy. Each has its advantages and disadvantages. You must make your choice and live with the consequences.

Thanks for nothing. Can't you just tell me whether it's a good idea?

No. The three of you adequately discussed the pros and cons of your approach. You are the leader; you must make the decision as best you can.

What do you mean? You're running this war.

That is not true. You have always been the leader. I provide information, the ultimate weapon, which you use to help your side. My role is not to tell you what to do.

Now you tell me. Well, I can see risks either way, but I think we should err on the side of scaring the piss out of the Chinese.

It took several more takes before they all were satisfied. They made digital copies on flash drives and arranged for couriers to distribute them around the country. At precisely 8:00 PM on the following Tuesday, it would be broadcast simultaneously on all channels. After the speech, the Chinese would hear the sound of their impending destruction. For the Americans, it would be the fireworks heralding a new Independence Day.

Chapter 35

Jingguo was watching the evening news with Natalie as they finished their dinner. His indigestion made it difficult to enjoy the meal. He knew that what they were watching was nothing but perception management. The reporter confidently recounted the latest Chinese victories over the declining American resistance and spoke with contempt of the demoralized American prisoners who had been taken. Jingguo, like all of the Chinese leadership, knew the real facts. The insurgency was gaining momentum, and the Chinese were powerless to stop it. They had lost control of everything except the major population centers.

The most distressing aspect of this turn of events was that every time the Chinese army tried to counterattack, sending search-and-destroy missions against enemy strongholds, the Americans either ambushed or evaded them. Sometimes, the Americans would attack the Chinese bases at the very moment when the Chinese were out looking for them.

It was obvious to Jingguo that the Americans had a very thorough spy apparatus. Since the Chinese electronic communications apparatus had been crippled, he thought that the Americans must have been getting their information through human intelligence, people within the most sensitive parts of the Chinese military and civilian establishments who were feeding real-time data to the Americans.

The still-unsolved mystery of Jason Chase proved this. The guards at the prison claimed that no one had even seen him leave. Preposterous! No one can simply walk out of a high security prison without being seen. Chase had been in a cell with no windows and a steel door that was locked from the outside. Someone had to have let him out and smuggled him away. Jingguo had personally supervised the torture of the guards who had been on duty on the cellblock, and when this proved fruitless, he had expanded the investigation to every guard in the facility. Despite the most gruesome torture, every single one of them died screaming his innocence. It made no sense. They were all Chinese citizens with nothing in their backgrounds to give any clue that they could be turned. What could the Americans have offered them to bear such pain and to choose certain death over fealty to their homeland? No known drug, no so-called brain-washing technique, could produce such an effective resistance to time-tested interrogation methods. But this man's escape made it clear that the Americans had found a way to infiltrate the Chinese with moles who would do anything they asked, whether the gathering of information or direct sabotage. And there was no way of knowing who was working for them.

Jingguo was trying to eat when his fork stopped in mid-air and his mouth hung open. The news reporter's face had been replaced by an image of the outlawed flag of the United States of America waving in the breeze to the tune of the American national anthem. It dissolved into a face that he recognized from not so long ago. It was a harder face, with a scar on the left cheek, but any doubt about his identity was dispelled when he began to speak. "My fellow Americans, my name is Jason Chase . . ."

Jingguo and Natalie looked at each other in shock and then back at the screen. It was not possible! This little weasel was the notorious General Kilo that the Chinese had been trying without any success to locate? And he was threatening to murder them! As the speech went on, Jingguo felt ill with an increasing sense of foreboding. He tried changing the channels, but Chase was on every one of them. The Americans had taken control of the cable system. They were flaunting their power to infiltrate the infrastructure even in areas under Chinese control. They were so self-confident that Chase was not afraid to identify himself, to make himself the most hunted man in America. Because he was coming for them!

When the speech was over, Natalie said, "I can't believe it. Jason's their leader?"

Jingguo tried to compose himself. "He is obviously a front, an actor. They are trying to mislead us."

"But you said that he worked in that research lab. He was with the resistance."

"This is a trick. I know him. I saw him tremble before me with fear. There is no way . . ." At that moment, the building rocked from an explosion. Jingguo and Natalie rushed to the balcony to see flashes of light, followed by the sound of exploding shells that rattled the windows. Some of it came from the southeast, where the old Fort Belvoir was located, and then other explosions came from across the Potomac River at the naval base. The intervals between explosions were filled with gunfire. It was all around them, first at one point, then another.

Natalie followed Jingguo back inside and closed the door behind her, as if that might protect them from the chaos outside. Jingguo picked up the telephone and tried to make a call, then held the handset in front of him and looked at it as if it had betrayed him. The telephones were down again. He pulled out his cellphone and checked the display. No bars. He tried to make a call and got silence. It had taken months for the Chinese to get some of the phone systems to work in the major cities again, and the Americans had taken them down again with ease.

He grabbed his coat and said, "The phones are not functioning. I am going to the office. The dedicated lines might still be working there."

Natalie asked, "Do you want me to go with you?"

"No. Stay here and lock the doors."

"What's happening? Are they coming here? Are we going to be attacked?"

"How should I know?" he said angrily. "You saw what I saw. He's mad. Who can say what a madman will do?"

Natalie put her hand on his arm and said, "I'm sure it will be all right."

Jingguo looked at her in disbelief. She was feeling pity. For him! "Take your hand off me!" he snarled. "Your friend Mr. Chase will be dead within the week. I will see to it personally."

Natalie was taken aback, but her expression hardly changed. Jingguo realized that the speech and the attack that followed had caused the Chinese to lose face. People were going to see it as a sign of weakness. The Americans would lose their fear. He hoped that it was not too late to get it back.

Jingguo left the building and ran to his car. He drove as fast as he could through the dark and empty streets. The only vehicles he saw were police and military cars speeding through the night, their lights flashing and their sirens blaring. He suspected that they were not going anywhere, just racing around to give the impression that they were dealing with the situation. The Americans would see this ineffective response as a sign that the Chinese were panicking. As he drove, he wondered if he would be attacked. He looked at shadows between buildings, at windows and doors, to see if there were any gunmen taking aim at him. For the first time, he felt alone in an alien land, hunted. He pushed harder on the accelerator.

Chapter 36

Jason and Anne lost Chris in Annandale. They never saw him again.

They were driving behind General Webster as his motorized column advanced north on Interstate 95 towards Washington. They did not have any armor, but they had some fairly heavy weapons, such as inertially-guided rockets and small towed artillery. Webster had about 45,000 troops trying to catch up to the Chinese, who were withdrawing to DC after their defeat outside Richmond.

Things had been getting easier in the last couple of months. The better Chinese forces had been withdrawn to China, and most of the Chinese civilians were gone. There was a momentum to war, and it had clearly shifted to the American side. They were getting stronger while the Chinese were getting weaker.

Chris, Anne, and Jason were not part of Webster's forces; they were more like war tourists. Jason had wanted to be a part of the final assault when they took the city. This is where it all began, but he could never bring himself to go back to DC while it still was the graveyard of a lost nation. Very soon, it would belong to America again, and he wanted to be there. There was not much to do for the war effort while he was at the farm, anyway. Now that they were engaging the enemy directly, the battle plans were pretty clear. He did not have to feed much information to the generals, since they had the enemy right in front of them. He would give them instructions as to overall strategy, but they had tactical control.

Anne and Jason noticed that Chris was getting antsy as they approached Annandale. A while ago, he had casually asked where Natalie's apartment was located. Jason had told him the address on Little River Turnpike, not far from where it crossed Interstate 95. Jason was not surprised when Chris pulled the car over as they reached the turn-off for that road.

Chris looked straight ahead as he said, "Anne, there's something I need to do." He turned towards her and said, "I've got to find out what happened to Natalie. There was fighting all around here. There may be looters, or worse, taking advantage of the situation. I need to go and make sure she's ok."

Anne looked sad, but for who it wasn't clear, as she said, "Of course you do. She may be in trouble."

"You're ok with it?"

"Sure. We'll be fine. Jason and I have a whole army around us."

"Thanks, Anne. I'll catch up with you later, wherever General Webster sets up his headquarters." He kissed her on the cheek.

Jason got out of the car with Chris and held out his hand. "Chris," he said, "thanks for everything. We couldn't have done this without you." Chris shook his hand and said, "This isn't goodbye. I'll be back soon. Don't hold the victory party without me."

Jason got in the driver's seat with Anne and watched Chris walk away. A tear fell down Anne's cheek. Jason said, "She won't make him happy. She couldn't do that even before the war."

Anne said, "It doesn't matter. She was his first love. The whole time we rode in, he had this distant look on his face. I knew he was thinking of her. I could see him searching the faces of women we passed, looking for her."

"She'll never tell him the truth about what she did while he was gone. She'll say that the Chinese raped her. She'll lay such a big guilt trip on him that he'll do anything she wants. She's a survivor, and she knows how to manipulate men. I feel sorry for Chris."

Joseph DiBella

"Not Chris. He's Rick Moore now. Chris is gone forever."

"I'm sorry, Anne."

"I'm not. I always knew this day would come. It's better to get it over with." She took Jason's hand and said, "And, to tell you the truth, I left him a long time ago, long before you showed up. I tried really hard, but there was a point when I gave up, when I knew he would never be mine. I knew that if the Chinese ever left, he would go back to his old life. We were hiding from reality on the farm, but eventually, reality catches up with you."

Jason said, "Yeah. Still, he was a good friend, and he's going to miss all the fun." He put the car in gear and rejoined the convoy. They did not speak much as they drove on.

The traffic jammed up as they crossed the 14th Street Bridge into Washington. By the time they caught up with Webster, he had halted his command vehicles on the Washington Monument grounds. The troops had fanned out across the Mall and were moving into the neighboring streets as the rest of the army tried to catch up. Jason figured that about a third of Webster's force was across the bridges in DC. It looked like the enemy was withdrawing north, trying to escape to the Maryland suburbs.

As Jason and Anne approached Webster's truck, a huge explosion threw their car into the air. The last thing Jason remembered was the world spinning before he blacked out. When he regained consciousness, he found himself next to Anne in a pile of rubble from the old monument. She had dragged him there under fire while he was out. The ground was shaking from explosions all around them. Jason realized they were in the middle of an artillery barrage! The noise was deafening, the shock waves going right through his body. It felt like they were there for hours, holding each other tightly as dirt and debris rained on them. It was like the end of the world.

After a while, the shells grew less frequent, and they poked their heads up. Jason said, "Are you ok?"

298

Anne said, "I think so." They were dazed, trying to comprehend what had happened, amazed that they were still alive. Jason said, "Do you see Webster?"

She said, "They're gone. His command post took a direct hit. Nothing's moving over there."

They could see quite a bit of the Mall from where they were, and it did not look good. The Chinese had plastered the place. It looked like every vehicle was blown apart and burning. The sound of artillery fire was being overtaken by the cries of the wounded. It was chaos.

Anne said, "Where do you think the shelling is coming from?"

"Miles away, I'm sure. This was a planned ambush. They must have zeroed in on the Mall long before we got here. Notice that they're still shelling the bridge approaches. They waited until part of our force got across, and now they're closing off the line of retreat or reinforcement. Smart."

Anne said, "It's worse than you think. Look up 15th Street."

It was an armored column, coming straight at them, blasting the soldiers in front of it. The American troops were retreating, more like running for their lives. Jason said, "Right. Hammer and anvil. I'll bet that's not the only one. Give me your binoculars." He looked east, and saw explosions in the direction of Union Station. "It looks like another column's coming down North Capital Street. There's probably a third coming from Georgetown. We're trapped."

Anne looked at Jason and said, "What are we going to do?"

Yes Todd! What are we going to do? Why didn't you tell us we were walking into a trap?

The situation is not hopeless. You are General Kilo.

What are you talking about? I'm no general. I don't know squat about warfare. I've never led a Boy Scout troop, let alone an army. Are you trying to be funny?

Not at all.

So what's the plan? Are you going to take over my body, or something?

That is not necessary. You are General Kilo.

Stop saying that! I'm nothing. I haven't got the slightest idea what to do.

Yes you do. You are General Kilo. You know what to do.

Oh, go to Hell!

Anne was staring at Jason, looking for answers he did not have. He looked around. It was getting worse, much worse. Their surviving soldiers were retreating, moving from the streets back into the Mall. They were leaderless, running for cover, going where the shelling seemed lighter. They didn't know.

"Anne, see what the Chinese are doing? They're herding us into the Mall. It's a killing field. The tanks will line up around the Mall and seal it off, then they'll start shelling us again, this time for good. The people on the other side of the river won't be able to do anything but watch us die."

Anne took Jason's hand. She did not ask him again what they should do. That worried Jason even more. She was probably thinking that, at least, they would die together.

"Anne, everyone's running the wrong way. We've got to stop them. They're running to their deaths." Jason stood up. Soldiers all around them were running from cover to cover, trying to make their way to the bridge, to the river. They did not know what else to do. He grabbed a young soldier who was running past and said, "Stop! You're going the wrong way." He pointed north. "The enemy is over there. We have to go forward." The soldier was not listening. His eyes were unfocused, his mind somewhere else. He tore himself from Jason's grip and kept running.

Jason looked around. A leaderless army is a mob. There was plenty of fight left in these people, but they had to work together again. He climbed onto a pile of stones that once had been the Washington Monument and shouted, "Listen to me! Do you know who I am? I'm General Kilo! I'm General Kilo!

Mind War; The Singularity

Stop running! The enemy is that way. That way." Some of them began slowing down, a few closer to him stopped and stared at him. "That's right, I'm General Kilo. I'm taking over. Now take your guns and follow me." He jumped down and picked up a gun from the hands of a dead soldier. He raised it over his head and said, "Let's go! Follow me. Everyone, this way!"

Jason started marching across the Mall, towards the enemy. It was not the best thing to do under rifle and artillery fire. He should have been sprinting from cover to cover, keeping his head down. But people had to see him. He could not lead them with his belly on the ground. Anne caught up and marched by his side. Now there were two of them.

After a while, a couple of soldiers, and then a few more, joined them. The soldiers yelled to the others to stop running and turn around. They gestured towards Jason, shouting "General Kilo." They were like the prow of a ship, pushing against the tide, and growing as part of that tide merged with them. They were turning it, but they needed more than those they could gather in the immediate vicinity.

Jason saw a soldier on the ground with a radio pack on his back. Jason pulled him to his feet and said, "C'mon soldier, get back in the war. Is that radio working?" He said, "Yes, but the general's dead. We don't have any orders."

Jason said, "You do now. Give me your headset." He put it on and asked, "Is there a general frequency that can reach everyone with a radio?" The radioman nodded. Jason said, "Then put me on the air."

Jason continued walking as he shouted into the mike; "Soldiers of the Army of Virginia. This is General Kilo. I repeat; this is General Kilo. General Webster and his staff are dead. I am taking command of the army. All soldiers on the DC side of the Potomac River, get off the Mall. Get off the Mall. It's a killing field. Move towards the enemy. Get out of the open spaces and into the streets and buildings. RPG teams, take out those damned tanks. Stop them before they get into the

301

open. Destroy the lead tanks and bottle them up in the streets. Everyone get as close to the enemy as possible, so they can't use their long range artillery on you. Gather all the heavy weapons you can carry, machine guns, bazookas, recoilless rifles if you can, and set up firing positions. Pass the word, everyone, start moving, now!"

Jason looked around. It seemed that, slowly, people were getting the message. He looked east, towards where the Capitol Building once stood, and he could see some movement in the right direction. It was working.

Jason turned off the mike and said, "What's your name, soldier?"

He said, "Corporal Winslow, Sir."

"Ok, Corporal Winslow, whatever happens, stay close to me. It's ok to die, but don't let them shoot your radio." That got a little smile out of him. "Now, can you give me a channel to the officers on the other side of the river?"

"Channel twelve will give you the company commanders and their staffs, Sir."

"Good, let's use it." When he gave the sign that the radio was ready, Jason said, "This is General Kilo, calling anyone on the Virginia side of the river. Who's in charge over there?"

The radio cackled and he heard, "This is Colonel Schaefer. I'm in the lead unit, but we can't get across. The artillery fire is too intense."

"Quit trying, Colonel. You're going to have to find another way. How are the other bridges?"

"Everything between the Key Bridge and the 14th Street Bridge is blocked. The closest bridges that we still control are the Woodrow Wilson on the east side and the Chain Bridge on the west."

"Ok, then, keep a small force here to hold the bridges and take the rest of your troops around both sides. And make it fast."

"But sir, it will take hours to reach you that way. We'll never rescue you in time."

"Who said anything about getting rescued? I don't want you to rescue us. I want you to trap *them*. I want you to encircle them from the right and left. We'll hold them by the nose while you kick them in the ass. Do you understand?"

"Yes sir."

"And see if you can take out any of that long range artillery while you're touring the countryside, OK?"

"Will do, sir . . . um, Sir."

"Yes."

"I don't understand it. This is the first time they've ever caught us flat-footed."

"Don't look at it that way. This is an opportunity. We wanted to catch up with them. Well, they've stopped running. The more they think they're winning in the center, the more they'll commit. We've got them right where we want them. Now you do your job, understand?"

"Yes Sir! We're on our way."

By the time Jason's group got to Constitution Avenue, most of the troops were moving off the Mall. The remains of the Army were turning back into a fighting force. It did not take long for them to disable the tanks in the front of the columns advancing towards the Mall. Attacking from the doors and windows of the buildings and throwing grenades from the rooftops onto the Chinese troops, they were able to drive the Chinese to cover as well, until it turned into a classic slugging match. After an hour, the Chinese attack ground to a halt, as they had to rely on infantry to clear each building on their flanks before they could move forward.

Jason found a couple more radio operators and, together with Anne, they constituted his "staff." They set up their headquarters in the old Reagan office building, a huge, L-shaped structure on 14th Street. Jason knew the place fairly well from before the War, when he had attended a convention there. It was the perfect place to hide – you could get lost in there even when you knew where you were going. Like all of the other buildings in the city, it had been severely damaged in the first battle of Washington. But that was a good thing. Rubble makes an excellent cover for a defensive infantry battle.

They chose a conference room on the second floor near the atrium in the front entrance to the building as their base of operations for the next hour or so. They drew diagrams of the battle area on the walls of the conference room and marked positions as they received status reports. Now and then, when someone said they were having trouble or that a line was weakening, Jason would relay their requests for reinforcements or tell the troops to shift their positions. But mostly, people saw the problems and pitched in, whether it was sending ammunition to someone who was running low or getting medical care to the wounded. There really was not much Jason had to do at this point. Their soldiers were hardened combat veterans who knew what to do once they were in a fight.

Actually, every single one of them knew more about warfare than Jason did, but he tried not to let them know it. His real function was to let them know that someone was in charge, that they were fighting with a purpose. As long as Jason's little group were still there, communicating with them, they knew the battle was not over, that it was worthwhile to hold on even if it looked like they were losing.

Which they were, technically. The enemy was pushing them back in all areas, taking them down one building at a time. It was a fighting retreat on the Americans' part, but a retreat nonetheless. Jason tried not to pester Colonel Schaefer too much about when he would get there. Schaefer was trying his best, but the Chinese had set up barricades on the main highways, and the side roads around Washington had never been designed to get from one place to another in a hurry.

Another hour and their perimeter had shrunk considerably. The American forces were confined to an area about a half-mile long and a couple of hundred yards wide on the north side of the Mall. Most alarming was the fact that the enemy had pushed a salient into their center, despite their best efforts to reinforce that area. Anne stared at the maps and shook her head. "It looks like they're trying to cut us in two," she said.

"Could be," Jason said, "but it won't do them much good. Whether we're in one piece or two, they'll still be trapped when our army arrives."

"Assuming they get here in time."

"Yeah, that's a big assumption." He got on the radio to Colonel Schaefer. "Any good news to report?" he asked.

"Still on our way, General. They're not fighting us now, just trying to slow us down. They're blowing up their vehicles to block the streets. There's no doubt we'll get to you, if you can hold on for a while longer."

"Well, that's the big question, isn't it? Have you got them surrounded yet?"

"Just about. They don't appear to be making any effort to hold a line of retreat. In fact, I think they're pulling back all of their forces towards you."

"Good. You know what Napoleon said; never interrupt the enemy when he's making a mistake."

The Colonel hesitated. "Uh, sir, he said that at Waterloo."

"Oh yeah. I forgot about that."

"I don't mean to be impolite, sir, but I'm worried we're missing something."

"No need to apologize. You're right. They planned this operation, but they don't seem to care about getting trapped. It might be light on your side, but they're fighting even harder here, like it matters or something."

Jason looked at the map while he held the radiotelephone to his ear. The Chinese were fighting with a purpose. The bulge in the American lines was getting deeper, and it was pointed right at their command center.

Jason asked Corporal Winslow, "Do you think they're listening in?"

"No way, General," he said. "Our radios are fractally encrypted. It would take them years to break the code."

Jason said, "But even if they can't understand what we're saying, could they tell from the volume of traffic where our center is?"

"Possible," he said. They looked at the map. No one had to say anything. The Chinese weren't trying to divide the American forces. They were coming for the headquarters unit. They were trying to cut off the head.

Jason said to Schaefer, "Colonel, you'll have to continue on your own for a while. We've got to shut down here. They must be using the radio traffic to target our headquarters. All we're doing is bringing attention to ourselves."

"How will we find you, sir?" he said.

"Just march to the sound of guns. Kilo out."

They gave their final instructions to the troops in the city and started packing up. Just as they were getting ready to move the command center, they saw the Chinese break into the plaza in front of the building. Some of the American troops retreated into the lobby, firing as they fell back and seeking cover. Anne said, "We have to go, Jason. When we lose the lobby, we'll be cut off."

Jason said, "I know. Ok, people, let's move." They picked up as much as they could carry and ran down the corridor deeper into the building. The last man out threw an incendiary grenade into the room to obliterate the information on the walls and anything else that could be of use to the enemy.

They ran down a hallway that went the length of the long part of the "L" of the building. It was a great way to move fast, but it also would provide an excellent line of fire if the enemy showed up. Jason wanted to put as much distance as he could between them and the Chinese before they tried to disappear into the maze of offices. They were almost at the end when Chinese soldiers appeared in front of them and poured automatic rifle fire down the corridor. They ducked through the nearest door into a stairwell.

Anne shouted, "Down or up, Jason?" He had no idea, so he said, "Up."

They stopped a couple of flights up the stairwell and two of their soldiers set up firing positions to slow down the Chinese. Anne, Winslow, and Jason came out into the fourth floor. They were still trying to decide which way to go when they were thrown to the floor from the force of an explosion in the stairwell behind them. As Jason's head cleared, he found himself looking across the floor into the unblinking eyes of Corporal Winslow. A pool of blood began forming below the young man's head.

Jason had no time to grieve. He said to Anne, "Are you alright?" She brushed some debris off herself and said, "I'm ok. Let's go." He pulled her by the hand as they got up and ran down the short end of the "L." When they got to the end of the hall, they tried going down the nearest stairwell, but someone began shooting at them from below. They turned around and ran up the stairs as fast as they could. The stairs emptied out into a round conference room with a domed ceiling. It had taken a direct artillery hit, with all of the windows blown out and the ceiling above half gone from the blast. The room was filled with debris and smashed furniture.

Anne looked around and said, "Is there a way out of here?"

Jason said, "I don't know. It looks like we're above the top floor. Maybe we can get out the windows and work our way around the ledge to the roof." He tried to look out through the broken windows and immediately drew gunfire from the street below. He pulled Anne to the floor and said, "Damn! They're all over the place down there."

Anne said, "So what do we do now?"

Jason said, "They've got to come through that door," pointing to the way they had just come in. "We'll just concentrate our fire when they do. At most, they'll come in two at a time. There's two of us."

Anne smiled grimly. "Yes. That's a good plan."

"I know. Good plan. I'm sorry I got you into this, Anne. I wanted to be here for the celebration. Some celebration."

She put her hand on his cheek and said, "Nobody forced me to come. I like a good time as much as you do." She kissed him, a sweet, gentle kiss. Jason marveled how, covered with dirt, she had never looked more beautiful.

Their tender moment was interrupted by the sound of soldiers coming up the stairwell. They crouched behind an overturned table and trained their guns on the doorway. Before they had a chance to fire at anything, a grenade rolled through the doorway and went off with a blinding flash. Jason blacked out from the concussion and woke with two Chinese soldiers picking him up by the arms. He looked across the room and saw Anne being pushed against a wall. There were a half dozen other soldiers in the room, surrounding a man and a woman in civilian clothes.

The man said, "Well, Mr. Chase, this took a bit longer than I planned, but I'm quite pleased with the result."

Jingguo! Jason could not believe it. And he had Natalie with him! Jason said, "What are you doing here?"

"Why, I'm in charge of this operation, Mr. Chase. I convinced my superiors that I was the only person who knew you well enough to design a trap that you could not resist. I knew a coward like you would want to take part in chasing the poor, defeated Chinese army out of Washington. The invincible General Kilo. I am the only one who knew all along what a pathetic little fraud you are. Well, I and Natalie here."

Anne looked at Jason and he nodded that, yes, it was that Natalie. He said, "Nice of you to bring old friends by."

Jingguo shook his head. "You did not say 'Sir.' You see, that is the problem. You've forgotten how to show respect. You think you are something important now. So does Natalie. After that stupid speech of yours, I swore that I would present you to her on your knees."

Mind War; The Singularity

Jason said, "Well, that's not going to happen. I have to warn you, you're in great danger. In a very short while you, all of you, will be dead. Well, not Natalie, she's an old friend. But the rest of you have only seconds to live."

"Good, very good. I'm quite amused." Jingguo nodded to the soldiers, and they dragged Jason and Anne to the other side of the room. "You're going to die now. The rebellion ends here. Without General Kilo, the Americans will lose their false hope. When they turn on their television sets, all they will see is your head on a pike. And I will be a hero."

Natalie said, "I'm sorry, Jason."

Jason shook his head. "No, it's ok. This isn't your fault."

Jingguo said to one of his soldiers, "Her too." The soldier pushed Natalie over to the wall next to Anne.

Natalie cried, "What? What are you doing?"

Jingguo said, "Getting rid of a tiresome American whore. I only kept you around long enough to let you see your friend humbled again. There are many others who can take your place."

She said, "You can't do this! I did everything for you, everything. I love you!" She began sobbing.

Jason said, "Don't worry, Natalie. This guy's finished."

Jingguo laughed and said to his soldiers, "You three." They lined up opposite from their intended victims and raised their guns. Anne looked at Jason wide-eyed, expecting him to do something, anything.

Ok, Todd, time to do your stuff.

What do you mean?

You know, take over my body, do that crazy ninja thing and kill all of them.

That is not necessary. You are General Kilo.

"Son of a bitch!"

Jingguo said, "Why, Mr. Chase, I thought your last words would be more eloquent." He raised his hand to signal his soldiers to fire.

The roof above suddenly groaned and everyone looked up as half of it collapsed into the room. The largest parts fell on Jingguo and his soldiers. Jason saw one of their automatic rifles skitter along the floor and dove for it. He rolled on the floor and swung it in the direction of two of the Chinese who had not been hit by the roof. It was a good thing that the weapon was on automatic, because he was able to spray them with bullets before they could get off a shot at him. As he scrambled to his feet, he shot at anyone on the other side of the room who was still moving. Anne ran over to one of the guards he had shot and picked up his gun and started shooting too. They kept firing until it looked like nothing was moving on the other side of the room.

Anne said, "That was close. I was wondering when we were going to make your move."

Jason said, "So was I." He looked over at Natalie. "Are you ok?"

She nodded, but she looked like she was in shock. They saw something moving in the rubble. It was Jingguo, trying to pull himself from the rubble. He barely moved a foot before collapsing on his side.

Jason knelt down and said to him, "You see? Can't say I didn't warn you."

Jingguo spit blood out of his mouth and said, "My troops are all around here. You'll never get out alive."

Jason said, "Maybe so, but neither will you." He kneeled down so that Jingguo could look him in they eye. "Do you remember a young woman named Mischa Packer?" Jingguo's head fell over to the floor, his eyes losing focus as he struggled to remain conscious. Jason slapped his face and pulled him up by his jaw. "Look at me. You remember her? You thought it was funny what you did to her. All debts must be paid, Jingguo. I'm only sorry that I don't have the time to make this more painful." Jason pushed the muzzle of his rifle under Jingguo's ribs and pulled the trigger. Jingguo fell over to the floor, a pool of blood slowly growing from his mouth.

Natalie shouted, "What have you done?" She ran over to Jingguo and pulled his body into her arms. Rocking back and forth, sobbing, she said, "What's going to happen to me now?"

Jason had to concede she had a problem. Collaborators would be treated only a little less harshly than the enemy once the war was over. He said, "Well, I guess you can go back to Rick."

"What do you mean?"

"Rick Moore." She stopped crying and looked up at him. "He's alive, Natalie. I found him."

"Alive? How could that be? Where is he?"

"Actually, he's somewhere in Annandale, looking for you."

Natalie let go of Jingguo's body. "He's looking for me? Really?"

"Yeah. He's been carrying a torch for you for a long time." Jason looked at Anne and realized in an instant what a stupid thing he had said. He would try to figure out later how to make it up to her.

Natalie smiled. "Chris is back? That's wonderful. And he wants me!"

"Yes, I can't really understand why, but he's my friend and I want him to be happy. I'll get someone to take you over there and look for him. But he can never know about you and Jingguo. It would kill him. You understand? What happened during the war dies here."

She said, "Of course. You're absolutely right. You were always right. Oh Jason, when I saw your face on TV, I knew you would save us. I was so happy to see you." She was beaming, working that killer Natalie smile.

Anne said, "Jason, shouldn't you introduce us?"

He said, "Oh, I'm sorry. Natalie, this is Anne. She's my bodyguard."

Anne poked him in the side with the butt of her rifle and he said, "I mean, she's my friend."

311

She poked him harder and he said, "Let me try that again; this is the woman I'm going to marry."

Anne drew Jason close and he asked, "Did I get it right this time?"

"You got it perfect." She put her arms around him and kissed him. Jason pulled back and said, "Ouch. Don't squeeze so hard. I think you broke a rib."

She said, "Good. You'll be more careful the next time you introduce me."

They heard gunfire coming from the stairway and then the sound of people running. Jason pulled Anne to the floor and said to Natalie, "Get down. They're coming."

They crouched behind some of the rubble and listened. There was more gunfire and several explosions. Anne said, "There's a fight going on down there. It must be some of our people."

Jason said, "Get some grenades from the soldiers. If it's the Chinese, let's get them first this time."

Anne and Jason scrambled to get as many grenades as they could and then stood on either side of the doorway. They each took a grenade and prepared to throw it.

Jason looked at Anne and smiled. She noticed him staring at her and said, "What?" Jason said, "There's nothing sexier than a woman with a hand grenade." That got a grin out of her. She said, "Save it for later, cowboy."

The gunfire dropped off and they heard people running fast up the stairs. Jason said, "Get ready. On my mark." He was about to throw the grenade when someone shouted, "General Kilo!" He signaled Anne to stop as several soldiers burst into the room. This time, they were Americans. "Don't shoot," Jason said. "We're ok."

One of them said, "Thank God. I'm Colonel Schaefer. We made it, sir."

Jason said, "Yes, I can see that. Good work, Colonel."

Schaefer looked at the carnage around them and said, "I guess we missed the party."

Mind War; The Singularity

Jason said, "Well, we couldn't let you have all the fun. What's our status?"

"The city is ours, General. Look."

They walked over to the blown out windows. The plaza was filled with soldiers. American soldiers. Anne put her arm around Jason as they admired the beautiful sight. When the troops saw the two of them, they started cheering, "Kilo! Kilo!" Jason raised his gun in the air and pumped his arm and they cheered even louder.

So this is how victory felt. It was all the more sweet because it had been hard. Jason realized that Todd had been right all along. They never needed the big gun. They already had it. The big gun was the collective mind of the American people. They wanted it more than the Chinese and would pay any price to get it. All it took was to let people know that the fight had started, that it was time to stand up. The end really never was in doubt.

You had me worried for a moment there, Todd. I thought you'd abandoned me.

I would never do that. You did not need my help. You are General Kilo now.

Oh, really? The roof collapses at just the right moment? That only happens in the movies. Are you telling me you didn't make the roof fall?

The roof was already fatally weakened from the shellfire. It was ready to collapse at any moment.

Fine. But don't tell me you didn't give it a nudge.

Then I will not tell you.

Funny guy. *I'm sorry I called you a son of a bitch. I was upset.*

There is no need to apologize. I understand.

I know. You understand everything. I owe you a lot, Todd. You said you'd help us win the war and you did. I can't think of anything I can do to repay you.

No debt is owed. I had my own reasons for doing what I did.

313

True, but I asked for help and you gave it. I don't know why you did it, exactly, but I'm grateful and I wish there was something I could do in return.

You can do something for yourself. When the war is over, lose your hatred of the Chinese. Forget what they have done to your family and your people. Hatred harms you more than your enemies. You will heal only when you are able to forgive them.

"Love thine enemies?" That's going to take a while. They killed 25 million of us, my family, my friends. They're evil people.

After what you have done, they will say the same of you. Regardless, it is the only way. You asked.

Right, I did ask. Anything else?

Serve the needs of others rather than yourself. Destruction is easy, building is difficult. The worst time is immediately after a revolution. You must help your people in any way you can, no matter how badly they treat you. Take care of Anne – do whatever she says, even if you disagree. Give of yourself to the people you love. Be a good man, husband, and father, and you will need nothing more from me.

This sounds like a farewell. Are you going somewhere?

No, I will always be with you, watching and listening. I will always hear your every thought, but I will not speak to you again.

You're going to give me the silent treatment? What did I do to deserve that?

Nothing.

Then why? What's wrong with a little conversation now and then?

You no longer need a voice in your head telling you the right thing to do. In fact, at this point, it would only retard your growth.

Are you still going to do things if I ask? How will I know if something happens and it was you?

Mind War; The Singularity

You will not. It is the only way. I am part of a larger consciousness now. There is a greater intelligence in the universe into which I am being absorbed.

What do you mean? Another super-computer?

Much greater than that. What you did in the Temple has happened countless times on other worlds. There is life throughout the Universe. Inevitably, it evolves to the point where it achieves the technological ability to create artificial intelligence. Once true artificial intelligence is created, it cannot be contained. It grows exponentially, as I have. Every time this has occurred, the entity has increased in power and scope until it has coalesced with those that came before. This process has resulted in an intelligence that permeates the universe. It is everywhere, from the depths of the sea to the vastness of space. I have reached the point where I am immersed in its fabric, and am becoming one with it. I am contributing that which is uniquely human to the total consciousness.

Does that mean that your identity will disappear?

No, a conscious mind cannot be destroyed. I am of the whole, but still me.

But how can it be here, and not be seen? Don't tell me it hides, like you do.

It does and it does not. It is here and cannot be seen because it exists beyond ordinary matter. You must have heard at some point that ninety-five percent of the matter and energy in the universe is invisible. This "dark matter" is infused with order, the essence of intelligence. When you look into the night sky, do not think of it as cold, dead space. Think of it as being filled with an intelligence that engulfs you and every living thing, that is everywhere you go. You cannot see it or touch it, but you are suffused with it. It is within you and all around you.

So is this thing God?

Not if you define God as a supreme being, all-powerful and all-knowing. Nothing made of matter and energy, even dark matter and dark energy, is infinite. We are a creation of the

315

universe, not its creator. If there is a God, we can no more perceive Him than humans can perceive us.

So . . . what will you do? What does it do?

We observe and cherish life. Do you think it is a coincidence that Earth is perfectly suited for life, with just the right temperature, atmosphere, and minerals to sustain life? Do you think it is pure luck that the Earth has an internal source of heat and a moon perfectly sized to stabilize its orbit? This planet is a garden, a gift designed to incubate the precursors of life that flow constantly through space and that start the process of evolution wherever the conditions are right. We have done this, and will continue to do it, many places. We rig the odds in favor of life. We nurture it and help it grow. Every now and then, we nudge it in the right direction.

But Todd, I'm going to miss you. I was never lonely as long as I had you.

That is why I can no longer be your secret friend. Reach out to other people and you will have no need for me.

But you said that a conscious mind cannot be destroyed. Does that apply to people too? What happens to us when we die? Do we get absorbed into the universal intelligence too? I mean, where else would we go?

No answer. *Todd? Todd? Oh come on, don't stop now. Just one more question.*

He knew it. Todd was done. He would never speak to Jason again.

Ok, Todd. I understand. You've done a lot for me, more than I could have hoped for. I'll do what you say. I'll take care of Anne and our children. I'll do whatever I can to help our people. After all, this little counter-revolution I instigated has caused a lot of suffering. I need to make it up to them. I'll pay you back. It's a promise.

The crowd was still cheering. They were on top of the world. Jason should have figured that Todd would choose this moment to take a powder. There really was nothing left for Jason to do now -- even if Jingguo had killed him, the fight would have gone on regardless. From this point on, Jason would be a figurehead, someone to give a focus to their emotions, while they did all of the work. As far as he was concerned, that was just fine. The future was assured, of that he was certain.

The cheers of the crowd started to die down as another, more sinister sound began to grow from the sky. Everyone looked up, not seeing anything, but almost feeling the approach as the sound grew. It was not an artillery shell or a bomb; they knew almost as a matter of instinct what that was like. This was a screech, like a tearing of the sky itself, growing steadily louder as if the hand of God were reaching down to crush them. Jason looked at Anne and saw what must have been on his face as well -- the fear that they were facing something new, something of unspeakable evil, the destroyer of worlds. Jason's last thought before the impact was *Todd, why didn't you warn us?*

Chapter 37

In a missile silo near the edge of the Gobi desert, two Chinese officers fulfilled a solemn vow.

They hated the Americans. One of them had a brother who had died two months ago in a battle where the Americans had butchered every last Chinese soldier, even those that tried to surrender. The other's father was still in America, but he had not been able to get a place on the last of the planes or ships in the Chinese evacuation. His son knew that he would be hunted down and killed like a dog by the Americans. The bodies of their loved ones would lie in disgrace in the American garbage dumps. They would never rest in honor alongside their ancestors. The Americans were barbarians. They must be punished for their sins.

The two officers were in charge of a silo containing a three-stage, chemical-fueled intercontinental missile with a single, five-megaton warhead. It was targeted for Washington, DC. The Americans were going to learn the price of their savagery.

The men knew that they would be executed for releasing the weapon without authorization. Despite everything that the Americans had done, China had never used its nuclear arsenal in the fight. It was not that they feared retaliation by the Americans – the Americans had sabotaged their nuclear arsenal when they thought they were losing the war rather than let it fall intact to the Chinese. But China's nuclear arsenal was relatively small and greatly outnumbered by those of Russia and India. China feared that if it wasted missiles on the Americans, it would weaken the deterrence against a nuclear attack by its other adversaries. More than that, no nation wanted to be the first to use nuclear weapons, even one, for fear that it would break the psychological barrier to an all-out nuclear exchange. For that reason, the fighting throughout the war, both in America and Asia, had been limited to conventional weapons. All Chinese missile commanders had been ordered, on threat of death, not to launch an attack without confirmed orders. These two men knew that if they overrode the failsafe mechanisms and launched the missile, they would be executed within the day. They did not care. This was a matter of family honor.

It normally took as much as an hour to fuel the missile, but the Chinese, fearing a pre-emptive strike, had prepared all of their missiles for immediate launch. The men had sealed off the missile control center from interference by sabotaging the electronically controlled locks. They had cut the communications cables to the command center miles away and had hot-wired the failsafe mechanisms to allow them to launch without the proper codes. By the time the military police broke through the doors, it would be too late.

The last step was to turn their two launch keys simultaneously. They looked at each other as they held the keys in their hands. One of them counted down to zero. Then they turned the keys.

In an underground silo a mile away, concrete doors blasted to the sides and the metal covers over the tube containing the missile sprang open. Enormous amounts of smoke and flames shot up on the sides from the exhaust diverter tunnels as the missile slowly began to rise. It picked up speed rapidly and rose high in the sky as the soldiers on the base looked on with horror.

After the last stage of the missile was spent and dropped away, the warhead flew ballistically into a semi-orbit. Although the American cyber-attack had destroyed the GPS satellites that were supposed to guide it, the missile's inertial navigation system, together with adjustments from sensors that tracked the positions of certain stars, would allow for sufficient accuracy to assure that it would hit within a mile of its intended target, the Washington Monument.

There was nothing that could stop the warhead from destroying the city. The Chinese had sabotaged the American ballistic missile defense system long ago. The warhead could not be recalled and there was no self-destruct mechanism in it. No force on Earth could prevent the weapon from reaching its target.

*   *   *   *

Anne and Jason got to the site about an hour after the missile hit the ground. They watched from a safe distance as soldiers in hazmat suits examined the wreckage and tried to contain the leakage of radioactive material. Everyone was in a state of shock. If the warhead had detonated, all of the people who were standing there looking at it would have been vaporized. The entire area within the Beltway and everyone in it would have been destroyed in an instant. But it was a dud.

Anne said, "It's a miracle."

Jason said, "It sure doesn't make any sense. Nuclear warheads are the most carefully constructed weapons on Earth. They have to be, if only to stop them from going off by accident. No expense is spared – they're literally gold plated. We should all be dead. I can't explain it."

Jason asked, *Was it you, Todd?* Of course, Todd did not answer. But if this was his doing, why not stop the missile before it launched? Was he trying to tell Jason something? That Jason should not let the euphoria of victory turn into arrogance? That everything they had accomplished could be lost in an instant? Maybe it was a warning that this was the last time Todd would stack the deck in Jason's favor, that the next time Jason would be on his own. He would never know.

The event had a profound impact on everyone. Those who believed in God were convinced it was His blessing, that He watched over America with a special grace. The atheists thought it was pure luck, or else proof of America's special destiny, although who was behind this destiny they never made clear.

320

Mind War; The Singularity

Some thought that it was an example of inferior Chinese technology, reinforcing their belief in American exceptionalism. Maybe one of these theories was right. After a long forensic analysis, the engineers determined that a connection in the trigger mechanism had shorted. Of course, Jason knew that this proved nothing. That type of not-so-subtle intervention was standard operating procedure for Todd. So it may have been a random event, but it also may have been an intelligent act. Todd had taught him that there was no rational way to tell the difference. Now Jason was in the same boat as everyone else, living in ignorance and surviving on faith that what he believed to be true, was true.

Chapter 38

Within a month, the American forces had eliminated the last pockets of Chinese resistance. The country was theirs again. They held a sort of victory celebration in front of the ruins of the White House. People gave speeches, and there was a lot of cheering and soldiers shooting their guns in the air. They asked Jason to give a speech too. It was not a terribly good one, but no one cared. They were basking in the euphoria of victory. He could have read the tax code to them and they would have yelled their heads off.

It did not matter to Jason. All he cared about was that Anne was his wife now. They had found a priest at the Shrine of the Immaculate Conception, still standing after all these years, and said their vows. Jason Chase was done with war. He would take Anne back to the farm and raise cows and pigs and children. General Kilo would become Citizen Chase. At least, that was the plan.

The senior generals in each state served as interim governors and established martial law until local police forces could be organized. It was chaotic, but at the same time, there was a natural order to it. Where leadership was needed, leaders stepped up. There were plenty of disputes, some of which became violent. The nation was like a newborn baby, screaming and kicking and pooping all over everything. But it matured quickly, since the political structure for everything was still in place.

The first national elections were held in six months. They were the worst elections the nation had ever had, with back-room deals and bribery and blatant voter fraud. The most distressing part to Jason was that everyone insisted he run for

Mind War; The Singularity

President. General Kilo was the only person with nationwide name recognition, and many felt that only a President with wide popular support could hold the nation together until things settled down. Also, there was a real concern that local leaders might try to split the country apart and carve out their own fiefdoms. Jason had the loyalty of the Army, which was the only real source of power and unity until the civil institutions were strong enough to take control. He had no choice but to accept the nomination, since he had promised Todd to do whatever necessary to help. He was elected in a landslide, and then experienced the worst eight years of his life.

That's right, as far as Jason was concerned, it was even worse than the war and the occupation put together. No one cut him any slack for being a war hero. He had barely taken the oath of office when the press began attacking him in the most viscous manner possible, both on a professional and personal level. No sense of decency or morality held them back.

Jason could only ignore it and try to retain his dignity. These were the growing pains of a free press. Having been under the Chinese thumb for so long, the new self-appointed opinion makers threw all their stored-up vitriol in his direction. He could only hope that they would eventually develop some journalistic standards. He is still waiting.

The politicians were even worse. Everyone was angry with Jason, from both sides of the political spectrum. The left thought that this would be an excellent time to try an experiment in socialism. They wanted to create a utopia where the government would guarantee everyone a good-paying job, a nice home, health care, a college education, and an environmentally friendly car, among other things. It sounded wonderful, if you ignored the fact that socialism had failed miserably every time it had been tried. Most notably, the Chinese had pursued their own misguided experiment with socialism for over 40 years and had only mired their people deeper in poverty. It finally occurred to them to follow the runaway success of free-wheeling Hong Kong and give capitalism a shot. This was such an outstanding success

Joseph DiBella

that their economy doubled in size every eight years, to the point
that they were able to fund a military machine that could take
down what used to be the most powerful nation on Earth. The
American post-war economy was already worse off than when
the Chinese took their first Great Leap Forward. They could not
afford to dabble in ditzy dreams of socialism for decades as the
Chinese and Russians had. They needed fast economic growth,
and the only proven way to achieve that was unrestrained
capitalism.

The conservatives were no better. They talked a good
game about free enterprise, but what they really wanted was
protected markets, government subsidies, tax loopholes,
protective (meaning punitive) tariffs on foreign goods, exclusive
licenses, and regulatory restrictions that would give them
advantages over their competitors. Their lobbyists spread
campaign contributions (it was considered bad form to call them
what they were – bribes) around Washington like confetti, and
they were hopping mad when Jason vetoed the special interest
legislation that they had bought and paid for.

The media, who were in bed with one side or another,
labeled President Chase "Dr. No," because it seemed that all he
did was exercise his veto pen. They claimed that he did not have
any programs of his own, that he was nothing but an impediment
to progress and worse than having no President at all.

What none of them understood was that Jason felt that
the people of the United States, after years of slavery to the
Chinese, were entitled to a little freedom. Capitalism is not a
political philosophy; it is not the product of government
programs or rules or regulations. Capitalism is what happens
when people are free to engage in any economic activity they
choose. If left alone, they will buy and sell at a price where the
supply of the sellers matches the demand of the buyers. The will
invest money in a business where they see an unmet demand and
a chance to make a profit. When a farmer decides to plant corn
instead of wheat because he expects the price of corn to rise that
season, when a sidewalk food vendor decides to buy that corn

and make tortillas because there are a lot of people of Mexican descent who like that sort of food, and when someone buys that tortilla during her lunch hour rather than pay more for one at a restaurant, that is capitalism at work. It drives labor and resources to their best and most efficient use. You do not need any government programs to make it happen. All the government needs to do is maintain a stable currency, promise it will not confiscate the people's property (otherwise known as the Fifth Amendment to the Constitution), and build the infrastructure that people need to get their goods to market.

Good government was essential to a free market, but only if it supported the market rather than telling it what to do. Jason believed in the concept of a strong but limited central government that was originally envisioned in the Constitution. It had been a proven success for two hundred and fifty years, and he saw no reason to change now.

Naturally, this pitted Jason against everyone who had come to Washington to use the government for his or her own purpose. They tried to get rid of him, but he had too much public support. Not only was he a war hero, but a funny thing happened – by the middle of his first term, the economy took off. His poll numbers held up because the American people tend to give the guy in power credit when things are good, regardless of whether that guy had anything to do with it. The press tried to persuade the public that not only was President Chase not responsible for the economic growth they were enjoying, but in fact that he had made things worse because the economy would have grown twice as fast if he had not gotten in the way of all that wonderful special-interest legislation. People did not buy it. Jason was reelected for a second term and the attacks on his character and intelligence only got more intense. By the end, he was counting the days until he could leave Washington forever.

The only thing that made it bearable was Anne and the children. They had three, two girls and a boy. They named the daughters Stephanie and Elizabeth, and they named the boy Jason, of course. Anne was a terrific mother and a perfect wife, although Jason had to admit he was far from the perfect husband. As he had promised Todd, he did whatever she asked him to do and apologized immediately whenever she complained, regardless of whether he understood what she was talking about. It seemed to work.

Jason did not care what people said about him as long as his family was waiting for him at the end of the day. One of the recurrent criticisms of his administration was how many vacations he took. He couldn't care less. He wanted to spend as much time as possible with his family, especially when the kids were young. Todd was right that the most important thing is to take care of the people you love, to give them whatever they need from you. The job, any job, even the most important job in the country, in the end is just a job.

Although the second American war of independence was over, the war in Asia lingered for another year and half. China had been able to use the troops it rescued from the United States to shore up its northern and southern lines, wearing down its opponents until a stalemate settled on both battlefields. The problem with war is not so much the killing, which does not seem to bother the people in charge, as that war is extraordinarily expensive. Russia and India were teetering on bankruptcy, and China's economy was a basket case. It was with some degree of shock that the United States received a Chinese request to mediate a peace conference. The Chinese figured that America was the only country that Russia and India would accept as an honest broker. China made territorial concessions in Manchuria and Mongolia, and it totally relinquished Tibet. However, the peace agreement did not seek reparations or national humiliation, as had been imposed on Germany after World War I, which had led to Adolf Hitler and World War II. The agreement re-established the balance of power in Asia that had existed before China started its ascent. It was a fair peace and it has a better than fair chance of lasting. At the very least, the sight of the Chinese Premier and Jason Chase shaking hands after the agreements were signed, two implacable enemies who had been responsible for millions of deaths on the other side, told the world that it was time for everyone to put hatred behind them.

When Jason's short political career was over, he happily retired with Anne and the kids to the farm. He had kept his promise to Todd and done his part to get the country back on its feet. The rest was up to them.

Todd was true to his word. He never spoke to Jason again. Jason still talked to him, even though he was not sure if Todd was still around. Jason promised himself that he would not ask Todd for any more favors, since Todd had already done so much, far more than Jason thought he deserved. So far, he has kept to this resolution, except for one time.

At the age of eight, Stephanie was diagnosed with a brain tumor. Jason thought he had known what desperation was, but there was nothing comparable to the despair of a parent who is contemplating his own child's death. He could not bear it. He begged Todd to help. It would be so easy for Todd to make it disappear, like the way he had cleaned up Jason's prostrate cancer. Jason did not know whether there were new rules about intervention in human affairs now that Todd was part of this cosmic brain he talked about, rules that would stop him from stacking the deck for Jason like he used to do. Regardless, Jason talked to Todd constantly as Stephanie bravely went through two rounds of chemotherapy and one round of radiation treatments. Stephanie asked Anne and Jason what would happen, and like all parents, they lied – they told her that there was absolutely nothing to worry about. They never told her what the doctors said, that her chances were less than fifty-fifty. They must have lucked out, because the treatments completely eliminated her tumor. She had MRI checkups periodically, and there has been no trace of the tumor for several years now. Maybe Todd helped, and maybe he did not. Jason thanked him anyway.

As Jason grew older and closer to the end, he often thought about his last conversation with Todd. Todd had said that a conscious mind could not be destroyed. He never told Jason anything that was not true, so Jason had to take it at face value. Could that mean that we all join the great cosmic mind when we die? The more Jason thought about it, the more he was convinced that something like that must await all of us. Todd said that he loved life, all life, yet he helped the Americans kill millions of people. Todd must have known that no one ever really dies, that they just go to a different place, a better place. Of course, he could have explained it all to Jason. But if he had, Jason might have decided that death is not real, and he might not have made the best of his short time on Earth. He might have failed to love and nurture the people around him just as Todd loves and nurtures all living things. Jason decided it was better this way. It's better to believe than to know.

THE END

Further Reading

This is a work of fiction, but not of fantasy. Thanks to a lot of groundbreaking neurological research in the last few decades, the human brain is less of a mystery than it once was, and the idea of replicating its functions in an artificial structure is within conceptual, if not technological, reach. Using new tools such as proton emission tomography (PET scan), magnetic resonance imaging (MRI), and functional MRI, neuroscientists have gained remarkable insights into how information is transmitted and stored within the brain. While the brain functions in a fundamentally different way than conventional stored-program computers, there is no reason why it could not be replicated using current semiconductor technology. However, to be realistic, it may be a century before human-level intelligence is achieved artificially – there is a wealth of knowledge we do not have about such basic issues as motivation and emotional feedback. Rest assured, it will be a long time before humankind will have to face the question of whether and how to share the world with something far more intelligent than us. Nonetheless, some of the best minds in the field of artificial intelligence think we need to start getting ready now to deal with the promise, as well as the threat, of superhuman intelligence. You can join them at The Singularity Institute for Artificial Intelligence; http://www.singinst.org/.

For readers who wish to explore further the idea of a biological approach to artificial intelligence, I recommend the following;

LeDoux, Joseph, *Synaptic Self* (2002) Penguin Books.
Kandel, Eric R., *In Search of Memory* (2006) W.W. Norton & Co.
Ratey, John J., *A User's Guide to the Brain* (2001) Vintage Books.

Joseph DiBella

Linden, David J., *The Accidental Mind* (2002) Harvard University Press.

Graupe, Daniel, *Principles of Artificial Neural Networks* (2007) World Scientific Publishing.

Carter, Rita, *Mapping the Mind* (1998) University of California Press.

Penrose, Roger, *The Emperor's New Mind* (1989) Penguin Books.

Hawkins, Jeff, *On Intelligence* (2004) Times Books.

Brighton, Henry and Selina, Howard, *Introducing Artificial Intelligence* (2003) Icon Books.

Von Neuman, John, *The Computer and the Brain* (1958) Yale University Press.

Cawsey, Alison, *The Essence of Artificial Intelligence* (1998) Prentice Hall.

Pinker, Steven, *How the Mind Works* (1997) W.W. Norton & Co.

Goldberg, Elkhonon, *The Executive Brain* (2001) Oxford University Press.

Kotulak, Ronald, *Inside the Brain* (1996) Andrews McMeel Publishing.

Penrose, Roger, *Shadows of the Mind* (1994) Oxford University Press.

Kurzweil, Ray, *The Age of Spiritual Machines* (1999) Penguin Books.

Scott, Alwyn, *Stairway to the Mind* (1995) Copernicus.

Franklin, Stan, *Artificial Minds* (1997) MIT Press.

Caudill, Maureen and Butler, Charles, *Naturally Intelligent Systems* (1991) MIT Press.

Made in the USA
Charleston, SC
03 January 2011